Animal Future

Robert McGraw * Darrin McGraw

Mondrian Books
San Diego – Riverside

Mondrian Books

San Diego – Riverside

For Nanci,

always our best fan, helper, and motivator

and

for Linda & Peter,

both irreplaceable

Chapter 1

Wrapped only in a towel, Autumn Winn fired a pistol at her new underwear.

The gunshot was loud, but at four in the afternoon nobody in the apartment building would be sleeping except the porcupine family upstairs. It was registered by the city of El Cajon as a diurnal apartment block, so in theory nocturnal animals were not supposed to be renting, but they knew the landlord and he had let all six of the porcupines take a one-bedroom. That sort of thing happened all the time.

Autumn was just a little too excited about finally finding the package in the mail when she got home from her shift. She had planned to put on her new underwear after she had a shower, so she could lounge decadently around the apartment in bulletproof lingerie. But then it occurred to her that after all, she ought to test her jaw-droppingly expensive purchase first. There were only 15 days for the money-back guarantee.

Draped over the chair, underneath a tall algoplastic houseplant, lay the knee-length split-leg chemise into which she had just fired a polisec-issue .40-caliber bullet. The Delicate Cider color option had been out of stock, so she had ordered Midnight Blue. It wouldn't match her skin but at least it was dark and wouldn't be obvious if her uniform shirt and trousers happened to separate at the waistband while she was fast-roping out of a burstcar or charging parkour after a suspect downtown. At five-foot-nine, she was glad they even had this style in her size.

Her contract with White Knights - San Diego Division had only five months left to run. But somehow that fact had made her anxious; she didn't want to end up as a Morning Heartbreak story on vidstream a week before she would have finished her career as a polisec officer.

She picked up the blue chemise off the chair and stretched it out. The shot had not left even a pinhole. Instead, the microdispersors had spiraled the bullet into a flat galaxy-shaped splotch of lead. She pinched its hot edge carefully and peeled the lead galaxy off the fabric like a decal. Then she checked underneath it on the chair. The ceramic mug she had placed on the chair was cracked into a small piece that said *San* and a bigger piece that said *Diego Padres*. So most, but not all, of the force was being spirally dispersed. The marketing for the SafeLite Tactical Wear company guaranteed zero penetration, not zero impact. She had had high hopes, that was all. That was OK. Zero penetration was pretty darn good.

And she had paid extra to have her name embroidered. Not the name her hopelessly American parents had given her, but her real name: *Nguyen Thu*. She had translated it out of a book. Even though no one would see it, having her Vietnamese name on the inside would guide her actions and her values. Maybe she would wear it under her civilian clothes tomorrow morning when she rode the maglev up to visit Great-Grandfather in Fresno. She already had her bag packed for the trip.

The front door musicated.

Oops. Autumn figured she knew what it was about. On second thought, it would have been better to test the chemise outside. She went to the door, brushing past the plastic tropical houseplants. She did not have a history of being great at taking care of plants so she didn't buy real ones. But she liked having things around that felt like Southeast Asia. Or what she imagined it might still be like there.

She checked the doorvid. It was Micaila, the porcupine family's oldest daughter. A few of her quills were poking out the back of her pink Asteroid Heroes pajamas as Micaila sleepily rubbed the pink vocoder clip on her ear with a broad fuzzy paw. Porcupines always looked sleepy anyway.

Autumn opened the door a crack and peeked out.

"Hi, Micaila."

"Hi Miss Winn," mumbled the girl animal's vocoder, which was set to overlay a cute child's voice on her actual pharyngeal output. "You hear loud noise?"

"Um, yes," said Autumn. "That was me."

"You okay? We got perps breaking in?" Micaila twitched her wide porcupine nose and blinked.

"Tactical equipment testing. It's part of my job." Which was vaguely true.

"My dad says you can't be shooting no guns inside building."

"Tell your dad he can't be sleeping in the daytime here. And don't gnaw on my door. The landlord is saying I keep kicking it or something." Micaila hadn't actually been gnawing, only clicking her teeth and looking wistfully at the door frame. Nevertheless Autumn had learned from experience that it was better to intervene early.

"Oh, sorry. Miss Winn, my dad real tired from night shift at Voxellity."

"Tell your dad he should get some earplugs. They worked for me back when I was on graveyard shift every night. In fact—wait." The porcupines might as well get some sleep. She went back in the studio apartment to her bedside table, then returned to the door. "I have some left over—give him this pair. I haven't worn them. They should squish to fit if you roll them between your paws."

"Thank you Miss Winn."

"You go back to bed now," said Autumn.

Micaila shuffled off, dripping a few spines from her tail onto the carpet. Autumn made a mental note to put on closed-toed shoes before taking out the trash.

She shut the door and headed for the shower. Tonight would be a good night. True, she might be washing her hair with antibacterial soap because she forgot to buy shampoo. And yes, she would be eating rice and spinach again because her attempted banh bao dumplings had been so soggy they fell apart. And OK, she might be spending the evening by herself at home trying for the fourth night in a row to get through *Emperor of the People: Lý Thánh Tông and the*

4

Making of Đại Việt. But she was darned sure going to read it while wearing the most expensive underwear in San Diego County.

She was not going to mention her tactical purchase to her coworkers. They tended to be easily distracted by any reminder that she wasn't male.

The wall vidscreen blared.

"Winn! You home yet?" said a familiar voice. The wall view panel flickered, then went to non-view blue except for her employer's logo—

* White Knights PoliceSecurity *
Full-service police/paramilitary security contractor
at a price you can afford.
* Subscribe today and get a 10% discount!*

It was Bickson, the team leader for Tactical Assault Command. Should she tell him she was just thinking about cops like him? No. He would probably think she was attracted to him. Anything any woman did meant that woman was attracted to him.

"Here. But I'm just getting in the shower."

"Hey, no problem. You don't have to cut vid on my account." She could imagine his smirk.

"You viding to tell me I won the soccer pool again?" She got out a TefPlas tumbler and poured herself a glass of reservoir water from the fridge meter, which read $0.70. The desalinated water from the tap had a slippery, slightly bitter taste, and she drank it only when she was running low on funds at the end of the month.

"I'm viding to tell you," said Bickson, "to have your freshly-showered body down here tomorrow at 5:00 a.m. sharp for a briefing. I'll have plenty of hot Protein-Caf for everybody."

"I'm T-O until Wednesday," said Autumn.

"Not anymore. Off-time's been cancelled. For the whole TAC."

"What! Bick, I applied for this over a –"

"Don't get that little button nose of yours out of joint. It's the real deal. Home tango is what we're talking."

"Again?" White Knights investigated domestic terrorism threats from half a dozen half-baked organizations on a regular basis. In her experience, not much had come of it.

"This time we got a tip something big is going down. Tomorrow morning we're gonna sweep Rug Land for some Free Lifers. So set your alarm, get your big girl underpants on, and be here on time. Or hey, show up commando if you'd rather."

"OK, Bick. And as soon as I get there, I'll file a Six-H on you. Sound good?" Filing a sexual harassment complaint against her supervisor wasn't something she would really do. It nearly always ended up in court and meant jail time for the defendant. But she had considered it.

"Winn! You don't need to go all tight about it." Bickson said. "Just trying to reduce workplace tension on the team. That's part of my job. I was only joking, that's all."

6

"I kind of thought that's all it was," she answered. "See you at the armory at 5 a.m. And I was only joking, too. Probably."

Without any further comments the wall flickered blue, then back to its usual off-white.

Autumn spent a few minutes telling her plastic plants unpleasant things about Bickson's probable nicknames in grade school, while pulling her clothes and toiletries out of the bag she now would not be taking to Fresno. She put the Yamato pistol back in its holster in her utility belt, which was hanging on the shoe rack next to her polisec BioBooster jumpboots and her one pair of really nice black heels. She went into the kitchen area and got the rice cooker started. Then she headed for the shower.

Chapter 2

It was just before closing time in the East Village when Mack Davis—exhausted—reached Mr. Brian's Fine Apparel and read the sign in the corner of the window: "Chimps Welcome (Class G and above)." *Animal-run,* he thought. *That's fine with me. It means they won't be likely to file a polisec report.* Plus, he was told the place had good clothing at reasonable prices. The other sign higher up in the window said "This Month! 20% off Men's Neckties."

Mack had unfortunately been forced to abandon his luggage in his hasty departure from the Incoming Security Checkpoint at Lindbergh Airport-San Diego Transport Control. But he wanted to look his best when he saw Maríqui again and gave her the necklace.

After he got the necklace checked out, of course.

Looking at his reflection in the window, Mack adjusted his open collar, pretending to check his appearance but actually reassuring himself that the jade necklace was still safe beneath his shirt. On the pothole-scarred street he saw no one who might be following him. He smoothed his sandy hair, gripped the shop's antique brass door handle, and went in.

Inside there were several male mannequins displaying pinstriped suits with pocket handkerchiefs. A chimp came out from behind the register counter. She was wearing an expensive cream satin blouse and maroon slacks.

"May I help you, sir?" she said. Her paste-jeweled vocoder clip was set to a soothing alto voice that reminded him of a woman named Audrey Hepburn he had seen once on a vidstream. "A necktie, perhaps? Many influential gentlemen feel that ties are beginning to come back in style again. We have natural silk, clone wool, and even synthocotton if you prefer something hypoallergenic...?" She was of course moving her mouth in the chimp way, but the vocoder filled in the phonemes for non-human vocal cords and produced the dignified accent she had it programmed for.

"Socks. Black," said Mack. "No pattern. And a fitting for a suit." To save money he had flown combined class from Singapore, with a sand badger next to him snoring like a human the whole way. He hadn't slept more than an hour on the flight, and he still needed to get to National City. He wasn't in the mood for conversation. He hoped the Provie chimp wasn't offended; it was just business. Anyway, he didn't know much about how thought processes worked with Provisional Citizens. No one knew for certain.

There were theories about what had caused the Elevation, but so far nothing convincing. In the last decade, dozens of animal species across the world, mostly mammals, had increased in intelligence to the point that they scored within normal ranges for human beings. Several smaller species had also increased in size and longevity, and behavioral changes were widespread. The world's best experts had

9

failed to discover why chimpanzees had largely abandoned knuckle-walking and started walking upright, or how dolphins had learned to build underwater housing complexes, or how mule deer had developed the ability to work in fast-food restaurants. Or why they would want to.

With the increasing involvement of animals in human society, many things had changed. Other things hadn't. There were still clothing shops. They just served a wider range of clientele.

"This way, sir." The elegant chimp gestured with her long fingers towards a doorway. The hair on the back of her hand was trimmed as short as the law allowed. "Step into our fitting room, and Mr. Brian will assist you."

Mack passed between the curtains into the next room, which was surprisingly spacious with a high ceiling and a skylight. There was a walk-through scanner frame and shelves with bolts of cloth in sedate men's colors; more well-dressed mannequins; some marble-faced glass display counters with floral neckties; and a series of glowing wall cases of shirts. To the right was a large mirror and a heavy wooden workbench with some cloth swatch sets, an electric needlerunner for easier sewing by non-H.sapiens hands, and a small V-shaped object that after a second Mack recognized as an ultrasonic hand shear.

Standing in the middle of the room was an impeccably dressed young adult male chimp. His Occupation Signifier —an antique cloth measuring tape—was draped around his neck and over a pair of noticeably beefy shoulders, but his sky-blue French cuff shirt fit him perfectly. That was a good sign.

"Good afternoon, sir," Brian said in a vocoder voice with a distinguished Mid-Atlantic accent. "I heard you tell Brianna you require gentlemen's stockings."

Brian. Brianna. B-Class chimps. *Unusually high intelligence to be working in retail, especially in the no-questions-asked end of town.* Probably a conjugal pair who had somehow managed to buy themselves out of their government-assigned jobs in the Consumer Stimulus Sector. They were clearly bright enough to have become statisticians, executive assistants, or even product sales analysts. Instead, they chose to risk everything for the tightly-regulated quasi-freedom of one of the few Approved Non-Government Employment Sectors, "Independent Business Owner: Limit 2 full-time employees, 1 part-time." Brian and Brianna were taking initiative in following their own path. They were setting themselves up for financial ruin, of course, but he respected them anyway.

"Actually, I require a full outfit," Mack said. Mr. Brian waved him courteously forward and Mack walked through the size scanner frame. It was an older model, so he paused for a moment until he heard the faint buzz that meant it was sending his complete body measurements to a clothes printer in the back room to await payment authorization before creating the clothing. "Shirts, briefs, couple of suits," he said. "And I have a slight tailoring challenge." Mack shrugged his left shoulder so Brian would see the bulge of the holster under his jacket.

"And what would that challenge be, sir?" The tailor never blinked. *He's very cool. Or very near sighted.*

"A tumor," Mack said. "I have another one in the small of my back."

"Ah...perhaps a doctor?" Brian blinked once or twice.

"AmeriCare doesn't cover my condition," Mack said.

"No, I would think not," Brian looked past him toward the front room, then glanced around, checking the windows. "I'm afraid I have neither the skills nor the tools to provide such service. You'll have to seek them elsewhere." He turned away and went over to the glowing necktie case filled with silks: lemon and scarlet and cobalt blue. "Perhaps you'd like to try a necktie. They are the latest retro new rage in men's wear, according to Milan."

Since Mr. Brian clearly wasn't stupid, he must have decided Mack was part of a sting operation. Mack followed him over to the glass necktie counter.

"I'm sure you have the skills," Mack leaned over the counter and pressed the back of his belt buckle. Two sparklies dropped out of the hidden compartment and tinkled onto the wooden countertop. "And here are the tools."

Mack had never been close enough to chimps—or wanted to be—to notice whether they sweat. They do. Dark spots were forming under the armpits of Brian's blue pinpoint Oxford dress shirt.

The counter was bathed in a soft light from the overhead skylight. It seemed familiar. Mack realized he had been here before: several years ago this store had been a florist's boutique. He had come here

12

once to send flowers to a woman he was dating. When he saw that a bouquet was twenty times more expensive than a greeting card, he skipped the flowers and just bought the card. *It's the thought that counts, right?*

"Relax, Brian," Mack said softly. "I'm not a prog. I'm freeman. Counter-gov. There won't be any polisec coming through the door."

"I do not want any trouble," the chimp tailor said. "Please just go."

"Those sparklies are worth a lot more than what I'm buying."

At this Mr. Brian's primate muscles tensed under the dress shirt. His face showed that under the dark fur, his pink skin was turning pale. "I operate," he said more firmly, starting to breathe faster, "a respectable business. If you don't mind, sir, I must insist that you please leave right now."

"I'm spending tonight at Huero's bar, if you change your mind. Ask for Mack Davis. You must know the place. Huero recommended you."

"Not allowed to enter liquor establishments." His vocoder crackled as the volume neared maximum. He waved Mack out hastily with his long French-cuffed arms. "Go, go, go!"

Brianna rushed into the room, her eyes wide, her upper lip curling back over her teeth.

Mack picked up the sparklies and sighed. *Time to perform my second vanishing act of the day.* In a fight with two chimps, he was bound to lose. Probably an arm.

Chapter 3

As she laid out her black uniform and set her bed to buzz her at 4:10 a.m., Autumn told herself it was no good feeling angry. Her trip to Fresno would just have to wait until next week.

She had planned the visit to Great-Grandfather because she wanted to do another oral interview about Vietnamese foodways from his childhood and try to get him to actually eat a bowl of pho with her. He hadn't eaten pho in forty years and insisted he wasn't about to. She kept trying.

Born and raised in America, she felt she hardly knew what it even meant to say she came from Vietnam. Her ancestors had become American quickly, so getting access to information had turned out to be harder than she had expected. She'd seen a few films, taken a couple of classes on the history of Asia, and read whatever she could get her hands on. One thing she knew was that she would need to build stronger family ties, but that sounded simpler than it was. Even at 94 years old, Great-Grandfather was still strong-minded and independent. Last month, for example, when she had told him about her plans for the two of them:

"You're only twenty-three, and you're gonna retire?" He put his spoon back into his taco-flavored minute rice, then double-blinked at the ten-foot-diagonal Mahindra MegaVid to make it go mute. "How can that be?"

"Quarter retirement, Great-Grandfather," she said, sitting across from him at the Everbliss Gardens dining suite table and trying to keep her eyes lowered to show respect. She had learned about eye contact from watching a viddoc series on "Vanishing Vietnam." Looking at the plastic table felt pretty stupid, and her parents in San Mateo would have been bewildered, but she wanted to believe that her Great-Grandfather was the one person old enough to appreciate her efforts to be Vietnamese. Especially because this no-eye-contact business was anything but easy for her.

"I graduated from EastPoint Polisec Academy at nineteen. Soon I'll be twenty-four. I'll have five years of service, so I'll qualify for one-quarter of a twenty-year pension. For life. Less union dues, of course."

"But you barely started being a cop."

"We're called Public Assistance Officers. It's a polisec, Great-Grandfather. A Police/Security corporation. 'Cop' is considered offensive. The last public police departments went out more than thirty years ago, back when a lot of the city and county governments went bankrupt."

"I remember. I'm old, not senile! OK, so the union forces the company to let cops retire after five years. But you haven't even shot anyone yet," Great-Grandfather said. "What kind of cop never shoots people?"

"No humans yet, no." Autumn was divided in her own mind about whether this was a sign of a successful polisec career or a lackluster one. "There was that dog that was about to attack my partner."

"A Shar Pei! How dangerous is a wrinkly little Shar Pei?"

"It wasn't that little. More like medium size. And we had no way of knowing if the dog was elevated."

"Dogs aren't elevated. Everybody knows that," he said. "A bunch of apes been getting elevated; that's almost understandable. Horses and deer a little. Lots of smaller animals, maybe a few kinds of birds, bunch of others, who knows? Cats, maybe. I saw an Animal World vidstream about elevation. Weird behavior means a species might be about to get elevated. But cats are weird anyway, so the scientists can't be sure. Anyway, dogs never got elevated. At least not yet."

"Dogs might be like orangutans," said Autumn. "Scientists think orangutans may have become so intelligent that they still do everything the same as always, just to make us think they haven't been elevated."

"Your partner wasn't being attacked by an orangutan. A wrinkly dog was barking at him, that's all! What do they teach at that cop academy anyway? The dangers of using common sense?"

"The point is, Great-Grandfather, with my retirement and your pension, we can rent an apartment. An older one." *Made out of real wood, not extruded plastic.* "I'll enroll full-time at Hi-Band University, study cultural history, and get certified as a Cultural

Reclaimer." She realized she was looking him in the eyes, and stared at the table again.

"Look, Autumn, if you want to watch streaming classes and become a low-level anthropologist trying to protect dying cultures, that's fine. But leave me out."

"You won't have to live here in the senior citizens home anymore. You'll have your dignity and honor again."

"I got plenty of dignity. I got a ten-foot video with synched phablet. My favorite meals are delivered every day by drone. I also got two girlfriends here. One of them is only seventy-two. That's all the honor I need. Why would I wanna live in a little apartment with one-quarter of a retired cop?"

"Because you're the only member of my extended family who can still be saved. Mom, Dad, the aunts and uncles—they've all been corrupted by modern Western life."

"I'm not gonna tell your parents you put it that way."

"They've heard it from me before." They were also mostly too busy running the accounting business to visit Great-Grandfather very often. "They don't care about the loss of our cultural heritage. They can't even see that the growing homogenization of the global One-Folk/One-World ethos is a bankrupt alternative to the mainstream." This came from a recent issue of the *Atlantic-New Yorker Monthly*, but even to her it seemed like grasping at straws. They'd been over this before. If Great-Grandfather had been somebody else's Great-Grandfather, she would have said he was a stubborn old coot.

"That crazy One Folk business again!" he said. "That's not a political party, it's a cult! Why is it whenever people start worshipping some nutty idea, they want to make everyone else worship it too?"

"Exactly, Great-Grandfather. That's why it's up to people like you and me to preserve our ancient traditions. The past is our future!"

"I don't need to be saved. I've never even been to Asia. I was born here in CentralValCal back before it split off from California. I'm happy here. If you want to spend your life wading through mud in the forest and going to the bathroom in the bushes, fine! You go to the past. I'll stay here in the future. The plumbing's better."

Chapter 4

"You kinda can't blame the little guy, when you think how far chimps have come," said Huero as he polished the martini glass with a more or less clean dishrag. "I mean, fifty million years in the jungle, eating bugs. Wouldn't know how to use a roll of toilet polymer even if they had one."

After Mack had left "Mr. Brian's Fine etcetera," he wanted to stay off the streets until he could be sure he wasn't being tracked because of that little misunderstanding at Transport Control. *And unless I get some sleep I'm probably going to walk into a lamppost.* So he had headed for Isla Huero, a bar owned by an old friend who had known him back when he wasn't whoever people thought he was now.

He was still hoping that the untraceable sparklies would make Brian the tailor change his mind. But he had now gotten a few hours of sleep in Huero's back room, and it was almost three in the morning, and there had still been no message.

Huero put the martini glass back on the shelf and locked the display case door. Fail to lock it, and a Federal Product Regulation agent might think he was actually using the glassware. Only TefPlas dishes were totally government-guaranteed against disease transmission. And totally government-produced and sold.

"Then, in one generation, they learn to talk." Huero ran the dish rag across the front of the display case. "Next the World Order declares them Honorary Humans and ten years later, they're promoted to Provies. They've come a long way to make it, mijo."

"I suppose," said Mack. "If Provisional Citizen status with 632 pages of restrictions and exceptions is making it."

He had tried to phone Maríqui, but kept getting her *Sorry I Missed You, Sweetie* vidmessage no matter who he phoned as. Still the same vidmessage as three years ago when she was selling bail bond insurance and they first met at the Cara Mia.

He then tried phoning her roommate, Eileen, and had caught her off guard. Eileen was sleepy and probably high, and let it slip that Maríqui hadn't been home in days.

"A ver," said Huero. "Think how many generations my ancestors had to pick fruit and be hospital janitors and restaurant busboys. A lot, that's how many. And *my* ancestors were humans."

"I'll take your word for that," said Mack. He hated it when bartenders shifted into history professor mode, especially when it was a 270-pound bartender with knife scars on his face and arms.

She might skip without telling me, but not without settling the rent with Eileen. She keeps accounts straight. Maríqui the Money. She was as well-organized as an ice crystal. Her coolness was one of the reasons Mack liked her, and one of the reasons they kept breaking up. That and the fact that he traveled so much. But she didn't ask questions about his work, so normally he tried not to ask about what she did when he was away.

20

"Animals have come a long way, mijo. Now they get all the crap jobs you Anglos used to make us do. Name your poison." He gestured toward the tablet screen embedded in the bartop in front of Mack. "Ten more minutes until it logs out. Then I can't serve you nothing until 5 a.m. It's now or no mas."

"Any idea where Urizen's headquarters is these days?"

"Muy chistoso," Huero said. "You in the comedian business now? Late night stream?"

"I'm serious."

"Yo tambien. You know people don't find Urizen. Urizen finds them."

Mack looked down at the bar. The polished surface reflected the unkempt outline of his hair and he pushed it back from his forehead. In one of the vid streams surrounding the menu screen, a smiling news-girl pointed to a chart showing that unemployment had risen to the government-promised goal of 36 percent. Tomorrow, fewer Americans than ever before would have to submit to the indignity of getting out of bed and going to work.

"I need Urizen to help me find an old friend."

"Maybe Maríqui's not such a friend anymore, mijo," Huero said. "She was in here with a new friend. Very touchy-feely with her."

Sigh. *What did you expect?* He had been out of the country for two months. But when Mariqui had messaged him and asked if he could pick up a little necklace she'd seen listed online, he'd had a moment of hope. "You know the guy?"

21

"Sorta. Big guy. Calls himself 'Ivan the T.' Used to be a bouncer at Lucifer's. Real bouncers use psychology more than muscle – you know I worked in that for a while, right? But with Ivan, give him the choice to break your left arm or your right arm, he'll break 'em both and smash your kneecap for luck." Huero set a large TefPlas glass on the bar. "Now are you depressed enough to want that drink? Or maybe you prefer some happy dust that you'll swear you didn't get from me?"

"No drink, no dust," Mack said, putting his right hand on top of the bar. "Just a buzz. Dame el mitt."

"Yeah, I remember. You don't do serious fun." Huero pulled the Cerebo-Mitt out from behind the bar and laid it in front of Mack. "Your grandma raised you, and she was pretty religious."

"Yes, she was. Even after religion was declared a mental health hazard." Mack performed a specific twitch of his left wrist to make his COR wristband come alive, turning from dull copper to a crisp pale green with tiny holodisplay options floating around it like the cars of a Ferris wheel. It showed the word READY superimposed over a miniature view of mountain scenery. With his right fingertip he flipped and scrolled the Ferris wheel to select an identity on the COR band, and then pressed his middle finger on the bar's PayPad. The COR band's proximity signal would override the system and tell the PayPad whose fingerprint Mack was going to have today.

IDENTITY CONFIRMED, said the PayPad screen. GEORGE W. BUSH. Funny how the system never spotted that one. Mr. Bush had been quickly forgotten after he lost the election to President Al Gore.

Mack slid his right hand into the mitt, and the warm buzz told him that in about thirty seconds his nucleus accumbens would start singing "Happy Days Are Here Again." No matter what the songwriters say, it isn't love that makes the world go round, it's dopamine. He pulled his hand out of the mitt and took a couple of slow, deep breaths. *Come on, neurochemicals, work your magic.*

Mack looked back down at the streaming vid. There used to be a way to mute the sound on a public vidscreen, but Federal Communications Control had outlawed it. Standing on a Hawaiian beach was some guy with huge teeth white enough to snow-blind a polar bear. He was promising that his "Secret of Magnattraction Thinking," would force health, happiness, and riches to come flooding into Mack's life just as soon as he bought a paid seminar subscription.

Mack was tempted to use the COR band to override the circuit and shut off the audio, but instead he just reached for the happy mitt again.

"Hey!" said Huero, grabbing the mitt. "Not yet. You have to wait twenty minutes, remember?"

"I'm trapped in the seventh circle of Hell. Gimme a break," Mack said. "If I OD on tranquility, you can dump me in front of any tax office. That'll rip me back to reality."

"I can tell you're rattled, mijo. Why do you need to hear from this chimp tailor anyway?"

"New clothes. In my haste, I mislaid my suitcase at a security checkpoint."

"It happens in the best of families."

There was a fluttery whoosh as an emu came through the doorway. "You've got mail," the bird squawked. "Smacks David, care of Huero's Island."

It still surprised him that emus could do any kind of job at all considering their brain was the size of a pea. *It just shows how effective the postal service's training program must be.*

Mack extended his left index finger and touched the red square on the bird's collar. The dot lights flashed and the square turned green to indicate that his identity had been verified. The emu had no way of knowing that Mack's COR band was helix-looped to feed back confirmation of any identity the bird's device asked for.

As the emu left, Huero tossed the dirty rag into the microwave to sterilize it. "Emus!" He spat out the word. "Spot 'em forty IQ points and they're still birdbrains."

"Watch your language." Mack's voice seemed to be coming from somewhere outside his head. He was rooting around in his jacket pocket for his ViewGlazzes, but the dopamine was beginning to make love to his subcortical network and things didn't seem so urgent all of a sudden. "Speciesism Offender List for the rest of your life."

"So now you're working for the Department of SpecioCultural Equity?"

"Ha! But walls have ears." As he fumbled in his pocket he felt the little hard shape of the jade figure on the chain around his neck. *I need to get this checked ASAP. Maríqui wanted this exact one from that exact shop. Why?*

Maríqui was not an art person: she could sit for a solid six hours day trading fashion industry stocks while she redid her nails and brushed out her long hair, but that time when he took her to the San Diego Museum of Art she couldn't stand and look at an Ukiyo-e woodblock print for 45 seconds. As long as he'd known her she wore 18-carat gold jewelry of the hoop-earring-and-bangle kind. Suddenly she wants to wear a quirky old piece of carved jade? It didn't add up.

"Not my walls," Huero said. "Every morning a GreenCleanBot slides through here with a zoombroom. You like how clean the place always is?"

"It's chaos. Like always." He found his ViewGlazzes and unfolded them.

"Because this particular bot isn't sweeping. It's a state-of-the-art bug spotter. If any of my walls grows an ear, I'd know it in two minutes."

Mack had known there was a reason he liked this place. He put on the ViewGlazzes. The text *1 New Secure Message* flashed green in front of his view of Huero straightening a rack of Caribbean flavor syrups.Mack double-blinked to view the words of the message.

Pick up clothes at 6 am. Brian.

"Mr. Brian has changed his mind about outfitting me," said Mack. "He wants me there and gone before normies are on the streets."

"You watch out," said Huero, frowning. "Might be something happening downtown tomorrow morning."

"How do you know?"

Huero glanced at him sidelong with a mysterious frown. "Tengo enchufe."

"Sure. But are your connections reliable?" said Mack. "Anyway, I can handle myself."

"Just come back alive," said Huero. "I like repeat business."

"No problemo," said Mack. "Coming back alive is a key part of my plan."

"Plans change, mijo."

Chapter 5

The SpeedRail ride to the White Knights Armory gave Officer Autumn Winn time to stroll-scan through several of the light rail cars, checking each passenger's readout on the display inside her Tactical Assault Command helmet visor. She was happy to find that her new underwear was quite comfortable.

Wearing her three-inch BioBoosters put her at eye level with the schematic rail map above the windows. In most of the cars the map animation feature was broken, so each car gave a different story about where you were on the route. She left a car that was almost all the way to Golden Hill and entered a car that was still stuck back in Santee, twelve minutes in the past.

She patted the stun baton on her belt in time with the music coming from the screens at both ends and both sides of the car. It was a trailer promoting a new vidstream challenge show. Twenty-five young men and women had been locked inside a disabled cruise boat, then set adrift in the middle of the Pacific. Several of them had multiple convictions for violent crimes, but no one knew which ones they were. The challenge was for the group to figure out who the psychopaths were and throw them overboard before they could injure anyone too seriously. The music was very catchy.

At this hour the train was mostly empty. There were only a few sleepy humans and Provies, both types mostly wearing earplugs. On one of the seats was an opossum in a little hard hat, curled up mournfully around its lunch box. A white-tailed deer in a scarf was standing by the door with one of the hanging straps gripped in her teeth. The torn scarf was covered with burrs and bits of grass, but it was at least something to demonstrate that the wearer was elevated. *One hoof barely in the new world,* Autumn thought. *But she still knows where she came from.*

In the next car there was a clearly male white-tailed prairie dog—the vocoder clip on his ear was blue and semi-triangular—wearing a New England Patriots sweatshirt and reading what seemed to be a novel on his phone. Like many nonprimates with decent incomes, he was wearing a Pawsall™ prosthetic grip on one paw, and he used it to hold the phone while swiping with the other paw.

When the train slowed and its robovoice called out "Spring Street-La Mesa", the prairie dog turned wearily on the plastic seat and popped up to glance through the window, as if fulfilling a species responsibility despite the early hour. But only a couple of people got on the train: a skinny long-haired human male with a battered suitcase and a long-tailed macaque wearing a kimono printed with a pattern of Andy Warhol "Marilyn" images. The newcomers sat down several seats away from each other under the bombardment of the vidstream screens and stared at their hands. Scooting back down into his seat, the prairie dog flicked open the khaki phalanges of his Pawsall and picked up his novel again. He didn't seem worried about terrorist actions today.

Autumn hoped her presence calmed and reassured people. That was one of the reasons she had enrolled in the polisec academy as soon as her government-mandated year of high school ended and she turned sixteen. Whenever civilians saw her in her black helmet and uniform with the high-jumpboots, multiple wrap restraints, knockout gas, and a palmprint-restricted Yamato .40 semiautomatic, they knew no harm would come to them. Yup.

Okay, maybe every single citizen didn't respect Public Assistance Agents, but surely some of them must. She worked for the White Knights, a top company with a top reputation, and that made her proud. Or it used to. Polisec work was necessary to society, but working for a charm school reject like Bickson was getting old. And these pointless animal sweeps were not the heroic missions she had expected when she applied for TAC. Neither were long patrol hours in areas where public vidscreen noise drowned out the ability to think not only criminal thoughts but almost any other thoughts as well.

There was something better ahead for her. She was going to bring back what it meant to be real. *I am Nguyen Thu,* she thought. *A real person with a real culture. I will live in serenity with Great-Grandfather in a wooden apartment building. It will have an antique coil stove, and no two-way vidscreens, and real plants that you have to water. And I will teach community classes at the library on How to Get Your Heritage Back.* In her mind, Vietnam was a quiet

29

landscape of rice cultivation and small villages, mostly free of motorized transportation and vidstreams and guns. There had of course been wars, she knew that much, but she hadn't yet gotten to the modern period in her reading list.

The train stopped at the Chollas Creek station. An hour from now, animals and some humans would pour out here to transfer northbound to Serra Mesa where, inside the Voxellity and JawJazz plants, thousands of mid-class workers would spend their days—or like Micaila's father, their nights—assembling vocoder units. Together with the Pawsall corporation, species vox was now one of SoCal's biggest tech industries.

Quitting the White Knights would disappoint her parents. They liked being able to tell the neighbors that their daughter was a successful polisec officer, whatever successful meant. She had hinted to them that she might have other plans, but she was waiting to explain things in detail until she got past the pension paperwork and signed the form with a separation date. She would probably leave right around Labor Day, in time for the fall semester.

At the far end of the next car, an elderly man sat napping in the corner. He was not nearly as old as Great-Grandfather, but he looked ancient, worn out, used up. As she neared him, her scanner showed his condition. *Subject deceased.*

She phoned SpeedRail Control and told them to send a pickup crew to the next station. Control said they would try to put a crew on as soon as possible, but considering recent budget cuts, it might take a few hours. Autumn sighed, then as calmly as she could told

Control that would probably be OK, since rigor mortis had already set in, and the body wasn't likely to fall off the bench before rush hour.

Chapter 6

The wall display said 4:30 a.m. when Mack walked into the Sleepy Daze Motel in a grimy back corner of National City. As he expected, there was a large binturong on the long shelf behind the counter. The animal looked up, his mouth full of something he was eating. Mack didn't want to know what. He did know the Sleepy Daze was said to be the most vermin-free flophouse in town.

"Mack Davis!" said Ten-ten, twitching his long white whiskers. For some reason binturongs always set their vocoders to sound raspy and low. He gripped the back edge of the counter with the tip of his furry prehensile tail and moved forward a few inches. "Heard you dead. Howzi?"

"Don't listen rumors. Mack Davis fine. Howzi Ten-ten?"

"Eating regular. All I care. Want room? Got female? All night all day cost ten-ten. Only night, cost ten-six."

"No room. Visit friend. Where room Shadow Guy?"

The bearcat turned back to his meal. "Not know person. Not guest here. Room or no?"

"No room." Mack slipped his hand into his coat pocket. Ten-ten noticed and immediately raised his tail and bared his teeth. "Relax," Mack said. "No gun. Gift for Ten-ten." Mack laid one fig on the counter.

"Strangler fig!" Ten-ten hissed. "Where get?"

"The tropics. Malaysia," Mack said. "Gift for friend Ten-ten. Where Shadow Guy? I have more figs."

"No Shadow Guy here. How many? Ten-ten?"

"No. Ten-ten too many sneak pass inspector. Got ten-two. Want 'em? I know Shadow Guy lives here a year or longer. What room?"

"Mack Davis friend?"

"Yeah. Mack Davis Shadow Guy friend. Where?"

"You friend OGA?"

How Ten-ten knew that Verhoven had once worked for OGA was anyone's guess. Maybe Ten-ten was taking a wild guess, too. However, binturongs are very curious animals, and if you put one in charge of every keycode in a motel, he's bound to poke around. Not that Verhoven would ever keep anything incriminating in his room, but maybe he still babbled when he had nightmares. Verhoven's nightmares were quadrophonic Astrocolor productions. He had earned them though.

"Not know any OGA," Mack said. "Just friends. Long time back." He jiggled both pockets so Ten-ten could hear the strangler figs rattling. "Mack Davis go now," Mack said as he turned to leave.

"Give figs," said Ten-ten.

Mack laid the twenty figs in a neat row on the counter.

"Shadow Guy room 18. Way in back." Ten-ten began pushing the figs down onto his shelf.

"Thanks," said Mack. "Mack Davis not tell Shadow Guy you talk." He turned and went to the door.

"Careful!" said Ten-ten. "Crazy dangerous!"

"Thanks, Ten-ten," Mack said without looking back. "I know."

Chapter 7

"I do not think we are inviting any trouble, dear," said Brianna. It was 4:45 am and she was meticulously grooming lint from Brian's blue-shirted shoulders, sitting behind him on the bed, in an effort to calm him down. "We are selling him a suit and some stockings. This is approved by law."

"I'm afraid those novogems are contraband," said Brian. "Almost certainly of asteroidal origin. He is probably a jewel thief. Or worse. He carries weapons. In the plural." They were keeping the conversation cool and normal by speaking English through their vocoder clips. There was one small lamp giving off a warm reddish light from the corner of their little bedroom above the front of the tailor shop.

"He was well-spoken, and I liked the smell of him," said Brianna. "He offered no violence. A human would probably consider him good-looking. Did you think his smell was all right?"

"It was acceptable. There was no blood and no gunpowder. I did however notice that he has been abroad recently. Southeast Asia, I'm sure of it. Tembusu tree was rank on his sleeves. With a little whiff of durian, I think. In any case we have sent the message, so we are committed to meeting with Mr. Davis."

Brianna reached over and slowly undid one of Brian's cuff links. "Whatever he is doing, surely he wishes to avoid polisec involvement as much as, or more than, we do."

"I am concerned that there will be risks to you," he said.

"I am not concerned." She stroked his back with long chimpanzee fingers. "Thank you for thinking of my safety. But you know I am safe."

"I know. I wish we did not owe so much for your safety."

"My safety has been guaranteed. As to the debt, this opportunity is what you have been looking for ever since we came to this country. Now we can finish paying off the loan."

He raised his long arm and briefly clasped hands with her overhead. "Yes. With this one sale. I could never have imagined it. But Brianna, I do not want to sustain false hopes because, of course, he may not come."

"He did seem to really want a suit."

Brian scratched his earlobe thoughtfully with the opposite hand stretched over his head. "We shall have to override the payment authorization input on the government revenue log in order to record his method of payment as cash."

"I can take care of that," she said. "Now you need to get some sleep."

Brian sighed and rolled onto his back on the bed. Brianna lay beside him, rubbing his knee comfortingly as he untied his necktie.

"Once we pay your brother back..." he said.

"Yes?"

"We'd have enough left to buy a little advertising."

"Oh, Brian, do you think so?"

"I looked at prices. We can get four vidscreen walls in this zip code for thirty-five hundred."

"And will local buildings be more effective than vidstream?"

"In downtown San Diego we can reach humans at the City Hall and the courthouse, and legal and financial offices where made-to-measure is in demand. It's better than paying for a streaming econobundle and wasting our vid time farther east in the county."

"That sounds good. You are so analytical."

Brian sat up from his pillow with excitement. "The Central Library wall screen has an EyeballRank of 85 for Homo sapiens south of the I-8. I think we should feature the Avventuroso clonewool line—"

"All right, all right," his wife laughed quietly. "We can talk about the details tomorrow after we have helped Mr. Davis accommodate his pressing…health concerns."

Chapter 8

"I'm going to sneeze," Mack said. "You oiled it recently, didn't you?"

The gun barrel was huge and cold against the tip of his nose.

"Every day," said Verhoven. "I should have shot you through the door and let Housekeeping haul you off in the morning. Trying to sneak up on me. That weasel out front told you, didn't he?" Verhoven jerked him inside the room, spun him around and slammed him face-first against the forty-year-old wallpaper with pale blue crocuses.

"I knocked. That's hardly sneaking," Mack groaned as Verhoven pushed his gun barrel into Mack's right kidney and began frisking him. "And he's a bearcat. Weasels are smaller. Don't kill him. Wasn't his fault. I used his addiction against him. Mrrm." The seam in the wallpaper was digging into his eyelid.

"Typical. You always *were* lazy," said Verhoven. He reached around Mack's armpit with two fingers, hooked the 9mm Hayakawa out of Mack's shoulder holster, ejected the magazine one-handed, and dropped the gun back in the holster. "I notice you still carry a backup piece in the small of your back. Still the Two-gun Pete."

He stepped back, kicking Mack's 9mm clip to the wall, and used his foot to slide a creaky wooden chair over to Mack. "I bet you haven't cleaned a gun in a year. Or fired one."

"You know I eschew and abjure all forms of violence." Mack sat down in the chair, slowly. *Do not give him a reason. Hair trigger. He hasn't been this edgy since Lesotho.*

"Really," said Verhoven. "Still a smart mouth, too. I always expected that would get you killed."

"It kept us both alive once or twice, I think."

"I haven't forgotten the Bahrain job, Mack. But even so, you make a move, hands or feet, I'll ex you. Without hesitation."

"Never doubted it for a second." Mack kept his hands on his knees, motionless and in plain sight. "Which conspiracy is trying to kill you this time?"

"Never grow up, do you? Still drifting along singing Life is Beautiful. Still avoiding the truth right in front of you. You are so predictable, Mack."

"Is it the Bilderbergers? The Whatabergers? The Illuminati? The Illiterati? The Ignorati? Or is there a new one?"

"Since I saw you last, I've figured things out." Verhoven allowed the gun barrel to point down toward the floor. "I should have realized it a long time ago," he said. "There has only ever been one conspiracy. Only one since the dawn of time. History, Mack. You have to study history. The truth has been out there all along. Right in front of us for twelve thousand years. Or more. If I told you half of what I know about the Great Pyramid of Giza, your brain would short circuit."

Half? Mack didn't think he could handle even a sixteenth. He looked around the hotel room. It was clean but plain, except for one wall with floor-to-ceiling shelves filled with exquisitely beautiful little ceramic figurines. "History. Well, I see you still love 18th-century miniatures. You're so predictable, Verhoven."

"I don't know that name anymore. Can you tell which are the authentic antiques and which are my work?"

"I never could," Mack said, "and I'm sure I can't now. Obviously your hand is as steady as it ever was."

"The discipline helps me relax. The discipline and the control. Creating art keeps me sane."

"I'm glad you're still sane." *Granting that for the moment at least.* "And I'm glad your vision is still keen. I need it." Mack reached, very slowly, into his shirt and took out the tiny jade figurine on a gold chain hanging around his neck. "I want to leave this with you for a day or two. When I come back, I hope you can tell me what it is."

"I can tell you right now," said not-Verhoven as he turned the piece over in his hand. "Quan Yin."

"How much is that in dollars?"

"Not yen, you imbecile. Quan Yin is the Buddhist Goddess of Compassion and Mercy. She's called Padma-pâni in Sanskrit."

"I knew that."

"Usually they are table figurines. It's rare to see one small enough to wear as a necklace. Probably made in Thailand around the year 2K."

"So it's real, then?"

"Yes. And a rather nice example except that the jade is poor quality. I hope you didn't pay more than fifty baht." Not-verhoven tried to hand it back.

"Keep it. I want you to study it a bit. I have an odd tingly feeling about it."

"Ah, yes. The feeling that nothing is what it seems to be. I feel it all the time," he said, looking more closely at the piece. "OK. I'll study it. Don't tell me it's a bomb."

"Probably not, but try not to drop it." Mack stood up. "Do you still have access to test equipment?"

Not-Verhoven went to a table under the shelves, sat down, and put a jeweler's loupe up to his eye. "No," his voice seemed distant and hollow now. Quan Yin had captured his attention. "But I have an animal friend who does."

"A friendly suggestion," Mack said. "Try not to talk in your sleep." As he turned the knob and stepped through the doorway, silently kicking his 9mm magazine across the carpet into the hallway, he looked back. "If I don't call you Verhoven anymore, what *do* I call you?"

"Nothing."

Chapter 9

"Captain, you say we know more or less where they are, right?" said Autumn's partner, Sergeant Bernard Carter.

Autumn and Carter were in the White Knights Armory briefing room with all the other TAC squad officers, everybody sitting at slightly awkward angles in the plastic chairs to accommodate the pistols and stun batons on their utility belts. Each of them had visored helmets in their laps or under their chairs, and each had a white knight chesspiece symbol on the left shoulder of the black uniform.

"More or less approximately, yeah." said Captain Bickson.

"Then why don't we go more or less approximately right *there*? Hit them hard and fast."

Autumn had never learned how to wink properly, so she smiled at her partner with one side of her mouth.

"You in a hurry, Carter?" Bickson said. "You have a previous appointment this morning?"

"Only my pedicure, captain." The others in the squad room did their best—but failed—to control their laughter. "If we take them by surprise," Carter went on, "we have a chance to at least get the big fish. That's what *I'm* saying."

Carter had enough years in the Tactical Assault Command that his bluntness was tolerated and even valued by the other officers. Being assigned to him as a partner was one of the best things that had happened to Autumn since she had switched from regular patrol to TAC two years ago. In that time she had also become good friends with Carter's sister, Lucille, who worked in the Tech division. But she had not yet told Lucille about her retirement plans.

"OK, OK," Captain Bickson said as the chuckles subsided. "The thing is, we're going to have to sweep the entire district because the tip didn't exactly give a definite location. Actually, the source,...well,...the tipster was able to hack into one of our CommTech server computers." Murmurs were audible throughout the room. He turned toward a pudgy man with retro chunky-frame ViewGlazzes seated beside him. "Sorry, Captain Heap. No disrespect intended."

"No offense taken," said the head of Tech Division. "Even our best geekers can't trace the source of the message. We have a department full of red faces right now. If we located the hacker, we wouldn't know whether to arrest him or hire him as a trainer." Captain Heap stood up and blinked twice to make his ViewGlazzes project a sliver of a street map on the wall. "So here's what we have. This is the area along Broadway referenced in the tip. The message says the Free Life Now movement has something big planned. The notorious Jiggs himself has slipped into town to coordinate things, so it won't be just civil disobedience and protests. It might easily involve destruction of property or other violence. Sorry we can't give you more to go on, Captain Bickson. "

Bickson motioned toward the wall, and the map zoomed out to show central San Diego divided into grid squares. "As you all know, the Free Life animals and the humans who give them aid and comfort demand—as their motto says—Equal Rights for All Life Forms," Bickson said. "Peaceful government-controlled protests are protected by the Constitution, but violence and destruction in downtown San Diego, that's not going to happen on our watch. This is White Knights territory!"

Autumn had worked a few Free Life protests in the past: a lot of apes and coyotes and humans out with cardboard signs on the Embarcadero, shouting and basically daring polisec to arrest them. Drone news cameras made certain her fellow officers didn't use unnecessary violence once the Provies were restrained with wrapsnakes. Destruction of property she had seen and plenty of it, but she didn't think the local Free Lifers were the kind of animals who would injure other creatures. On the other hand, the "notorious Jiggs," whoever he—or she—might be, that was quite a different matter entirely.

"Sir, are we going to be wrapping all un-IDed humans as well as Provies?" asked a newer recruit—Henderson or some name like that. *Nice looking*, Autumn thought as she reached back briefly to adjust her ponytail.

"Damn straight," said Bickson. "Bring 'em in. The Secure-Tek Company would love for us to mess up, so they can steal our contract with the City of San Diego. They wouldn't be above planting some shills in the crowd. Sorry, Secure-Tek, but the White Knights are going to find out who this Jiggs is, and lock him in a suspended life capsule for the next twenty years."

Secure-Tek had contracts in towns outside the City of San Diego, including Chula Vista, Santee, Encinitas, and Oceanside, in addition to smaller contracts with private institutions. Autumn had heard from fellow officers that the pay at Secure-Tek was bad, and the company was disorganized and heavily reliant on part-time help. Otherwise she might have looked into making a jump. As it was, Secure-Tek was one of those companies that gave the polisec industry a bad name. Bickson was a bit of a rotten apple, but taken as a barrel, White Knights still looked pretty good.

"Excuse me, Captain," Lieutenant B. Dylan Chavez raised his hand. "From the standpoint of intelligence analysis, do we have corroboration on this tip? What if it's some other fringe group trying to mislead us? It could be the Open Source Party. Or the One-God movement. Why would a Free Lifer betray his own group?"

"A dissident, obviously!" Bickson said. "Groundlickers can hold grudges against other groundlickers." There were a few scattered chuckles. "Hey now," Bickson held up his hands. "Nobody get offended by a little humor to reduce tension."

Autumn glanced at Chavez, who was frowning and sitting back in his chair. Chavez seemed to be asking more questions lately and looking increasingly frustrated. She wondered if maybe he had applied for a raise—he certainly deserved it—and been given the standard line about how he needed to add more value to the company.

Bickson started off on a tangent about Provies and city politics, things she didn't need to hear. She began thinking about who might want to buy her BioBoosters when she left. She wore a larger size, so she was optimistic they would work out for somebody. Money would be tight as it was. Financially the SafeLite underwear hadn't been a good idea, but lately she had kept thinking she might need it, for reasons that didn't make sense logically.

She wondered if leaving by Labor Day was really doable. She needed to look at current rental rates for apartments in Fresno. Plus, recently she had gotten the sense that Great-Grandfather was going to be harder to convince than she'd hoped. Having her trip canceled this week didn't help.

"We think the Provisional community is as much a potential target as the humans in the downtown area," Heap was saying. "There have been reports of sales of unregistered all-operable weapons to Free Life agents."

"White Knights policy is to protect and serve rugs—I mean, Provisional Humans," said Bickson, "just the same as if they were actual people. Hey, just kidding. Everybody relax. Sometimes less-seasoned officers," he swung his gaze over toward Autumn, "can get unnecessarily tight about innocent banter."

This was the sort of moment where, in previous meetings, Officer Autumn Winn would occasionally get herself into trouble by opening her mouth. Even now Bickson might be deliberately baiting her into saying something he could use against her. She kept her mouth shut, but made eye contact with Bickson and glared at him.

His eyes narrowed. She held her stare. He looked away. She took a deep breath and looked at Carter next to her. He gave her his "atta-girl" wink.

"OK then," Bickson said, hitching up his utility belt and looking down at his notes. "We don't want the Free Lifers to realize we've been tipped off, so keep things non-threatening. Remember our Extreme Friendliness program. Just run your scanwand over their hairy bodies, log their ID chips, and check out the premises," Bickson went on. "Avoid the use of forced compliance techniques."

He swiped his phablet sheet to switch off the record function. The meeting was over, at least officially. Then he smiled a little as he said, "We can always go back in and crack a few skulls if some critter fails to show the appropriate humility."

Chapter 10

Mack crossed his legs for the seventy-eighth time and laid the plastipage magazine down beside him on the bus stop bench. The readout in the top left of his ViewGlazzes showed it was a quarter to six in the morning. If someone had been watching him as carefully as he had been watching the tailor shop, they would have been justified in wondering why he had let four different shuttles pass him by. They might have assumed that "Classic Bimbo Weekly" had riveting editorials.

While walking here from the transit station he had noticed an unusual number of polisec burstcars whirring through the streets. They were in hover mode, with the jets retracted, but at any time they could switch to bounce mode and jump clear over accident scenes, protester barricades, or even low buildings. He would have expected to see two or three burstcars; there had been more like ten or twelve. And here across from the tailor shop, no polisec presence at all.

Huero was right: something pasará.

At this hour the street was empty. Most of the signs were targeted to elevated animal consumers, with huge lettering to reach species with poor eyesight.

UpRite Primate Shoes, All Sizes

Vocoder Fitting for Less—Specializing in Hard-to-Fit Species
Clínica Médica Nocturna Para Ciudadanos Provisionales
Parfumerie des Bêtes Elites

Overlooking the business district was a row of high apartments a few blocks away. One of them had been retrofitted with large-capacity animal elevators, gray-white tubes running up the outside of the building, to appeal to quadrupeds looking to live downtown. The elevators looked like they'd been Rapidfabbed onsite, instead of being built with factory parts. Mack wasn't sure he would want to ride in them himself.

Down the street, a polisec horse turned the corner and headed Mack's way. He remembered she had trotted across the same intersection more than thirty minutes ago, and if she recognized him, he could be in for some trouble.

In the old days before the Elevation, when police horses had riders, you had an even chance of talking yourself out of a situation. Now their riderless saddles carried only armaments: freeze gas to immobilize you until a burstcar arrived, or, if you were too far away, stop-rockets to bring you down and keep you there until the horse got close enough to gas you. Horses could walk a beat for several hours, and they had a great awareness of changes in their surroundings. They were not, however, flexible thinkers.

She stopped in front of Mack and gave him the big-eye. "Miss bus?" she snuffled. The vocoders provided by polisec were barely adequate for communication.

"Yeah, well, you know." He tried to make borderline panic sound like mere embarrassment. "I guess I was too engrossed in reading an article." He nodded toward the plastipage. The horse lifted her head to bring her binocular vision into play, then turned sideways a little to focus on the title of the mag.

"Mmph! Right!" she snuffled as she saw the girlie gifs cavorting across the page.

"No, really," Mack said. "A story about this year's Olympic Marilyn Monroe Team. Nine absolutely perfect clones." He swiped his finger across the plastipage, trying to get the article to come back up. "And four alternates."

The horse tossed her mane and snorted hot breath in Mack's direction as she checked his face against her memory of mug shots.

After a longish moment, she said, "Pay more attention bus!" followed by some word under her breath as she trotted away. It sounded like "Berf," but considering the trouble horses' lips have with bilabial consonants, it was probably "Perv."

I think it's time to pick up my new clothes and get the heck out of downtown. Preferably before 8:00 a.m. And definitely without wearing a wrapsnake.

Chapter 11

"It fits nicely, overall," Brian said as he adjusted the shoulders of Mack's coat. "The Astrozzoli was a good choice of fabric, and the suit color is perfect with your light complexion. We've also concealed those little bulges. The shirt, however…"

"What? It looks great in the mirror," Mack said.

"The left sleeve placket is bunching up. Quite unsuitable. Do you always wear a COR wristband? I thought they were obsolete long ago with the advent of ID chips."

"I like vintage items. This one has extra storage capacity. Family photos, my address book, maps, customer information. You know, things I couldn't do my job without." *Not in my line of work.*

"I see," Brian frowned as a passing cloud darkened the skylight over the fitting room. "In that case, I will simply have to adjust for it. Please remove the wristband so I can mark the sleeve. Brianna," he called out, "bring me the laser pen, please."

Brian slid the coat sleeve up a few inches to expose the shirt as Mack gently laid the weathered copper COR band—containing 45,000 fake IDs, thirteen security override utilities, a miniaturized FJÖLSVIÐR 277 quantum computer, and a neuroimmobilizing projector/proximity antenna —on top of his old suit neatly draped on the glass counter.

Brianna entered and handed her husband the marking device. He said something quietly to her in French.

Something about staying in the room? Probably still nervous about me.

"Lovely craftsmanship, isn't it, Mr. Davis," she said. "Mr. Brian has a real gift for fitting clothes to any customer's body."

"Just keep your arm still for a moment, sir, while I mark this. This fabric has some stretch, one of our most durable selections, but –"

A musical sound signaled that the front door had opened.

Brian scrunched his face in exasperation.

"I'll see who it is," said Briana as she went through the curtained doorway

A man's voice came from the front showroom. "Morning , Ma'am. Just a routine safety check of the building. White Knights, keeping everybody safe from trouble-making punk deer and intoxicated raccoons and such. Who else is here besides you?"

In the workroom Brian bared his teeth at Mack and hissed, "Polisec! You gave your word!"

"No, I swear!" said Mack, stepping closer to a full-length cheval mirror standing near the doorway. "Don't worry, it's not about you. There's a lot of generalized polisec activity today." He buttoned his jacket and tugged a bit at the bottom hem to smooth out the fit. *Of all the tailor shops in all the towns in all the world....*

There was the clomping noise of polisec jumpboots. "Look, Sergeant," said a woman's voice. "These suits are Neo-European French and Italian. Wow! This shop has great cultural authenticity."

Just some beat pollies taking a look, thought Mack. *Not in wrap-and-arrest mode. Odd conversation, though.*

Brian snatched up his dark blue suit coat and put it on. Brianna came back into the main workroom and took Brian's hand in hers. Mack made himself busy looking in the mirror, frowning sideways at his collar. *Italian? Mariqui loves pasta. I'll take her to Sparzzatella's.*

The officers followed Brianna through the curtain. They were wearing black TAC outfits rather than the standard blue uniforms. Their riot helmets had the visors up, and Mack saw that one was a smiling Aframerican man of average build; the other was a tallish Asian woman with a look of curiosity.

"Morning, sir," said the man. His badge said CARTER 382-AS. "Public Assistance. We apologize for the interruption."

"I am the proprietor," said Brian quickly. "The shop is DOL certified, and I can show you the paperwork. This is my wife, and this man here is a customer. We are authorized Provisionals with four years residency."

"There's no problem, sir." Carter said calmly as he leaned over to look behind the counter. "We just need to verify that there are no un-IDed citizens on the premises."

The female officer glanced at the counters full of neckties. "What is a tailor shop doing open before 8:00 a.m.?" she asked.

Brian opened his mouth and it moved a little, but nothing came out. His tongue licked his teeth nervously and he adjusted his tie with the hand that wasn't tightly gripping Brianna's. "It's, ah, Early

53

Bird Sale day," he said. "We wish to capture the morning City Hall custom –"

"Way over here in East Village?" said the female officer.

"People come to, to the Library," said Brianna, her vocoder crackling a little.

"For parking, you know?" said Mack in a bland tone. "Many of my colleagues prefer, like myself, to park at a distance from the crush of Broadway and get a bit of exercise. We find the old Central Library parking lot ideal for our purposes."

"Best-kept secret, hey?" said Carter with a smile. "Guess I hadn't heard about that." Overhead, the skylight darkened again. "Winn, looks like these three are all we have here."

"Everyone stand still, please, while we scan your IDs," said the female officer. The boots made her a good inch taller than Mack. He casually put his hands together behind his back to flip his COR band to an identity compatible with a job at City Hall.

His wrist was naked.

Holy floating carp. Wherever he went, at the gym, in the shower, in bed, rappelling up office buildings during carefully engineered power outages, the COR band never left his arm. But now when he desperately needed it, it was on the counter fifteen feet away.

"You!" she pointed at Mack. "Step closer. I'm not picking up any ID signal from you."

"Be happy to," said Mack, weighing whether to rely on some fast talk or simply knock over the cheval mirror to cause confusion while he ran for his life.

His decision was preempted by an even greater chaos.

There was a crash of thunder and lightning overhead. Screams from both chimps and shouts from the officers.

That's not lightning, Mack realized. *It's gunfire.*

The skylight shattered and he dived behind the workbench as the shooters began to drop through.

Chapter 12

Crouched behind the workbench, Mack already had his 9mm out.

The timing of the attack wasn't as bad as it might have been. At least he still had the deadly bulges under the new suit.

In the edge of the full-length mirror at the front he could see a little sliver of the room. Armed members of some smallish bandy-legged species in black biostrong suits with black-visored helmets and tail pouches. Another one, this one with human body proportions, appeared from above somehow…oh, there was a rope.. A second human came down, this one tall and scarecrow-lean even in his biostrong armor.

Where did the Knights go?

The biostrongs had their weapons up. Bullpup stocks with thumbholes. *Yup, KXD full autos. Big suppressor tubes on the barrels. Sounded like it..* The mirror image slanted but it looked like the machine guns were pointed toward the front of the room.

BOOM

That was a polisec gun. The muzzles would now be pointed towards it.

BOOM again and return fire rattling from the biostrongs who seemed to be backing up. A shred of the door curtain flapping and torn.

So at least one polly behind the doorframe.

Another door in the back of the room. *Can't get there from here.*

Am I in this? Did they see me dive?

Something shiny flashed in the mirror. A fat little metal tube. Brianna's face. A bluish-white smoke.

Freeze gas.

The two White Knights' visors would have already auto-lowered in response to their increased heart rate, and they were equipped with resp filters.

Mack had no filter.

BOOM

Return fire rattling, now with the muzzles turned away to the other side of the room. So the other polly was behind one of the display counters. The bluish-white smoke was curling toward the front of the room.

Freeze gas will drift. If I freeze, I'm helpless, I get shot.

BOOM

Can't just wait it out. I'm in this. He got the 9mm settled just right in his hand.

There was a yell of rage. Not human. Mack leaned to look past the edge of the workbench. The biostrongs had grabbed Brianna, now limp, and Brian had grabbed one of them. Brian was yelling and flailing his French-cuffed fists and grabbing and biting at the smooth black visor, hammered and smacking it. You would think the bluish-white freeze gas drifting upward would at least be slowing Brian down.

One of the biostrongs on the side of the struggle was the tall human. Mack shot him. The shot opened a gray flower on the black armor protecting the tall man's skinny stomach, and the man staggered but did not fall.

Dammit, you just popped that one off. Take your time. Mack grabbed a corner of paisley gabardine from a roll on the top of the workbench and then was back behind, with the big plastic roll clattering down on top of him and with it the little ultrasonic shear bouncing and skittering on the floor, and he pulled the whole cloth cylinder against his mouth and breathed through it as the wall behind him split and withered under machine gun fire, big chunks tearing out of the plaster to leave an intact rectangle where the workbench was. The shop was an old twentieth-century building with actual brick underneath. Solid. That would be why the polly behind the doorframe was still in.

There was a scream from somebody not human, maybe a biostrong, whatever they were, but not synced with a shot.

BOOM BOOM BOOM

In the cracked fragment of the mirror he saw one of the pollies, the woman, come up from behind the marble necktie counter and get off those three shots with her polisec cannon and then duck back behind the necktie counter and one of the biostrongs was on the floor and out. *Nice!*

The black figures swiveled at her and all together they laid fire and Mack peeked over the top of the bench with a wad of paisley over his mouth and nose and shot one of the black-suited apes, or

58

whatever they were, in the back of the neck just under the helmet and the ape went down.

At the back of the room Brian had been thrown down and was struggling on his back on the floor with something thin and gray around him, scrunched around his arms and feet.

The tall man saw Mack. He reached for a long gray cord running down the sleeve of his suit and threw it at the workbench. The thin gray thing writhed in the air as it came. It was a wrapsnake.

HOLY. MOTHER. OF. PEARL.

Mack rolled back in panic, losing his hold on the gun, just trying to get seated with his back against the workbench. He splayed his arms straight out against it and kicked his heels temptingly a little. *Don't move except the feet.*

The robot slithered around the corner of the workbench, hunting, and it went straight for his moving feet. It shot one end of its carbon-fiber body between the back of his knees and the floor. Then both ends of the wrapsnake, with their little stainless steel mouths, whirred around and around his legs and then his waist and wriggled up his body.

BANG.

Loud. That was something else. A weapon not fired before.

The wrapsnake drove its two mouths repeatedly against his arms and the wood beneath them, trying to drive in underneath and around while Mack kept his outstretched arms and palms jammed against the deliciously flat side of that old workbench. *Eight, seven, Don't Move! six...*

There wasn't any more gunfire.

Four, three, Stay Flat! two…

Grunting noises. Shuffling. A tinkle of broken glass and a heavy thud.

Zero. The wrapsnake search routine timed out and the mouths curled back down around his chest and nuzzled into each other with a click. Mack was tied up. But only from the armpits down. That meant he could get out.

He dragged himself over the floor like a mermaid until he could see the skylight.

The biostrongs were going back up the rope and out the skylight, hands and feet all a-climbing. One of them had a big grey lumpy bodybag. The next one had a limp black ape-shape under one arm. And then the rope was slurped up, leaving only a jagged rim of glass with a little mist drifting toward the blue sky.

Chapter 13

Autumn Winn couldn't move. Thinking wasn't going so well either.

She was lying stretched out on her left side on the culturally authentic linoleum floor and she felt a sharp pain when she breathed deep.

One of the shots had cracked her visor and after that she had inhaled a big bluish-white gust.

She tried to breathe as deeply as she could. *Get the freeze gas out. Get moving.*

Things weren't very clear right now. Her head was full of mud. Stunned. Why would a Free Lifer betray his own honorable Great Grandfather? This was a good question. It should be on morning vidstream. She wanted to call in to the Armory but her helmet display was dark. *I got ten foot video with synched pho.* She couldn't move her mouth for some reason that she couldn't remember right now. *Secure Tek, that was it. Secure Tek and banh bao dumplings on the side.*

Through the dim visor and the bright open crack down the middle of it almost parallel to the floor she was lying on, she could see a chimpanzee across the room struggling with the wrapsnake. He was wheezing and panicking and getting nowhere.

Every polisec officer in East Village ought to have heard that fight. Except that every polisec officer was over in the sweep zone. Looking for a mysterious Free Life terrorist named Bickson.

She and Carter had been off zone. That much she remembered. Her mind was starting to come back now. A quick stop for coffee at Pam's Place. Trust Carter to pick the one spot to sweep where they could live in a little wooden apartment.

In her field of vision there was a writhing gray flash of a wrapsnake in the air. Her head was sideways ninety degrees on the floor, so the snake traveled upwards, but that really meant horizontally. The snake flailed and whirred against a bullet-riddled mannequin and wrapped it up tight with a robotic satisfaction.

Then from the same direction the customer in the suit walked into view and knelt over the tailor. As far as she could tell while rotated ninety degrees, he wasn't especially tall or short, not fat or skinny, not very old and not very young, not really anything. She thought she had seen him somewhere. Dark blond hair, pointy nose, and a well-honed look, like there wasn't much that would surprise him.

The man started talking real quiet. Not much else now to hear. Nice and quiet. A real wooden apartment with an antique coil stove.

"Brian, relax. Relax," Mack said. "It's not a real snake. This isn't the Tai forest." He was speaking in soothing tones and stroking the chimp's back. "We can get this off you. Trust me. Relax. Hey, hey, hey…hey, hey, hey. Yeaaah. I'm going to have you slide your hands very slowly up and put them flat against your face. Like that. See?

The wrapsnake will avoid your neck and head. Polisec don't want lawsuits from prisoners being accidentally strangled."

In her fog Autumn wondered how many civilians knew that. What exact percentage do you suppose. Lucille could find that information.

"Good. OK, it's in holding mode. I'm just looking for the connect point. Hmm. Where is it?"

Who was this guy? Did he have hands very slowly? Therapy kind of sounding like sounds, like vase. Oh, her head.

"See, because you put your hands on your cheeks, the snake had to settle for the area around your elbows. Aha, there's that little steel place. You could do this yourself. Straighten your arms and they'll be free. Then disconnect the mouths. No, not like that. Hey…hey. I'll do it. Like this."

The snake came off and began flopping wildly. The man threw it away and it made a slithering whirring noise as it wrapped something she couldn't see.

The tailor got to his feet, shakily. "They took her."

"I know," said the man.

"No, they TOOK HER! I was trying to get them, but they just pulled me off. And that SNAKE thing!"

"Yes, they took her. Do you have any idea why?"

"I don't know." The chimp was staring up at the broken skylight. Then he turned back and bared his teeth. "What do you mean, Mr. Davis?" The chimp's vocoder was distorting and buzzing with

63

anguish. "What do you mean, do *I* know? Isn't this all about YOU? You and, and your—*bulges*?"

"No," said the man. "It's not. I'm pretty sure that if it had been all about me, I would have been in that body bag. And possibly for good. Whereas your wife—"

"*Brianna*!" wailed the tailor.

What bulges, thought Autumn. Get those bulges off. Phys C every morning. Treadmill. Dad jogging to St. Bartholomew's every morning in his orange track suit. *Emperor of the People,* page 71.

"Hey…hey…hey. Brian, she's okay. I'm sure your wife was alive, and I really think they wanted to keep her that way."

Autumn could flex her feet now. Those old manicured BioBooster toenails.

"That's why the freeze gas, understand?" the man called Mr. Davis went on. "They could have simply shot her, but they didn't."

"My goodness. My goodness. I'm sorry." The chimp sat down on the floor and rested his face in one French-cuffed hand.

She was starting to get a movementy sort of feeling back in her shoulders. She twisted them a little. She decided that she should just see, because being able to move would be a culturally authentic activity, whether her outflung left arm was capable of sliding very slowly and quietly toward her. It was. So obedient. Congratulations! You have completed the requirements for this Hi-Band course. And the breathing pain didn't get worse.

"Brian, you're going to get her back. It's going to be okay. Probably a ransom situation. I know some great lenders who will help out anybody, and I do mean anybody. Hey…hey. Don't worry, it's OK. Could easily have *been* me, though. A lot of people might have wanted to do that. Come to think of it, I was in a body bag once. Didn't intend it, but it worked out all right. Kind of a funny story. Friend of mine, we'll say, wanted me to go to Karachi and kind of pretend I was somebody who –"

Davis suddenly stopped talking. He walked quickly across the room, upward and out of Autumn's field of vision, his shoes crunching on broken glass and pieces of marble. His shoe sounds stopped.

What bulges, thought Autumn. Mr. Davis. Mr. Mr. Mr. Davis. We had no way of knowing. You barely started being a cop. Wrinkly little cop barking. She realized that the stun baton on her utility belt was poking her leg.

The shoe sounds started again, crunching furiously, back and forth and around.

OK, let's think. Where was Carter? Her had been blasting away from behind the doorframe, changing the height every time, and then the tall perp fired a longbarrel and then, what? Carter didn't fire back. Carter should have popped them off that rope like grapes. But they just got away.

"What's wrong, Mr. Davis?" said Brian the tailor. "What are you looking for?"

"My—I mean my—I'm looking for my—that is—well, where's my SUIT?"

"They took it," said Brian. "With Brianna. She was lying on the counter. They just scooped her and everything right into the bag. Bits of glass right in with her. Oh, I'm so worried. Mr. Davis, are you all right?"

There was a long pause.

"I'm fine," said Mr. Davis.

Autumn thought she could probably get up. She thought about where her gun might be. She couldn't see it on the floor by tilting her chin. It could have fallen behind her. Or maybe it was on the shattered countertop.

Carter should be saying something by now. He ought to be getting up and staggering in from the next room with a couple of busted ribs and an atta-girl wink and his smoking Yamato .40 in his hand.

"That old suit had acquired some bullet holes, I'm afraid," said the tailor. "You didn't lose much."

"Right."

She could definitely move her hips now. And the pain wasn't really that bad.

"Oh Brianna, my sweet Brianna."

Davis came back down into view. He was rubbing his bare left wrist with his right hand. "Right. Just an old suit." He stared around as if not seeing things. "I need to look around."

Autumn flexed her fingers and it turned out they were around something. She realized that her gun was still in her hand. And Carter was still in the next room.

Davis walked quickly downward past her chin, which meant back across the floor and toward the front room. Yes, she had seen him before: right here in the tailor shop, before the fight. She heard the sound of his footsteps change as he walked through the doorway.

From the front room he gave a low long whistle. His footsteps stopped. "Man, oh man," he said.

She knew what he was looking at.

With a slight pain in her side and an awful feeling in the pit of her stomach, Autumn rolled back and forth like a rusty freighter wallowing in a hard sea, and after about three hundred years she came to her feet.

Chapter 14

"Brian, I'd stay out of the front room right now," said Mack as he returned to the fitting room. He had picked up a new pink silk shirt and was wiping off the edge of his palm and his naked COR-less wrist. "Those exploding rounds have a tendency—"

"Freeze gas!" said a voice.

He stopped. There was a gun muzzle leveled at him by the female polly. She had a crack in her helmet visor and she was standing with feet apart, both hands holding the pistol. She looked a little unsteady.

"Freeze, I mean," she said. "Freeze!" Her black uniform was smeared with salmon-colored brick dust.

"Officer, I'm not part of this chimpnapping operation. I totally don't understand what just occurred," Mack said calmly.

"What bulges?" she said. "White Knights!"

"Don't move, Davis!" It was Brian. The chimp was pointing a gun at Mack: his own Hayakawa 9mm.

Oh yes, that bulge. I dropped it when the snake came. Sloppy. "Hey, Brian, thanks for finding my property. You can just hand that —"

"Don't move!" said the officer, swiveling to aim at Brian. "So shoot me, I'll help you!"

"You'll help me what?" said Brian, tilting his head and waving the gun in her direction.

"I meant shoot you," said the officer in a slightly muffled tone.

"Nobody's going to shoot you," said Mack. "Put the gun down, Brian." Mack drew his his backup revolver from the small of his back. "Officer, I'm on your side. I just–"

"Drop your weapons," she said. "Both of you. Right now." Her hands were shaking, and she was hunched forward and clenching her gun almost against her body, rotating her upper body to shift back and forth between Brian and Mack.

"Everybody calm down," said Mack.

"I am perfectly calm!" Brian shouted. Having absolutely no experience in how to aim a gun, he was waving it from side to side as if watering a lawn. "My shop is ruined and my wife has been captured. Officer, this man –"

"Drop them," she said, "…or I'll shoot you down like a…" She shook her visored head slowly. "…like a Shar Pei."

"A what?" said Mack, shifting his aim from Brian to her.

"It's a wrinkly sort of dog," said Brian, shifting his aim to Mack.

"Brian, put my gun down. Right now!" Mack said. "It's OK, Officer. We're putting them down." He slowly knelt and laid his gun on the floor while motioning with his other hand to Brian. "She doesn't want to shoot us. But she's a little jittery."

"Officer, it isn't mine. Honestly. It was on the floor." Brian fumbled with the gun as he lowered it. "See, I don't even know how to hold it. I almost dropped it. I'm just a tailor. They took my wife! We must go after them!"

"Stay right where you are," she said. "And back away from that gun!"

"How can I back away if I have to stay?" said Brian.

"You!" She swung her aim over to Mack. "Hands on your head. How are you licensed to carry two guns?"

"I do some work for a jewelry investment broker, " said Mack, smoothing his tousled hair back and letting his hands just stay up there. "I often transport loose gemstones. I have two permits because, well, a certain politician's wife was one of my customers, and she told her husband..."

"I want to scan your permit chip! Now!"

"Sorry, but my body is allergic to implants, so my ID is in a COR band, and those guys took my belongings."

"A COR what?"

"A digital storage wristband. I guess they were before your time."

"Shut up! What's your name?"

"Mack." He smiled at her from under his hands. "Mack Davis. And you are...?

"Shut up, Davis!"

"WINN 626-AF," Mack read from the ID tag above her shirt pocket. "I love those old-fashioned names."

"Public Assistance Agent Autumn Winn. Keep your heads on your head. You! Tailor!" She turned to Brian, whose pink-skinned

70

face was strained with anxiety. He was nervously stroking the fur on the back of his neck and rocking from one foot to the other.

"My clients call me Mr. Brian," he said.

"I didn't ask your name. They just murdered my partner. Who were they?"

"I don't know. They took my wife." His rocking became more agitated. "We must go after them!"

"Stop bouncing! Tell me everything you know about those chimps," said Autumn.

"They were not chimpanzees. Not the right smell. Smaller. And with tails. We must go now!" Brian was becoming frantic. "They may come back. We must leave."

"Great idea. Let's all leave," said Mack. "Officer Winn, we'll come to your office this afternoon and file a report. Is two o'clock good for you?"

"Stay right where you are." Autumn said. "You're both under arrest."

"For what?" Mack said. "Buying a suit with two pairs of pants?"

"Officer, I'm the victim," said Brian. "You can't arrest—

"Calm down. We'll sort it out in the interrogation room," Autumn said. "My team will be here as soon as they realize I haven't reported in."

"In that case, maybe you should report in," said Mack with a sigh.

"A bullet hit my helmet. Smashed my communicam."

"All right," said Mack, looking around. "How about if I loan you my ViewGlazzes to phone in?" He reached inside his coat slowly, pulled out the glasses, and held them out to her.

"Put them on the ground and kick them over to me," Autumn said.

"Oh, come on! They'll get scratched."

"Just do it. Now."

"OK, OK. I'll enter my password for you." Mack slipped them on and multiblinked to zoom in on the woman. Meanwhile she managed to pull off her helmet with one hand and disentangle it from her ponytail. She let her busted helmet drop on the floor and roll away.

Asian, thought Mack, *but not quite Han-looking. Large dark eyes. Winn. Taller than average.*

Mack laid the glasses on the ground and gave them a gentle, precise shove. "Here you go. But eighteen hundred dollars is a really expensive hockey puck."

She kept her gun aimed at Mack and Brian as she picked up the glasses and got them onto her face one-handed. In a moment, she was talking to someone at the White Knights armory, telling them that her partner had been killed and a Provisional Citizen kidnapped by well-armed assailants.

"Mr. Davis," Brian whispered. "You run out one door, I'll take the other. She won't know which way to shoot."

"She's the type who decides quickly," Mack whispered back. "She'd drop us both before we got to the corner."

"I'm very fast," said Brian.

"With those BioBoosters on, she can run forty miles an hour for short distances."

"Both of you be quiet!" Autumn took off Mack's ViewGlazzes and put them into a cargo pocket on her pants. "I've got my orders. You're under arrest."

"We already were," said Mack. "Do the two cancel each other out?"

"You have the right to remain silent, so shut up."

"Oh dear. I think we have a problem," said Brian. "I've –"

"We *are* the problem!" said Mack. "We witnessed everything, and those guys may not want to leave witnesses alive."

"Don't panic. The White Knights have a solution." Autumn nodded toward the door at the back of the room. "The department says that door opens into the alley, and there's a vacant factory next door. All vacant buildings are required to have polisec-approved lock codes, so my code activator will open it. The plan is for us to stay in there until an extraction team gets here to pick us up."

"Listen to me!" said Brian, more firmly. "I've remembered the smell."

"What smell?" said Mack and Autumn.

"Baboons. Vicious. If they come back, we are dead."

"I should have read my horoscope," said Mack, "and stayed in bed this month."

"Let's move," Autumn ordered. "We're going across that alley as fast as possible."

"Yes, Officer," said Brian.

"Hold on!" Mack said. "If the boons are outside, we'll be sitting ducks."

"You are both witnesses to the murder of a polisec officer. If you resist or attempt to escape, I'll wrap you. If I can find an unused wrapsnake around here. Now move!"

"We're moving," said Mack.

"You two press flat against the wall, but not too close to the door," said Autumn. "I'm going to crack the door open and take a look outside."

"Listen, Officer Winn," said Mack. "To make a daylight attack by fast-roping through an antique glass skylight, that's not something a team improvises. They needed a staging area, and the building next door was probably it. The boons might be inside, regrouping."

Autumn unlatched the door, then crouched down and opened it a crack. After a moment, she opened it a little more. Then she took a male wig head from a nearby table. She thrust it through the opening, then quickly pulled it back. There was no gunfire. She tried it again.

"Everything seems normal," she said finally. "Maybe they're gone."

"Or just patient," said Mack.

"We need to get this show on the road." She snapped open one of her cargo pockets and pulled out a metal disk. "This is a distress beacon. I'll toss it through a window. When it hits the floor, it will activate, and the extraction team will know we're in there. But we'll stay here in the doorway until we see them arrive. Fair enough?"

"Fair," said Mack, "but which window did you have in mind?" He was looking at the brick wall of the vacant factory. There were no unboarded windows on the first two floors. The only thing reachable on the second floor was a ventilator duct.

"Hmm," said Autumn. "My boots will bounce high enough to reach that metal duct. But then how do I get to the window level?"

"Hang on a sec." Mack turned to Brian. "I realize this is an imposition, Brian, but would you mind helping us? The sooner we're picked up, the better."

"Mr. Davis, I am a certified bespoke tailor. Not a circus performer!" Brian said. His eyes narrowed as he studied the side of the building. "But I suppose, if it gets us out of here so we can track Brianna…give me the thing."

The chimpanzee removed his coat and shoes, then held the beacon disk between his teeth. He carefully put his head through the doorway and looked up and down the alley. Then he took a loping run across the alley and jumped for the ventilator duct. His first jump was two feet short, and he fell back to earth with a thud. But as he got up, he looked around and saw a bricked-in doorway with a protruding lintel. He jumped, took hold of the brick lintel, swung back to grab a metal brace with his chimp feet, then swung in an arc toward the window, his necktie flapping. As he reached the top of his arc, he threw the disk hard. It smashed through the window glass. Brian slid down and loped back to the tailor shop.

"I did it," he said, breaking into a chimpanzee grin as he pulled his shoes back on. "I got the disk inside."

"You were outstanding, Brian," said Mack.

"Great job, Mr. Brian," said Autumn. "We won't have long to wait now. The extraction team is really fast. I estimate twenty min…"

She stopped when she heard a high-pitched scream like the death cry of an enormous steel mosquito.

"Get back!" She yanked Mack and Brian back inside.

The drone-fired missile ripped into the alley and smashed through the wall of the second floor next door. Immediately an explosion shook the whole block. As the vacant building burst into flames, Mack leaped forward and slammed the door shut.

Officer Autumn Winn, Mack Davis, and Mr. Brian stood side by side in the shop staring at the little line of flame outlining the chink of the door, their hair riffling in the thin blast of heat.

"You're right," says Mack. "Your people really *are* fast." He opened the door enough that they could see that the alley behind the burning building was still relatively free of flames.

"That missile was definitely not protocol," said Autumn.

The three of them were six blocks away from the shop before they slowed down.

Chapter 15

At a line of rental garages Autumn flicked a switch on her utility belt to activate her polisec code for the lock, and they all piled into the nearest unit, squeezing in behind the rear bumper of an old ToyoFord. With the garage door closed again behind them it was dark. The place smelt like dust and oil.

At first the only sounds were the hiss of Autumn's BioBoosters whirring down and the rasp of Mack's breathing. *I thought I'd already had enough exercise yesterday at the airport.* After a minute he could breathe enough to talk. "Why do I have this feeling that the slogan 'Protect and Serve' is no longer working in our behalf?"

"It's the chimpanzee," said Autumn. A little crack of light from the underside of the garage door showed the outline of her bent elbow and her hand on the butt of her holstered pistol. "Someone wants to kill him."

"If that were true," Brian said, sitting on the trunk of the car, "they would have done it when they attacked the shop." His cufflinks glinted in the darkness.

"He has a point," Mack said.

"Then it has to be you." Autumn glared at Mack. "Something about you says I shouldn't trust you for two seconds. I'm not turning my back on either of you until we get picked up."

"We won't *be* picked up. They think we're dead," said Mack. "Don't you get it? That missile was meant to kill all three of us. Nobody has those missiles except polisec. It was your people."

"No, the Free Lifers must have stolen one. They're terrorists," she said, as the sound of sirens came from the direction of the tailor shop. "Listen, when the White Knights don't find us there, they'll comb the area, and I'll bring you in. We could even walk to the Armory from here, but I can't afford having either of you escape. We should be safe this far from the shop. We'll wait for a bit and then I'll wave down a polisec car."

"Or catch the next passing missile," Mack said. "No thanks. My eyebrows are still singed from the last one."

"You look normal to me, Mr. Davis," said Brian, straining to look at him in the low light.

"Just a joke, Brian. And call me Mack. Listen, Officer Winn. You still have my glazzes. Which, by the way, I loaned, not gave you."

"You'll get them back eventually," Autumn said.

"Just put them on again. Blink two left and one right," Mack said. "You'll get a news stream."

"I don't have time to watch streams," she said. "Let's go find a polisec car. That's an order."

"OK, sure. But let us find out what's happening back there? Or at least let Brian use the glazzes to find out."

"Yes, please!" said Brian. "Perhaps they've found Brianna. Please look!"

Autumn took the glazzes out of her pocket and put them on. Mack leaned against a stack of old magazines. They were printed on a crinkly, crumbling stuff which he realized was wood-based paper.

"Just political news," she said after a moment. In the dark the glazzes were glowing against the upper half of her face. "An executive order about increasing chocolate rations."

"I've heard *that* one before," Mack said.

"Wait," Autumn said. "There's a headline crawl." She was quiet for a moment, then began reading the crawl. "A White Knights officer was murdered by a chimpanzee tailor," she said. "The tailor was a Free Life terrorist who was caught by the dead officer setting a bomb in a building. The tailor chimp was killed in the explosion."

Mack gave a low whistle.

"More coming. Wait. OK, polisec is tracking down two escaped terrorists," said Autumn. "And— wait, this isn't right. "

"What?" said Mack.

"And a rogue officer accused of helping them escape."

Brian sheltered his head with his hands. "What a terrible mix-up."

"It's not a mix-up," said Mack. "I know a black op when I see it."

"Hold on, hold on," said Autumn, holding the glazzes on her face. "Public advisory…" After a moment Autumn took off the device slowly and said in a quiet voice, "Polisec is cordoning off the area north of Island Avenue. Everyone is ordered to stay clear of the East Village."

"That is an absolutely wonderful idea," said Brian.

Mack reached out in the dark and took his glazzes from her, touching her hand gently. "They know we're still alive."

Autumn shook her head. "I'm experiencing...cognitive dissonance. This can't be the way it looks."

"You're right," said Mack. "It's probably worse."

"We can't go back to the Armory."

"I'm afraid I have to agree with you. I suggest we split up and look for those –"

"Both of you stay where you are! You're not just witnesses anymore. If either of you are captured, they'll say you're terrorists and murderers."

"And they'll say *you* are the rogue cop," said Mack.

"Then you two are the only way I can prove I'm innocent."

"In fact," said Mack, "we are each other's only witnesses."

"That means we have to stick together," said Brian. "And find whoever took Brianna."

"We have to stick together," repeated Autumn slowly.

"I was planning on a candlelight dinner date tonight," said Mack. Outside the garage, distant sirens howled, but not distant enough. "Under the circumstances, maybe I'll take a rain check."

"It won't run." Mack slammed down the hood of the ToyoFord in the open garage. "They've drained the gas out. Probably storing the car until it becomes more valuable."

80

"Too late," said Autumn, standing in the sunlight. She had brushed some of the brick dust off her uniform and was taking out the elastic in her hair and regathering her ponytail. "It looks like scrap."

"No, it's a classic," said Mack. "ToyoFord went bankrupt and was taken over by a bus manufacturing plant in India. And who knows? Gasoline may come back in style someday."

"For a jewel broker, you know a lot about cars," she said. "Did you use to be a mechanic, too?"

"Nope." Mack chuckled. "Grew up on one of the last family ranches in the Southwest. Lots of old equipment that had to be kept operating."

"So what is our next step?" asked Brian. He was looking around anxiously and smoothing down his suit coat with his long-fingered hands.

"Davis, use your glazzes to locate public transport stops nearby," said Autumn. "It'll take a while before polisec gets enough officers on duty to check every bus and taxi."

"And we go where?" asked Mack.

"There's only one person at White Knights that I can trust. We'll contact her from my apartment."

"You have a vidscreen, right?" said Mack. "White Knights will have it bugged. Not that we could even get inside your apartment. By now, polisec has officers, horses, and drones watching the building from every angle."

"You're probably right," she said. "Plus we would be endangering everyone in the building. " She sighed.

"Surely they wouldn't fire a missile into a packed apartment building. At least I hope not. In fact, it may be that they've changed their minds about wanting us dead," Mack said. "Here's my thinking: They're looking at this as an operation that went wrong. Now they need us alive so they can figure out why the mission almost went down the drain."

"I can tell you why," Autumn said. She looked down the street and sighed. "Polisec officers weren't supposed to be in the tailor shop."

"Meaning what?" said Mack.

"That shop was six blocks outside our search grid," she said. "But my partner wanted to go in anyway."

"Merciful Heaven," said Brian, throwing up his hands. "Your poor partner is dead because we were running our sale, 20% off men's neckties. Oh! I feel so guilty."

"That wasn't it," said Autumn. She looked at Brian. "We were out of our area because of my cousin. She owns a pastry place a block away from your shop. It was one of Carter's—my partner's—favorite places whenever we needed to sit at a table and write our shift reports. This morning we stopped in just to buy something since we were close. But when we left, he said we might as well scan the animal-owned tailor shop down the street. Just to be thorough."

"Your cousin owns the bakery? Pam's Place?" said Brian. "What a small world."

"Well, we can't go to your cousin for help," said Mack. "Polisec will be swarming all over that street now. By nightfall they may be in full search mode all over town. We have to have a place to hide out, at least until tomorrow."

"I know! We'll go to *my* cousin at the San Diego Zoo!" said Brian. "It's not far."

"The zoo?" said Autumn. "Nobody keeps chimpanzees in zoos anymore, do they?"

"Not exactly." Brian grinned. "He runs the place. He's the Assistant Director. The director is some human political appointee who never shows up. Charlesworth owes me a favor because I make his suits."

"Well, we can't stay here much longer," said Mack. "So…any zoo in a storm."

"The sweep zone is between us and the Park Boulevard entrance," said Autumn. "Crawling with officers. We can't just walk. We need a vehicle."

Mack put on the glazzes. "I'll do a search for transportation."

"Meanwhile, Mr. Brian and I will have a chat." Autumn pulled out her stun baton and pointed it at Brian. "You know more than you've told us. Why would Free Lifers attack a chimpanzee-owned shop?"

"I can guarantee you they weren't Free Lifers," said Brian. "We are off limits to Free Lifers."

"Don't test my patience, you," Autumn said, brandishing the baton. "Why off limits?"

"Because of Brianna," Brian said quickly. "Or at least her brother."

"What about her brother?"

Brian didn't say anything.

"We gotta have it now, Brian," said Mack, blinking behind his glazzes. "Don't clam."

"Well," said Brian. His lips curled nervously. "The truth is that her brother is an activist. With Free Life. But Brianna and I never had anything to do with them. Never."

"How long has he been involved?" asked Autumn.

"Before we came to the country. So five or six years. He calls himself Jiggs VI, after a famous ancestor."

"Jiggs!" said Autumn. "An activist? Our intel says he's one of the leaders. It was Jiggs we were looking for in this sweep this morning. Supposedly he creates the plans that others carry out."

"That's possible," said Brian thoughtfully. "He's very intelligent. Very tough and disciplined. But he adores his little sister. Anyone who hurt Brianna would disappear the next day."

"So Jiggs had that troop of baboons pick Brianna up and take her to him," said Autumn. "Makes sense."

"Only to a human," Brian said. "My people will have nothing to do with baboons. We are mortal enemies. Besides, Jiggs has always been adamant that Brianna can have absolutely nothing to do with the movement. She doesn't even know how to contact him. He sends us an untraceable message a couple of times a year."

"Who would do this, then?"

"I have no idea. I really don't," said the chimpanzee, rubbing his teeth in agitation.

"Time for us to go," said Mack, taking off the glazzes. "I've located transport to the zoo, but we'll have to run to catch it. Back up on 7th and J, past Pawsall Park."

"We can cut through Lui's Wrecking Yard," said Brian. "It will keep us off the open street."

"Good. We need to stay as inconspicuous as possible," said Autumn. "Davis, please tell me you've located a SoloCar. Or at least a taxi."

"Nope," said Mack. "We'll have to take the bus."

Chapter 16

The trio stood close to the wall in the shadow of the Great Society Work Relief building. Once the sun set, one-hundred-seventeen million tiny, algae-powered twinkle-lights would turn the conical building next to them into something resembling a huge, glittering, stylized Christmas tree, capped by a golden dollar sign. The Great Society building was the perfect symbol for the public largess available to any full-status citizen who entered its massive lobby. It was also a favorite with sightseeing tourists.

A polisec burstcar was cruising a block ahead, its black side panel showing a white chess knight with an impassive expression. They watched until the car turned a corner and the *bwwrshh* sound of its ringjets faded away.

Autumn wondered how many TAC personnel were converging on the tailor shop right now. She wasn't sure Bickson had ever handled an actual terrorist bombing incident. Which of course this wasn't.

Was that missile fired by mistake? she wondered. *Or was it deliberate?*

"According to the published schedule," Mack said, "the bus has left the Star of India naval museum and should pass here soon."

"Then how long until we get to the zoo?" Autumn said. She had gotten a glimpse of the burstcar and seen that Chavez was one of the officers inside. They all looked grim. She wasn't sure what protocols were required for dealing with a rogue cop, but she wanted it to be something she could look up tomorrow on her lunch break rather than experience personally.

"There are no more scheduled stops before Balboa Park," Mack said. "The schedule just said 'Pass-by of scenic architecture.' I guess we'll be at the zoo in twenty minutes or so."

"OK, listen up, you two," Autumn said. She was starting to feel increasingly anxious. "When I stop the bus, get on as fast as you can after I get the passengers off. Then I'll order the bus operator to go straight to the zoo. San Diego Transit hires mostly opossums and even if they hiss a little they'll do what they're told."

"Actually," said Mack, "it's not a city bus."

"Well, what other kind…," Autumn began, but Mack interrupted her by pointing down the street.

Pulling around the corner and coming towards them was a flaming red, double-decker, open-topped London Transport bus. On the front and sides, signs said "See Scenic SanDi" and "San Diego Tours."

"Wow, that's quite a bus," said Brian.

As the bus drew closer, they could hear a pre-recorded tour lecture, but the only words they understood were "Great Society" and "Work Relief."

"What language is that?" Autumn said. "Chinese?"

"Mandarin, in fact," said Mack. "Before I handled jewels, I used to be a…"

"Never mind!" she said. "Look! The thing is full of..."

"Pandas!" said Brian.

The red bus was bursting with black and white furry passengers in Bermuda shorts and ViewGlazzes.

"Tourists from China," Mack replied. "Pretty common this time of year."

"I never saw so many pandas!" said Autumn. "There must be forty or fifty." Several of the pandas had hats and T-shirts saying "SanDi = Paradise" and "Star of India." Many of the pandas seated on the top of the double-decker were turning their fuzzy round heads back and forth as they took pictures.

"This is lucky," said Brian. "You'll be able to speak to the passengers."

"I am *not* Chinese!" snapped Autumn.

"Oh, I do apologize. To us, humans all look very much alike."

She stepped off the curb and held up her polisec ID badge for the driver to see. Being a totally automated, GPS-controlled bus, it had no driver. The computer's camera eyes locked onto the device on her badge. Autumn jumped back onto the curb as the bus made a sudden stop.

The pandas now were moving and twisting around in the seat harness bars to try to see what was happening, growling and whining to each other in Mandarin. The top of the bus looked like a forest of black and white fur blowing in a high wind.

Autumn jumped onto the front access step and climbed aboard. "Off the bus! Off! Off!" she yelled, waving her baton as she started pushing pandas towards the exit. "In the name of White Knights Polisec, I commandeer this…Aw, just get the hell off my bus! Off!"

The automated tour lecture stopped abruptly in mid-sentence as the computer evaluated the changing situation and generated a new message. Unfortunately, it was also in Mandarin.

"Speak English, bus!" she yelled. "Polisec orders code G6L4. Speak English, and get these animals off the bus!"

"Your attention, please, honored guests," the bus's computer voice responded. "We have made an unscheduled stop at the request of local authorities." The steel harness bars on all the bus seats clicked open to let the pandas out. "Please proceed carefully but immediately to the nearest exit and disembark. Upper deck passengers, please watch your step coming down the stairs."

The upper-deck passengers, understanding little or no English and being quite alarmed by the sight of an armed and apparently insane woman pushing pandas out the door, took the expedient course of ignoring the stairs completely. Instead, twenty pandas began climbing over the side railings, dropping heavily to the ground, and ambling down the street. Meanwhile, Autumn was suddenly trapped in a fuzzy mass of pandas exiting the lower deck and pushing her back off the bus. She fell to the pavement as the pandas ran down the street to catch up with the others in their party.

"Well, Officer Winn," Mack said as he helped her to her feet, "at least we're managing to stay fairly inconspicuous."

"I don't know where my baton is," she said. She looked around on the asphalt. "And my badge got torn off."

"Got it," said Mack, picking up the ID badge. But instead of handing it to her he started after the pandas. "You two get aboard. Be right back," he said over his shoulder.

"Where are you going?" she said to his back as he ran.

Mack caught up with the nearest panda and said, "Souvenir, souvenir," as he dropped the badge into the animal's shoulder bag.

"That's my badge, you complete babbling idiot!" Autumn yelled to him.

"Thank you. Souvenir of San Diego. *Jiniàn pǐn,* yes? *Xie xie.*" Then he ran back to the bus.

If she had still had her baton she would have bashed him. "What the hell do you think you're –"

"On the bus! On! On!" he yelled as he pushed her back onto the bus and into a seat. "Bus! GO! San Diego Zoo. Polisec orders code G6L4. Now go!" He sat down heavily in a seat across the aisle from her and said, "Yeah, it was your ID. And I want that badge as far away as a panda can take it. So they don't find us." The bus pulled away from the curb and into traffic.

"Oh, damn. I forgot," Autumn said.

"What did you forget?" said Brian.

"Polisec badges have a locator chip," she said. "In case an officer is wounded or stranded." She looked down the street toward the retreating black and white fur storm. "The Armory could have been tracking us all this time."

"Not immediately," Mack said. "Not until they realized you weren't killed by that missile. I should have thought about your badge sooner. Anyway, from now on they're tracking a panicky panda from Pindu. We should be able to move freely."

"No, wait," she said. "That's not the only one. A couple of years ago, polisec put chips in all our service weapons, in case one gets lost or stolen."

"Makes sense. We'll need to ditch your gun too."

"I can't. We might have to use it."

"If you keep it, I *guarantee* we'll have to use it," he said.

"We are not throwing away my gun!" said Autumn. Carter was dead, she didn't have a helmet or a badge anymore, and White Knights was saying she was a terrorist. Her lack of sleep because of the early morning meeting was hitting her, and she felt like crying, but she refused to let it show. "I'm responsible to see that it doesn't fall into the wrong hands."

"If it's incinerated on your person by another missile, it won't fall into anybody's hands ever again. That what you want?"

"No." What she *wanted* was to go back to 6:30 this morning and not go inside the tailor shop. She was furious at Carter. She was the junior officer. She was the one supposed to be making stupid moves.

"Look, I have to stick with Brian," said Mack. "But if you'd rather go it alone that's OK. Are we dropping you and your drone-attracting pistol off at the next bus stop?"

"The hell you are," she said. She pulled the Yamato from her holster, ejected the magazine, and handed the gun to him as if it were a citation. "But you're still under arrest."

"Thanks," said Mack, and sprinted with it up the stairs to the upper deck. Autumn was close behind him. *Funny,* she thought, *last night I couldn't wait to get out of uniform and now losing it bit by bit scares the baiji out of me.*

"Now what we need is some kind of…Ah! Perfect!" he said. As the bus slowed to a stop at a red light, Mack held the railing tightly and leaned far over the side of the bus. Stopped beside the bus was a large maroon, white, and blue cargo van. Mack dropped the gun, and it landed with a clunk on the center of the truck's roof. As the truck made a right turn, they saw the logo on its side: *U.S. Federal Postal Express.*

"Who knows?" Autumn said with a sigh. "Maybe it's headed for China too."

Chapter 17

"I hope there's not a problem." Brian was peering out the window as Mack and Autumn came back down the stairs. "We're not going toward the zoo. We're getting on Imperial Avenue eastbound."

"According to the schedule we should be on Park Boulevard," said Mack with a frown. He tried to remember if Huero had mentioned anything specific that would shed light on the general polisec situation.

Brian's concern was overheard by the bus, which generated a spoken reply. "Attention, passengers. Because of polisec activity in a cordoned-off area, we are forced to make a detour. This means we must forego our drive through one of San Diego's architecturally quaint older business sections. We are now plotting a new course that will include attractions we believe you will find stimulating and exciting. Please remain seated at all times. We apologize for the inconvenience. Thank you."

"That explains that," said Brian. "A good thing, too. We would have been coming frighteningly close to my tailor shop."

"Zamparanelli and Offspring for all your fine menswear needs," the bus announced, "at prices to suit all species. Contact code is now being downloaded into all of your devices."

"Quiet." Autumn said. She didn't look happy. "Busses have ears."

"It's OK, Brian," Mack said. "The computer only responds to passenger comments about things on the tour. If you mention food, it will recommend restaurants on the route. You know, paid endorsements. But do be careful what you say."

"Zamparanelli, indeed!" Brian muttered to himself, with some comment about bad needlework.

Suddenly the automatic steel seat harnesses closed over each of them.

"Attention, passengers," the computer voice said. "You will notice that for the next few minutes your seat restraints will not open. This is because we are about to enter a highly-restricted area where you are required to remain seated at all times for your own comfort and safety. Please sit back and enjoy the sights."

"Mack, what's going on?" asked Autumn.

"Uh, bus? What area that would be, perchance?" Mack tried to force his hand under the restraint.

"Again we apologize," said the bus, "for any inconvenience caused by our unplanned change of route. We have located a nearby building with remarkable architectural features, where a representative will board the bus and give you a brief history of the structure."

"Bus!" Autumn said. "Polisec orders code G6L8! Return to zoo route!"

"Passenger's polisec order has been placed in queue," the bus informed her. "We have almost reached our next interesting building, the recently-remodeled White Knights Armory."

"Stop! We've got to get off this bus!" Autumn said loudly in her command voice. "Now!"

"All passengers must remain on the bus for your own comfort and safety…" the bus responded, "as we turn the corner and approach the gleaming white facade of granite and titanium across the next intersection. Notice, please, the image of a white knight chess piece emblazoned on the impenetrable carbon steel gates that open into the armory courtyard."

"Mack!" Autumn hissed. "Brian! Somebody!"

"Give me just a moment…" said Brian. With his powerful chimpanzee arms he was straining to force the harness bar away from his body, with little success.

The bus was only one traffic light from the Armory entrance. Ahead to the left and high above the street, there was a little flash of reflected sun off the windscreen of a polisec burstcar at the top of its jump over the roof of a small office building. The burstcar descended, ringjets whirring underneath and the internal gyrotrain swiveling the vehicle into line with the cars in the right lane. Its underlights began flashing blue and white as it merged smoothly downward into a gap in traffic ahead of the bus. Once at ground level, it pulled around the line of cars and zoomed past, toward the Armory gates.

"Soon, we too will pass through those gates," the bus said cheerily, "and into the safe and protective confines of a top-rated police/security company. Once inside, surrounded by well-armed professionals, we will be pleased to be joined by a top White Knights officer..." the voice paused. "One moment, please. Retrieving information."

"Probably some Public Affairs rookie who hasn't even heard about the tailor shop yet," Mack said quietly. He drew his gun.

"Attention passengers," the bus resumed. "Once inside the gates, we will be joined by a top White Knights officer named Captain C. J. Bickson."

"We're dead!" said Autumn.

"Not so loud," Mack whispered as the bus began a short message from the *Heavenly Rest Mortuary and Cemetery*. "Here." He reached inside his coat to the small of his back for his second gun and then passed it across the aisle to Autumn. "You may need this."

"One moment please, passengers," the bus said. "We are instructed to wait here at the corner until the officer boards. Then we will drive across the intersection, through the gates, and into the armory."

"Wha — how did you get your guns back?" Autumn whispered to Mack as she stared at the gun in her hand.

"I retrieved them while you were busy trying to get a wig head shot up." Mack took out his Hayakawa and put the muzzle against the restraint hinge. "Better lean the other way. I'm probably going to blow off my leg."

The bus said, "Attention, passengers. I am informed that Captain Bickson has unfortunately been called away to a fast-breaking polisec operation, and no other officer is available to speak to us."

"What a disappointment," said Autumn, almost smiling. Mack slumped back into his seat.

"No need for disappointment, honored passengers," the bus responded. "We will still be allowed to drive through the gates and park long enough to take a good look around the inner courtyard." The bus's solar-powered motor started up again. "Everyone get ready for a stimulating experience inside one of the most secure facilities in all of the fifty-four United States."

Mack suddenly looked at Autumn. "Winn! Get your shirt off!" he whispered.

"What?" Autumn somehow managed to keep her voice down. "Are you crazy?"

"Even if nobody gets on the bus, some cop in the courtyard may see you."

"OK, right," said Autumn, unbuttoning her black uniform shirt as quickly as possible. Underneath was her dark blue bullet-proof underwear.

"If a button tears off, I can sew it back later," said Brian. "Assuming there is a later."

Autumn squeezed the shirt out from underneath the metal harness bars.

"Drop it on the floor. The bus is moving!" said Mack, sliding his Hayakawa partly under his thigh and laying his hand on the gun to conceal it.

Autumn threw her shirt on the floor and kicked it under the seat in front of her. She pulled out her elastic hairband and let her hair fall so it would at least cover her shoulders. Then she held Mack's backup gun out of sight, pressed between her knee and the wall of the bus.

The bus had just reached the intersection when a voice called from the corner, "Stop, bus! Open door for inspection. Polisec orders code G6H2."

The voice was very familiar.

Chapter 18

"Routine inspection." It was the polisec horse that had questioned Mack earlier that morning. She stuck her big head inside the bus entrance. "You again? Finally caught right bus? Who these people? Not tourists' clothes. Something strange here."

"Oh, no, Officer," Brian said. "Everything's fine and normal. We're just, uh…"

"Going to a photo shoot," said Mack. "Fashion photography."

"Photo shoot. Yes!" said Brian. "At the San Diego Zoo. But we must get there immediately, Officer. This beautiful bus will be the backdrop for the photos."

"Photos from Lorenzo's Fine Portraiture will make this vacation memorable," the bus intoned. "Purchasing Connection now being downloaded."

"Where camera?" said the horse. "Show me camera."

"We're not the photographers," said Brian, as he ostentatiously adjusted the silk handkerchief in the pocket of his suit coat. "We're the fashion designers. The human gentleman is Mr. Mizrahi, and I am Mr. Lagerfeld. And we're running terribly late."

"Why girl dressed like that?" the horse asked. "Look like underwear."

"MamZelle, the latest in lace lingerie for all sizes and species," the bus offered. "Connection being downloaded."

"She's our model," Brian said. "She's Miss…uh,"

"Miss Autumn," said Autumn.

"Yeah, Miss Autumn. Right," said Mack. "She's done a lot of centerfolds. Miss Autumn. Miss February. Miss Bambi. You know."

"No, don't know," said the polisec horse. "But her face very familiar. Seen her somewhere."

"That's because she has appeared on so many plastimag covers," said Brian. "She's been on the cover of, let's see, *Celeb*, and *Wide World of Fashion*, and what else, *Synthetic Fibers Quarterly,* and uh…"

"*Deadly Weapons Annual,*" said Autumn. "*Asian Heritage Journal.*"

"*Home and Tractor,*" said Mack. "Or you might have seen her in *Equine Enquirer.*"

"You have photo location permit?" asked the horse.

"Mr. Lagerfeld's assistant is bringing it from Hillcrest," said Mack. "There was a mix-up this morning because of all the polisec traffic restrictions, and I couldn't get a SoloCar. That's why we're so late, you see."

"Miss Autumn still has to get hair and makeup," said Brian. "We'll send you a scan of the permit as soon as we reach the zoo. But we simply must dash now."

"This delay is simply *unbearable*," Autumn said haughtily. "The traffic. The schedule. The, um, the grueling life of a professional model. You think I want to be seen in public with hair like this? Wait until I tell my agent that I had to walk out of the hotel without my second-stage creamy texturizer."

The bus interjected "Protect your delicate skin from the ravages of air pollution with Delightie…"

"No more bus talk!" the horse said loudly. "Polisec orders code G6H9." The bus instantly became quiet.

"Oh, Miss Autumn, please don't start throwing one of your internationally scandalous tantrums," said Mack. "I'm sure Captain Bickson would be very embarrassed by a public scene right here in the Armory, what with everything else that's happening today."

"No talk!" the horse said. Then she gave them all the equine big eye for a moment. "OK. You can go," the horse said. "But girl cover up until photo shoot. Not shock children." The horse pulled her head out of the doorway and said, "Bus, you go straight to zoo now. Cancel normal procedures. No stopping anywhere. Polisec orders code G6H9, Urgency 6R. Now go!"

The bus turned the corner and headed north, away from the White Knights armory.

"Attention, passengers," the bus said. "We sincerely apologize that you were not able to go inside the polisec facility. Our final stop will be the world-famous San Diego Zoo and Botanical Gardens in beautiful Balboa Park." The steel harnesses clicked open. "Your seat restraints are now disengaged, and you are free to move around. Thank you for enjoying your afternoon with us."

Autumn and Brian and Mack didn't move. They looked at each other in exhausted silence. The bus passed a building with a huge vidscreen ad for *Ramirez Hoof Wax: Ace That Job Interview*. It featured the video of a beautiful Appaloosa horse displaying her hooves.

Autumn glanced over at Brian and said, "Mr. Lagerfeld, will my feet show in the photo? I don't have nice-looking toes."

All three of them began to laugh.

Chapter 19

When Autumn had finished buttoning up her uniform shirt. Mack moved across the aisle into the seat behind her.

"Nice work," he said.

"You, too," she replied while looking out the window.

Up front Brian was watching the tall apartment buildings tick past row by row. He absent-mindedly stroked his neck and the furline around his face.

The last time Mack had been in this neighborhood, some of the buildings were still under construction. Grant Hill, Golden Hill, Sherman Heights—the whole area had been razed and converted into mass housing for Provisional Citizens. These were not Rapidfabs, but buildings built by human construction crews under the Species Opportunity Act.

Nocturnal buildings were the ones with tiny, autoshuttered windows. The diurnal buildings had long outthrust balconies where the occupants could install a little climbing gym, or keep a few potted trees to browse leaves from while they watched a vidstream, or simply rest in the San Diego sunshine. They would be tired after working at low-paid jobs in the service sector or manufacturing and construction or increasingly even in the medical and white-collar sectors.

A lot of Homo sapiens had picked up and moved north to Orange County where animals were restricted to specified zones; or, if they spoke some Spanish, they might move to Ciudad La Raza. Maríqui kept talking about that as a possibility. Or they went to the neighboring states of CentralValCal and Greater Arizona. Anywhere to get away from the Provie tide. But of course, the fewer humans there were to work in San Diego, the more animals were needed to pick up the slack.

The bus was stopped four cars behind a red light. Rush hour had come early and traffic was oozing. Things were probably confused and tied up from here to Little Italy with people fleeing or being directed away from the area of the sweep and the explosion. Mack looked around at the packed cars headed in both directions. No polisec presence that he could see. A few animals were ambling down the street, or doing a double-take at seeing a big red bus in what was normally just a neighborhood, not a tourist attraction.

San Diego's natural harbor had shaped the city's destiny once again, and it was now a key port of entry for animals from nearly everywhere. Immigrants from Africa and Asia who had struggled over land and sea to reach the Asian side of the Pacific Rim might work at grunt jobs in the booming economies of India or Australia while saving up to pay for their first vocoders. Of the ones who failed to find permanent places there, or who hoped for more, some made their way eastward across the ocean. They came on ships in converted cargo/sleeper containers with a few holes punched for light, spending two weeks sipping from plastic water jugs. Or they traveled by air in the rattling seatless insides of used-up jetliners, breathing from oxygen masks and clinging to the webbed harness belts that ran the length and width of the plane.

The bus rolled with agonizing slowness past a small building with the sign *ALL-CLEAR Provisional Legal Services*. Outside the door lingered a giant tortoise, one of the few nonmammals known to be elevated. It was munching a lettuce leaf and reading a plastimag spread flat between its front feet on the sidewalk. On one side of its shell there was some graffiti in what looked like Korean.

Some of the animals making that Pacific crossing went to the megalopolitan corridors of Chile; others struggled to compete with native species of elevated animals in the Amazonian countries; many went to Canada and worked on the pipelines. But the once-magnetic dream of the United States had not faded away completely. And since the wealthy state of Siliconia kept an almost complete lock on entry through San Francisco, the main entry points on the West Coast were Seattle and San Diego.

They passed a building with a full-wall vidscreen ad in bright orange and green: *VidCall Kenya, only $14.99/Minute. Encrypted Vocoding at Both Ends.*

Increasingly, Lindbergh International was turning into an immigrant processing center. Long lines of primates and quadrupeds and mustelids and others waited with their big or little duffel bags to be tested for viruses while being asked what was America's last officially-declared war (World War II), or which branch of government controlled the news media (Legislative), or what was the federal penalty for operating an unlicensed drone ($70,000 fine plus eight years of community service). At last they were told whether they would be allowed in as Provisionals.

There would be some humans entering or leaving the country at Lindbergh, the ones who couldn't afford the quicker and nicer terminal on New Island offshore from Coronado. This week Mack had guessed based on his experience that while animals at Lindbergh were subject to wearying scrutiny, humans using the airport would get almost a pass from the overworked authorities.

He had found out otherwise.

And now without his COR band he was now ID-less, in a world where being able to make a computer believe that you were who you said you were was essential for survival. Even if he bought a cheap deepweb fake ID and found a little hole-in-the-wall motel like the Sleepy Daze, he still couldn't ply his trade without the tools he had on that COR band provided. He would never be able to retire from the madness of modern life.

Not getting the COR back wasn't an option.

I really am *going to need Urizen now,* he thought.

Meanwhile he was on a tour bus with a weirdly formal chimp and a shaken-up polly woman. She, at least, might be worth getting to know better.

"I would never have thought you were the type to become polisec," Mack said to Autumn, leaning forward a little over the back of her seat. "You seem more, what? Intellectual. More studious."

106

She smiled slightly. She was still looking out the window. "I do my job," she said.

"You probably find you don't have much in common with the other Public Assistance Agents."

"I actually like most of them," she said. "It's just a few that ruin it."

"You have hobbies outside of work?"

She ran her thumbnail across the grip chequering on the revolver he had given her. "Sorry you got caught up in this, Mack."

"I'm sorry, too."

"Next time you should buy suits during business hours."

"Hey, have you noticed that you haven't called me Davis all afternoon. If I call you Autumn, that could be part of your disguise."

"Maybe. As long as it's not *Miss* Autumn. I will totally Six-H you."

"Six-H." Mack thought for a moment. "'Sexual harassment or verbal assault while acting under color of law.' Probably a real hassle for a woman working in polisec."

Autumn turned to look at him. "Hang on, how do *you* know this stuff?"

"Oh, I was a law student for a while," he said. "But I switched to Art History."

"And the tracking chip in my badge?" she persisted. "And the fact that only polisec uses whiner missiles. How do you know all this?"

"To be perfectly honest, I used to be a proofreader for a publisher that did military and polisec manuals. Well, a few. Mostly we did children's picture books," he said.

Autumn tilted her head, sized him up, and then a slow smile crept over her face. "OK, I've met your type before," she said. "I should have spotted you right from the beginning."

"Um, meaning what?"

"Meaning you can stop the act now. You're not at all what you've been claiming to be."

Mack hoped his antiperspirant was living up to its advertising. "I'm not?"

"Sheesh. you're not even smart enough to be subtle about it, are you, Mister Polisec Street Expert?" she said. "You're just another polisec wannabe. You're a badge groupie. A siren sweetie. Trying to chat me up and everything."

"Guilty as charged." he said. "But from now on I promise to be faithful only to you. I swear off even looking at any other polisec ladies."

"Not interested." She sighed, turned forward and stared out the window again. "You can leave the bus if you want. But I'll need to hang on to your gun."

A moment later the look on her face suddenly changed. She quickly looked down at the small five-shot revolver in her hand.

"Holy shelduck." She spun back around and pointed the gun at him. "What would happen if I pulled the trigger right now? Should I pull it and see?"

"I'd rather you didn't," he said.

"Because it will fire, won't it? I bet there's no palmprint safety lock." she said. "If it *did* have one, I wouldn't have been able to fire it at all, and you would have had no reason to give it to me. Which in turn means this is an illegal weapon. Isn't it?"

Mack stared down the barrel of his own gun. *Time to switch to a better brand of antiperspirant.*

"But you *did* give it to me," Autumn said. "Hey, I know what! I'll pull the trigger, and we'll find out."

"No, don't shoot. You're right. It will fire. But that's only because I had it before the palmprint lock law was passed," Mack said. "It was grandfathered in. It's kind of an heirloom."

"It's no heirloom, and you didn't get it from your grandfather. This weapon has only been in production for about four years. No ordinary wannabe would have the contacts to get an firearm like this at all, much less illegally."

"Honestly, Autumn, the way the laws keep changing…"

"That's Officer Winn, to you, scum! Now I really *do* have you dead to rights." She glared at him for a moment, uncertainty on her face. "You're one of those sleazebags from Secure-Tek polisec. You're trying to steal our contract with San Diego County!"

"No, honestly," Mack said. "You yourself said my attitude is too rebellious to be in the polisec profession. You're absolutely right. Hey, could you maybe put that down? This is the second time today someone has pointed my own gun at me."

"Your attitude is exactly what I expect from Secure-Tek rent-a-cops. You're snarky, slippery, sloppy, and unprofessional. You accidently got swept up in a White Knights operation, so you decided to tag along and look for officer mistakes or improper procedure. Anything you could scrape up to make us look bad to the County. Admit it!"

"Seriously, Autu…Officer Winn, I'm not trying hurt anyone. I'm a victim in this thing just like you and Brian. All I want is to get my property and go back where I came from. Honest."

"If I shot you right now, you think White Knights wouldn't back me up one hundred percent? Think again! Now, who are you?"

When all else fails, tell the truth, he thought.

"OK, OK. My name's not really Davis."

"Go on," she said.

"I'm a former OGA operative, but now I do mostly industrial espionage. You know, product spying to help companies keep up with the competition. I'm tired of it, and I'm saving up to buy a small mountaintop in Idaho and paint watercolors. Unfortunately, my bank account is still about a million dollars short of even a log cabin, so I have to do five or six more jobs before I can retire. That's the honest truth. I swear it."

"You? A spook? Not in a million years." Autumn glanced out the window as the bus came in sight of the zoo parking lot. "You're not disciplined enough to be a spy. You're nothing but a no-class Secure-Tek scum." She settled the little revolver into her big Yamato holster. "Stay out of my way."

110

Mack smiled.

World-Famous San Diego ZOO, said the big grimy letters on the corner of Park Boulevard. The bus turned into the enormous empty parking lot.

The zoo facilities had been built in an earlier era, when you couldn't see a warthog or a Thomson's gazelle just by walking past a laundromat. The bus passed over the asphalt between widely spaced light poles that had faded pictures of animals mounted on them. With a puffing of brakes the bus slowed and swung its double-decker bulk in line with the curb of the entrance plaza.

The three of them stood and waited in the aisle to disembark. Brian turned around to face Mack and Autumn. "I'm worried. Suppose this bus keeps a record of where it's been. Could it be used to track us down?"

Mack instinctively reached toward his wrist to connect to the bus computer and wipe its memory using his COR band. But his wrist was bare.

"Don't worry," said Autumn to Brian. They stepped off the bus and she turned around. "Bus! New polisec orders."

Mack was thinking about this code business. The White Knights orders code probably changed constantly to keep anyone who might overhear it from being able to use it. The first part, G6, had not changed today, so that was probably the month and day. The last part was what kept changing.

"Polisec code G6J5. Disable live link to bus company. Drive non-stop to Yuma Arizona Zoo," Autumn commanded. "Pick up passengers and return. Do not return without passengers. Wait for passengers!" She turned back and smiled. "That should keep the bus company from retrieving their bus for a while."

The bus snapped its doors shut and rolled away, back out through the parking lot, looking like a red toy bus as it diminished in the distance.

"Look!" Brian said. "Overhead! Drones!"

"Relax. They're only traffic spotters," Autumn said. "It's afternoon drive time, and Balboa Park is surrounded by six different freeways within two miles. Those drones aren't polisec."

Mack hoped she was right, and as their eyes met for a moment he saw she was hoping the same thing.

They walked past rows of overgrown bushes to the zoo entrance and came up to one of the ticket booths. It looked empty

As Mack raised his fist to knock on the ticket counter, there was a high-pitched scream from somewhere down inside the booth.

Chapter 20

"Yaaarrrrgh! Victims!" the voice squealed, and a dark-eyed white ferret popped up on the shelf behind the counter.

"Not victims, Leroy!" said a black sable ferret, as it popped up in the booth's other window. "Guests! Visitors! Patrons!"

"Customers!" they both squealed and did an excited ferret war dance around the counter top.

"At last," Autumn said. "Someone who's happy to see us."

"Welcome, consumers of zoological culture!" said the sable ferret. "Attendance is very low today. No crowding, no waiting. How many tickets, please?"

"Use your eyeballs, Larry," said Leroy, the white ferret. "Three customers, three tickets."

"But maybe someone's joining them," said Larry.

"Or meeting them," said Leroy.

"Or hiding behind them?"

"Hiding in their pockets?"

"How many tickets?" both ferrets said in unison.

"No tickets," Autumn said. "We've here to see the Assistant Director."

"Do you have an appointment?" said Larry.

"Have an appointment?" echoed Leroy.

"No," Autumn said, "but we don't need one."

"Sorry, no appointment, no Director," said Leroy.

"How many tickets, please?" said Larry.

"Look, Leroy," Mack said, "we don't need an…"

"He's Larry," said the other ferret. "I'm Leroy."

"It's easy to remember," said Larry, "because I'm slightly bigger."

"Yes," said Leroy. "Mother said I was the lesser of two weasels."

The ferrets screamed in laughter and broke into another short happy dance.

"Both of you!" Mack used his authoritative voice. "We don't need tickets. She's a polisec officer. We just want to go to the main office."

The ferrets disappeared into the darkness of the ticket box.

"Where'd they go?" Mack said.

"You scared them," Autumn said. "Let me handle this." She tapped on one of the ticket windows. "Hey, fellows, we're in a hurry. Three tickets, please."

"What kind?" Leroy said as he popped up in the other ticket window.

"Which package?" said Larry, popping up beside him.

"What do you mean, 'package'?" Autumn said.

"Do you want the One-day EZ-Pass," said Leroy.

"Or the One-day Special Plus Pass," said Larry.

"The Three Day-One Pay package?"

"The Summer Fun Extended Package?"

"The One-Year Introductory Membership Offer?"

"Or the Select Member with Full Benefits Subscribership?"

"OH!" Leroy gasped. "How about the Gold Patron, Lifetime-Plus Ten, Anything, Anytime Offer."

"PLEEEASE," begged Larry. "We've never sold a Gold Patron, Lifetime-Plus Ten, Anything, Anytime Offer. Not ever!"

"PLEEEASE," the ferrets both squealed in unison and did another excited dance.

"Listen!" Mack said, rapping his knuckles on the counter. "Give us the cheapest tickets you have."

"OK. Three Full-day-No-privileges passes," said Leroy. "Price now showing on the pay screen."

"Press your PayChip against the touchpad on the screen," said Larry. "Ninety-four dollars each, please."

"Total is $282.00," Leroy and Larry said together.

"WHAT?!" said Autumn and Mack together.

"But we only want to see the Assistant Director," Brian said. "He's my cousin."

"Sorry, no tickets and no appointment…" said Leroy.

"…means no entry through the security gates," said Larry.

Brian grabbed Mack and Autumn by the arm and pulled them to one side. "Just pay it, and I'll get it back from my cousin," he said. "I've been watching those drones overhead. One of them is hovering in place, and it's not near a freeway. We've got to get inside quickly."

"Well, we can't use our PayChips," Autumn said. "A PayChip transaction would identify our location almost immediately. We'll have to come up with cash."

"Can't help you there," said Mack.

Autumn scowled. "What? I suppose you'll say you left your money in your other pants."

"In this particular case," Mack said "my other pants are with a troop of baboons carrying machine guns. But you're polisec. Order them to override the security gate." He had no intention of pulling out his sparklies just to get into the zoo.

"This isn't like the tour bus," said Autumn. "The zoo is part of the city central facilities network. The override will place an automatic call to the Armory to get confirmation."

"I'm afraid I don't have any cash," said Brian. "When I'm in the tailor shop, I leave my things in my desk."

"Oh, brother," said Autumn, digging down in her uniform pants pocket.

"How much cash do you have?" Mack said.

"Counting the change from buying the donuts," she said, "almost twenty-five dollars."

"Let me work on this. Almost $25, huh?" said Mack as he turned and stepped back to the ticket window. "'Scuse me," he said to Larry, "you forgot the Senior Citizen Discount."

"No Senile Citizen," said Leroy. "Two adult sapiens, one adult chimpanzee."

"Chimpanzees are Provisional Humans. Don't you know it's a crime to discriminate against Provies?" Mack said.

"Chimps are Provie Citizens, yes," said Larry. "But not Senile Citizens."

"If a chimp is a Provisional Citizen," said Mack, "then an old chimp is a Provisional Senior Citizen. So he gets the twenty-percent discount. That's only logic."

"Maybe logic," said Leroy, "but he's not old."

"Listen," said Mack, "chimpanzees have a lifespan only two-thirds that of a human. You work in a zoo, you should know that. Two-thirds means this chimp is old."

"Looks young to us," said Leroy.

"Just look at him!" Mack said. "Those loosely dangling knuckles, that bald spot on top. And wearing a *necktie*. Who does *that* anymore? A geezer if I ever saw one!"

"Wait just a minute!" Brian said behind him. "I resent…"

"Shhh!" said Autumn. "Let him try. That drone's starting to move this way."

"So he'll need the discount," said Mack firmly. "Or do I report you to the Assistant Director?"

"Who happens to be my cousin," Brian called over Autumn's shoulder.

"OK, OK," said Leroy. "Revised total is now on screen."

"Two-hundred-sixty-three dollars and twenty cents," said Larry.

"You can't forget her, though." Mack pointed to Autumn. "She's his caregiver. Caregivers get the same discount. That's the law."

"She's not caregiver. She's in polisec uniform!" Leroy bounced excitedly on the counter. "He's not very much old. Doesn't need any caregiver!"

"Then what do you think she's doing here? Directing traffic? Giving parking tickets?" said Mack. "Of *course* she's his official uniformed caregiver! Are you saying that she's *my* caregiver? Are you implying I look so decrepit that I need a caregiver? That's highly offensive! I could sue the zoo for that!"

"You not old! He not old!" Leroy bounced into a full ferret war dance until Larry nipped him on the neck. Leroy disappeared into the depths of the ticket booth and could be heard bouncing and scrabbling against the walls.

"Alright! OK," Larry said as he popped back up. "We give two discounts. Total now $244.40. Everybody settle down."

"Great. Thank you," said Mack. "I can see that you are a very reasonable and very…Wait a minute. Hold on!"

"Now what?" said Larry.

"What now?" Leroy's head popped up into view.

"There's some mistake," Mack said. "The screen shows the price for Full-day Passes."

"You wanted the cheapest ticket," said Larry.

"Full-day is cheapest," said Leroy.

"Look at your sign," Mack said. "Right there on the wall. Zoo hours. What does it say?"

"Zoo hours, 11:00 a.m. to 6 p.m." said Larry. "Used to be longer before budget cutbacks."

"And not many customers since the Elevation," said Leroy. "Now humans are used to seeing animals everywhere."

"Look at the sun," Mack said. The two ferrets craned their necks to see around him. "Lower," Mack said.

Larry scrunched his body lower and pressed his nose pressed against the ticket booth window. "Sun going down soon. So what?"

"Mack, close the deal," hissed Autumn. "The drone is sweeping the parking lot."

"We've wasted a lot of time making sure you guys don't overcharge us," said Mack. "By the time we actually get into the zoo, it will be almost closing time. But you're trying to sell us full-day passes!"

"Cheapest thing we've got!" yelled Leroy.

"You seem like nice guys," Mack said in a more conciliatory tone. "Would you deliberately try to cheat zoo visitors? Larry, would you?"

"No! Plenty nice," said Larry.

"Not as nice as me," said Leroy, scooting up next to him.

"I could tell how nice you were," said Mack. "You'd want your customers to get the right value for the price they pay, right? You love customers."

"When we get them," said Larry.

"So what time is it right now?"

"5:30," said Leroy.

"And the full day pass would start at eleven. But six and a half hours is nine-tenths of seven hours, right?"

"Wait," said Leroy. "Need pencil."

"Just simple math. So the day is already nine-tenths over and we have one tenth left. Just charge us one-tenth of the full day price, and we'll call it fair."

"We don't do that!" Larry said, his voice becoming even higher pitched. Leroy began bouncing more wildly than ever while making unintelligible ferret noises.

"You can't charge us ten times what we should pay!" shouted Mack. "That's against the law!"

"We don't want to see the zoo!" shouted Brian. "We only want to talk to my cousin."

"We gave you discount already!" Larry's voice was now almost a scream.

"And a second discount!" Leroy squealed.

"I demand to the see the Assistant Director right now," Mack shouted. "Right this second, or I'll call my attorney."

"Stop yelling," yelled Leroy, "or we call polisec!"

"I *am* polisec," yelled Autumn. "And we want the Assistant Director!"

"My cousin!" yelled Brian.

"The law! Discounts! Senior abuse!" yelled Mack. "Polisec! Scandal! No more customers *ever*!"

"OVERRIDE!" screamed the two ferrets in unison. "Override on register two!"

The numbers on the screen changed to $24.44, and the words "Override Authorization Required" appeared. Larry slammed his paw on a button as Autumn thrust her almost twenty-five dollars through the opening under the window. The metal security gates began to swing open.

"Keep the change!" said Autumn, and the three rushed through the gate.

As they walked down the path, Mack took a nervous glance over his shoulder.

The two ferrets were bouncing in a full-frenzied happy dance. "We keep change!" they were squealing. "We keep change!"

Chapter 21

"Brian! Dear cousin! What a thrill!" the Assistant Director said as he rushed across the office to meet them. He grabbed Brian's hand and shook it as any executive would, then immediately shifted into more typical chimpanzee behavior, rubbing his hands up and down Brian's arms and shoulders and giving Brian a big kiss on the cheek.

"Charlesworth, this is a new customer of mine, Mr. Davis." Brian pointed to Mack. "And the lady is Officer Winn. She has been helping me."

The Assistant Director bowed to Autumn, then gave Mack a business-like handshake. To Mack's relief, he omitted the kissing part. It was clear that the alpha male in this situation was Brian.

"I wish you had called first," said Charlesworth, "Fortunately I am wearing one of Brian's suits, you see, very nice, isn't it? And I could have had the snack bar prepare a dinner before they closed. Since the last cutbacks, the zoo is only able to have the snack bar open for a few hours. I'm very sorry."

"That would have been nice," Brian said. "We were forced to skip lunch. But no matter. We have much greater needs than food."

"Ah, but there's good news, dear cousin," said Charlesworth. "I have keys to everything in the zoo. So we can let ourselves in. I happen to know they received a shipment of fresh fruits today. Come! We'll make it a party to celebrate your visit to the zoo. I've been wishing that you would stop in."

"Food will be welcome," said Brian, "but this is not the time for a party. We are in very big trouble. We need your help."

"What has happened, dear cousin? I will help you any way I can."

"This morning my shop was attacked."

"Gang activity!" Charlesworth gasped. "If only you could locate in a better part of town."

"No. It was baboons," said Brian. "They were dressed like military or polisec. They killed a polisec and kidnapped Brianna."

"Brianna! Baboons!" Charlesworth leaned against the desk in shock. "Now I understand why this officer is here. Tell me what I can do. Anything!"

Brian quickly told his cousin about the attack, the explosion in the vacant building, and their escape from the area. "Charlesworth, we've come to you," he said, "because we need a place to hide until tomorrow."

"Oh, Brian. I am very afraid. What if polisec comes here looking for you?" said Charlesworth. "I could lose my job. I am very frightened about all this. Or the baboons! What if they've followed you here!"

"We don't think any of that will happen," Autumn said. "We've covered our tracks, and there's no reason to think anyone knows we're here."

"But I shouldn't help fugitives. I could lose my job." Charlesworth began rocking from one foot to the other. "But you're family. I must help family. Oh, what should I do? You're my family, but I could lose my job! What if I lose my job?"

"Charlesworth!" Brian looked the Assistant Director in the eye. "They're trying to kill us."

Charlesworth stopped rocking and stared at them for a moment. "Wait!" he said. "I know the perfect place. As soon as it's dark, I'll take you there."

Autumn, being originally from the Peninsula up in Siliconia, had never actually been to the San Diego Zoo before. The zoo was a winding, forested complex of terrain on higher and lower levels that made her feel surprisingly peaceful. Animals were something she had to deal with every day, but the variety of trees here was nice. The wide paved path curved repeatedly out of sight, overhung by branches bursting with leaves. And every single one of these was a real plant.

She would have liked to take off her gear and walk barefoot among the trees and dig her toes in the earth. But this wasn't the day.

They walked up a little path behind a boulder-looking wall and stopped. Mack looked with interest at the seam where a door handle protruded from the fake rock. Brian was squatting hands-down in a chimpish pose which looked natural even for him in his suit;

Autumn wondered if the forest called to his primate side, or if he was just tired.

"In there." Charlesworth pointed through the trees at the lion area, separated with a moat from the broad visitor walkway. "You should be safe tonight."

"How many lions are in there?" Autumn asked.

"Only the two females," said Charlesworth. "I'm afraid the San Diego Zoo long ago fell upon hard times. We had an older male once, but he died. Now, two lions are all we can afford to feed."

"That's the part that worries me," said Mack. "How hungry are they, exactly?"

"Oh, no, no. You won't be in with them," Charlesworth said. "You can't see it, but in the rear of the enclosure, behind those large artificial boulders, is a storeroom."

"Is there a whip and a chair?" asked Mack.

"I don't believe so. Why would there be?" said Charlesworth. "The lion keeper uses the room for cleaning supplies and repair tools. The point is, if polisec did come to the zoo, they would never notice the storeroom."

"And we won't have to worry about baboons," Brian said. "Baboons stay as far away as possible from the smell of lions."

"I can't actually blame them," said Autumn. "Come on, campers. Let's get to base."

"Yes, get settled into the storeroom. Move whatever you need to," Charlesworth said. "I will bring you food and blankets. If you need to leave the room during the night, one door goes outside to the path, but the other door opens into the lions' area. Don't get confused."

Chapter 22

There was no light in the storeroom, so Autumn propped up her polisec flashlight on the apple box and bounced the light off the wall. She cycled through several settings including superbeam, spotlight, and double flash until she found the low setting.

"Except for the occasional lion noises," said Brian, "it's almost like a quiet candlelight dinner." He was trying to sound cheerful but his quavery vocoder tone showed he was trying to hide his fears.

They sat down on the concrete floor of the storeroom with their backs against the walls. Each of them had a large napkin on the floor, covered with apples, papayas, carrots, nuts, and a left-over chicken sandwich. To wash their dinner down, they had single-serving boxes of some drink called Ecology Juice, which had an unidentifiable but clearly artificial flavor.

"Your health," said Mack, raising his juice box. "Cheers."

"Santé," said Brian, toasting in return.

Autumn just sipped through the plastic straw and ate her sandwich. She had never actually been to a candle-lit dinner with wineglasses and silver forks, and did not know how to offer any toasts. She would have liked to attend a top-tier university, perhaps overseas, get at least a Master's and perhaps even a Ph.D in cultural heritage. But for the daughter of small-time CPAs helping to support their extended family, it hadn't been within reach—not in Siliconia, anyway, where housing alone could take up to seventy percent of the average person's salary.

She had grown up knowing she would be expected to prepare for a practical career, so that she could do her part in contributing to the family. These days she was trying to catch up on her education by reading books during her treadmill sessions. Polisec work had turned out to be, well, not what anyone would call fascinating. It seemed like it consisted mostly of bossing people around and filling out endless forms. Until today.

She had more or less reconciled herself to the idea that until she could retire, she would simply work to be the best Public Assistance Officer in the whole of White Knights. She hated people like Bickson, who dragged down the whole enterprise, and she hated outfits like Secure-Tek that gave polisec work a bad name. If Mack was in fact connected to Secure-Tek, she was almost sorry she'd saved him in the tailor shop.

On the other hand, he had really tried to help with the problems of the bus and the ticket booth. Maybe he was in fact the one good apple in a rotten barrel; the inverse of Bickson. Time would tell.

"Officer Winn, how are you doing?" said Brian. He was looking at her with an expression that was hard to read by reflected flashlight.

"What? Oh, I'm fine."

"I am very sorry about your partner," he said. He bobbed his head in some kind of reassuring chimp gesture.

"Thanks," she said. She had been trying not to think about Carter. "And try not to worry about your wife. I'm sure we'll catch up with them. Somehow. We're not going to give up."

Which reminded her of another positive thing about this Mack Davis. He was resourceful and tenacious. *Actually, that's two positive things.*

"I was just distracting myself for a minute by thinking about other things," she said. "Books and stuff."

"Oh, do you like to read?" asked Brian.

"Sometimes. Well, a lot, actually."

"Brianna is a wonderful reader. She's reading Charles Dickens' *Bleak House* right now." This would have been no small boast for a human, let alone a Provie, given that even college classes involved mostly learning by vidstream.

"So what do you read?" Mack asked her, crunching a bite out of his apple.

"Asian history and culture, mostly."

"You mentioned," said Brian, "that you weren't Chinese."

"No. I'm Vietnamese. Ethnically, that is. I was born here."

"Vietnam! I have met some animals from there," Brian said. "Very nice, very hard-working. Your parents emigrated from Vietnam?"

"Well…my family came from there in the 1900s." She wasn't sure how to explain why Vietnameseness mattered so much to her when her family had been in America for four generations.

"Very interesting. Do you speak the language at all?"

129

No, of course she didn't. Not yet, anyway. "Well, I can say things like "hello" and 'thank you very much,' *Cám ơn rất nhiều.*" She had wanted to get into intensive first-year Vietnamese at Hi-Band, but the classes never fit around her work schedule. She turned the conversation around. "Where are you from, Brian?"

"Côte d'Ivoire," he replied. "Ivory Coast."

"Your wife as well?" Having said this, Autumn immediately kicked herself. Brianna was undoubtedly a painful subject right now, and Autumn should be trying to deflect the conversation, for Brian's sake. But he seemed happy to answer.

"No, Brianna's family is from Gabon; now they are in Hong Kong, working in import-export. I came to Hong Kong on a ship from Mangalore with only a vocoder and a size 18 raw cotton shirt. I'm still amazed a girl like Brianna spoke to me at that first Primate Association dinner."

"Côte d'Ivoire," said Mack. "*Vous parlez francais* then?"

"*Naturellement*," said Brian. He made a funny French expression with his eyes and mouth that seemed more chimplike than he usually was, but also somehow more human, and it made Autumn snort a little of her Ecology Juice.

Quickly she tried to cover it. "So is Brian the name you were born with? Or …got at some point, if you weren't born with it?" She realized she didn't know how to ask animals about how and when they became elevated.

"No. Brianna and I received our names from Immigration here in San Diego."

Autumn nodded emphatically with understanding. "And your *real* names?"

"Animals don't have names before Elevation. Not in the way humans think of. We simply know each other." He picked up a carrot and pulled off the leaves. "My real name is Brian."

"It is? I mean, it was only—assigned to you," Autumn said. "There's no heritage or legacy behind it."

"Given by your parents, or assigned by the state, what does it matter?" he said. "What's real is whatever I can use. For elevated animals, the past is useless. Everything is about the future."

"Oh." She had never thought about what it would mean to be an intelligent creature without a cultural heritage to reclaim. Yet in spite of that, Brian had a certain quality that reminded her of Great-Grandfather. Well, no, it didn't. It reminded her of what she wanted her Great-Grandfather to have. A kind of dignity, she would call it.

Mack seemed to notice her puzzled expression and he asked Brian another question. "You didn't feel Hong Kong was exactly what you were looking for?"

"That's what's so upsetting," said Brian. His voice did seem more agitated now. "If you come to this country, you spend a great deal of money to get here, you wait a long time for your Provisional status to be confirmed, you start work before dawn every day, and meanwhile people call you a rug, and a groundlicker, and other names. But when we think of all the advantages we will have here, we just work harder. We don't complain."

Well, you *don't,* she thought. *Jiggs and the Free Lifers would disagree.*

His face twitched and he went on a little more slowly. "My mother was only partially elevated. But she knew that for me and my sisters a life in the forest would not be enough. During harvest she earned money by beating cocoa pods with a stick and picking out the beans for the growers."

"Was that good?" asked Autumn. She couldn't tell from his expression.

"She was able to get us on a transport through South Sudan for Nairobi," said Brian. "It turned out the route had been compromised. We were under a tarp in the truck when the human driver was shot. He survived. In fact he drove the truck another eighty kilometers to the Kenyan border with only one good arm. But at that time I thought, all this doesn't happen in America. In America we would be *safe.*" He paused. "That's what I mean by upsetting."

"Yes," said Autumn. "Sorry."

"I get what you're saying," said Mack. "This country isn't what it used to be. Hardly even related, in fact."

"Why don't you do something about it, then?" she asked.

"Me? I'm not all that patriotic," said Mack. "Last refuge of a scoundrel, they say. Half the dirty deeds in history have been done in the name of patriotism."

"Is that your excuse?" said Autumn.

"I think patriotism means being the kind of citizen your country ought to deserve," said Brian, "even when sometimes it does not."

132

Mack shrugged. "Could be."

"You mean being patriotic for the nation, not just for your own reasons," said Autumn.

"How would one be patriotic not for the nation?" asked Brian with a puzzled look.

"Well, you said it's about being that kind of citizen. I've been preparing to...." She stopped herself. Somehow Brian seemed easy to talk to. But explaining her future hopes and dreams with a Secure-Tek agent present was not what she'd planned. She'd put her foot in it now, though, and both of them were waiting for the rest of the sentence.

"OK," she said. She wouldn't include anything about leaving White Knights. "This is just an idea, not fully worked out or anything. But I want to get certified as a Cultural Reclaimer and teach classes about Vietnam. The history, culture, tradition and customs, stuff like that. To boost people's sense of who they really are."

"They don't know who they really are?" said Brian.

"I can't speak for animals," said Mack, "but human beings do have trouble with that."

"How does knowing about the past help?" asked Brian. "Not that I doubt you. My wife finds her reading of books very rewarding. But I am curious how you see it as a human."

"Well..." she cast around for an example. "I've been reading a book about an emperor of Vietnam in ancient times. Lý Thánh Tông."

"What makes him interesting?" asked Brian, cocking his head.

"How he grew up, I guess. When he was young, before he took the throne, his parents had him raised among the common people so that he would understand what their lives were like. So he became a very compassionate ruler. There's a story about how he ordered blankets to be given to the prisoners in his palace. He said he felt cold himself wearing his robes in the palace, and that had to mean the prisoners were even colder."

"That's fascinating," said Brian.

"Not what you think of when you hear the word Emperor, I guess," said Mack.

"They took on the title of Emperor to imitate the Chinese system," said Autumn. "But when they dealt with China, they only called themselves kings."

"Political expediency," said Mack. He smiled a little.

"Anyway, I think studying the history of my culture is inspiring," said Autumn. "But I can't say it has anything to do with being patriotic to the United States." She was not all that much stronger on U.S. history than on Vietnam, she realized. Graduating at sixteen from the mandated one year of high school like everyone else, she hadn't had time to learn much about history before going into the polisec academy. That seemed a shame.

"I tend to believe," said Brian, massaging his long hands in his lap, "that encouraging compassion surely makes people better citizens, whatever the country."

She expected Mack to say something clever in response. But he was quiet, and looked like he was thinking hard. "Mack, what do you think?" she asked.

"About what?" he said.

"Whatever."

He was silent for a minute. Finally he said, "I think once we get Brianna back, she and Brian are going to have some terrific little American chimp kids. The first generation. They're going to ride bikes too fast all over the neighborhood and scare the feathers off the postal emus."

Brian smiled a big smile, mouth wide open, but with the teeth covered, and he seemed to relax a little. "That will be good," he said.

"I want to check around the area," Autumn said after they had balled up their dinner napkins and put them in an empty bag marked BIG CAT LITTER. "To make certain the perimeter is secure. Both of you stay in here."

"Sure thing," said Mack, in a way that she could tell meant he had no intention of staying put.

She sighed. She put her hand on the doorknob. "On second thought, Mack, I want to talk to you. Follow me."

"Officer, nothing on earth could induce me to follow you through that door."

Not the Secure-Tek attitude again. "Why the hell not?"

"Because that's the wrong door."

"Oh," she said, letting go of the knob. "The other door, then."

She went out onto the path, and he followed her. There was a fresh cool feeling from the bushes around them in the night. She was feeling some irritation because her life plan had sounded so flimsy in her own ears when she described it over dinner, but that wasn't Mack's fault. Even if he did work for Secure-Tek.

"You know," she said. "I wouldn't really have shot you on the bus."

"I appreciate that."

"You're not going to run away, right?"

"No, Officer Winn," he said.

"I guess you can call me Autumn," she said. "This isn't a normal situation. We're going to have to work together. But I need to know you won't desert us."

He made an odd little expression with his mouth. " No," he said. "I'm sticking around. For my own reasons."

"That's fine. I'll meet you back here. But as long as you're with us, you're with us. No scumbag attitude, and no dirty tricks. Make one false move, and –"

"You'll ex me. Without hesitation."

"Um, right."

"Never doubted it for a second." He smiled and faded off in one direction, leaving her to reconnoiter in the other.

Mostly what she wanted to do was walk around and breathe among the plants. *Soak in some horticulture.* It would calm her down. If Brian didn't get her almost twenty-five dollars back for her, maybe she could deduct it as a medical expense. Mental health therapy.

Chapter 23

Mack walked around to the front of the lion enclosure and leaned over the railing.

"Yoo-hoo," he called out in a loud whisper. "Hey, lions. Let's have a chat."

Very few lights were left on in the zoo after closing. Mack could see no motion inside the lion enclosure, not even shadowy forms. The enclosure might as well have been a flat black wall. As he opened his mouth to speak again, he suddenly had the feeling he should turn his head to the right. When he did, he saw two large cat eyes shining in the darkness.

"Hello, there," he said. "How did you get across the moat?"

The lioness remained still and silent. Mack remained still and tense.

"I need to find Urizen," he said. "Can you understand me? Look, I know that some animals are elevated but hide it from humans. Do you understand? I must talk to Urizen. This is very important."

The lioness opened her mouth, but didn't speak. She only yawned, the points of her teeth flashing white for a second, then disappeared back into the darkness. As Mack walked back down the path, he felt sure he was being watched by someone, or something, else.

He returned to the storeroom. Brian was methodically cutting a strip off the end of one of the blankets using the V-shaped ultrasonic shear from the tailor shop.

"When did you have time to grab that thing?" Mack asked.

"In the shop I saw you retrieving your weapons, so I thought this might be useful too."

"Is it?"

"Yes. I am going to tie this piece around the doorknob to the lions' area. We will know which is which if we have to get up in the night."

"Good thinking. You wouldn't want to meet a lioness in the dark," Mack said. "They aren't very sociable."

The next morning. Brian was sprawled on his side on the blanket, his suit coat draped over him.

"He's exhausted," said Autumn.

"He's not the only one," said Mack. "I was waiting for you to get back. You spent a long time checking things out last night."

"I'm not tired. I'm pumped. I'm going outside the zoo to get us an ally," Autumn said.

"You'll be spotted," said Mack. "The search may have slowed a little now, but in that uniform you're hard to miss."

"You could never be a spy, like you claimed. You Secure-Tek guys aren't very observant. Look behind you. What you failed to notice is a pair of zoo overalls hanging on the back of that door.

They're way big, but that's good. I can wear them over everything, and my belt and gear won't make lumps."

"I do notice I've been promoted from scum to guy. Life is improving," Mack said. "Who is the ally?"

"Sergeant Carter's sister, Lucille. She's a top geek in the White Knights CommTech division. She'll be off work today helping his widow arrange for the funeral." Autumn said. "Maybe she can trace who initiated the drone missile code. I may be gone all morning."

"Me, too," said Mack. "I'm going out to work a couple of angles of my own and see what I can learn. I'll meet you back here tonight. What should we do about Brian?"

"We'll write a note and let him sleep." She pulled on the overalls. "He needs rest. He's trying not to show it, but he's worried sick." She zipped up the khaki overalls and adjusted the material around her holster and the various pouches on her accessory belt. "How do I look?"

"Lumpy," said Mack. "In a cute way."

Autumn opened the outside door a crack and looked out. The zoo was not open yet, and there was no one in sight except a large wallaby picking up paper trash.

"Hey kiddo," said Mack seriously, "be really careful."

"You, too," she said as she slipped out the door. "Scum."

Mack took his time walking to the zoo's front exit. It was still early, and Verhoven—or whatever he called himself now—was a night owl and would still be asleep.

As Mack passed the rhino and giraffe enclosures, the rhino was munching out of its feeding trough, and the giraffes were snarfing leaves from high up on the acacia trees. Not being elevated didn't seem to bother them in the least.

Still no messages on his ViewGlazzes. He had sent Maríqui his flight arrival time, and normally she would at least send a welcome-home note—even if she'd been seeing somebody in his absence. Did she have a hunch that *he* had a hunch about the Quan Yin? Did she think he'd skipped with the figurine? But why not call? Why not play the game out? Was this Ivan guy putting pressure on her? Maybe she was just too distracted to return a call. *Very touchy-feely,* Huero had said. It sounded like she had feelings for Ivan, or at least had started. Mack was no longer sure exactly what Maríqui had feelings about. Or whom.

As he strolled, Mack noticed he was being paced by that Bennetts wallaby wearing a zoo employee cap. The animal was hopping along picking up pieces of waste paper and putting them into a canvas bag strapped to its side. Mack was passing a park bench when the wallaby suddenly jumped against Mack's thigh, pushing him down onto the bench. As Mack sat up, the wallaby took a quick look around, then reached into its bag, pulled out a napkin, and shoved it under Mack's leg. The animal hopped a few feet away and turned to watch as Mack retrieved the napkin and uncrumpled it.

On the napkin, in beautifully looping feminine handwriting, were the words:

Let not search and inquisition quail. Tonight, Cosmopolitan Hotel. 9:20. All three of you.

Mack crumpled the napkin up into a tight ball, let it drop, and kicked it so that it landed exactly next to the wallaby's large foot. The animal looked around carefully, then quickly picked it up, stuffed it into the bag and hopped away at top speed.

Interesting, thought Mack. *It's not often you see a nervous wallaby.*

"Brian! Wake up!" Charlesworth shook Brian's shoulder. "I need to help you!"

"What's wrong," Brian said as he rolled over.

"Nothing's wrong. Your friends have left, and I've had a good idea," Charlesworth said. "I had a sleepless night worrying about you and your friends. It's not safe for you to stay here."

"What is your idea?" Brian said.

"You remember my younger brother Clifford?" said Charlesworth. "For two years now he has been manager of an avocado orchard up in the foothills. You could be safe there for days, perhaps weeks, if necessary."

"Have you phoned him?" said Brian.

"Oh, no, no, no," said Charlesworth. "It may be that the polisec is already tapping phone calls. That's why you must take my place today. I will take a truck from the botanical garden and drive out to

142

see Clifford. If polisec are watching, they'll think I'm going about trees for the Zoo."

"What do you mean, 'take your place'?" Brian asked.

"You can sit in my office and pretend to read reports. There are no appointments today, and I gave my admin assistant the day off. If the desk rings, don't answer it."

"But what if somebody comes?" said Brian.

"They won't," said Charlesworth. "Just stay in the office for a few hours. I'll put a sign on the door saying an accountant is auditing the books and must not be disturbed."

Chapter 24

Lucille waved her hand to make the kitchen timer stop beeping, then pulled on a silicone glove. Most of the family would be gathered around Denise at the house in Poway by now to plan Bernard's funeral, except for herself and her other brother Steven, who was flying in from Oakland.

She had to get the Polish kielbasa casserole out first, then she would log in and do a few minutes of remote work on that mileage-comp module for the Armory payroll system while she waited for the dish to cool.

She opened the oven door, removed the hot dish, and started to turn when she heard a familiar voice behind her say, "Put the dish down on the counter. Put it down slowly, Lucille."

Not breathing, Lucille managed to set the hot dish on the counter without dropping it. Once she turned around, she took hold of the refrigerator door handle to steady herself.

"It's all right, Lucille," Autumn said, waving her arms in her baggy zoo coveralls. "I'm not a terrorist."

"They said you went rogue," said Lucille, staring at Autumn. "Bernard was dead and you ran with Free Life. You know you could be shot on sight?"

"I'm so sorry about Bernard. There was nothing I could do. It was a surprise attack, and I got hit by freeze gas. I've never even talked to a Free Lifer."

"How'd you get in?" said Lucille. "I got my own locks and prox sensors on the front porch."

"You left the garage side door open."

"Oh. When I emptied the trash." She let go of the refrigerator door handle and took a deep breath. "Bernard—did he…"

"He didn't suffer at all," said Autumn. "He was hit with an exploding round and died instantly. And Lucille, it wasn't his fault. He followed every protocol. He died with his BioBoosters on. There was a surprise ambush. Then the missile, and I had to get out."

"I knew it! I knew all that stuff about you shooting Bernard just couldn't be true," said Lucille. "But I'm glad to hear it from you."

Autumn walked over to her. "Bernard, and you, have been the best things about the White Knights for me, you do know that, right? He was the best partner anyone could had."

Lucille held Autumn's hand tight. After a minute she spoke again. "We gotta go to Denise. She'll want to know."

"You can tell her later, but I can't. I'm on the run." Autumn zipped herself out of the coveralls. "I need your help."

"Looks better to see you in uniform," Lucille said.

"Yesterday the uniform was both a liability and a help. But it was too risky this morning. In fact, I had to flirt to get some guy to swipe his chip twice on the robobus to Mira Mesa." Autumn looked around quickly. "Hold on! What room is your vid screen in?"

"The living room, but don't worry about it," Lucille said. She let herself down heavily on a chair at the kitchen table. "I hacked it so it can't turn on without me knowing. Damned if White Knights going to snoop on me in my own home. Now, what in the world have you done?"

Autumn gave her a quick summary, with little about Brian and less about Mack.

Lucille puffed her cheeks and exhaled very slowly. "Worst mess I ever heard of, honey, and I've been with White Knights twelve years." She got up and drew two glasses of water from the fridge meter. "So how can I help?"

"First of all, in all this mess my parents up in Siliconia might gotten a next-of-kin call from HR. I need you to get a secure message to them, so they know I'm still alive, but they can't try to contact me yet. Maybe tell them I'm working undercover, and they have to pretend I'm dead."

"Done."

"Thanks," said Autumn. "Then I want to find out who fired that missile. I need to know who they were trying to kill and why."

"You're sure now it was a whiner missile? D'you hear it?"

"Positive. Do you think Secure-Tek has them?"

"That rinky-dink outfit? Secure-Tek is lucky to afford bullets, never mind whiners. Nobody in five hundred miles has them except us."

"Maybe the Free Lifers stole a missile somehow?" Autumn asked.

146

"Not from us," said Lucille. "I supervise the gal who keeps all the armaments inventory data. I can see everything White Knights has in six states, and we don't have very many whiners. If one had been stolen, I would know about it immediately. However, I *can* find out if one of ours has been used."

"If the missile *was* fired by someone in the company," said Autumn, "that still doesn't tell me who they wanted to kill. Maybe the chimpanzee is mixed up with the Free Lifers. Or this Secure-Tek guy, Mack, might be involved in something bigger than just angling for contracts."

"Or it could be *you* they want to kill," said Lucille. "You know you can tell ol' Lucille the truth. Have you done anything to make the company go really ugly on you?"

"The only thing I've done is apply for early retirement," said Autumn. "Have they started killing people for that?"

Chapter 25

As Mack walked up, an old fellow was sitting on the low cinderblock wall in front of the Sleepy Daze Motel, trying to light a cigarette. Mack pretended not to notice the ambulance at the motel entrance, or the gurney with a sealed black body bag being loaded into it. He checked using his ViewGlazzes, but the media had nothing on this. He walked closer to the cinderblock wall.

The man's cigarette was the old-fashioned kind with little bits of actual tobacco. His gnarled hands were shaking so badly he couldn't keep the electromatch steady.

"My dad had that problem, too. So he'd let me light them for him," Mack said as he sat down on the wall near the old man. "Want me to help?"

"It's only in the mornings," the man said, handing him the match. "I'll be steady as a rock by one or two o'clock. Maybe three."

Mack struck the match and held it under the cigarette while the old man took a drag to get the cigarette started.

"Same with my dad," said Mack, "and he lived to be a hundred and one."

"Hell of a thing," the old man said. "Used to be you didn't need a prescription to buy cigs, but they cost you an arm and a leg.

Government said that was to keep people from smoking too much and catching cancer."

"Hell of a thing," Mack agreed as he watched the paramedics lift the gurney and flip the rolling wheels out of the way.

"Now you gotta have a prescription to buy cigs," the old man said, "but any pharmacist will give you one."

"Wonder who died," Mack said.

"Some guy lived on the same floor as me. The groundlicker maid found him this morning when she went in to smooth out the bed sheets and pretend she had actually changed them," the old man said. "Y'know, the pharmacist doesn't even write the prescription out. Just has you sign a line in his book."

"I used to know a guy here," said Mack. "Ed McTavish. Or maybe it was Ted."

"Naw, this guy was a German or something. Kept to himself. Dutchman, I think," the old man said. "To top it off, now the government has bailed out the tobacco industry so much that cigs are practically free. Just sign the drug store's book and pay a few bucks. Get a whole box. They're not nearly as long as they used to be, though."

"McTavish might have been a German on his mother's side," said Mack. "Maybe a Dutchman."

"Wasn't no McTavish on my floor. Dead guy had a kraut name," the old man said between coughs. "Hell of a thing. Maybe the government hopes we'll get cancer and die sooner. Everybody wants old people out of the way. Health care costs are bankrupting the country."

Mack stretched his legs out and wiggled his feet. "Guess I'll get back to my walk." But he stayed seated on the wall.

"Freeloafen," said the old man. "Or maybe it was Far Offen. Some kraut name. Wore sunglasses indoors. He never talked much to anybody."

"Verhoven's a Dutch name, I think," Mack said as he watched two uniformed polisec come out of the motel.

"Yeah, it was something like that," the old man said. "Maybe that was it. I think that was it."

"Died of a heart attack?"

"More like a brain bleedout, you might say." The old man took another drag. "Better than cancer, though. Personally I'm hoping for a sudden death heart attack. Go quick. Pretty painless."

"He had a stroke?"

"I didn't say it was a stroke," said the old man. "He shot himself in the head. Covered the gun with a sofa pillow so nobody would hear the shot. Hell of a thing."

"This Verhoven guy committed suicide?"

"Wasn't nearly as old as me. Probably had cancer and didn't want to suffer for years sitting in the clinic waiting for a doctor. But it was his choice. I don't judge."

"You wouldn't expect a guy committing suicide to hold a pillow over the gun," Mack said. "Guess he didn't want to wake people up. That's pretty thoughtful."

"Pretty agile, too," said the old man. "I couldn't do it like he did. I'm too stiff. Got arthritis everywhere I've got a joint. Can't bend much anymore."

"Why do you say he was agile?"

"Would have to be, wouldn't he?" said the old man. "Have to be flexible to hold a pillow behind your head with one hand and hold the gun back there with the other."

"*Behind* his head?"

"Yeah. Shot himself in the back of the head. Twice! Hell of a thing." The old man stubbed the cigarette out against the top of the wall and reached into his pocket for another one.

"Hell of a thing," said Mack.

Chapter 26

Brian was reading zoo documents on Charlesworth's screendesk, trying to keep his mind off Brianna.

Memories of her haunted him. Reading Proust in French together at night. Shopping for fruit together in Kowloon. Loping down the beach in Point Loma.

The note Officer Winn had left in the storeroom said she knew someone who might help them. She said Brian should definitely not search for Brianna by himself.

Not that he would have any idea where to start. Even if he went back to the tailor shop, her scent would be gone by now. So there really was nothing else to do except sit behind the big desk in the Zoo Director's office, read giraffe breeding reports on the out-of date screen reader, and wait for Charlesworth to get back.

Several times he had looked at the big photograph on the wall, and the brass plaque on it that read: "Aubrey Tiberius Singehoffer, Director." The human had a pleasant-enough smile; graying, perfectly-coiffed hair; and what appeared in the photo to be a rather expensive suit that didn't fit quite right. This was the political appointee who phoned in twice a week, showed up in the office only rarely, and in general left Charlesworth to do all the work of running an under-staffed, under-funded organization struggling to manage with an ever-decreasing flow of customers and revenue.

If Director Aubrey T. Singehoffer came into the tailor shop, Brian would tell him, "Sir, the parts of your suit are fighting each other rather than achieving coherence. The sleeves should flow from the shoulders, but they're just tacked on. The lapels must seem as natural as the petals of a rose."

He looked at the map of the various animal exhibits and enclosures, showing what remained after the Elevation and the cutbacks of the past fifteen years. The current locations of the various animals didn't seem to have any rationale.

Brian thought again of Brianna and remembered a walk in Hong Kong Park before they were married. He had told her his dream of someday having his own tailor shop where he could create clothing his own way. "No matter how good the cloth is," he had told her, "if the various parts of the suit are not fitted together precisely, the final effect will be a disappointment. Customers may not recognize what's wrong, but unconsciously they will find the results displeasing. And they won't come back."

He found himself wondering about Brianna again. Autumn had said there was some kind of Free Life action expected. Would Jiggs have had Brianna evacuated to safety during a protest? He would have simply sent both of them a message to stay out of downtown. No, Brianna had been taken by an unfriendly force. Brian didn't want to think about that right now.

He browsed through at the zoo files on the screen. *Aviary nutritional protocols annual update. Promotional events staffing plan. Visitor Information Kiosk repair. Veterinary service—pygmy hippos. Maintenance—camel exhibit perimeter. Organic fertilizer purchases.* They seemed to be handled as an assortment of disconnected tasks, each of which could have been outsourced to a subcontractor. *A lot of good things,* he thought, *all individually necessary. But what's their overall goal for the institution? There is no coherence. No strategic vision.*

Then he found an image of an old map of the Zoo from the 1900s. It looked completely different. Not only was the old zoo much larger, but it was organized to have animals of similar type or habitat together on walking trails. He studied the map intently. *This was before the Elevation. When they had to release species seemingly at random, the place was devastated. Whoever was in charge cobbled together what was left.* He knew nothing about zoo management. But maybe the older files would show how things used to be. *Perhaps in this case, the past actually* is *useful.*

The files told a story of crisis. A surge of research and international involvement at the beginning of the Elevation as the San Diego Zoo contributed to the international race to understand what could be happening in genetics and the environment. Collaboration with scientists from various institutions, including records by some graduate interns in neuroscience from UCSD, back when the campus was still a functioning university of the old face-to-face type. And then—a zoo attendance collapse, followed by

154

desperate rounds of fundraising while boosting ticket prices to compensate.

Clicking through the documents, he found an old file named *San Diego Zoo Master Plan*. It was short and more than twelve years old.

That is what's missing, he thought. *They have no master plan from the more recent years. They have lost sight of what the zoo used to be.* He went further, absorbed in the material. He read for a long time.

There were sounds outside the office. At first Brian hardly noticed them, but they came closer until they finally broke through his concentration.

"My Assistant Director," a man's voice was saying, "will give us a tour of the facilities, Senator. A short tour, of course, since you have to get back to the Capitol in Placentia tonight."

The office door opened and two men entered. One was a tall, stocky African-American. The other was the man in the photo, the man with the perfect hair and the badly-tailored suit.

"Hello, Charlesworth," Aubrey Singehoffer said, then stopped and stared at Brian. "Charlesworth?"

Chapter 27

"I can access the drone missile log, but not alone," said Lucille. "Security level on that data is too high. It takes two ID chips for clearance."

"So you need a second person," said Autumn.

"It can be me and one of my superiors, Captain Fahey or Captain Heap. Or me and the other IT supervisor, Lacey. Or me and a uniformed officer, but only someone from Tactical Assault Command. Chavez maybe?"

Autumn frowned and chewed on her lip. "There's no TAC officer I can trust. I just don't know what's going on." She was starting to think this was all a bad idea.

"Then it has to be you," Lucille said. "You have to come back into the armory to my office so we can access the data. No other way."

"No dice," Autumn said. "Not going. And anyway, I can't because I don't have my ID badge anymore. I got rid of it so I couldn't be tracked."

"Hmm. That does pose a problem. Maybe there is one other way," said Lucille, "but it's very dangerous."

"Unlike my current lifestyle."

"If you got inside the armory, you could go to the basement and pick up Bernard's badge. It should be in the Evidence Lockup by now."

"I wouldn't get past the ground floor before someone recognized me," Autumn said.

"Wear your helmet."

"Don't have it. It was thrashed anyway." *The real problem is, I'm scared.* Not that there weren't good reasons.

"Well, honey, I have a present for you." Lucille went to the hall closet and came back with a heavy algoplastic trash bag. She opened it and took out a brand new helmet.

"Lucille! What do you have that for?"

"It was going to be Bernard's birthday present. You know what standard issue is like. Denise wanted him to have something a little better quality. This one's got the silicone pads inside. She asked me to keep it here so he wouldn't accidentally find it."

Autumn took the helmet in her lap and chewed her lip again. In the tailor shop Brian had jumped in with no weapons and no SafeLite underwear, going hand to hand against armored attackers with machine guns. As a Provie he didn't even have anything like a tradition of family honor to uphold. She, on the other hand, was afraid to walk into a building and pick up a badge.

But they know me. I'll be caught.

"What's on your mind?" said Lucille.

"This is not going to work. Even with my visor down, I still have to get through the checkpoint, and that means putting my hand on a DNA scanner."

"You said they know you aren't dead, " Lucille said. "What else do they know?"

"Well, they know I'm on the run," said Autumn, "and if they're tracking my chips…"

"They are. Depend on it," said Lucille.

"…they also know that I know that they know."

"How?

"Because I sent my badge and my gun in two different directions," Autumn said. "Or at least the Secure-Tek guy did. Mack."

"That means they know you're running scared," said Lucille, "and that's good."

"Because?"

"Because they'll figure you're either heading out of town, or you've gone into hiding."

"Which means the last place they'll expect me to go is into the belly of the beast," said Autumn. "OK." *I can do this.* "I just hope they haven't put a watch flag on my DNA file."

"They hadn't when I left work last night. I would have seen the alert," said Lucille. "Why would they? They aren't expecting you. Let me phone one of the church ladies to deliver the food to Denise's house. Then you and I will work out details."

Chapter 28

"Your girl hasn't been here since, oh, a week or so," said Huero. "But her big ugly boyfriend was here last night. Be careful, mijo. He's looking for you."

"Por que why?" Mack took another sip of his spiced tomato juice.

"Por que you were due back in town two days ago with something that belongs to Monique. They're nervous you've maybe skipped."

"Maríqui," Mack said. "Her name is Maríqui."

"No le hace," said Huero. "However you spell it, it still means trouble. So, do you have this thing they want to get back?"

"No, I don't," said Mack. It was the truth. Verhoven had the necklace last. Who knows where it might be now. Maybe polisec. Maybe the trash man. Maybe the housekeeping maid.

Or Ten-ten.

That was a possibility Mack would have to check out as soon as the crime scene cooled down enough that he could return to the motel without tripping over polisec crime scene investigators.

"Funny he would be so concerned about an inexpensive necklace," said Mack. "This Ivan guy seem like the sentimental type to you?"

Huero laughed. "Oh, sure. Probably has 'Mom' tattooed on his chest in letters two feet high."

"So he *is* big."

"Almost like me," said Huero. "Don't say I didn't warn you."

"OK, I got you." Mack's mind was elsewhere. Ten-ten might have said something to polisec about him coming to see Verhoven. Or they might dig his DNA out of the wallpaper. Or they might have picked up his ViewGlazzes on the general network this morning, if they had brought a polar-coordinate tracer to the site.

This was utter paranoia. But if someone had taken down Shadow Guy, anything was possible.

"Do you have a phone I can borrow for a couple of days?" Mack asked.

Huero opened the cash drawer behind him and lifted an almost-invisible flap. "This one is anonymous, but it's got only thirty dollars on the chip. I'll add that to your tab." Huero handed Mack the small button phone. "Watch that tab, mijo."

"If you have a nice safe place, I'm going to give you these ViewGlazzes to hold onto till I get back."

"Sure. I never say no to a little collateral."

Mack tested the button phone in his ear, and then dropped it in his pocket.

"When you're through with it, wipe it clean and drop it in a trash chute," Huero said. "Or in the ocean if you're close enough. It's biodegradable."

When Mack left Huero's place, he decided to pay a visit to Ten-ten. It was early afternoon and Ten-ten, being a nocturnal animal, would be sound asleep. With humans, raiding someone at three a.m. was a good way to catch them off guard and get the truth. The same approach, shifted twelve hours, might work with a binturong.

After he had walked a few blocks toward the Transit stop, however, Mack wondered if he should save himself some effort and ask for a lift from the car that had been following him ever since he left Huero's.

But he had a hunch he knew who was driving the car and thought it might not be the most pleasant ride he had ever hitched.

He resisted the urge to duck down a side street. *Stay on the main drag. Find an out right here.* Signs said *Store Closed. Store Closed.* A lot of shops had closed since humans started moving to get away from the animals. Hair salon: too small to hide in. Antique store: no clear exit. Vet clinic with big gray Rapidfabbed annex: too busy.

When the car was delayed by a turning delivery van and a stop light, Mack ducked into a recessed doorway by some flower boxes and hastily got himself in through the door.

"Welcome to Karma Kebab, the café of right livelihood," said a graceful female voice.

Mack blinked as his eyes adjusted slightly, and he saw the sharply triangular muzzle of some kind of ungulate. It was kind of smiling at him, to the extent possible.

"One for lunch?" It was a bharal—a Himalayan blue sheep. The pink vocoder in her ear was decorated with a tiny eightfold wheel sticker, and she wore a loose saffron smock which did not go well with her naturally slate-blue wool.

"Would you mind if I just used your restroom? In the back, I assume," said Mack, walking to the right and into the café. There was one occupied table, a Latino human couple and two children playing with their salad. The smells of the food hit him now, curry and coriander and cardamom and clarified butter, and reminded him he was hungry.

"Oh, I'm afraid the restrooms are for customers only."

He heard a car outside screech to a stop down the block and thought he knew which one it was.

"Well, I'm a customer." There would be a back exit for the kitchen past the restrooms. He would go straight out the back.

The bharal used her mouth to pick up a cloth folded over a menu and led him to a table at the side of the café, her four white and black legs clicking back and forth. The wood-paneled café was decorated with thick cotton wall hangings and a high wall shelf near the front window holding a seated Buddha and a battery-powered bubbling garden fountain. Over the flower boxes outside he saw now there was a rope of prayer flags fluttering. Eastern religions were popular among animals who had spiritual inclinations, either because of their country of origin or because philosophies involving reincarnation had inherent appeal.

Mack was about to head straight to the back but he saw that the back hallway was to the left, behind the table where the human family was eating, and there was a meek-looking waiter sheep

162

nudging forward a stainless steel serving cart draped with an embroidered cloth and loaded with plates of jasmine rice. The cart was blocking the path to the back door.

The bharal ewe was holding the menu out and waiting for him to sit at the table. So he sat down and took the menu from her mouth. The sharp ridge of her muzzle was defined by a thin black stripe and she had a refined look, like a lady whose big nose makes her seem even more delicate. Her ridged little horns were polished and waxed, a concession to worldly fashion.

"Can I tell you about our special kebabs today? We have halloumi cheese with peppers and cherry tomatoes. We have squash and potato in a Dijon sauce." *Makes sense that grazing animals, of any religion, would choose a veg restaurant to work at.* "We also have a ginger vegobeef with mint chutney. And we have a mushroom and zucchini with couscous."

"They all sound amazing." He wasn't lying. He realized that he hadn't eaten with a knife and fork for three days, since before he got on the plane in Singapore. "Give me a moment."

"Of course."

His stomach was rumbling. He wished he had enough cash to buy lunch. Last week in Raffles Place, on the 38th floor overlooking the darkening golden waters of the Singapore Strait at sunset, he had ordered an ayam buah keluak that literally melted in his mouth. He expensed it directly to the client via a securely scrambled connection without even knowing how much it cost. That was life with his COR band.

He wished he didn't have to disappoint these nice Himalayan sheep folks and run out the back. But when the ewe's back was turned, he slid out of the seat and pushed past the rolling cart.

Down the hall he passed the kitchen and the restrooms, which were a typical converted set saying "PROV" and "SAP", and found a rear exit with a steel-barred screen door.

On the other side of the black screen door, sitting on the concrete back step by the milk crates, was a red steppe fox with a machete in its Pawsall. A craggy look around his eyes and the scars crisscrossing the top of the sleek muzzle suggested that this fox did not conquer purely by stealth and cunning.

Minor problem... thought Mack. *Ivan's brought friends.*

The fox met Mack's gaze through the black screen and shook its head tightly, just once.

From the front of the café a voice bellowed, "Davis!"

Chapter 29

Autumn felt her palms sweating as she switched the gym bag full of rocks to her other hand. She hung back a little to let a few more citizens get between her and Lucille as they neared the public entrance to the armory. Officers seldom used this entrance, so there was less chance of someone recognizing Autumn here, but she had her visor down over her face.

"We'll go through gate number one, nearest the duty officer's rostrum," Lucille had told her. "Duty officers pay more attention to the gates farther away from them because that's where an activist would try to slip in. Anyway, duty officers won't waste much attention on an officer in uniform."

Over the shoulders of the citizens in front of her Autumn could see Lucille place her fingertips on the DNA scanner. It analyzed the body oil and dead skin in her fingertips and in a few seconds flashed the "Proceed" light.

Lucille passed through the gate and headed for the rostrum with its bank of screens mounted overhead for the duty officer to keep an eye on.

"What's up, Sergeant Thatcher?" Lucille said. "Thatcher, right? I think we met at the last holiday party."

"Oh, yeah, you're …uh…the lady in charge of the computer system. Miss …uh…."

"Lucille is fine," she said. "That's what everybody calls me. How is that T-4?" She boldly joined the officer behind the rostrum and peered at the monitor for Gate One. "Some of these screens are starting to show vertical variance."

"Vertical…?

"You know. When vertical lines suddenly wiggle for a second, then settle down. You seeing any of that?"

"I haven't really noticed any, no," the officer said.

Autumn allowed an old man to enter the three-foot square security cage in front of her. He stepped on the scale plate verifying that his weight was on the cage floor. The high barred gate behind him would remain open, but the gate in front of him would stay closed.

When Autumn placed her fingertips on the DNA scanner, the computer would scan the data base and, if it found nothing amiss, the front gate would swing open. But if the computer found an outstanding warrant or any kind of hold-for-questioning against her, the rear gate would quickly snap shut without warning. She would be trapped inside the cage while officers tossed in a couple of wrapsnakes, and then she would be searched and thrown in the lockup.

Autumn stepped with the bag into the cage just far enough that her feet were on the scale floor. As the display screen reading changed to *Please Step To X on Center Spot* she quickly leaned

166

forward and set the bag of rocks down in the center of the cage. The cage display panel registered *1 Occupant* even though her feet weren't actually on the center spot. She leaned backwards as far as possible without falling over so that, if the rear gate suddenly slammed shut, it would hit her right shoulder first, giving her a split-second's warning to squeeze through and flee at top BioBooster speed before her fellow officers started shooting her in the back.

The display changed to "Please Place Fingertips On Pad." Even leaning backwards, Autumn could reach the pad. But before she touched it, she looked over towards Lucille, who was studying the monitor screen without blinking. Lucille was toying with her left earring. If she suddenly dropped her hand away from her ear, it meant that Autumn's DNA had been flagged, and the computer was showing "Detain Cage One." That would happen only one second before the cage door slammed shut. If her body was tensed and ready she might get out.

As Lucille had instructed her, Autumn placed her fingertips slightly above the pad, but not quite touching it. The rest would be up to Lucille.

Staying focused and motionless was not at all difficult. Autumn was, in fact, almost paralyzed by fear.

Especially when the security cage display panel suddenly went blank.

Chapter 30

I'm starving, thought Mack as he walked quickly from the back café screen door. *I wasn't planning to have to meet Maríqui's friends before lunch.*

"Davis!" bellowed the voice again. Barging into the café at the front was a mountain of muscle wearing an expensive pinstriped satin dress shirt.

"Hey! Ivan!" said Mack, coming out of the hallway and throwing his hands out. "It is a *really* small world. Met you down in the Gaslamp a year ago. You were –"

"She don't want you, Davis!" Ivan was accompanied by another fox slinking at his big heels. This fox was pure white, a highly groomed Siberian variety wearing a brocaded blue vest and a machete in an underslung sheath against his chest. He had a fluffy cloudlike tail, a chill eye, and a mincing step.

"You know, both you guys are looking *sharp*," said Mack, moving to the other side of the room, away from the family eating, and pulling a table in front of him.

"You 're yesterday's vid," said Ivan, coming into the center of the room. "But you still got her property. Give it!"

"I'm actually catching up with Maríqui tonight. Did you get her vox yet?"

"Give it to me, Davis," said Ivan. "Now!"

"We should really talk. It's too bad I've got this courthouse appointment right now with the D.A.," said Mack. "Maybe I could come meet you at the bar tonight–"

Ivan looked at him, then gave a little shrug of his huge shoulders like a horse flicking off a fly. He jerked at his sleeves and in a moment had them rolled up on his thigh-sized arms as he came for Mack.

Mack slalomed around the tables, pulling out chairs into the path. "Don't hit me, don't hit me, you might break it."

"Break what?"

"The thing you want."

If he drew his 9mm, the restaurant staff would definitely call polisec. He had seen burstcars on the street on the way from Huero's. And there were bystanders: the parents at the table clutching their children; the slim lady bharal; the waiter at both ends of the café.

"I'm not gonna to hit you," said Ivan. "I'm gonna give you a big hug. And then lay you nicely down on a table where Vlad's gonna dice up your face."

The white fox jumped fluidly up onto a table, tail billowing. He reached under its chest with his Pawsall and drew the machete.

The family jumped and ran, plates scattering, and the front door banged behind them.

Ivan picked up two wooden chairs and flung them both behind him; they smashed through the cafe's front windows.

"Heeey!" yelled the bharal waiter. The bharal ewe at the front had let the menus drop from her mouth onto the floor and was standing dumbfounded.

"I'm really sorry," Mack called out to both of the sheep.

A ram ran out from the back office. He had the huge bharal horns that curved out and down like a majestic upside-down handlebar mustache. One of the horns had a pencil clipped onto the tip. He interposed himself in the middle of the room between Mack and Ivan.

"Owner here is a human," growled the ram. "Has clout. Take your rutting clashes someplace else."

Ivan said something back. The bharal cocked his horned head for a second and then nodded slowly, slate-blue jaw clenched. "OK," he said, looking back and forth at Mack and Ivan with a cold determination. "All right. All of you. Karma coming to YOU." With a toss of his horns he flipped a chair out of his way.

We have lost the strategic imperative for limited war, thought Mack as he drew his Hayakawa 9mm.

The white fox sprang off the table top, brandishing the machete, and closed his jaws over the gun and Mack's index finger. It burned. Mack flicked his wrist and the gun, the fox, and the machete all clattered onto the floor. The fox snatched up the gun and ran out of reach.

Ivan threw a chair at Mack, who rolled out of the way. The ram slammed into Ivan and knocked him down.

As Mack stood up with his shoulder aching and his hand on fire, he heard banging and scratching coming from the back door. *Red fox. Trying to reach the doorknob.*

He looked to his left, toward the front windows. While Ivan was trying to get up and a grip on the ram, Vlad the white fox was up on the Buddha wall shelf with the gun, working clumsily to get his small Pawsall around the human-sized grip and inside the trigger guard.

You know, thought Mack, *I'm getting a little tired of people appropriating my sidearm without even a range permit.* He moved to the right, toward the back wall of the café, to put Ivan between himself and the fox.

A scraping noise came from the back door, suspiciously like milk crates being dragged across concrete.

There was a little cry from the female bharal huddled over by the hostess lectern, looking on wide-eyed with her delicate mouth open.

Mack looked and saw that the white fox on the shelf had the 9mm braced against his blue vest, lining up a shot at the male bharal.

The back door banged open.

Mack dived forward, grabbed Vlad's machete off the floor, and threw it. It wasn't a balanced throwing weapon but the back edge of the blade did hit the fox, who yowled and flailed and lost the gun. The whole shelf and the Buddha and the bubbling garden of peace came crashing down, bringing the curtains and curtain rail with it.

Ivan landed a punch on the ram's shoulder, and the ram stumbled and went down. The ewe screamed.

From out of the back hallway bounded the red fox, machete flashing like an oncoming dragonfly wing.

Mack smacked the back of Ivan's skull with a chair.

Ivan grunted and staggered, but he didn't fall down or do anything else helpful. Mack turned and used the chair legs to parry the red fox's machete.

Where Vlad was all white cloudy flow, the red fox moved like a string of firecrackers. The machete blade hacked into the wood once, twice, three, four times. Mack shoved the chair at the fox and dashed to the front of the cafe where his gun was lying somewhere under the curtains.

On the way he stepped on a plate of mushroom kebabs and his foot slid, the plate scooting like a hockey puck over the wood floor.

Mack went down hard and when he hit the floor it knocked the wind out of him.

A moment later, Ivan picked him up.

Chapter 31

Out in the sunshine, Brian looked nervously at the zoo's solar-operated cart. It had a canopy roof and a front end made to look like a galloping zebra. In his entire life he had never even driven a car.

But The Zoo Director said, "I'll drive, Charlesworth. I want you to concentrate on giving the Senator a fact-filled tour in the brief time he has graciously been able to give us."

"Very good, Aubrey," the Senator said as he sat down in the front and slapped Singehoffer on the shoulder. "In that case, once around the park, driver."

An hour later as they neared the end of their drive around the grounds, Brian was gaining confidence.

"In summary, Senator, since the Elevation, humans are having to learn to think about animals in a completely different way," Brian said. His underarms were soaked with sweat under his suit jacket. But the two men in front of him in the cart actually seemed to believe that he knew something about zoos. "Humans daily work side by side with a wide variety of intelligent, articulate animals. They interact with them at a level unlike any time in history. It is a different world now. The zoo's raison d'être can no longer be to provide basic encounters with nonhuman species at high prices."

"I'm impressed by your level of culture and insight, Mr. Charlesworth. Go on," said the Senator.

Brian adjusted his tie. "I believe—that is to say, Mr. *Singehoffer's* example has caused me to realize that we can no longer think of a zoo as a set of individual enclosures, no matter how up-to-date they may be. It leads to a static, unnatural presentation. And since modern visitors associate with articulate animals every day, they find the zoo experience uncomfortable and unpleasant. Consequently, attendance drops each year."

"But the solution," said the Senator.

"Yes, Charlesworth, what's the solution?" said Singehoffer, leaning over intently from the driver's seat.

"Yes. The zoo, of course, will need to return to a strong focus on, uh, conservation biology and scientific collaboration with other institutions. But fundamentally what people need today is help making sense of things. They need to understand a world in which relationships with animals are more complex than ever. They need a relevant vision."

"I think you're absolutely right," said the Senator. "Civic knowledge. How to interact with Provisional Citizens."

"Yes, they'll need to see how animals' lives and backgrounds and natural behaviors are related to their current interaction with human society. And I do not just mean humans; elevated animals need the vision too."

"And you think we can do that here."

"Absolutely. The San Diego Zoo has the expertise and the authority to provide this vision. The zoo can take a leadership role in…um…creating meaning in a post-Elevation world. And as part of this we must present non-elevated animals as part of a complete landscape, just as elevated animals are in everyday life."

"Amazing," said Singehoffer.

"With today's technology, we can maintain a subtle, almost-invisible separation of animals. Living areas can flow naturally and invisibly from one to the other. Notice your suit, Senator, which I must say is extremely well made. The sleeves seem to flow naturally from the shoulders, but at same time, the sleeves are kept in their proper place by invisible stitches. Similarly, a zoo must have subtle connections and separations, and most of all, coherence and a sense of flow."

"Excellent analysis!" said the Senator. "Innovative and progressive."

"I must give the credit to Mr. Singehoffer," Brian said as Singehoffer parked the cart near the front door of the office. "His style of management is what inspired me."

"Why doesn't that surprise me?" the Senator laughed as he shook hands with Singehoffer. "Aubrey, I'm happy to go back to the committee and report that you are a forward-thinking executive whose appointment should be renewed."

As the Senator got into his chauffeured car, Singehoffer turned to Brian. "You and I need to have a little chat," he said. "In my office. Right now."

Brian wondered if he had left the office window open. He might still be able to escape.

After they entered the office Singehoffer closed the door behind them. "This visit," he said, fixing Brian with an unblinking stare, "has really caught me by surprise."

"Me, too," said Brian.

"That was an impressive performance you just gave," Singehoffer said. "Even your manner of speaking is more refined. Now tell me the truth."

"It's a long story," Brian said. "But please don't –"

"Right now I only want to know one thing," said Singehoffer. "Charlesworth, who is your *fabulous* tailor?"

Chapter 32

After an excruciatingly long moment, Autumn saw the "Proceed" notice came up on the Armory cage display panel.

"That is *so* sweet, Sergeant," Lucille was saying as she picked imaginary flecks of lint from the shoulder of the man's uniform and with her other hand tapped the button for

Cage Release - Test.

"My policy is not to date anyone from work," Lucille went on. "However, you just never know." She patted his shoulder, smiled, and walked away.

Autumn grabbed her bag of rocks and walked through the inner gate and past the rostrum, being careful not to look in Lucille's direction.

She half expected to hear an officer yell "Stop!"

She forced herself to walk past the row of elevators and to the door marked "Stairs." Uniformed officers seldom took the back staircase; they preferred the elevators on the off chance their scanners might detect a passenger with an outstanding warrant. Officers got paid a commission for every warrant evader they captured, and commissions made up a large percentage of their paycheck. Commissions were a silent reminder that law enforcement these days was a private enterprise.

The other reason Autumn took the stairs was that she couldn't simply set the bag down and walk away, or someone would call the bomb squad and the building would immediately go on lockdown. Under the stairs there was usually a large trash can.

At the bottom of the stairwell the trash can wasn't there.

I'll have to keep schlepping this thing until I get to a trash chute.

Things in the Armory looked excruciatingly normal. A couple of patrol officers were passing each other in the starkly-lit basement hallway which looked even starker through her helmet visor. Every officer in the building would have a duty to arrest her if they knew she was here. And the reason she was here was because she suspected that at least one of them had tried to kill her.

As she passed the room with the holding cells, she noticed a fair-haired officer looking through the window of one of the cell doors. He was someone she had never seen before. His light blue uniform told her he was a new officer assigned to an internal job in the armory. His shoes were highly polished, and his suit was obviously brand new.

Just out of the academy. It's worth a try.

She made an about face and walked back to the room. "Officer," she said, flipping her visor up halfway. "I need to leave my gym bag behind your desk for a few minutes while I use the john."

"Oh, yes sir. I mean, yes ma'am. I was just checking on my prisoner. He's a DUI they put in the cell to sober up." He came forward quickly and took the bag from her. "Whoa, this is heavy. Do you have weapons in here? I'll write out a receipt for them."

"It's just rocks. Take a look if you like. For my friend's flower garden."

"Oh, I get it," he laughed. "Maybe I should put a note on the bag with your name. In case I get called away, I mean. That is, if you don't mind telling me your name."

"Denise," she said as she walked out the door.

The young officer leaned out the door and called after her, "Denise what?"

Autumn turned her head and called over her shoulder, "Denise...uh...Casseroli."

"Italian, huh?"

"Polish," she said, and disappeared around a corner.

Autumn had never been to the Evidence Room, and the best she could remember, had never seen the gray-haired sergeant before. He was well over the maximum weight for a White Knights officer, and she was certain she would have remembered him.

She had no choice but to take the risk of raising her visor, at least to the halfway click. To leave it down would seem highly suspicious, even to a man who was almost surely only a few months from retirement and marking time keeping evidence records in the basement.

"All we've received from that tailor shop incident so far is boxes of broken skylight," the sergeant was saying, barely looking up from his screendesk. "The officer's uniform and such must still be at the morgue."

"Then I guess I'll go over there," Autumn said.

"Don't waste your time. They won't release anything to you," he said. "Chain of custody. It has to come here first and be logged into the evidence records. But I'm almost done logging everything else. Why don't you try back in a couple of hours."

"OK. Thanks. I'll tell my team leader." As she turned to leave, a metallic glint caught her eye from the mouth of an open evidence envelope in the logging stack on the desk behind the technician. A familiar kind of glint.

"Almost forgot," she said, turning back to the technician. "I also need to look at a clue used in the trial for the Pratt multiple murder. About two years ago. A metal pipe."

"I remember that case. Bad business," he said. "OK, but those boxes will be way in the back. Might take me a couple of minutes."

Autumn listened as his footsteps faded. Then, boots whirring, she jumped over the countertop and dropped on the other side right next to the desk.

Without touching the envelope, she bent down and looked inside. The glint she had seen was exactly what she thought. The envelope contained a TAC officer's badge.

It could only be Carter's. Any other badge would currently be on some officer's chest. She grabbed the badge and tossed the envelope back. It slid over and went down between the desk and the wall.

In another four seconds, she was back over the counter and walking quickly down the hall to the stairs. Lucille's office was up on the fourth floor.

She unbuttoned her shirt pocket and started to drop the badge in when she noticed the number on the badge. *626.*

It wasn't Carter's badge. It was hers.

Chapter 33

Mack's feet barely touched the floor as Ivan lifted him up with one hand, his thumb on Mack's trachea. His other hand was patting Mack down in search of the little jade figurine of Quan Yin.

Behind Ivan in the middle of the room the red fox had the male bharal pinned on the floor with a machete at the sheep's jugular.

Wonder Verhoven found secret of Quan Yin before died, thought Mack as his vision clouded red with little stars. *Would been nice to know.*

Suddenly Ivan yelled and Mack felt his throat released; he fell and partly caught himself on a table by the window, scraping his hipbone. Plates and kebab skewers scattered.

The ewe was backing away, shaking. Ivan leaned down with a grimace and held the back of his right knee where she had stabbed him with her polished horns.

Ivan turned toward her. "I'm going to snap off your little hare krishna rug head," he snarled.

Still backing up, she stumbled in terror.

Okay, we're done. Holding the edge of the table to steady himself, Mack drove a kick straight into the side of Ivan's left knee.

As Ivan screamed and went down, Mack shoved himself off from the table and up onto his feet. He corkscrewed his fist back and snapped it into Ivan's left eye. Ivan groaned and ducked away on his knees.

A pain flashed up Mack's leg. Out from under the curtain mess Vlad the white fox had clamped his jaws onto Mack's left shoe. Mack stumbled, grasping frantically for one of the kebab skewers on the floor and came up with a Dijon-squash-slathered plate. He hacked down with the edge against Vlad's snout, and the fox jumped backwards.

Meanwhile, Ivan had gotten to his feet. His face was bleeding.

"She's not a rug. She's a Provie," said Mack as he spread his feet. "And we're breaking her restaurant."

Ivan charged.

You just don't get it. Mack retreated around the left side of the café, weaving to move out of line, and feinted two or three times until Ivan tried another roundhouse. *You lost the chance to walk away.*

Circling out of Ivan's punch, Mack snap-kicked him in the solar plexus and landed another face strike. Ivan roared, but this time there was more distress in the roar. He swung wildly and then started to reach out to grab a chair. Mack rolled underneath the swing, the chair smashed against the back wall, and Mack came up and kicked Ivan in the knee at the spot where the ewe had stabbed him. Ivan bellowed, stumbled, and swung again.

Mack sidestepped, spun and trapped the arm, and twisted Ivan's hand till the chair fell and bounced off the floor. With a strong hip thrust Mack put him reasonably hard into the wall, turning him so as not to break his neck. Ivan slid down heavily, back against the wall, into a half-upright sitting position. His head bounced like a pocket rag when he hit the floor. His eyes stayed closed.

"I'll tell Maríqui," said Mack, panting, "you can't make it tonight."

He then turned to face the craggy red fox guarding the bharal on the floor, and swiveled into tiger stance. The fox jumped backward, snarling, holding the machete pointed forward at arm's length. Mack shook his head tightly. Just once.

The red fox looked him up and down, then flipped the machete in the air and caught it in his teeth as he used all four feet to flash out the front door.

Vlad the white fox was already gone.

The bharal ram came to his feet, staring at him, and then moved to the café front, protecting the ewe. Mack realized that his own mouth was still fixed in something like a snarl.

He brought his face back to neutral and straightened his jacket. His shoulder throbbed, but seemed intact. He could feel that the back seams of his brand new suit were partly busted out. The fox had chewed up his shoe and before that, his index finger. He swished his burning hand around in a puddle of cooling water on a table. He stepped through the overturned chairs and dug his gun out of the pile of curtains.

"Really sorry about everything," he said to the dazed sheep, who only stared at him. "Great cooking. I'll recommend the place. But guys, next time you might just let a person use the restroom."

Outside the front of the café there were sirens and the *bwrrshhh* of a polisec burstcar touching down. Mack holstered his gun and as the bharals continued staring, he ran out the back hallway, through the screen door, past the milk crates, and down the alley.

Chapter 34

"You telling me they got your ID back by tracking down a panda tourist before he left on a cruise plane?" said Lucille. "I'm impressed. But I guess that proves White Knights *is* looking for you."

And here I am, looking for them, thought Autumn, standing in Lucille's office. *Makes us even.*

While Lucille finished working at her standup desk, Autumn took a deep breath and looked around. If Lucille couldn't help her, this might be her last time at the Armory. At best, assuming her family could raise enough money for bail, and assuming a judge would even grant her bail on terrorism charges—*Wow, that's a lot of assumption.*

At best she would be unemployable until the courts finally got around to hearing her case maybe a year from now.

On the other hand, if Lucille's search gave Autumn the name she needed, it would all get settled. Bickson would have some self-serving story about how mistakes were made but not by him. She might get a reprimand for leaving her post, maybe even a short suspension, but they'd let her go back to work and then she could say she was leaving anyway.

Now that she was in danger of being forced out, though, she felt like pushing to stay. Had she really learned all there was for her to learn at White Knights? Carter had taught her a lot, but one thing he hadn't taught her was what it would be like without him. She wasn't sure she wanted to start again with a new partner.

Anyway, if she wanted to get her Cultural Reclaimer certification, it would help to have some leadership experience. Maybe if she didn't get an official reprimand, and if she stayed for a while, she could apply for a small-team leader slot. Heck, another year and she'd be eligible for Sergeant rank, if a vacancy opened up. Could she last that long?

No; not under Bickson. It wasn't going to happen. Autumn didn't like the idea of quitting just because of this walking cement block with gold railroad tracks on his collar, but he'd never sign off on her promotion, even if she stuck it out for two years—or for ten.

"OK, I'm firing up the big boy now," Lucille said. "Central Data, Top Level. This is something not many people get to see." She left her desk and walked over to the blank wall.

"Identify," a voice said. The word IDENTIFY appeared in midair about two feet away from the wall. Lucille held her left hand toward the wall and pulled up the sleeve of her blouse to expose the invisible UV tattoo on the inside of her wrist and the chip implanted under it.

Suddenly, the space in front of the wall began to be populated with dozens, then scores, of ghostly images moving in the air in several planes of distance. Lists of names, report pages, flurries of database screens floated past photographs of officers, suspects, crime scenes, evidence. For a moment Autumn felt overwhelmed as if she were floating in space with clouds of information rushing toward her. She took a step backwards.

Lucille laughed. "I would say you get used to it eventually, but truth is, even *I* don't." She made a set of purposeful gestures. Some images disappeared, new images appeared, and things orbited into different positions. "Honey, a hole in space is going to appear in front of you now. Hold your badge in that hole. You won't feel anything; the hole isn't really there. Don't drop the badge or it'll fall on the floor."

Autumn watched as the air in front of her seemed to swirl like water going down a drain. In an instant, a shimmering golden rectangle opened in midair. She inserted her badge into the opening, and it sparkled in the golden scanning beam.

"There is only one level of White Knights security higher than this one," Lucille said as she once again exposed her wrist to the view-wall. "And I don't know who has access to it. In fact, no one does. It's a level nobody seems to know how to get to." Both of them were standing with arms extended into the glowing swarm. "I'm beginning to retrieve the Tactical drone archives now." A head shot of Captain Bickson in uniform flashed past with the letters T.A.C., and then disappeared.

"Ah. Here it comes," said Lucille. "That cloud just off your right shoulder. I'll pull it closer to me, and we'll soon know what this missile business is all about."

When the cloud was in front of Lucille, she flicked her fingers apart and the cloud tripled in size. "Come over here by me," she said. "If you'll look down here on my left, Tuesday's scheduling data…"

Suddenly all the images disappeared and were replaced by large flashing words—"RESTRICTED ID BADGE. DETAIN BADGE HOLDER."

"Damn!" Lucille said. "Damn, damn, damn!" She grabbed the badge from Autumn's hand and began making gestures to the blank wall, using both the badge and her wrist. "Get the hell out of the building, Autumn! Move it!"

"What about you?" Autumn said, trying to pull Lucille away from the wall.

"Don't worry, I'll think of something." She made more gestures. "Use the west employee exit!"

"That's all the way across the building!"

"You have to! It's the only door you can use without needing an ID scan to exit." Lucille stared at the small blue spot hanging in space in front of the now otherwise blank wall. The blue spot was pulsating as it grew larger. The room was filled with a high-pitching hissing sound.

"I have no idea what's happening," Lucille said. "Autumn, get out of here RIGHT NOW."

Chapter 35

Mack arrived at the motel for the second time that day, this time with his bleeding right hand wrapped in a fuzz-polymer hand towel in his coat pocket. He was surprised to find Ten-ten on duty so early and said so.

"Polisec come. Stay long," said the binturong, popping something into his mouth that looked like it was probably even more disgusting when it was still alive. "Mess up everybody hours. Got figs?"

"Sorry. Figs gone," said Mack. "Mack here about Shadow Guy."

"Shadow Guy gone, too," Ten-ten said.

"I know. I saw," said Mack. He lightly bumped against a lampshade, on the exact spot on his shoulder where a chair had hit him, and he winced. "Mack want to ask about him."

"Gone for good this time," said Ten-ten.

"Yeah, I understand that," said Mack. "He had something of mine. A small necklace. I want it."

"All gone," said Ten-ten as he checked the countertop for any crumbs he might have dropped. "Shadow Guy gone. All stuff gone."

"The polisec took everything?" Mack asked.

"Shadow Guy took all stuff."

"Shadow Guy took nothing. They carried him out. Now listen! Mack very angry if Ten-ten holding out on Mack. Where is necklace? Ten-ten have necklace?"

"Ten-ten have nothing!" The binturong bared his teeth and raised his tail. He was tired and losing patience. "Shadow Guy take everything! Leave nothing! Not even leave tip. Everything two suitcases!"

"What do you mean suitcases?" Mack bared his teeth, too, to show Ten-ten that he was also out of patience. "Mack saw Shadow Guy wheeled out, put into polisec death car! Shadow Guy in body bag, not suitcase!"

"That dead guy! Not Shadow Guy!" Ten-ten hissed. "Shadow Guy pay bill six a.m. Leave with two suitcase. Not give tip!" The animal was clearly becoming exhausted by having to talk so much more than normal. "Mack get lost!"

"Calm down," Mack said. "Mack say sorry-sorry. Mack not understand. Sorry-sorry." Mack took two steps backwards and turned forty-five degrees to indicate submission and retreat. Ten-ten glared at him for a very long moment, then lowered his tail.

"If necklace, Shadow Guy still got. Room all empty." Ten-ten said. "Ten-ten know nothing else."

"Mack go now. Sorry-sorry. Next time Mack bring food for Ten-ten," Mack turned and took a few steps towards the door to allow Ten-ten to calm down. Then he looked back over his shoulder. "Who was dead guy?"

"Old guy live one floor below Shadow Guy," Ten-ten said. "Blind guy. Live here long years. Never go out. His name Verhoven."

Chapter 36

As she walked quickly down the Armory fourth floor hallway Autumn was passed by a couple of clerical staff, but they paid no attention to her. Reaching the door to the staircase, she took a quick look behind her. Everything seemed normal. She went through the door and ran down the steps.

Two floors down she had just slowed to a walk when she heard a door open behind her.

"Officer Winn!" a man's voice called. "Stop."

Her hand went to her sidearm as she turned. The unfamiliar feeling reminded her that she was carrying Mack's revolver. She let her arm hang casually over the holster.

It was Jaime Dela Cruz from Pathology. "Hey, Autumn?" he said, coming down the stairs toward her. She had worked with him on a couple of cases. "Miss me?"

"Should I have?" she said.

"Well, I've been on vacation," said Jaime. "Thailand! It was a fantastic trip. Travel's what I live for, you know. I'm just putting in a half day on my first day back."

"Hope your work hasn't stacked up too much. I'm sure you'll have to be buried deep in the lab for a while," said Autumn.

"Nah, the secret is you take a long enough trip that they can't afford to wait, and then by the time you're back, you get all new cases instead of stuff you have to catch up on. Coming to the first floor? We're going to lunch."

Damn. "No," she said, "I'm, um, needed downstairs right now. Sorry."

"No problem," said Jaime. "Drop by the lab sometime, and I'll show you some great photos. Telling you, long vacations are the best. You've got time accrued, right? Anyway, see you round."

In about five minutes he was going to go to lunch and hear the news from his lab mates about yesterday. He would then probably call Bickson's office.

At the basement level again, Autumn carefully opened the door leading into the hallway. Two TAC officers were just walking into an office. Farther down the hall, another appeared to be chatting with a secretary in a doorway. A woman from the motor pool walked up and handed a paper to the officer, who smiled and said something.

This is unreal, Autumn thought. *Twenty minutes ago, this hall was almost deserted. Now there are people all over the place.* Behind her in the stairwell a door opened and she heard multiple voices echoing.

"Excuse me, Officer," a voice at her side said. She turned to see a custodian wheeling a large trash can. "I have to put this can under the staircase." Autumn had to come out into the hall to let him get the can through the door. *Too bad I don't have a bag of rocks right now.* He closed the stairwell door and left her there.

If she followed him up this stairwell to the first floor she would run right into Jaime and his lab mates. But she could get to the first floor by taking the other stairs. She'd need to get all the way down the hallway.

She became painfully conscious that she wasn't wearing a badge, her sidearm was nonregulation, and Bernard's helmet was a size too large for her. She passed several people in the hallway, but none of them were TAC officers.

Turning a corner, Autumn saw the evidence lockup ahead of her. She made sure her visor was down all the way and walked a little faster. She could hear angry voices coming from the lockup.

"If the envelope is wedged in between the desk and the wall, the badge must be there, too!" It was Captain Bickson. "Now get down on your damn hands and knees, and look again. I want that badge!"

She got past the door and down the hall. But now coming toward her were three TAC officers. It was Henderson, Deang, and somebody else carrying a lunch sack. They were bound to greet her, and she would have to say something in return. Even if she only nodded, they couldn't help but recognize a tall female figure in TAC gear.

There were only two doorways coming up. She was going to have to run. She might make it as far as the elevator.

Then as she passed the second doorway, she heard a man's voice, "Hey, Denise!" She turned to see the fair-haired rookie in the doorway.

"Oh, hi." Autumn quickly stepped into the holding cell area. "Almost walked right past you, didn't I." Behind her, she heard the three TAC officers talking as they passed the room. They were saying something about Free Life and double guard duty at the Linda Vista power substation and how nobody was getting paid enough for this.

"I was wondering why you hadn't come back yet," the rookie said. "Is it OK to say 'Officer Denise?' I mean, that's not against the rules, is it?"

"What's your first name?" Autumn asked.

"Brad."

"Well, Brad," Autumn said, "you just keep right on calling me Denise. The more you say 'Denise,' the better. In fact, you can say it in every sentence, if you want. I love the way you say it."

"Great, Denise." Brad smiled as he bent down for the gym bag behind his desk. "Here's your gym bag. I'm still impressed by you carrying this over. It must weigh fifty pounds. I bet you'll create a really nice flower garden with this. Denise."

"Do you like gardening, Brad?" Autumn pushed her visor all the way up, so that Brad could see her dark eyes. "You like flowers?"

"Uh, yeah. My mom is really great with flowers. I wish I had time to tell you more, Denise," Brad said, "but I just got phoned to escort my DUI guy up to the entrance level to meet with his lawyer. Then I take them to the judge's chambers." He smiled. "Denise."

"The entrance level," Autumn said, lowering her visor. "Well, Brad, maybe you can help me kill two birds with one bag of rocks." *If Jaime hasn't picked up the phone by now.*

"What'nell is in this thing, anyway? Cement?" the prisoner said, lugging the gym bag in both hands, as they reached the stair landing.

"Be quiet and keep moving," Brad said. "Remember our deal. You carry the bag out the front lobby, and I note on my report that when you were brought in, you were courteous, cooperative, and seemed reasonably in control of your motor functions."

"Don't even *remember* being brought in," said the prisoner.

"Nearly there," said Autumn, and went ahead of them to open the door leaving the stairwell.

Everything looked safe in the lobby. People were entering and leaving the building normally, and there were no extra officers watching the exit doors. Maybe Jaime had not called, and Lucille had somehow managed to cancel the detain order. On the other hand, maybe the guys with laser-sighted rifles were just very well hidden.

Autumn, Brad, and the DUI passed the elevators and crossed the lobby in no particular hurry, just two uniformed officers escorting a prisoner and his bag of personal belongings. When they got to the exit, Autumn reached for the gym bag.

"Thank you for the favor, Brad," she said, taking one last look around the lobby. If a TAC team was watching her, they'd make their move now. "And sir, we do appreciate your good citizenship, assisting law enforcement officers in their responsibilities."

"Ow," said the prisoner, squinting at the light from the glass outer doors. "Can I getta aspirin, or a happy mitt, or something?"

"It was great meeting you, Denise," said Brad. "Officer Casseroli.I hope we meet again soon."

"I bet we will," Autumn said. "One way or the other."

She took the bag and without looking back, walked out the front door of the Armory and crossed the street.

She forced herself to walk for a block and a half before she dropped the bag into a dumpster and went into a 40 mph sprint with her BioBoosters.

Chapter 37

Aubrey Singehoffer had been gone for almost an hour, but the underarms of Brian's shirt were still soaked. He had swung around from the ceiling molding and the light fixture for a while to help himself calm down. Then he brushed off his coat and sat at the desk and stared at the map again. Singehoffer had made very clear that he, that is, Charlesworth, had a bright future at the zoo. Brian hoped that even a quarter of his tour spiel would turn out to be feasible.

He wasn't terribly clear about what humans thought was weird, but today seemed as if it would qualify. Nevertheless, there was the hope that perhaps Mack and Autumn were getting closer to finding Brianna.

Thinking of her situation again was sobering, however. Was she even still alive? His blood ran cold at the thought of her being taken for cloning experiments or anything of that kind. But that didn't make sense; they could abduct chimpanzees off the street at any time without having to break into a tailor shop. They wanted Brianna for a specific reason.

Did the baboons and their masters think Brianna knew where Jiggs could be found? That seemed uncomfortably possible, if there was a hunt for Jiggs underway. She would be unable to tell them anything. They might not believe her. The thought was awful.

He checked the desk's voice mail. There was a message from Mack Davis that had come while he was giving the tour. He wrote it down on an envelope and erased the message. It sounded promising. This Urizen might be what they needed.

He hoped Briana wasn't hurt, that they were giving her food and water, that she knew he was looking for her, that even if tonight didn't work out, no matter how long it took, he would never stop.

The desk phone chimed. On this old desk there was no textifier display screen. He let the message go to voice mail.

It chimed again and he let it go.

It chimed a third time. Maybe it was Charlesworth. Maybe Brianna had been found, and it was on the news.

"San Diego Zoo," he answered. "Director Singehoffer's office."

"It's me," Autumn's voice said. "Is Mack Davis back yet?"

"No," said Brian. "but he left a message. We're supposed to meet him at eight tonight in Old Town. He has a contact who can help us locate Brianna."

"Old Town's a big area."

"He said the east end of San Diego Avenue by the clock shop."

"Can do," said Autumn. "Everything nice and quiet there at the zoo?"

"One might say that," said Brian. "As of now."

As he hung up the phone, he suddenly thought, *I have my work cut out for me.* He had to leave notes for Charlesworth on what he had said to the Senator and the Director. Before he forgot everything.

He switched on the desk vocode transcriptor and looked at the control screen. It was an older model with an entirely different layout than any he had used before.

Forty minutes of tinkering later, he was finally able to get the machine to record a sentence. *It would have been faster to write with chalk on a piece of wood,* Brian thought, *the way I did at first in the forest; il y a très longtemps en Côte d'Ivoire.* But at least now the machine was working.

He began dredging up from his memory, and repeating aloud for the transcriptor, all the wild things he had found to say about the future of zoos in America.

Chapter 38

At 8 p.m. Autumn was standing under a tree on San Diego Avenue across from the sign saying

-RECOVER LOST TIME -

OLD TOWN CLOCKS & WATCHES

REPAIRS - CERTIFIED HOROLOGIST

There were evening tourists walking in both directions, but no Mack or Brian yet.

To cover her uniform, Autumn had found a torn-up piece of green plastic behind a loading dock and punched a hole to make it into a poncho. She had Carter's helmet in an oversized plastic shopping bag. Nobody looked at her boots, and it was dark anyway, sort of, a slightly queasy semi-darkness mixed with light from shop windows and street lamps and algae-light ropes wound variously around the scattered trees.

A taxi swooshed past.

If she moved to Fresno she would have to buy a car. That could make finances tighter. Great-Grandfather got around without a car of his own, but that was because he got free SoloCar credits as part of his Everbliss Gardens membership. A lot of things were covered by his membership that he would lose when they shared an apartment.

Unfortunately, Autumn would have to take up the slack. She had figured she could make ends meet with a retail job. Except she had been reminded this afternoon, as she took the long way round to Old Town, how many of those jobs these days were now going to Provies.

If she had a car she would also need an apartment with an auto charger, and she didn't *want* a new apartment building. She wanted the old kind made of wood. Termites and all.

She spotted Brian in his suit and tie coming along the cross street. He moved low and fast between parked cars. *He's getting pretty good at this secrecy stuff*, she thought. *For a tailor.*

"Pretty good, isn't he?" a voice whispered in her ear.

"Mack!" she said. "You scared the hell out of me!"

"Shhh," Mack whispered. "We need to stay as inconspicuous as possible, remember?"

"What's with the finger?" asked Autumn. Mack had his right index finger taped up in thick gauze.

"Got it caught in one of those personalized birthday card vending machines. Had to get something for a friend of a friend."

Mack led her onto the side street where Brian was crouched beside a late model Kalana'i 350 sedan. Mack nodded and Brian got up and strolled nonchalantly over to them. "Hello," he said, with a chimpish pursed-lips expression that made it sound like "hloo." He was doing his best to appear in a good mood.

203

"OK. We have a 9:20 audience with the king of the night," Mack said. "His name is Urizen, and there's little that happens in San Diego that he doesn't learn about sooner or later. Sooner, usually."

"He says he knows about Brianna?" said Brian.

"Well, he didn't say that in so many words," said Mack, and then seeing Brian's face begin to fall, he quickly added, "but I think he does. He knows we're looking. I've done deals with him before, and he wouldn't agree to meet unless he's got something."

"Why did you tell us to be here at eight?"

"First, to scout the area and make sure it isn't a trap. I've made a circuit of the plaza to check the west end where our meeting point is. We're going to walk the shops like tourists and keep our eyes open for trouble till thing close at nine. But when you have an appointment with Urizen, you better not be even one minute late."

"Who is this Urizen?" said Autumn. "I've been briefed on local shady characters, but…."

"He manages to stay off polisec radar. He has a lot of help. Women of all ages and descriptions love Urizen almost, well, like cats love catnip. Rich widows, homeless women, business owners, teenagers, you wouldn't believe. Cat magic or something. They'll do anything to make him happy. As a result he has the biggest intelligence network on the West Coast since the Apple-Google War. But he's a little crazy. And he doesn't give anything for free. Let's go."

"I still don't know who this guy is," said Autumn.

"Told you already," Mack said as he started walking back to the main street. "Urizen isn't a guy. He's a cat."

They went westward down the sidewalk. Across the street, outside the Casa del Corrido, there were beautiful Latinas in frilled blouses passing out flyers. Autumn had eaten there a couple of times for holiday office parties; White Knights got a good group discount, and there were a lot of junior Public Assistance Agents who were, like her, not originally from SoCal and who thought of Mexican food as inherently a party cuisine. As they walked past the restaurant they were enveloped by the smell of tortillas cooking and wood smoke from the grill.

"You said this Urizen gives nothing for free," said Brian, sniffing with interest. "How are we going to pay for the information?"

"Got a loan from a friend," said Mack. "Don't worry. We'll be all right."

As they walked on, the old-timey norteña accordion music across the street was replaced by a somewhat more modern salsa-hop beat from the cantina. Above the bar in the cantina was a twelve-foot vidscreen playing a stream live from Buenos Aires, labeled as the second ever Antlers America Cup. Teams of well-muscled marsh deer playing for Uruguay and Peru were sprinting on an enormous field and passing a ring back and forth to each other with tosses of their heads. The ring sailed for five seconds in a forward pass and was finally caught, spinning, on one antler tip by a buck in the red Peruvian uniform at the peak of a majestic leap. Immediately the camera cut to a human and a deer commentator nattering away in the studio.

Across the street was the Whaley House, with a sign saying *America's Most Haunted.* These days Autumn was feeling a little haunted herself. Visiting a mysterious cat was sounding like a sketchy idea. But that made it just like everything else they'd done over the last two days.

They passed a window full of pinewood toys and mugs decorated with ears or noses of different animal species. They had a display of printed plaques for pet owners showing various small dog breeds, Pomeranians and Bolognese and terriers and Chihuahuas—no Shar Peis, though—each one with the motto:

WHO NEEDS TO BE ELEVATED
WHEN YOU'RE THIS CUTE

At the corner of Twiggs Street was the whitewashed 19th-century Church of the Immaculate Conception with its tile roof and mission-style bell tower surrounded by palm trees. Farther down the street in a brightly spotlighted dirt corral was a shaggy black bison, a mountain on tiny legs munching grass out of a bucket and occasionally lifting its massive horned head. There was a huge sign saying BUFFALO and OLD WEST in, apparently, five or six languages, and another sign she could barely make out that said

Buffalo Rides

Very Gentle

(something or other she couldn't read)

Certified Non-Elevated Animal. SCE compliant

Tourists were getting their pictures taken in front of the animal, unperturbed by the historical fact that wild bison had never roamed west of the Sonora Desert.

There was a bench by some little faux covered wagons where two mariachis were resting between sets. One of the mariachis was a Latino human, and standing beside him was the other, a midsize ungulate Provie of a species she couldn't quite make out in the dark. They both wore black suits with silver buttons. They were looking together at something on a palmphone screen, the very different faces of the man and the animal glowing in its small rectangular flood of blue light.

As they crossed the street Autumn noticed uneasily a sharp little movement in the starless downtown night sky.

"Don't look now," she said to Mack, "but I think that might have been a drone."

"Where?" he said.

The black buzzing thing ducked behind the roof of the Old Town Theatre down the street. "It's gone now." *Haunted is right.*

"Polisec?" asked Mack.

"Didn't look like it, at least not the kind I've ever seen White Knights using."

"Hm. They probably can't pick up our faces if we stay out of the light. But keep your eyes open, and let's not hang out on the corner. Things seem normal around here to me."

They ducked past some half-size covered wagons into the Old Town Market – a walled collection of smaller stores – and found a brightly lit gift shop. It was a big space full of small things jingling on display racks in rows and rows and rows, all possible colors in uproar. The walls were hung from floor to ceiling with shirts and hoodies and imitation leather jackets.

"You two stay here while I do another scouting run," said Mack. "I'll be back."

Brian and Autumn began to walk around separately, almost in a daze, surrounded by what seemed like every souvenir ever offered for sale in San Diego.

Mostly plastic stuff made overseas. Maybe sometimes real isn't what people will buy, thought Autumn as she wandered the crowded aisles, her shopping bag containing the helmet in one hand. She wanted something in her life to be real. Was the Vietnamese name embroidered on her bulletproof chemise real?

She had told Great-Grandfather about the name. His response was "OK, you want your friends to call you Thu for a while, fine. I can't keep track of stuff like that."

"But this is Vietnamese, it's original, it's Autumn in translation."

"Sure, but you're the one decided to translate it. You could pick from an old list of Russian baby names or something and decide that's you, just as easy."

She didn't like thinking the choice was arbitrary. "There's also the connection to my people."

"Your people? You don't have nothing to do with Vietnam. I don't have nothing to do with it. You think if you went there you'd get along good with 'em? You can reboot that right now, girlie."

"But the heritage. Genetics at least."

"Seems like genetics hardly matters any more. I take a Solocar to the clinic and there's a little raccoon with a striped tail and a pink girl-voice thing in her ear checking my hemo levels and giving out my pills. Tells me she got elevated eight years ago and can't remember nothing before that. You think she's going around saying her genes are what she's all about? And all the cloning stuff we got, baby blueprints, everything. You pay and you get what you want. Big improvement in general, is what I say."

"But what about –"

"Without some of the stuff we got now, I'd be dead. My dad's heart gave out on him when he was sixty-three. Now I could live to a hundred and five, no sweat." Great-Grandfather was smart, but he just didn't seem to need to *think* about things.

She saw Brian in the next aisle, looking at seashells with plastic eyes glued on them. *Can't remember nothing before that.* She had thought that elevated animals were born that way, but apparently not always. One of the things, probably, that refuted the simple mutation

209

theory and mystified scientists. She'd read something about what they called latent mutation theory, but really everyone was still groping in the dark to explain what was happening, or predict what would happen.

For a lot of people the future was the biggest thing to think about. Autumn was hungry for the past. But she hardly knew anything about the heritage she was trying to commit to.

Her parents were so American they could get matching his-and-hers picket fences. She had never figured out how two people with shared Vietnamese ancestry but with absolutely no interest in it had even found each other. The story was that they met at a college "face-to-face" mixer, the sort of thing colleges organized to make students feel like their school lives weren't totally online. Maybe what drew them together was their post-ethnic attitude, the shared perspective of people who arrived at turbo-Americanness by similar paths.

Her dad belonged to the Rotary club and had built her a closet with his woodworking tools when she was twelve. He watched comedy streams and grilled lean burgers in the back yard—heedless of those who warned that pretty soon cows and turkeys were going to become elevated. Her mom read biographies and made a mean sachertorte and maintained a popular multistream about 3-D knitting projects. They had taken Autumn and her brother Kyle on Solocar vacations to Yosemite and the Grand Canyon and they had been there for at least some of the kids' soccer games. Kyle was nine years older and slated to take over the family accounting business;

he ran marathons and he was dating a cute Jewish girl, to whom he was going to pop the question any day now, and he was a chip off the old block. The American dream in a nutshell, for what it was worth. That was OK. Today that dream was rare enough that it was a real accomplishment.

She wanted a bigger picture, though, a sense of what it all meant. It seemed like her heritage was the doorway. But the culture was very different. The books she was reading kept bringing up the importance of Confucian values. Filial piety. Respect for learning. Honor. Community. There had to be more to it. What wasn't merely "Asian,"—if that even meant anything—but specifically Vietnamese? Why did that matter? And the question that confused her even more: what were those things going to mean in an Elevated world where half your neighbors were a different species than you?

She would have to figure it out over the long term. Maybe five months was too soon to leave her job. Or maybe she just needed to get out and hustle and get started taking Hi-Band classes in earnest. She wasn't sure any more.

Right now she had to deal with…right now. She was liable to get blown up by a real missile for fake reasons, and that was why she was hiding her uniform, which didn't even feel like her anymore anyway, under a tarp she'd made to look like a poncho. *How deep into fake do you have to go before you get to real?*

She walked past a couple of women trying on huge sombreros and talking about getting through the border checkpoint from NorCal, and a pronghorn antelope nosing through a rack of beach-themed postcards while talking about airline prices to somebody on his earbud phone. The pronghorn tourist's vocoder spoke with a Texas twang and he was carrying his belongings in tooled-leather saddlebags. It struck her that maybe some animals actually didn't care about what had been called, in one *Atlantic-New Yorker Monthly* article, the Leather Question. Maybe it was a "circle of life" kind of thing. And maybe, like humans, animals didn't always ask big questions even though now technically they could.

She didn't like feeling like a tourist. What did that mean? *Basically, a tourist is somebody who's willing to take accessible over authentic.* She certainly didn't want to be a tourist in, or about, Vietnam. But so far she had had to take what was accessible. And being all real all the time wasn't an option when she was undercover.

She needed to figure out what was going on before she could go and explain it to the White Knights. And she had some friends to help her, at least, kind of. She saw that Mack had returned and was walking the aisles. She ought to have a talk with him before they went to see this Urizen.

Chapter 39

Autumn caught up with Mack near the back of the store. He was turning over a beautiful colored glass vase in his hands.

"Wonder if she'd like this," he muttered aloud, his brow furrowed, as she walked up and stood next to him.

"Who?" she asked. She realized that his name and possible employment were the only things she knew about his life. In fact, she didn't even really know those.

Mack glanced over his shoulder and smiled. "Oh, my grandmother, on my cousin's side. Think they could print 'Phyllis' in gold lettering?"

Autumn sighed and nudged his elbow with hers. "Mack, I was in the Armory today."

"You were *what*?"

"They'd already picked up my badge. From the panda."

"You were in the Armory." Mack looked at her. "Does the Armory know that?"

"I think so. My badge—I retrieved it, but it triggered an alert. Lucille was helping me when the alarm went off. I'm worried about her. In normal times, she'd ping me an icon message when things calmed down, but with us on the run I have no way to retrieve it."

"But you got out. We'll focus on that. Could you have been followed?"

"I don't think so. I hopped SpeedRail behind a baby stroller, went past Lindbergh all the way to Rosecrans, went into a lumber yard office and came out the loading dock. I didn't see anyone, so I jumped from the loading dock onto the back of a passing recycling truck full of electronics junk, then doubled back later. I think that would throw off pursuit."

"Wow. OK." He put down the vase and looked at her again. "That's actual dry cleaning. You're not as much of a rookie as I thought."

"Me! A rookie!" She felt she had been quite generous in trying to forget that he was with Secure-Tek, or might be. "I am a White Knight, top honors in my Academy class, with five years on the force, *Mr. Davis*, and you are –"

"Let's pretend we've already had that conversation for the day and skip ahead."

Simmer down, she told herself. *He's got nothing against you personally. It's just that occasional outbreak of bad attitude.*

"Did you get anything good?" asked Mack. They started to stroll around the shop.

"Not really," she said. "I was trying to track down the drone missile firing order. But when we tried, the system locked up."

Mack frowned. "Let me ask you something," he said, tugging the gauze bandage back into place on his finger. "Have the White Knights ever employed baboon deputies in the past?"

"Not that I know of. Maybe over on the Drug Enforcement side. But I think I would have heard."

"I hate to say this, but I think something is dirty at White Knights."

"You mean something deep." Autumn ran her fingers over a *SoCal* T-shirt showing a human surfer silhouetted against a gorgeous sunset. When she moved to San Diego she had wanted to learn to surf, because surfing seemed like the real SoCal, but work just hadn't left time. "I thought at first the missile was Bickson mad at me because I made a crack about 6H-ing him. But that's crazy, and the more I think about it the crazier it is."

"Could Bickson in fact be crazy?"

"Not literally. He's got an ego like the Lightyear Blimp, he harasses women, and he kind of hates me, but he wouldn't blow up an officer and two civilians for that."

"Maybe he's hiding something."

"What?"

"Use of polisec authority to commit crimes, maybe. Kickbacks, embezzlement, drug trade, undocumented animal trafficking, who knows?"

Autumn thought for a while. She browsed through a rack of jingling keyrings saying *San Diego*, dozens of different permutations of the same basic item. "He's been on Chavez's case lately too. I thought it was just because Chavez is smarter than him. But maybe Bickson's afraid for a special reason."

"They did scoop that badge up very quickly for a polisec facility that supposedly thinks you're dead. You saw—we all saw—something we weren't supposed to see in that tailor shop."

"Why would corrupt polisec abduct an ordinary Provisional Citizen? There's no ransom money in it. That tailor shop was nice, but they aren't wealthy by any stretch."

"Brianna's not ordinary. She's got a tie to Free Life."

Autumn stopped and looked at him. "You think polisec would interrogate her? Brian says she doesn't know anything."

"They may not believe that."

"The Brians have been in the country for four years. Why now?"

"I don't know." He picked up a Virgen de Guadalupe Vanilla Lime votive candle and sniffed it. "Another option is that she had encountered something polisec is up to and they're afraid she'll talk. Maybe even Brian doesn't know. Maybe they want to plant some evidence, get her deported, or at least frighten her enough to keep her from playing canary. They took the trouble to keep her alive, but there's always the risk they might come around to exing her later."

"Holy shelduck." *This is my supervisor we're talking about.* 'But that doesn't clear things up at all. Why do it in secret? If they wanted Brian's wife, even on false pretenses, they could have just shown up and taken her off in a burstcar. But the tailor shop wasn't even included in the sweep zone."

"That could have been on purpose, to clear the area around the extraction," said Mack.

"But they got an anonymous tip telling them where to sweep."

216

"So they claimed."

"Man, I can't trust *anything* anymore," said Autumn. *Was the tip fake? Were previous tips fake? Is Free Life even a real organization? No, of course it is, Brianna's brother runs it. Or so she thinks. Aaa!* "I gotta get away from you. You are the king of paranoid."

"There might be someone still left who has me beat there," said Mack quietly. "I hope."

They walked around the corner and found Brian. He had picked up a tiny coin purse shaped like a piñata and was trying to get the metal twist clasp open. It was stuck and when he applied more torque, the cheap fabric underneath just tore apart. He looked around guiltily and put it back on the shelf.

"Careful. Damage to merchandise, code section 2538," said Autumn archly.

"Perhaps we can find the proprietor," said Brian anxiously, adjusting his gold cufflink, "and explain that it –"

"We can't call attention to ourselves," she said. "Be honest on your own time."

"Aha. Understood," said Brian, backing away from the shelf.

"It probably cost 35 cents from India," said Autumn, surprised to hear herself talking like this. Brian smiled a little and nodded. He moved on and began looking at refrigerator magnets with his hands behind his back.

Wasn't a White Knight someone who enforced the law? *Am I still a White Knight?* Her sense of what her values and actions ought to be was getting bent a little by circumstances. *Being on the run does things to you.* Whether those things were all bad she wasn't sure. If yesterday hadn't happened she would never have realized that something was fishy at the Armory. And maybe nobody else would have either.

She turned back to Mack. He was looking at a pair of little sparkly earrings.

"Have you ever wondered about a relationship you're in," he said, "and you think, maybe the biggest problem is that it just Tires You Out? You know, it sounded great at the beginning, but at this point what you're getting out of it isn't worth the effort? And there's no trust there anyway?"

"I'd say you're hitting the nail on the head," said Autumn. She browsed through a stack of painted ceramic trivets. "To be honest, I've already started the retirement paperwork."

"Huh?" said Mack, giving her a bewildered look.

"White Knights," she said. She hadn't actually meant to tell him, but OK, maybe speaking her goal out loud would help to commit to it. "I'm officially getting out. I told you about the whole Cultural Reclaimer thing, right?"

"Ohh." Mack nodded vigorously.

"What was it *you* were talking about?"

"My chiropractor," said Mack. "Guy can't return a phone call to save his life."

"Really?" she said, but went on. "I'm looking to get out. But I don't want to be fired, and I don't want to be celebrating my twenty-fifth, thirtieth, and forty-third birthdays in a cell in max security out at Salton City."

"Stands to reason," said Mack.

"I have to make the Knights see what really happened. Supposing we don't get blown up or something, Mack, will you testify if I need you to?" Yesterday in the garage she had assumed he would, because telling the truth was just what witnesses did. A lot had happened since yesterday. "I need to know. Can you tell them the truth?" She stopped herself from putting too much emphasis on the word *can*. It wouldn't help to get insulting.

Mack didn't respond immediately. He put the earrings back. "The problem is," he said slowly, "suppose I do? Are they going to believe me?"

She looked at him. He seemed unusually serious. "I guess I wasn't considering that issue," she said.

"Autumn, I'm not what you call an upstanding citizen. Brian, on the other hand, *is* upstanding. But he's a Provie and juries can be funny about that. Plus, it was his wife that was abducted, so he's not an impartial bystander. I don't know." Mack scrunched his mouth to one side and shook his head a little. "The way to really clear things up with White Knights is if you find whoever's responsible on the inside."

Brian came back to them. "It will be 9 p.m. soon," he said. "Don't you suppose we should get going?"

"Let's do it," said Mack. "The Cosmopolitan Hotel."

They left the shop and walked through the Old Town Market to get to the exit on the north side. It was a slow night and the vendors were already beginning to wrap up their carts. They passed a glass case set into the pavement which revealed the original market foundation rubble below ground level, a window into the place's past.

The market gates were set in high wooden walls that looked like a recent addition, topped with ornamental barbed spikes made of wrought iron for a vaguely authentic touch. A lot of businesses had put in extra security measures a decade ago when species like weasels and raccoons started to steal things besides food.

An employee pushed the big wooden door shut on the market courtyard, locked it with his code, and trudged off to the parking lot.

The three of them turned west and strolled down the wide concrete path past the Theatre, heading toward the grassy plaza and its surrounding historic buildings. At various junctions were wooden barrels serving as trash cans and strengthening the feeling that as you crossed Twiggs Street you were walking back into the 1870s. Some of the buildings actually dated back that far, and others had been rebuilt, and not all the merchandise was cheap imported goods. Autumn wasn't sure whether she would call Old Town real or fake; it was both, or maybe it lingered between, as a kind of twilight zone of authenticity.

The air was cool and the night sky had no moon; the street lamps threw wedge-shaped blocks of yellowish light on the pavement, and on the left a huge pancake cactus cast a gnarled chaos of shadows on the long adobe wall of the Casa de Estudillo. Mack was looking around cautiously.

Ahead beyond the stables, the two-story pillared façade of the Cosmopolitan Hotel was the best-lit thing in the vicinity, glowing like a ghost ship on the right side of the path across from where the plaza lawn started. From the plaza the white shaft of the central Old Town flagpole rose up through the trees at least thirty meters in the air.

"Will Urizen come to meet us?" asked Brian.

"No, he'll send somebody," said Mack, glancing around the stable wall. "She'll take us—yeah, it'll be a she—to wherever his local spot is. He's a cat, he's got lots of places. I didn't know he had one here in Old Town these days."

Once they reached the hotel and climbed the stair risers that went all around the base of the building, they were in the narrow wooden veranda area under the hotel balcony, with narrow wooden columns holding up the upper level. A sign hanging from the blue-painted underside of the balcony said *RESTAURANT and SALOON* with a 19th-century-style hand pointing inside. The lower level was lit by hanging lamps and there were wooden dining tables and chairs for the hotel restaurant's customers during business hours. Everything was styled to show the frontier town San Diego used to be and, in a way, had become again.

Brian adjusted his tie and paced down the boards anxiously. Mack sat down heavily in a chair.

"Long day?" asked Autumn, putting the bag with the helmet on the table next to the napkin dispenser.

"Same 24 hours as usual," said Mack, rewrapping the gauze and tape tighter on his finger. "But some days you can only handle about ten."

"Ain't that the truth," she said. She wondered how Lucille had managed things back at the Armory. Lucille could do anything, though.

Brian came back from the other end of the veranda. Autumn took off her makeshift poncho and draped it over a chair. She was about to sit down.

"I need to explain something about Urizen," said Mack. "Cats aren't often elevated, and when they are, well, their brains are…different. This one especially–"

"Mack…?" said Brian so softly it was barely audible.

"Hm?"

Brian didn't respond. Autumn and Mack looked at him. His eyes were huge.

"I smell baboon," Brian whispered.

Chapter 40

Mack saw Autumn staring at him. *A trap?* she mouthed.

"Urizen wouldn't," he whispered. He slid out of the wooden chair without making a sound. *Damn drone found us,* he thought. "Which way?"

Brian lifted his nose and sniffed as he slowly turned around. He shook his head a tiny bit. "Don't know. Really strong, all around."

"Brian, we have to know."

Brian took a deep breath, then went stiffly down the hotel steps, one slow step at a time, sniffing. On the second step he turned back and glanced up. He froze.

Mack glanced overhead toward the second-floor hotel balcony, and then back at Brian.

Brian gave him the faintest little nod, looking around coolly and sauntering slowly back up the steps.

Mack looked back toward Autumn and she locked eyes with him. She jerked her head a little to the side, toward the Casa de Estudillo across the street. On top of the long adobe wall was a long glinting tubular shape, a slightly shinier black than the shadows, bobbing as it moved closer behind the trees.

Mack and Autumn stood on the wooden boardwalk, breathing in sync. She let her right hand dangle and silently pluck open the retaining strap on her holster. Brian was breathing in and out shallowly.

Mack looked at Autumn, then for a deliberate two seconds at her boots, then up overhead. *Get. A. Machine. Gun*, he mouthed.

Autumn glanced up. She sidled slowly over toward the corner of the hotel boardwalk. She leaned one shoulder gently against a pillar, facing the hotel windows. Then she hopped backwards into the street, drawing her sidearm; her boots landed whirring and she shot up off the dirt like a rocket.

Without waiting Mack drew with his bandaged right hand, middle finger on the trigger, aiming across the street just behind the black tubular shape. His shot cracked the quiet night like thunder. The black shape dropped back and fell inside the adobe wall.

There were three more gunshots over their heads on the balcony.

Mack grabbed Brian's arm and they leaped off the hotel boardwalk and ran away from the hotel, back east toward the market. They heard another gunshot behind them and then machine gun fire. "She'll catch up," said Mack. "Come on!"

In fact he could hardly keep up with Brian running on all fours. Ahead of them the stained-glass windows of the Church of the Immaculate Conception burned warm and orange around the sacred blue figures in their centers. But as they reached the market on Twiggs Street, something high up across the street in front of them flashed and bullets tore up the sidewalk, spattering up chips of concrete. They jumped back and flattened themselves against the north market wall.

"The hell—! Where did that come from!" said Mack.

"The church roof," said Brian. He scrambled to climb the wooden double doors of the market, but they were too high for him to reach the top, and his smooth shoe sole slipped off the thin iron door handle.

"Oof," gasped Autumn, landing next to them with her boots whirring. She had the revolver in her hand.

"Where's the machine gun?" snapped Mack.

"Two more boons on the balcony. Not a good place." *Nice to see you too,* she thought, having barely made it off the balcony with bullets flying.

"Neither is this. Get us inside!" They could see black forms with guns loping from the hotel towards them, low on the ground.

Autumn flicked a switch on her utility belt and the lock on the big market door clicked open. Mack pushed her and Brian inside and pulled the door after them. Autumn flicked the switch on her lock activator and the lock clicked shut again just as the door began to splinter with small groups of holes from machine gun fire at ground level.

The three of them zigzagged in the semi-darkness around the now-shut stalls. Machine gun fire from the high angle of the church tore into racks of leather handbags on their right, and they swerved left to hug the east shop wall.

There were sounds of scrabbling at the doors and walls around the market. It now felt like a very small place. The iron security spikes on top, whatever their level of cultural authenticity, were blessedly solid. Outside they heard a kind of open-and-shut call like a bark ending in a snort: *Raaa-hu. Raaa-hu.* The barks repeated and moved in different directions around the market walls. *Raaa-hu.*

"We can't stay here," said Autumn. In front of them the dark ragged shapes of the shot-up handbags were swinging wildly. "They'll surround us."

"Brian, can baboons see in the dark?" asked Mack.

"No better than you," said Brian.

"They weren't wearing visor helmets, probably for visibility," said Autumn. She had left Carter's helmet at the Cosmopolitan hotel next to the napkins. It didn't stay on very well anyway. But she had her new underwear. She had never been more thankful for express delivery.

"The boon up on the church spine is framed against the sky," said Mack. "He's in a tank suit. Polygraphene armor. With almost 180 arc of fire. The bell tower is partly blocking that though." He switched the gun to his left hand. "Follow me." They followed him between the shops to the gift shop they had been in before on the market's south side.

Another burst of machine gun fire ripped at the north gate.

Autumn quickly opened the shop door, and they piled in and she relocked it behind them. There were now only a few minimal lights in the darkened shop. They tried not to knock over the racks of merchandise as they hurried to the door that led out of the market complex.

"I thought they wanted us alive," said Brian.

"Looks like they reclassed it as a wet op." said Mack. "Here, Annie Oakley, for you." He shoved a 9mm magazine into Autumn's hand.

"But that's for your other gun, not the revolver," she said.

"Both pieces take the same caliber. I carry that way for a reason."

Raaa-hu, came the roar behind them.

"Gotta go!" said Mack. "Let's head left, down Twiggs to Congress Street."

Autumn was squeezing the magazine, trying to pry the bullets out. "Hang on!"

There was a crash from the north gate. "We have to go!" said Mack.

"Hang *on*!" Autumn flicked her utility belt switch, and the lock to the gift shop's south entrance clicked open.

Holding his pistol in his left hand, Mack kicked the door open a few feet so they could see the concrete-paved pedestrian street of the Old Town central area and the DENTIST sign across from them. The concrete street ran to the right along the south side of the plaza, parallel to the street up on the north side where the hotel was. There were no baboons visible.

"Wait," he said. He picked up a sombrero off the hat rack and tossed it out into the street. It spun lazily halfway across the dirt street, then bucked and flapped midair as it was shredded by a burst of fire from the church to the left.

"Oh no!" said Brian.

"OK, to the right then," said Mack. "We'll get out through the south parking lot. Autumn, with your boots you're the fastest. Cover us and then catch up."

"Do we even have a chance?" asked Brian, his shoulders slumping.

"Absolutely," said Mack. He was speaking quickly, but he patted the shoulder of the chimp's suit. "Remember in the tailor shop, you fought to get Brianna back? What happened?"

"I was punched, and then I was wrapped," said Brian. Behind them at the other end of the gift shop there were pounding, crunching noises at the door.

"Minor details, Brian. You nearly ripped the arm off a baboon in a biostrong suit. After *you* got to him, they had to carry his moaning body up the rope."

"I guess I did," said Brian.

"So if they get close, do it again! Remember: if and when necessary, *you're an ape*. You may have to *go* ape."

"I may? I am?" said Brian. He blinked. "I am."

The pounding on the other door stopped.

"Autumn, stay cool and concentrate on your shot placement. Brian, we'll cross the street at –"

There was a burst of flame from the far end of the shop, an explosion that rocked the building. Shells with little glued-on eyes and spinning keychains mixed with wood fragments and plaster rained down on their heads.

Mack blasted off two rounds, screamed like a banshee, and ran out the door. Brian scrambled to get out with Mack.

"Oh, sure. Stay calm," said Autumn, furiously stuffing each of the 9mm bullets into the five revolver chambers. *Wish I had my Yamato*, she thought.

There was a second explosion and the north door of the gift shop was replaced by a blooming black cloud. Dark shapes with fangs came tearing through the forest of gifts and shirts and purses all now jangling smoky and aflame. The fangs seemed to be approaching in slow motion. She got the fifth bullet into the chamber and snapped the cylinder shut. She pivoted her body edge-on to the line of attack.

The walls and windows next to her shredded under machine gun fire. There was a lightning bolt of pain as two bullets smacked her in the thigh, stopped by the SafeLite underwear. Autumn gasped, staggered, and then got her stance back. With her arm straight out she fired twice at the fangs.

The first dark mouth dropped away. Then the second. There were more coming.

She shot again, and with her boots a-whir, ran out of the south entrance.

Chapter 41

Running at top chimp speed, Brian made it safely across the street, but Mack got only a few yards when a spray of concrete splinters hissed on the concrete ahead of him and forced him to return to the near side of the street. He ducked behind a barrel.

Not seeing him, Autumn flashed past at 40 mph. *Ahh, no, come back,* he thought.

Bullets punched through the window glass over his head and went into the Printing Office Museum. Bits of lead type spilled and clattered out of a tray, and a group of bullet holes smacked through a replica 1869 San Diego Union newspaper sheet hanging on a printer's drying line.

Those hits on the concrete arced in the opposite direction. They couldn't have come from the church. Where? Down the street, in a huge and luxuriant tree, a certain branch hanging over the center of the street bounced a little. *From there he's got me. Move. Go go go!*

Firing toward the tree as he ran, Mack sprinted across the street toward the wooden fence of El Emporio Artesano. As he frantically tried to climb its smooth wall, a well-groomed, French-cuffed chimpanzee hand reached out and pulled him up and over as bullets chunked into the fence where his feet had just been.

Autumn reached the grassy plaza before she realized that she had outrun the others. She paused behind a huge gnarled tree trunk and reloaded.

Baboon shapes were pouring out of the market door she had just left, each running with a gun in one hand while the other front paw snapped with the back legs, open and shut, like scissors. Their tails stuck up a few inches and then beyond that dangled free. Down at the end of the street, silhouetted against the blazing windows of the church, stood a very tall, thin human with a long-barreled revolver in his hand.

She turned to see two more baboons coming around the Casa de Estudillo from the direction of the hotel. She heard more barking from east of the plaza: *Raaa-hu. Raaa-hu.*

Mack tumbled into the Emporio courtyard, knocking over a shelf's worth of candleholders.

"Thanks," Mack said to Brian, and looked around. The wood-walled courtyard of the Emporio, dimly lit from the streetlights outside, was a forest of artisan wares: hundreds of hanging wind chimes and carved parrots and seagulls and pots and bowls and huge patio planters and fountains and toys and tiles and wall art and old decorative cartwheels and vases with great bursts of plastic flowers.

A row of pots dangling on a line high over their heads exploded in a sweep from one end to the other under a burst of machine-gun fire. Fragments rained down. "The tree gunner," Mack said. "He can't hit us. But they'll come over the fence."

231

Baboons barked outside: *Raa-hu.*

Suddenly above the fence a fur-maned head lifted up, its mouth opening to bare its top canines. Mack fired and the animal dropped backwards.

Brian slipped his arms out of his suit coat and laid it carefully on a shelf.

"What are you doing?"

"Preparing for battle," Brian began rolling up his pinstriped shirtsleeves. "This is chromostabilized natural wool. It's important to take care of quality fabrics."

"Great. What about MY suit?" Mack said, as he saw another baboon mounting the fence, and shot it.

"You selected Astrozzoli, a glossier but more durable synthetic fiber," said Brian. "I have high hopes for it."

Brian cleared his throat and bared his teeth a couple of times, as if experimentally. Then in his shirtsleeves he picked up a huge painted clay *horno* oven larger than himself, heaved over his head like a boulder, and threw it over the fence. As he did so he gave a terrifying scream. For millions of years in Africa, such a scream would have made a troop of baboons keep a respectful distance from a chimpanzee encampment. It made a chill run up Mack's spine.

Mack fired once more, and all scratching on the other side of the fence now stopped completely.

From behind the tree trunk Autumn saw a dark shape climbing swiftly up the plaza flagpole, a gun slung on its back. At the top he would command a 360-degree angle of fire.

No, you don't, Autumn thought, sprinting to the struts at the flagpole's base. Her boots lifting her like a springing leopard, she sprang up and landed on the pole's lower section, which was lined with wooden climbing blocks for raising and lowering the flags. Standing on a block she looked straight up and fired a shot up along the pole. The shot missed and the baboon scurried upwards.

If she retreated now she'd definitely get shot in the head.

She jumped up onto the pole and started to shinny upwards.

"Stay here," said Mack. "I'm going out the back. I've got to cover Autumn, or she's dead."

"But –"

"Take this." He thrust the Hayakawa 9mm into Brian's hand. "It has six bullets left. Look at the sights."

"This is no time for tourism!"

"The *gun* sights," said Mack. He was padding a brightly painted tin wall sconce on the inside with bandannas. He poured a bowl of little souvenir pewter crosses into a bandanna and stuffed it under the padding, then put the whole thing over his bandaged right hand. "Hold the gun in both hands. Make this little prong thing on the front show up" —he took Brian's other hand and touched it to the iron sights—"in this V notch back here. When the prong thing is on the baboon, squeeze the trigger."

233

Brian sighted awkwardly along the top of the gun.

"The kick's not bad, but be prepared for the muzzle to buck upwards just a little," said Mack, gesturing with the sconce on his hand as he ran toward the back office and jumped the fence.

The side street was lit by ghostly yellow street lights. Mack crawled on his belly to avoid casting a long shadow within sight of the tree gunner. Once behind the next building, he ran past a sprawling spiky agave plant to a swath of dry river rock on the ground.

On his left was a building with a sign saying MASON STREET SCHOOL. On his right, past the swath of rock, was the back of the little courthouse and the old original jail, a little free-standing closet-sized iron structure made of rusted plates and gratings.

To be safe from the tree gunner he passed behind the jail and the Wells Fargo building with its towering flat false front, the fake-it-till-you-make-it architecture that had sprung up to settle the West. He came back around to the concrete street between Wells Fargo and the cigar store, the side wall of which read TOBACCO * PIPES * CUTLERY * GENTLEMEN'S FURNISHINGS.

If I can sneak up on Tree Shooter, we should be in much better shape. But I really need to borrow a baboon's machine gun. He adjusted the wall sconce on his fist.

In the street lights he saw the lamp-lit covered boardwalk of the cigar store. A few meters away, Mack saw, not a baboon but a tall thin man in tactical gear aiming a long-barreled revolver at the flagpole.

Through the plaza trees Mack could see, climbing up the flagpole after a baboon, the unmistakable figure of Autumn.

Mack sprinted up onto the wooden boardwalk and hit Tall Guy in the head with the metal sconce as hard as he could.

Chapter 42

Tall Guy went down, and his long gun spun into the street.

Mack started for the gun, but only went two steps when he took a hard blow in the kidney. Tall Guy hadn't stayed down. Mack gasped and fell. The tin sconce flew off his hand, glanced off a rain barrel, and rolled several meters down the concrete street.

He rolled to his feet again, ducking under a jab. The two faced off, fists guarding their heads, circling each other. Up in the stratosphere loomed Tall Guy's thin craggy face; he had studious-looking eyes, a long jaw, and a tight cruel mouth.

Tall Guy launched a barrage, and Mack had to block fast. The men filled the air above their waists with flashing fists. Mack kicked at those long legs, but Tall Guy was moving his feet constantly, weaving like a skateboarder. Tall Guy was pushing Mack farther down the boards where an antique dry good scale stood, and Mack almost tripped backwards over its big metal foot. Tall Guy used that moment to dive for his gun in the street. Mack tackled him.

They fought on the ground, rolling across the gap in the buildings toward the Wells Fargo Museum and the tiny courthouse.

Tall Guy got up, but Mack trapped the leg with his feet and took him down again. Tall Guy punched him on the shin repeatedly, pang-pang-pang like a trip hammer. Mack screamed.

Autumn fired up again at the baboon. She had only two more rounds before she had to reload again.

Something dropped past her to the ground. It was a machine gun. *Now we're talking,* she thought.

She holstered her revolver. "*Cám ơn rất nhiều,*" she said and dropped off the pole.

When she hit the ground, wincing with pain from the bullet bruises on her leg, she found herself facing a baboon that was running to get the weapon. On his fur-maned black muzzle she saw the nostrils close together, side by side, pointed at her. Her boots whirred as she jumped the three meters, snatched up the machine gun, and fired off a burst. The baboon turned and ran.

In the absence of a good Vietnamese war cry she screamed, "You better run, monkeymouth!" The baboon leaped up onto the roof tiles and she jumped after him.

Tall Guy turned back down the street to find the long gun. Mack heaved himself up, adrenaline fighting the pain, and looked for cover. What was available was the brick corner of the courthouse. He could crawl there.

With blistering nineteenth-century Conestoga speed he crawled on the wooden boardwalk. Once he got around the corner to safety he would surely enjoy resting at the courthouse where he would jaw with the cowpokes and ranchers of this quaint little port town of San Diego and take a hearty chaw of Virginia tobacco shipped all the way around the Horn, or sip a jigger of whiskey brought by rail to San Francisco and carted right here to these gritty rough-grained boards under his fingertips. He really felt like getting around this corner that was coming up a few inches away. He would aim his tobacco confidently at the brass spittoon; inquire after any news of the health and sartorial splendor of our dear ol' Gentleman President Chester A. Arthur; wonder if the Butterfield stage would be bringing any ladies this week; declare his infallible plans to attain land and riches here in California and listen to the preposterous plans of others. Having a fine old time, yes siree.

As Mack scrambled and rolled around the corner into a bush, a hole exploded behind him and took a bite out of the brick.

Chasing the baboon over the slippery tile roofs of the Casa de Estudillo complex was taking Autumn eastward.*I have to get back to Mack and Brian,* she thought.

A machine gun flashed in the big tree to her right. There was a thick-bodied baboon in it; he was firing in the direction of the cigar store. She jumped to the tree, spraying it with her own machine gun as she landed on a thick branch amidst the foliage.

She couldn't see the gunner now. The tips of the curving branches shuddered and she turned wildly but saw no one. She crouched and began creeping forward; her steps shook the branches more. Something rustled.

This wasn't a sapiens she was fighting. *Think vertically.* She looked up through the foliage. She was afraid to stay in the tree, but afraid to move.

Leaves. Leaves. Dark shapeless shapes. Then, a dark straight non-leafy shape.

Autumn dove left as a roaring burst devoured the tree bark where she had been. She spun, jumped, and with her gun muzzle practically touching the baboon's chest, she blew him away.

Brian had Mack's pistol tucked behind him in his Italian leather belt and was throwing terracotta planters and any large thing he could get his hands on toward the bushes. Suddenly to his left a baboon with a machine gun slung on his back swung down from a tree and dropped into the courtyard.

Brian quickly drew the pistol, pointed it more or less at the baboon, and pulled the trigger. The noise made him jump; the shot had in any case gone uselessly high. He ducked through a jingling grove of wind chimes while the baboon ducked behind a stack of gorgeously painted pots.

At least I didn't drop the gun.

Brian slipped off his shoes, hunched low behind the counter, and crept around into the next aisle, ready to fire again. From outside the Emporio art corral he heard a burst of machine gun fire. The light from the streetlights on the artisan wares coated everything with fantastic shadows. On the rack next to him the propeller of one of the little metal biplane sculptures revolved lazily.

He heard a scraping sound in the darkness high and to his right. Brian pointed in that direction and pulled the trigger. The sound of the gun was enormous, and his ears rang as a dark form fell to the ground at his feet. It lay wet and still in the crazy shadows.

Brian looked at the gun and then at his shaking hands. *That is for Brianna. And my friends,* he thought. *And me.*

The courtyard wasn't safe anymore. And Mack and Autumn needed him.

He slung the baboon's machine gun over his shoulder and held Mack's pistol in one of his flexible chimpanzee feet while he swung up to a low rafter, his shirt cold and damp with sweat under his arms, then climbed over the pottery racks to the roof.

Mack ran to get behind the jail. Behind him a bullet hammered a dent in the cast iron.

Across the little dirt hollow to the south was the old Mason Street schoolhouse. Mack fired from the left of the jail and then sprinted to the right across the dirt.

He slipped around the corner of the school. *Where's Autumn? I need to double back.* He broke out a small pane of glass in the school door, reached in, got the doorknob open, and slipped in to the dark school, closing the door behind him. *Stay low and noiseless. Let them think I ran off.* He quietly took hold of a chair and pulled it against the door.

Light filtered through the windows from the street lamps outside. He could make out white-chinked wooden plank walls, clustered rows of benches, old books and quill ink pens, a poster entitled *RULES*. To his left, at the back, an iron stove. The other way, at the front of the room, a chalkboard; and upright on poles in flag stands were the flags of the United States and Mexico.

Keeping his head below the levels of the windows, he shuffled forward on his knees past the benches. A banner overhead said, *SAN DIEGO'S FIRST SCHOOLHOUSE.*

Darkness. Silence. Had he lost them?

And then at the rear of the schoolhouse the windows exploded under machine gun fire.

Chapter 43

As the dead baboon tumbled out of the tree, the gun snagged and bounced through the branches. Autumn grabbed it by the barrel.

It was hot, and she dropped it. But she jumped down, rubbing her burned fingers fiercely on her shoulder, and picked up the weapon. It was a heavier-duty machine gun than the one she had already captured. She took them both and ran back, limping a little, toward where she had seen baboons attacking the fence.

More fire from the church. She dropped down behind a wagon and returned fire with the heavy-duty gun, raking the church tower. *At last I have some fire power.* To her right, baboons were still scaling the fence to the Emporio Artesano. She blasted away left and right at the church roof and at the alley, a machine gun in each hand, ejected shells flying.

Behind her she heard the crack of some other weapon, not a machine gun, something high-powered.

Brian dropped down from the roof next to the candle shop.

A baboon came loping around the corner, almost knocking Brian over. The baboon's eyes widened and he raised his gun. Brian grabbed the baboon by the throat and slammed him into the ground. He didn't get up.

Another baboon was bounding up toward him from the plaza. Brian tried to fire the machine gun at him. It didn't fire. *Empty? Maybe there's a safety catch or something.* He snatched up the pistol and fired. The baboon skittered away and ran up into the tree.

Brian stepped cautiously into the street. Just then he saw two black shapes coming from the far northwest corner of the plaza. One of them was huge and shaggy, not a hominid. It veered toward him and rumbled like a mountain on four little legs over the plaza grass, under the trees, and shot away again past the cigar store. The other shape was big and long, feline. It ran gracefully, long tail streaming, and disappeared north of the Casa de Estudillo.

Two baboons jumped in through the schoolhouse windows and up on the benches, their half-up tails swinging in outline against the window light.

One of them was immediately knocked to the floor by a force of a *McGuffey's Reader*, accurately thrown against its head.

The other baboon fired, but without knowing where to aim. Mack was back behind the teacher's desk, but the blackboard cracked and the flags clapped and tore as the baboon's burst of fire ended abruptly. The animal grabbed at the underside of his weapon, and there was an audible click.

He's changing magazines.

Mack surged out and tackled him. The baboon, only half the size of a man, tumbled off the bench in one direction and the new magazine went in the other. Mack used his bandaged hand to

243

grabbed the still-hot barrel machine gun. He swung it and knocked the baboon across the room and against the stove.

Then Mack heard a snarl at his feet just in time. He hammered down against the teeth that were trying to bite his legs, again, again, until the second baboon sagged and crumpled.

He turned back to see the first baboon already up again in the back of the room by the stove, shaking himself and making high-pitched snarling noises and snapping his long black head around. He stopped, his snout pointing at an angle. He had seen what he wanted on top of a bench, and he sprang for it.

Mack lunged to the front of the room. He stumbled against the teacher's overturned desk, banging the shin the Tall Guy had punched. The pain made his mind turn blank red for a moment, but he kept going and clutched at the flagpole.

The baboon had gotten to the gun, but was tugging at it repeatedly. The gun sling was caught under the foot of the bench. A more elevated creature would have simply fired the gun from where it was. But the baboon had been trained to fire the weapon a certain way.

O Say...Mack grabbed the flagpole -- *Does that*-- out of the flag stand --*Star-Spangled Banner*-- pulling the flag tight around the pole --*Yet Wave*...

As the baboon got the gun's strap clear and brought the machine gun muzzle up in line, Mack swept the baboon and gun clear off the benches with one backhand swing of the pole, then charged with the pole in both hands and let out a wild Fort McHenry yell, leaping up

244

on the benches and stabbing down with the little painted pewter eagle decoration on the point. He kept stabbing again and again after the eagle snapped off until the baboon groaned with half-bared teeth, then rolled halfway over and lay unmoving.

Mack stood panting on the school benches, holding the pole upright. *–and the Home of the Brave.* He let Old Glory unfurl to the ground.

In the pale light from the window he saw on the banner a mighty eagle defeating a snake.

A snake?

What he had actually grabbed was the Mexican national flag.

OK then…Viva Mexico.

He set down the flag and started to clamber painfully down to pick up the machine gun. He had to go help Autumn.

"You just stay up on the pedestal, Lancelot," said a human voice.

Outside the window was Tall Guy with his longbarrel, and he had a crooked half-grin of triumph on his long bloodied face.

The machine guns were empty and Autumn was taking shots from behind the wagon with Mack's revolver. The hammer clicked. *That was it. I'm empty.* There was a burst of more distant fire off to the south. *Mack's going down fighting.*

She had to try to get to Brian before they overwhelmed him. She wished she had paid SafeLite the extra $83.95 and gotten the long-john style underwear.

Suddenly from the top of the church there was a scream. Over the peaked roof of the Church of the Immaculate Conception, toward the baboon in heavy armor, flashed a huge catlike form with a long tail. The baboon scrambled away and managed to dive through one of the openings in the bell tower. The big feline body poured in after him. There was a clanking bell ring and a short, interrupted baboon bark and then a very low BONGGG. Then silence.

Chapter 44

"You're out," said the Tall Guy at the window, aiming at Mack.

Suddenly a thunderous noise rounded the corner of the building. Tall Guy's head turned, his mouth opened in a flash of panic, and he half-tried to aim and acquire this new target, but the threat was too close and too fast. Tall Guy broke and ran.

A pair of horns and a shaggy hump swerved just short of the wall and rushed past the lower edge of the window, skidding hooves throwing up clouds of dust.

Mack grabbed the loaded machine gun with his left hand and stumbled to the window's edge. Pursued closely by the huge four-legged shape on small feet, Tall Guy was far off already, long legs pumping, getting out of Old Town.

The shape rumbled to a stop and let Tall Guy go. Then it turned and trotted back to the schoolhouse.

It was the supposedly non-el bison from the buffalo-rides corral.

The bison pulled up underneath the window. He looked at Mack and with a toss of his head he pointed with his horn toward his own back.

"Taxi?" said Mack, leaning his good shoulder against the window frame.

The bison nodded, a hard downward jerk of his head and horns.

Mack stepped out the window and climbed onto the hump of the bison's back, grunting unhappily as he bumped his shin.

Clinging to the back of the trotting bison, Mack made it jerkily around the candy store and back onto the south street. He saw Brian standing nervously by the covered wagon, clutching a machine gun. Autumn was nearby; she was talking to a big mountain lion.

"Are you Urizen?" Mack heard her ask as he came trotting up on the bison. The mountain lion just gazed back and yawned. From its lower teeth dangled a shred of black material.

"Mack!" Autumn said when she saw him. "You're—you don't look so good. But you're here. The situation seems under control. Urizen won't talk though."

"Because that's not Urizen," said Mack, swinging his legs off to dismount. The bison let him down and trotted off quickly in the direction of the northwest corner of the plaza.

"No, it is not," said a female voice behind him, with a marked Spanish accent. "In any case, you are unfortunately late."

A lean young woman in a white off-the shoulder blouse and flounced skirt walked toward them from the grass of the plaza. As she pulled goggles off her face, Autumn recognized her curved nose and strong Aztec features. She was one of the servers from the Casa del Corrido back in the tourist district. Except that here, instead of carrying a tray of fajitas, she was holding an assault rifle and infrared night vision goggles.

"Señor Davis, the Special One instructed you what time to come," said the woman. "If you don't respect El Especial, why not just stay home?" She looked toward the mountain lion and said, "Sheila! Acércate." The big cat swished her tail and padded over to the flounce-skirted woman, who did not pet her, but clipped the night goggles to the lion's collar.

"Cut us some slack," said Mack. "We were at the hotel on time. We got distracted by a slight massive paramilitary attack."

She raised her black eyebrows. "Habéis causado muchos daños aqui."

"I know. We'll pay for the damage. Compenso. Promeso. We really need to see him!"

Sheila the mountain lion dipped her nose and sniffed at Brian, who drew back.

"What is all this baboons business?" asked the woman, looking around and sweeping the street with a tiny powerful light.

"We're hoping Urizen can help us figure that out," said Mack. "Something very dangerous is going on in town. He'll definitely want to hear what we know."

The woman raised her eyebrows incredulously, showing her large brown eyes. "You trying to sell? To the one who knows all?"

"No," sighed Mack. "We came to buy. But he's *definitely* going to be interested. Believe me."

"Then come," she said. She turned and walked back across the grassy central lawn.

"Hey!" called Mack to Brian, who was heading toward the shambles of El Emporio Artesano. "Where are you going?"

"To retrieve my coat and shoes," said Brian."I'll catch up quickly. Then I'll give your pistol back." He seemed only slightly wary of the possibility of baboons still lingering about. "Your coat sustained some damage, I see. No matter. I still have some needles and my shear. I'll repair it when we have a moment." He loped off quickly toward El Emporio.

Sheila and the Aztec woman were headed for the northwest corner of the plaza. Mack caught up with Autumn, who was picking up something from the grass of the plaza lawn.

"Mack, look at this." She handed him an empty machine gun magazine

"Vámonos!" The Azteca called back to them sharply.

"Momentito," Mack said as he examined the magazine in the yellow light of the street lamps. On its side was an engraved serial number and the words *Property of Secure-Tek.* He gave a low whistle.

"What does this mean, Mack?" Autumn was now pointing her revolver at him. Her hand was shaking.

"Oh for—," said Mack. "Give it a rest, Autumn."

"Again! What does it mean?"

"Did I actually *say* I was with Secure-Tek? That was your assumption! Look, you need to make up your mind pretty quick if I'm on your side or against you. Or did I just save you and your little rice paddy finishing-school future?"

"That's not cool!"

"No, *officer*, it's not. Yes, I brought you here tonight and it turned out to be a near disaster. I'm sorry about that. But remember: I'm the one who shot two perps blasting away at you in the tailor shop and killed one of them, then got you out of area to escape your own people, gave you a weapon, and arranged for us to see probably the only creature who can help us. So I'm a little tired of being treated like your biggest problem in life!" His hands were shaking too.

Autumn lowered her weapon, but only a bit.

"Maybe I'm scum," said Mack, "but am I really Secure-Tek scum? Really?"

"Tonight I thought we were running from White Knights," she moaned. "But now…?

"Maybe it's both. I don't know! Maybe there's a backroom deal, a merger in the works. But it's time right now for you to decide either to trust me or to shoot me. I'm sick of this, so decide now! Are you going to shoot me? Or not?"

"Um." She gestured with the gun. "Actually, I'm out of ammo."

"Oh, well, here." Mack shakily handed her his 9mm. "I think there are two rounds left."

She lowered the 9mm in her hand. "Oh, *Mack*. Honestly!" she said. "You're right. I haven't believed you. But now…."

Brian caught up with them. carrying his shoes in one hand. He stopped to put them on. "Are you two all right?" he asked, but they didn't answer.

Autumn gave Mack back the 9mm.

"I'm sorry, kid," he said, breathing out slowly. "I'm a little hopped up."

"Me too," said Autumn. "Sorry, Mack. We're both coming off adrenaline. I should have kept my mouth shut."

"I'm sorry, you know, what I said about your culture. I've been to Vietnam twice, once for weeks. Your ancestors are an ancient and noble—"

"Relax. It's OK. Anyway, I've been throwing trash at you from the start." She stood hunched with her arms folded across her uniform. "A habit I've picked up from an unhealthy work environment."

They were standing awkwardly a few feet from each other, both with their arms folded, both silently looking sheepishly downward.

"Ahhh. Humans are all crazy," said Brian, knuckle-walking wearily past them. "Just groom each other and get it over with."

At the northwest corner of the plaza they left the grass and came to a great round tiled fountain. They passed between adobe pillars into the torchlit brick courtyard in single file, Sheila the mountain lion leading the way and the Aztec woman at the rear holding her rifle at low ready.

Ahead, past the covered galleries and shuttered shops, was the gate to a café patio with the sign *Casa de Reyes*. But Sheila turned to the right, going around the patio wall, past a bench painted with skeletal ladies of the *Dia de los Muertos* type, and led them to a hedge-lined with a little door at one end marked CUSTODIAN.

When Sheila breathed directly on the center of the lock, the door clicked open. Sheila stood aside.

Once inside the door they were in a storeroom full of extra brooms and broken chairs.

"Weapons, please," said the riflewoman. Mack handed over his guns.

An apparently solid section of the storeroom's back wall clicked apart—*nice touch of craftsmanship there*, thought Mack—and they passed through the opening into an inner courtyard lit by indirect light with a huge round stone planter in the center. Behind them the door clicked shut. The riflewoman had not followed them in.

Sitting on the planter under a weeping tree was a huge grimacing sculpted head, a glossy white papier-mâché skull at least four feet high painted with red and yellow and blue flowers. Brian jumped a little when he saw it, but the painted head did nothing, except continue to look as if, deep down in the earth, it had just stubbed its toe.

Past the stone planter, in front of furiously curling wrought-iron gates shot through with bursts of green foliage, stood a delicate young woman in a thin pink dress beckoning them.

Chapter 45

The belle in pink motioned them forward. She stood pale and tall and graceful, almost as if she were suspended from a point on the top of her head. Autumn thought she had probably had ballet training.

"Y'all are really lucky, y'know," she said in a thick Appalachian accent. "He almost never, I mean that, lets customers come in here."

"Honored, I'm sure," said Mack.

She turned and touched the large wrought iron door handle, then stopped.

"Don't y'all go thinking you're something hot, now." She looked Mack up and down, then the others with less scrutiny, but more curiosity. "Urizen knows what's been happening." She opened the gate and went before them. "He always knows."

"Where did he get the name Urizen?" whispered Autumn.

"Crowned himself. Like Napoleon," whispered Mack.

Inside the wrought iron forecourt was a kind of garden space flourishing with shelves of plants and hanging plants and vines and wreaths and dry twisted branches. Old wood rafters and latticework overhead were supported by square wooden posts, and there was a massive brass chandelier. At the left was a wide door frame, and here the ballerina stopped and stood like a theater usher. Brian and Mack nodded respectfully to her as they stepped inside.

Following them, Autumn noticed a little side court where a card game was going on lit by a single stark table lamp. She realized with a start that the big rough shape at the table was the bison that had given Mack the ride. *No wonder he was so quick to drop Mack off; he had to get back to the game.* She caught only a glimpse of the other players: the dark little nose of some small and lithe animal sniffing at the cards in its hand, and a rear view of the ear and gaunt cheekbone of a man who in that light might equally well have been Tibetan or Japanese or Kenyan and who wore a bandolier covered with cartridges.

The bison used his hoof to slide a card from a slanted display holder beside him up onto the felt table, and as he did so, he shot her a dark glance with his beady black eye. At once she looked away, ahead into the chamber they were entering. *Bison aren't supposed to be elevated at all,* she thought. *The scientists agree. But this one…?*

"Here," said the ballerina to Autumn, and handed her a big plastic shopping bag. Inside was the helmet she had left at the hotel.

They were in a narrow chamber full of various items on cabinets and shelves, with tiles on the floor and a low ceiling of boards and snaking electrical conduit all painted white. There were more hanging plants and dried flowers; sparkling glass ornaments; sheet metal silhouettes of angels, little shrines, geodes, tiny silver *milagro* charms in a basket of woven bark.

On the right was a wide open door frame with a step leading up into another chamber. As they entered, it became clear they were in the first of a set of three similar chambers joined by doorframes like a succession of proscenium arches. The middle chamber beyond had magnificent, although stained, Persian rugs on the floor, with armchairs and a mission-style church pew and a baroque carved round table. Packed around the walls and crammed into corners, were shelves crammed floor to ceiling with old books.

Autumn had never been this close to so many books on paper. The musty smell of books blended with the smell of herbs and soap from the cabinet behind them.

In the farthest chamber of the three, in a small open space lit by an ancient chandelier with three naked bulbs, was a big frowsy old woman in a rocking chair. She was wearing a bathrobe and reading aloud from a book in her hand. She was reading quietly and rather rapidly, and Autumn could not make out exactly what she was saying. She wondered if it was a foreign language or just a strange kind of English.

Autumn wanted to ask the old woman where to go next but Mack didn't seem in any hurry. He was just standing there looking around, not with the sharp all-around curiosity Brian was showing, but with the air of someone who has arrived at the meeting place. She put down the bag with the helmet.

As Autumn touched a silver candlestick with her finger, her pant leg caught on something. Or was caught.

"Rose, thou are sick," said a voice echoing around her, not too loud, but penetrating. It was a tenor voice with a rich and complex range of overtones, more than might be expected for a single voice, and it crackled and quavered just a little in a way that made her take notice; a voice that would not be ignored. She looked around but couldn't see anything except the old woman who was mumbling away from her little book.

Something was tugging on her leg. She looked down and saw that it was a large cat. It had blotchy gray-and-brown-and-cream-and-white tufty fur of medium length, with a whitish ruff.

"Poor rose," said the cat, and Autumn realized that the voice was the cat's, that it was being piped wirelessly from his vocoder into a sound system running throughout the rooms. His mouth was clearly opening and closing with the syllables resounding from the speakers. "Such a suitable pair to divide the desolation between us." He was a just little larger than average for a domestic cat, not fat, but stocky, with wide ears.

"What about *me*?" said Mack, with a hint of indignation.

"Old flesh, old flesh," said the cat, walking on and blinking languidly at him. "These be new comers. Fresh from the field. It would have been an empty stage if it were not for a few corpses that lay thrown and twisted into fantastic shapes upon the sward."

"Right. Sorry about the mess out there," Mack said.

Autumn had been slow in processing the scene; cats were not an animal she was used to thinking of as elevated. *This has to be Urizen,* she thought with a little bewilderment. *This is the big noise, the kingpin of underground intelligence in SoCal. Well, El Especial's coat use a little brushing.*

"Thanks for seeing us," Mack was saying. "We were waiting for you when they made their attack."

"Terrible tragedy," said the cat, hanging his head a little. "A terrible waste. Over a hundred killed."

"A hundred baboons?" said Autumn, incredulous.

"Mice," said Urizen, curling his body around and strutting away. "Deafening explosion. Soon lay a heap of stone, bricks and mortar; a hurricane now raged of heat and perfect sleet of coals." He jumped lightly up the step into the middle chamber, then turned and looked at them again, whiskers outstretched. "And backward on the city bent his gaze, bright with the flames of Dido. Thus are you come. Hunted. Javert on your tracks." There was a certain savor in the way he said these last few words.

Mack said, "We're counting on your usual guarantees of safe-conduct. And I'll pay for the losses to your neighbors, of course."

Urizen leaned back, tail up, stretching out his front legs and digging his front claws into the faded Persian rug. "Mater Dolorosa. Most damage covered by insurance. *Double Indemnity*, James Cain, shelf forty-six. Yet shall I require some ointment to smooth their tongues." He rolled, showing his furry white belly, and came back to his feet. "You breached the checkpoint at Lindbergh. People are looking for you—more than usual. *V sostoyaniye boyevoy gotovnosti.*" He swung his tail slowly from side to side. "You've brought friends."

"Yes. This is –"

"Oh, I know them." Urizen paced smugly. "I stand and look at them long and long. They do not sweat and whine about their condition. *Herzlich Willkommen.* On the Edgar A. Guest list."

He came up to Brian and sniffed the crease of his pant leg. "Perfume of the East. The brave little tailor; Grimm number 20. Shirts of sheer linen and thick silk and fine flannel, shirts with stripes and scrolls and plaids in coral and apple green and lavender and faint orange with monograms of Indian blue. Such beautiful shirts! He needs will be"—Urizen yawned, showing his pink tongue and little teeth—"Absolute Milan."

Watching the cat, Autumn noticed that he wore no clothes of any kind, not even a collar, only a little black stud in one ear. That would be his vocoder, a type she had never seen. Urizen turned back, seemingly in time with her thought; his luminous pale-green eyes met hers as he now spoke in a high, sing-song miaoing voice and paced around the rug.

"Someone asked a beggar, whom he saw in his shirt in the depth of winter, as brisk and frolic as he who goes muffled up to the ears in furs, how he was able to endure to go so? 'Why, sir,' he answered, 'you go with your face bare: I am all face.'" The cat circled, shaking his head slowly from side to side. "And on their naked limbs the flowery roof showered roses. So you see I'll wear no rags forever then, for every hair's an ear."

"I don't know, Mack," whispered Autumn. "Does he get more lucid?"

Over his shoulder Urizen looked back at her as he walked. "We're all mad here," he said in his normal tenor voice. "You're mad too, or you wouldn't have come. I am only mad north-northwest."

259

"In and out," whispered Mack in her ear, almost below the threshold of hearing. "But he gets things across the best way he can. Right now he's just warming up."

"Much learning hath made thee mad. *Disarming the Narcissist*, Behary, shelf eighteen. If no other in the world be aware I sit content; I show that size is only development." He paced in front of a bookshelf with his legs stretched straight and alert, and slitted eyes. "*Selah*."

The old woman, who had not stopped reading quietly in the background all this time, suddenly closed the book, stood up, and walked out through a door in the back.

"My library," said Urizen, sniffing at the books, "was dukedom large enough. I listen, I listen; I listen. When one lives in an *edzecate* country, one must live like *edzecate peoples,* said Mrs. Kavarsky. Your huddled masses. A human hodgepodge with its component parts changed but not yet fused into one homogeneous whole. Any strange beast there makes a man." He made a snarly kind of a face, held it taut for a second, and then let his expression return to neutral.

A short black woman in a crisp naval lieutenant's uniform, carrying a stack of books, entered from the back without speaking and began filing them away in the shelves. *How many books are there,* wondered Autumn.

With a protruding claw Urizen pulled one of the books from the lowest shelf and gazed at it open on the rug. Autumn noticed with some curiosity that he had the print upside down. He reared back to stretch himself and then walked right over the book with his ears up and pointed forward. "I have no time for seeming," he said. "There's a light on this tree that won't light on one side. I'm taking it back to my workshop, my dear. I'll fix it up there. Then I'll bring it back here."

He stopped at a Chinese statue covered with characters diagramming the meridian lines of the body, and pawed briefly at it. Then he began walking slowly and deliberately back toward them. "The daughters of Albion weep: a trembling lamentation. *One Hundred Great Opera Stories: The Bartered Bride,* Smetana." Then of a sudden he took a flying leap and sprang up onto Brian's coat sleeve and shoulder, startling him, holding on with his claws, but Brian did not shake him off.

"She yet lives," said Urizen, looking Brian directly in the eyes. "*N'est pas morte.*"

"*Sans doute?*" said Brian, his eyes wide as he strained his short neck to look at the cat on his arm.

"A hostage. Safe! Rest assured."

"*Merci,*" Brian exhaled heavily and pressed his free hand against his brow. "Thank you."

"Happy to help," said Urizen, leaping off again onto a round armchair of split wooden stakes and coffee-stained white leather. "Trippers and askers surround me. Apart from the pulling and hauling stands what I am, amused, idle, unitary." He sat on the chair and contemplated his guests.

Autumn wondered why she'd never heard of this creature. *He must have a lot of influence to stay this unknown.* And that blotchy coat would be ideal camouflage for all the places he might sneak around to.

"I sat studying at the feet of the great masters; O that the great masters might return and study me. No dainty *dolce affettuoso* I: bearded, sun-burnt, gray-neck'd, forbidding, I have arrived." Urizen chattered his teeth a little. On a shelf above him there was a decorative many-pointed star made of mirrors. He looked at the spiky reflections of himself. "*De quién es la casa de reyes?* I am large, I contain multitudes. *Soy el rey.*"

The old woman in the bathrobe now returned with a different book and heaved herself back down into the rocking chair. Urizen hopped off the chair to come back down to his visitors, stepping with feathery lightness, and twined his liquid body around Autumn's calf.

"Pure, lonely and unconquerable knight," he said to her, then switched again to a strange high voice of incantation. "To the twelve gods of Asia, the spectres of those who sleep…" He stopped to stage a mild bite at her BioBooster boot, then resumed twining.

"So did fair Britomart, of constant mind,

pursue her journey, through that parlous pace,

With steadfast courage and stout hardiment;

No evil thing she fear'd, no evil thing she meant."

The old woman began reading again, as quietly and unintelligibly as before. Urizen looked up at Autumn and mewed softly. *All right then*, she thought. She picked him up.

He rolled in the crook of Autumn's arm, licked his paw, and stared into her eyes. He spoke now in his normal voice, though

Autumn found it unnerving that it came from the speakers all around rather than from the cat in her arms. He licked his fur between sentences. "Full of homeseekness. Slurp. *Đại Việt*. Click your ruby slippers three times, darling. You don't want to be *ma đói*. Slurp. Robber ghosts. Unnatural, premature, or violent deaths far from home. Slurp. "

She felt the power of him, something that did not need to attack in order to conquer. He held the fascination of an ordinary cat, multiplied many times: something both brutal and soft, sinister and blameless, sinuous, arresting, seductive.

A blonde woman in a purple sleeveless dress came up from behind them and stepped past Brian politely, bringing what looked like an optical storage cylinder in her hand. She went up and conferred in whispers with the naval lieutenant.

Urizen tensed, got into a crouch in Autumn's arms, and jumped down. *"Clear and Present Danger.* Baboons withheld by the shortness of their chains. America is darkened; and my punishing Demons terrified crouch howling before their caverns deep, like skins dried in the wind." Now he stood perfectly still, his ears turned back, looking off in the distance as he said, "Secure-Tek."

Autumn stirred herself. "It must have been a Secure-Tek drone that sighted us in Old Town," she said, digging in her cargo pocket. "We found this."

The woman in purple came and took the machine gun magazine from her and carried it over for Urizen to sniff. *These women are his hands,* Autumn thought. *And his converts.*

Urizen's elevated intellect was beyond any animal she had met before, but it was irregular, like a huge misshapen pearl. *Something different's happened with him. Even normal elevation they can't explain, but this?* Unlike most elevated animals, Urizen had not settled into the drab background of workaday citizenship, riding SpeedRail to work every morning. He was still wondered at, still mythic, like the animal deities of Egypt or the Americas.

"Security. Unalteration. Immobile. *Jane's Book of Drone Armaments*, shelf thirty. The mind-numbing drone of the bagpipes. Newspeak. The Panopticon." Urizen was rolling his neck and looking around. "Society will develop a new kind of servitude, a network of complicated rules, through which the most original minds and the most energetic characters," he said as his tail lashed, "cannot penetrate. It does not tyrannize but it compresses, enervates, extinguishes, and stupefies a people, till each nation is reduced to nothing better than a flock of timid and industrious animals, of which the government is the shepherd." There was something hungry, predatory, and yet fearful in his tone. "The essence of it consists, then, in the centrality of the inspector's situation, combined with the well-known and most effectual contrivances for seeing without being seen."

He crouched low and began a slow sneaking advance upon a miniature porcelain artichoke lying on the floor. He pounced on it and then opened his paws. "When I search for Man in the technique and the style of Europe, I see only a succession of negations of man." He pawed at the glazed object and then batted it away.

"Let's get *to* it," whispered Autumn.

"Just wait," said Mack. "With two new people here, he's a little wound up."

Women entered in the back, but remained in the shadows, organizing things on a shelf. Urizen thrashed his tail. "Sometime am I all wound with adders," he said, whiskers angling sharply forward, "who with cloven tongues do hiss me into madness." He glanced at Brian and then pounced on something invisible on the rug.

"We're ready to buy, old boy," said Mack. "Come on down."

Urizen stared at the rug and began muttering; the speakers around the room flickered with white noise. The murmur of the old woman reading continued. Autumn tried to catch Mack's eye and saw that he too was starting to frown.

Brian crouched and made some soothing, smacking noises with his lips. He dangled a sprig of dried rosemary from one of the shelves. But the cat was now not talking at all. He lay on the rug and tilted his head in a distant look, seeming to have lost the key to speech or at least the thread of his own thought. He licked the back of his paw intently.

Wait, mimed Brian to the others with his hand. He undid one of his gold cufflinks and tossed it onto the Persian rug.

Urizen's eyes gleamed, and he pounced on it. "Aha! Aha!" said the cat, his mental gears apparently restarted, and he rolled the cufflink back and forth on the rug. "Take care not to look upon finite particles as such. We are to conceive them as the just nascent

265

principles of finite magnitudes. Nor do we in this Lemma regard the magnitude of the moments, but their first proportion as nascent."

He jumped onto a cushion on the elaborately carved round table, arranged himself sitting on his haunches, and faced them.

"To the present business," said Urizen.

Chapter 46

A middle-aged Japanese woman in slacks, with little reading glasses on top of her hair, appeared from the murky back area. She walked up to Mack, her open hand extended.

"Here comes my mistress the soul," said Urizen. While the woman crossed the room the cat remained like a statue from a pyramid tomb, but he looked over at Autumn: a deep and sly look with slitted pupils. "You know he gave her the ring yesterday?" he said to her with a sudden lucid casualness.

"Who?" said Autumn.

"Your brother Kyle."

Autumn froze. For the first time since they had entered Urizen's chambers, her chest tightened with genuine fear. "How—you couldn't possibly know—"

Urizen shivered and his whiskers pulsed. "Why should I not speak to you? Every atom belonging to me as good belongs to you. I hear America singing, I have heard what the talkers were talking, O I perceive after all so many uttering tongues. She seems to have said yes, by the way." His tail twitched and his ears swiveled.

I'm starting to get it, thought Autumn, her heart pounding. *It's not just cat glamour. He's powerful enough that he could provide people with meaning; something to serve. He's a risk, a gamble in every way. But he feels...real.*

Mack had slid open his belt buckle and turned his hand so the woman could see the five sparklies in his palm. She took the sparklies from Mack and walked over to show them to Urizen.

"You had those all the time?" whispered Brian. "And that whole routine with the ferrets?"

"I wasn't going to blow one of those on a measly ninety-dollar zoo ticket. Now I'm officially a pauper," said Mack. He snapped his belt buckle shut.

As the woman showed Urizen the sparklies in her palm, his eyes gleamed and his tail thrashed. "Mack's been a-roving. Offworld assets. *Solomon's* Haggard *Mines*, Sturgeon's *Dreaming Jewels*. Shelf forty-two."

The women seemed to change now, coming to attention, seeing Mack, Autumn, and Brian for the first time as VIPs, and they beckoned the three visitors up the step into the middle chamber.

"Mediccelerants for you?" asked a young woman in a pencil skirt. She opened a case with a skin patch kit.

"That would be *amazing*," said Autumn. She took two Acceloheal patches to cover the bruises from the bullet strikes dispersed by her underwear.

"Sure," said Mack, letting another woman clean and rebandage his finger.

"Take off your shirt," Urizen said. "Wash and press. *Collected Tillie Olsen*, shelf twenty-two."

Mack glanced at Autumn, then shrugged and began to unbutton his shirt.

"Not you, idiot," said Urizen. "Born in Abengourou Department, parents partially elevated, escaped past Mogadishu. *The Naked Ape.* Desmond Morris."

"Looks like you get free laundry service," Mack said to Brian.

"Now this is the life," said Brian, as he pulled off his coat and unbuttoned his shirt. The blonde woman took the shirt and scooped up the cufflink from the floor, now forgotten by her master. Brian put his coat back on over his tank undershirt.

The Japanese woman was still holding the jewels before Urizen. Gazing at them, the cat intoned: "*In Great Eternity, every particular Form gives forth or Emanates Its own peculiar Light, and the Form is the Divine Vision. And the Light is his Garment; This is Jerusalem in every Man.*" The women all shut their eyes together, as if ritually.

Autumn glanced at Mack for a cue. He merely leaned on the doorframe and played with the frond of a hanging plant. He shrugged. "When you pay cash, you don't have to pay homage," he said quietly.

The Japanese woman took the sparklies and disappeared again into the gloom.

"This hour I tell things in confidence," said Urizen. "I might not tell everybody, but I will tell you." On his cushion he assumed a position like the Sphinx with his forepaws out and his head up. He made a noise that might have been—in a human, at least—a chuckle, then said, "Ask."

269

"Where is Brianna?" said Mack.

"The Poison Tree," said Urizen. "Large pillars round the Void. Castles and high spires where kings and priests may dwell."

"The poison tree?" said Autumn. "Do the baboons live in trees?"

"I think he's talking about something else," said Mack. "Wait."

"Now the serpent was more subtle than any beast of the field. In opposition dire, a warlike cloud the myriads stood upon the margin'd ocean: the Jewel, ahoy. La Hoya."

"The jewel, the ocean, La Hoya." said Mack. "La Jolla, Southern California."

"Salomon's House!" cried the cat. "Books and abstracts, and patterns of experiments. These we call merchants of light. Demonstration of causes, means of natural divinations, and the easy and clear discovery of the virtues and parts of bodies. *The Fall of the Ivory Tower.* The Atlantic mountains where giants dwelt in intellect; now given to stony druids, and allegoric generation." He brushed his ear with one paw.

"Some sort of scientific place?" said Brian, rubbing his chin with the back of his hand.

"A university," said Mack. "The ivory tower. The old UCSD campus, I'm thinking."

"It was Secure-Tek that won the UCSD security contract," said Autumn. "They have a facility on campus."

Urizen smiled a little cat smile and licked his nose. "Assurance doubly sure. Oxford is the dust of her walls. A very tall man, a sufficient man. Here, said they, is the terror of the French, the scarecrow that affrights our children. A good tall fellow."

"The tall man in the tailor shop," said Autumn. "And tonight. He killed Carter. Secure-Tek."

"Their fell captain," said Urizen, nodding and flexing his whiskers. "The Witch-King. Reinhardt."

"Reinhardt," muttered Mack.

"Why did they kidnap her?" asked Autumn.

The cat sat up and assumed a learned air with one paw outstretched, as if about to diagram something on a classroom touchscreen. "Ahem. Everything depends on the manipulation of water. Were it not for a century and a half of messianic effort toward that end, the West as we now know it would not exist. The lone and level sands stretch bare away. One does not really conquer a place like this. One inhabits it like an occupying army and makes, at best, an uneasy truce with it." His eyes now opened very wide and he sat still facing something they could not see. "Seven lean and famished cattle. Albion's coast is sick silent; the American meadows faint! Why then 'tis time to do it. *The Monkey Wrench Gang*."

"Something about water," said Autumn. "What? Why?"

"The Game is so large that one sees but a little at a time. Patience, little Friend of all the World. Kipling. Clouds obscure my sight. But 'twill be done. Tomorrow, and tomorrow, and—that's all," said the cat. "You have less than thirty-six hours."

271

He jumped into the hands of the blonde woman and began rolling around as if enjoying an imaginary pile of laundry. More women entered the room.

"Less than thirty-six hours until what?" asked Brian.

"To get her back, I'd say," said Mack.

Five or six women were now walking around in the room with their hands out and as Urizen rolled luxuriously he was passed from hand to hand, as if borne on clouds, the women following each other in a circle, and ecstatically he chanted:

"I see a Serpent in Canada, who courts me to his love;

In Mexico an Eagle, and a Lion in Peru;

I see a Whale in the South-sea, drinking my soul away.

Water, water, everywhere, nor any drop to drink."

"He's not telling us anything," said Autumn in exasperation.

"Sometimes that happens," said Mack, resting his hands stoically on his belt buckle.

"There is a limit of Opaqueness," said Urizen as he was deposited by the women onto the round table. "There's nothing you can know that isn't known, nothing you can see that isn't shown." He was now bobbing his head and warbling, and Autumn realized he was singing, after a fashion:

"There's nothing you can make that can't be made

No one you can save that can't be saved

Nothing you can do but you can learn to be you in time

It's easy: all you need is Jiggs."

"Jiggs!" said Brian. "Where is he?"

"You want it. What you need is Jiggs. You got it." The cat stepped forward and back again on the glossy tabletop, twisting his shoulders at a jazzy angle.

"Does he know about Brianna?" asked Autumn. "Can we contact him?"

"Better than that," said Urizen, tossing his head and turning away. "I'll show thee every fertile inch o' th' island." He clambered onto the bookcase behind the table.

"Where?" asked Brian.

The cat climbed up and across the bookcase by shelves, one by one, and then finally jumped into the lap of the old woman in the rocking chair. There he padded around in tightening circles like a whirlpool draining down. "My obedient hand shall take you there. To Agamemnon's ample tent repair. Bid him in arms draw forth the embattled train, lead all his Grecians to the dusty plain. Declare, e'en now 'tis given him to destroy the lofty towers of wide-extended Troy."

He shut his little mouth firmly as if he had finished. He began to knead the old woman's robe with his paws thoroughly, slowly, drowsily, then curled up in her lap. She stopped her background reading.

"Jiggs. Tonight?" asked Mack.

"*The Sun Also Rises. Chitty Chitty Bang Bang.* Follow the yellow brick road...." Urizen yawned. He closed his eyes. His last utterance sounded like "*I been there beforrrre....*" It blended into a long rich purr that grew and surged and then fell off slowly and interminably like a retreating wave of the sea, until Autumn and the others found themselves listening only to the faint background hiss of the speaker system.

A pregnant woman in a pale green smock appeared from somewhere and motioned for Mack, Autumn, and Brian to follow her. They went back out through the court of wreaths and vines. Behind them they heard the sound of the old woman reading aloud again.

"Sleeping rooms have been arranged," said the woman in green. "Your car will be ready tomorrow morning at 7:30."

"A car? Sleeping? Hold on." Mack's voice was strained. "Ma'am, we can't afford...."

"Urizen is pleased with your generous contribution. Follow me." She disappeared between two bookcases.

As they were following her up a dimly lit staircase, Mack suddenly stopped. Climbing up behind, Autumn almost ran into him.

"Yo there," she said. "You all right?"

"Damn!" Mack slapped himself on the side of the head. "I forgot to ask about Maríqui!"

"Who's Maríqui?" asked Autumn.

"I'm not sure," said Mack. "Name tossed around. Random person in the case."

Chapter 47

"Wow," said Autumn.

Mack didn't disagree. The three of them were standing on the sidewalk in the morning light, in the process of sliding into the spacious walnut-paneled back seat of a classic silver Rolls-Royce. Gasoline-powered vehicles were legal only for certain military and polisec vehicles, and high-end automobiles like this were for use only by very high-ranking government officials.

Mack got in after Brian and pulled the door closed with three fingers, protecting the index finger and the new bandage. Otherwise he didn't feel too bad given all that had happened yesterday. In a few minutes before breakfast Brian had made his suit look practically brand new, if you weren't standing too close.

That dead guy not Shadow Guy. So Quan Yin, Goddess of Compassion and Mercy, was not dead either and apparently there was still a chance of getting her back. And the COR band too.

The most comfortable part of the morning had been when the pink dancer belle woke them up with breakfast. They had not seen Urizen again, but his message last night had been clear enough about at least one thing: they were going to see Brianna's brother Jiggs, chief strategist of the Free Life movement.

The stunningly coiffed person in the driver's seat turned to face them, placing her arm across the back of the front seat. Her dress was simple, classic, and made of silk velvet with hand-beaded cuffs and collar. The emerald ring on her right hand looked like it was worth more than an average San Diego human would earn in a year.

"If you're all comfortably settled, we'll leave now," said the Lady, her pink smile revealing perfect teeth.

"Ready, thank you," said Mack. Brian sat up straighter and adjusted his tie. Over on the left side Autumn was looking all around at the car's interior. Under her arm was a folded raincoat the ballerina had given her to cover her uniform once they arrived.

The Lady smiled and continued. "I know absolutely nothing about your identities or your mission, so there is no information I can give you. Please be gracious enough not to question me or even speak to me during the short trip. My instructions are to drive you to the New Island Ferry Pier near the Hotel del Coronado. I will drive past the security checkpoint and right up to the passenger loading ramp, so that you can walk directly onto the ferry. Your fares have already been paid. Don't worry about the security people; they will not stop us. This vehicle is very familiar to them, as is my face. I am told that once you reach the transit center on New Island, someone will meet you there. Wherever you're going, I do hope your trip is a pleasant one."

The Lady steered the car out of Old Town, where the buildings' wood and adobe facades at this hour of the morning looked drab and hung over, and took Taylor Street to the freeway. She observed all traffic laws meticulously.

They cloverleafed onto Interstate 5, and as they headed into downtown, Mack looked to the right and caught a glimpse of Lindbergh and the air traffic control towers. He had been there on Monday just before lunchtime—*is today only Thursday?*—when he entered the country on Singapore-Qantas-Mundial Flight 452. That was where he had left the international terminal without his luggage while making a rapid detour through the hoof-and-mouth medical examination booths, hoping the startled nurses and animals he sprinted past would have the sense to get out of the way of the large men in BioBoosters and assault gear who were following only moments behind him.

When Autumn, Mack, and Brian began speaking to each other in the back of the car they did so in quiet, reverential tones, as if they were on the back pew of a mobile altar to the faith of the world's elite. Our Lady of Pecuniary Substantiality.

"I don't understand about all the books," Brian said softly. "I didn't even know there were cats that could read." He now had on a freshly-washed and immaculately-pressed shirt under his coat.

"They can't," Mack said, "Not even him. The women read everything to him aloud. His memory is phenomenal."

"Oh," said Autumn. "That explains the upside-down book."

"Cat's eyes are built for seeing in the dark, but they have trouble with the detail required for print. And Urizen likes old books, the original copies with the paper smell. So there's a doctor in China

277

who will perform illegal retinal surgery on nocturnal carnivores, but it's expensive. I mean, those sparklies are nothing." *Nothing comparatively speaking, that is.* Mack didn't want to think about how far back it had set him to let them go. It would add quite a few jobs to his list before he would be able to retire in the Idaho wilderness and concentrate on making art instead of dodging bullets.

"Urizen's saving up for an eye operation?" said Brian.

"That's why he sells information. The real trouble is that he can't resist spending most of it on books, so he's not getting ahead."

"All these women of his," said Autumn quietly. "Why doesn't he just ask for money from them? This driver could afford it, I'm sure."

"You're talking about a cat. Fiercely independent. He'll take their adoration, but not their cash."

"What a remarkable person," said Autumn. "I mean, crazy, but with all that— charisma."

"Oh, brother. Not you, too," he muttered. "We got out of Urizen's place just in time."

"Hey, knock it off," she said. "I can keep my feet on the ground." She said it stiffly, as if her certainty might have just the tiniest crack in it.

Mack sat back and looked out the window. They had already passed beneath the overpasses at the interchange for Balboa Park and the Zoo and were getting in the lane to exit onto the Coronado Bridge. Off to the right, the bridge's slender blue curve soared high over the bay between the mainland and Coronado Island, which was really a peninsula. But just south of it was something else.

I'll show thee every fertile inch o' th' island, Urizen had said, and he was often surprisingly literal. Mack was starting to have a pretty good guess where they were going: the one place in San Diego where the Free Lifers couldn't possibly have a base. Or so one would think.

Elites, thought Mack, *always want to separate themselves in space and time.* They live behind walls and travel in private airplanes housed in private hangars at private airstrips. If they are super-mega-big-time-ultra-rich, they buy their own private islands. But if they are only average ultra-rich, they allow the vast human and animal working class to build their islands for them. Through a ballot proposition, for example, to "provide much-needed improvements to Lindbergh International Airport, including construction of a separate restricted-traffic private aviation strip and facilities."

In the end what did the taxpayers get? At Lindbergh, some repainted terminals and new pre-fabricated immigrant processing buildings surrounded by twelve-foot-high razor-wire fences. But the rich folks got New Island.

Brian leaned over to Autumn and whispered, "Do you *see* what the lady is wearing?"

"Um, clothes?"

"Top -name designers!" Brian struggled to keep his voice down in spite of his excitement. "*THE* top-names! Labels I've never seen in real life, only in the fashion mags."

"Okay, then," Autumn whispered back. "Really fancy overpriced clothes."

Brian looked at her in disbelief, then settled back in his seat.

Their car was now driving up the lower slope of the Coronado bridge. Past the low concrete wall Mack saw the clumped skyscrapers of downtown San Diego some ways off. Closer to the bridge was the great spread of commercial dockyards with massive loading gantries all in a row, angling their necks above the water like long-necked antelope ready to drink. Above was a great blue sky flocked with puffs of white cloud.

After a moment they were up on the curve of the bridge, driving on a thin shaving of concrete two hundred feet above the calm blue water, with the knee-high sections of concrete wall and lamp poles flashing past. Mack felt Brian stiffen.

"First time, right?" he said.

"Yes," said Brian, clutching his trouser-creased shins tightly with his long hands.

"Always feels like those little walls aren't even enough to keep a skateboard from rolling off."

"Yes," shuddered Brian. "Exactly."

Almost as soon as they had peaked they were losing altitude again and beginning to curve to the right. The shadow of Autumn's head glided off the back of the Lady's headrest as the car neared the low finishing ramp of the bridge on its increasingly squat forked pylons next to the sailboats of the marina.

Brian was calmer on the downhill stretch. "Urizen said Brianna was a hostage," he said quietly. "But none of what he said indicated why?"

"There's something going on with water," said Mack. He glanced at the wrinkled blue surface of the bay below them. "I thought at first it was somehow about farming, but then if I understood where he was going with it, it's actually about the sea. That's all I got. If Brianna's connected, I can't tell you how. But I bet Jiggs can."

Out the left window past Autumn's calm profile Mack caught a glimpse of the little sparkling buildings and airstrips of New Island, only three miles over the water to the south. Then they curved completely and bore straight down toward the gentle streets of Coronado. To the side of the bridge, sudden bursts of bushy green trees and then flat park grass let them know they were back over solid ground. The car turned left at the light and headed to the south side of the island, only about eight blocks away.

Yup, Mack said to himself. That was where the New Island ferry would dock.

The New Island Transportation Hub project involved something like a billion dollars' worth of dredging. They repacked the sand and rock around a skeleton of geotextile tubes filled with concrete slurry, which gradually hardened into a lasting monument to the principle of rugged self-sufficiency through the use of other people's tax money. The little artificial island had four landing strips and a six-story, two-million-square-foot duty-free mall where no one had to share shopping space with unpleasantness such as animals shedding hair and speaking ungrammatical English.

New Island people are, in fact, exactly the kind of people I tend to work for, Mack thought.

As they veered onto Silver Strand Boulevard the gleaming glass profile of that duty-free mall loomed across the short stretch of water dividing New Island from Coronado. They turned onto and passed under the signs telling them NEW ISLAND FERRY—PRIVATE ACCESS ONLY, MEMBERSHIP REQUIRED.

The car approached the pier entrance and waited.

Brian said quietly, "There's the ferry. But we seem to have stopped."

"Why is the barrier gate not retracting?" said Autumn.

"Everyone please remain completely silent," said the Lady in the driver's seat. "Things are not proceeding as planned." She lowered her window as a security guard walked up to the car. Autumn slipped her helmet over her head.

"Good morning, officer," she said cheerfully. "I believe you were on duty the last time I came through."

"Good morning, ma'am," said the guard. "Yes, I do recognize you, but we have orders from polisec to check all vehicles. Who are your passengers, please?"

"The gentleman seated directly behind me," the Lady said, "is the Cultural Attaché from the Limpopo Republic. He's been my husband's guest for a few days." She handed him a sheaf of documents Mack hadn't seen before, none of them probably in existence before 10:00 p.m. last night. "The uniformed officer is a bodyguard kindly assigned to us by polisec. And this man is an official interpreter."

Another guard had now come up to the opposite side of the car and was looking carefully at everyone in the car.

"Get them all out of the car," he ordered, "and line 'em up. Now."

As they stood in a row squinting in the sun beside the guard box, salt wind whipping their hair, the senior guard walked past the Lady and stopped at Brian.

"I understand you are with a foreign government. Is that correct, sir?"

Brian only smiled and shrugged his beautifully tailored shoulders.

"You're the interpreter?" The senior guard looked at Mack, who was at the other end of the row. "What's with the finger?"

"That? Doggone skin reaction from eating processed food again," said Mack. "Whenever I come back to the U.S. I break out. Last July I was wall-to-wall hives from the navel down."

"So what language does the VIP here speak?"

"Southern Limpopese."

"Ask him to tell me his name."

"Ah... yangon phnom wantanama hahale," said Mack.

Brian took a deep breath and said, "Gabbana. Dolce ay Prada Gabbana." He smiled and extended his right hand.

"Pleased to meet you." The officer gave a quick limp handshake. "You understand?"

"Uh…lilidaché," Brian replied, trying to smile even wider.

"And the purpose of this trip?" the senior officer asked.

"E gobi lumpur walla penang, uh, bayanhongor?" said Mack.

"Mbolo Versace Kawakubo, mmm, Schiaparelli Herrera Lacroix." Brian seemed determined to keep up the smile even if it resulted in temporary paralysis of his facial muscles. "Ooee-ooah-ah Ferragamo Blahnik."

"He says," Mack translated, "that his government is looking forward to finally signing the trade agreement with your country. Assuming he's in time to catch his flight."

The senior guard looked down at Brian's finely-groomed chimp hand, then shook it again. He saluted for good measure.

"Right. Sorry for the inconvenience, sir."

"I believe you may be new here, are you not?" said the Lady, with a practiced smile on her pale pink lips.

"No ma'am, I am not," said the senior guard, "and I do know who you are. Unfortunately, we have orders from high up, and it would mean my job to disobey. Sorry for the inconvenience."

The senior guard then stepped in front of Autumn. Slowly, his eyes went down to her BioBooster boots, then back up to her helmet.

"Raise your visor, please," he said. Autumn obeyed.

"Your helmet looks too big," he said.

"That's what I get for buying online," she answered. "They're sending a replacement."

"Step over here, please," the senior guard said, motioning Autumn to walk to the side of the car.

Mack estimated the distance between him and the senior guard: one and a half seconds. The other guard was farther away and might have time to draw his weapon, but fortunately he was bent over, looking inside the car's trunk. That might provide the extra two seconds Mack needed. Or maybe not.

"You're tense, Mack. Relax," whispered Brian. "Listen."

"So then let me ask you, if you don't mind," the senior guard was saying quietly to Autumn. "When you White Knights people land a bodyguard assignment, do you get a per diem with expenses? Or is it just straight salary?"

"Since when are you the relaxed one?" Mack whispered to Brian.

"Since I found out Brianna's still alive."

"The car's clean, Sergeant," The other guard called out as he closed the trunk lid. "Registration paperwork is all in order. Nothing in the car except a box of nose tissues and the lady's purse."

The senior guard turned around to speak to the Lady. "If the attaché is going to the airport, where's his luggage?"

"It was sent on ahead, of course," she said. "I don't mind playing chauffeur; it's a pleasure with distinguished guests. But I'm not going to be a luggage porter, even for my husband."

The senior guard smiled, probably for the first time today, and said, "Sorry for the inconvenience. You're all free to leave now."

As the car drove forward onto the pier, the Lady spoke first. "Well, my darlings, that was all deliciously thrilling, wasn't it?" she said. "However, this necessitates a slight change in our itinerary. Now that the guards are aware of us, I can't simply drop you off at the pier and go home. They know I would never do that with a real attaché. Therefore, I will now go to the auto loading ramp and drive aboard the ferry. Once it shoves off, you will exit my car and go into the passenger seating area. I will remain in the car. Please do not say goodbye to me, and do not, I repeat, do not return to this car. I wish you all the best. I'm now driving up the ramp. We shall not meet again."

"You'll have to stay a while on the island," Mack said. "If you go back on the ferry too soon, it will look suspicious."

"How considerate of you to think of that," she said, looking at the rearview vid screen to see Mack. "Don't worry. I plan to spend an hour or so in the terminal shops. I may even buy a pearl necklace. All in a day's work."

Chapter 48

They agreed they would attract less attention if they sat in different areas of the passenger deck. Mack chose an empty seat on the port-side passenger deck near the forward stairwell and leafed through a stack of plastipage mags. He skipped *Vogue* and *Human Elegance* in favor of an abandoned copy of *Universal Enquirer*.

"How Lee Harvey Oswald Murdered Elvis and Marilyn: 100-year-old Mystery Solved!" the low-res cover splash said. Mack finger-swiped the cover to see what other articles the mag had. He already knew about the Oswald-Marilyn-Elvis love triangle. He had seen Hoover's files on the subject. The next article was "LBJ and JFK's Secret Love Child: Their Test-Tube Baby Became President!"

That article looked mildly interesting, and Mack might have started reading it, if it hadn't been for the young Neo-Hipster in ViewGlazzes and a little sandy-red goatee who walked up and sat down at the other end of the bench.

The young man had slicked-back hair and wore a shiny aluminum-finished blazer. He sat with his arms folded, blinking heavily behind his ViewGlazzes as if selecting a vidstream. Then he flicked an imaginary dust mote off the razor-sharp crease in his suede trousers.

"My man," he said softly, looking at the sea, "you are très, *très* hot. Y'know? I mean, busting security at the world's third tightest airport checkpoint. Woww. How did you get the scanner to show Arnold Schwarzenegger's DNA, anyway? That is exponentially cool. Bummer that some security agent had actually heard of ol' Arnold."

"Sorry. You speaking to me?" Mack unbuttoned his suit coat and glanced over the top of the plastipage at the undulating blue surface of the water. Swimming for his life might need to be an option.

"Just frisking my whiskers, man. I come bearing gifts. Vital information you need. You won't be able to get through the New Island passenger gate. Your two friends should be solid. But *you* will be copped."

"Information?" said Mack, swiping quickly through a few more mag articles. "What do you mean? Photographs?" *Rule One,* Verhoven liked to say: *all men are created equal; don't trust any of them.*

"Naw, your pix were all blurred. That's another trick I'd like you to teach me. Mucho admiration, man." The hipster pulled a tissue from inside his shirt sleeve and leaned down to wipe a nonexistent speck off his mirror-finish shoes. "But that sec agent at Lindbergh saw your face. The ports have an idbuild holo circulating now. This is the bible I'm giving you."

Mack folded the plastipage. He could jump from the side rail and kick off. He looked at the waves and hoped the wind did not pick up.

The young man pushed the tissue back up inside his sleeve. "But hey, it's copasetic, Jack: we have a plan B."

"Who is this *we*?"

"You're just going to go down these stairs to the auto deck. Then all the way aft to the luggage holding area. There's a chimp baggage handler down there with *Danny* on his shirt. He'll get you safely onto the island. No fret, no sweat." He stood up, and as he walked past Mack, said, "The boss is looking forward to meeting you. See you later, Terminator."

Autumn was leaning on the top railing on the starboard side, wearing the long raincoat she'd been given and looking over the water at the tiny brown trails across the green slopes of Point Loma. She was trying to figure out what was bothering her. In her mind hung the beady black eye of the bison last night playing cards.

Clearly there were animals who were elevated but did not admit to it. She had heard of that before. But apparently there were animals who only admitted to it some of the time; in certain circumstances; with certain people. It was required by law for elevated animals to register with the DSCE. It seemed as if the bison had not, and she had a feeling Urizen hadn't either. On the streets, Urizen probably posed as non-el.

The baboons worked for a polisec, but maybe it was under the table. They must sleep somewhere and eat something. Did they have apartments? Barracks? She had killed some of them, and might have to kill more. If they were registered as elevated it would count legally as personicide. Of course, they had been trying to kill her and others; and they were certainly elevated, whether they were DSCE compliant or not. But how elevated were they? It wasn't clear that the baboons could speak. Or the bison. There might be different levels of elevation in daily life. She didn't know the state of legal theory on this. One thing she was pretty sure of was that the law expected a Provisional Citizen not to be acting elevated in one place and non-el somewhere else.

She reached up and drew a wind-whipped hair out of her face. Ahead of the ferry the shoreline of New Island was looming larger. They were headed to the edge of the world, or the beginning of it, a global launching pad for wealthy SoCal humans like their driver this morning.

Urizen's women were living double lives of their own. For that matter, Autumn herself was wearing a different name—in a way— under her polisec uniform, which in turn was covered right now by the raincoat. Most officers did have some sort of separation between their uniformed selves and their life off-duty. And she had thought of her Vietnamese name as the beginning of a transition to the next stage, not as one self living alongside another.

Maybe Great-Grandfather would like Vietnamese stuff better if it *could* be lived in parallel, if it didn't have to be an everyday thing. If she could pursue cultural studies without having to quit her job, she wouldn't have the big money worries. But it would be very slow. She was afraid she might never get past skimming the surface, never be more than a tourist.

The bison was working two jobs, but that didn't make him a tourist. If he was on Urizen's team he probably didn't need to give rides to families to make ends meet. Maybe he enjoyed both gigs; maybe he preferred not having to act elevated all day. There were clearly many different experiences of elevation. In a sense, Autumn herself was trying to become elevated. Maybe there was more than one yellow brick road.

New Island was coming up quickly. There was what looked like a glass stadium but she understood it was some sort of shopping complex. She could see individual people on the upcoming pier now. A jet swooshed in on the left, making its landing. Another one had apparently just taken off and was diminishing to a speck against the clouds.

If Lucille was right about whiner missiles, someone in the White Knights was apparently leading a *real* double life. If it was Bickson, what was he up to? If someone else, how did they get access to drone control? Could Secure-Tek have planted a mole in the organization? A recent hire?

Or maybe the Secure-Tek mole was someone she knew?

The ferry speakers buzzed. They were about to dock.

"You can be honest with me," Mack said to the beefy chimp wearing the dark green EasyShip outfit with *Danny* embroidered on the chest. They were standing in a low-ceilinged area of the hold crammed with boxes and luggage and shipping cases. The chimp was shoving a locked plastic shipping bin across the steel floor plates.

Mack continued: "Do I look like a total and complete fool? Or merely a patsy with the IQ of a tube of sink cleanser? Which is it? Be frank. I can take it."

"It's all...the same...to me, buddy," said Danny-on-the-shirt, wrestling with a box marked FITNESS EQUIPMENT. His vocoder was set to produce a gentle tenor that sounded like a kindergarten teacher offering carrots and a nap. The circuit was a little out of phase, so his soft voice ebbed and flowed in volume, which he apparently tried to offset by saying his words in sync with the volume.

The chimp hoisted the box onto a plastic-wrapped wooden desk. "Frankly? I already think... you're an idiot."

"Can we just re-examine this so-called plan?" said Mack.

"We dock in six minutes. You can...get inside the shipping case...or you can get handed to polisec." Danny-on-the-shirt picked up a four-foot suitcase and threw it like a Frisbee. It sailed across the baggage space, landed flat on top of a wobbly stack of suitcases, and stayed there—barely—as the stack swayed back and forth.

"How do I know they're not the same thing?"

"Because I'm telling you...moron," said the chimp's vocoder sweetly. "You get into...the case, I lug it...onto the conveyor belt. Then I walk...alongside and just before...we get to the...luggage scanner, I...slide the case off the belt and onto a...transport cart that will roll...past at the right moment." He tossed a box marked

MERLOT and it landed with a crunch on top of a box marked CHANDELIER—EAST WING. "You'll be…opened up again inside a secure parcel van…Whole trip takes maybe…nine minutes, and you're…outside the terminal."

Mack looked at the open mouth of the splintery wooden case. The outside was marked OFFICE SUPPLIES. "Don't you have a box of couch cushions or something?"

"I'm just…following orders…It's your call. Did you feel…that thump just now?"

Mack nodded.

"That's the …starboard engine reversing to…swing us around broadside to…the pier." Danny-on-the-shirt flipped a wooden case right side up and slammed it onto the top of another one. "In two minutes, the…ramp will go down. Then, before anyone … can get off the ferry, the…security people come aboard. So you…have about four minutes…You leave in the case, or…you leave wrapped in a…restraint bag. Makes no difference…to me."

Mack felt a second bump as the side of the ferry knocked the edge of the pier.

"Which end is up?" he said.

Chapter 49

Carrying her helmet in the shopping bag, Autumn reconnected briefly with Brian on the main deck. Many of the ferry passengers were going back down to their vehicles on the automotive level to disembark, but there was a small crowd of people queuing up for the exit gangway: knots of simply and expensively dressed women, fathers holding children's hands, a Chinese-looking couple English to each other with Australian accents, a South Indian family with several small children. All Homo sapiens.

There were a few glances in Brian's direction. But no one said anything, perhaps because he was the best-dressed male passenger on the ferry. *You can go a long way if you look like money*, she thought. In her raincoat and chunky boots on a beautiful day she actually stuck out more. She wondered if Urizen, or the Lady, had needed to pay off the ferry crew to keep them from turning her in.

"So do we have to go through something like Customs?" Brian asked quietly.

"I think there's a gate," she said, scanning the pier below. "Everybody just goes through and on their way." Their way seemed to be, in virtually every case, toward the mall. "Go down separately. I'll meet you there."

"Where's, um, our other friend?"

"I suppose he'll meet us on the dock."

They shuffled down the gangway in line. Brian was several people ahead of her. When she reached the bottom the two of them left the pier and pulled off to one side of the disembarkation area, near the street corner where car after car was zooming out of the ferry's automotive level and turning to the left as instructed by the signs saying *To MALL OF THE PACIFIC*. She did not see the Rolls-Royce they had come in; perhaps the Lady was already gone.

"My goodness, did you see those women with the Freña purses?" said Brian. "I think that red blouse was a Coriola-cashmere blend."

"No, I didn't. What's Coriola?" She was looking around to see if Mack was sitting on one of the concrete walls. Maybe he had disembarked early?

"It's a graphene fiber. Extremely strong. The major supplier is in Santiago."

She wasn't seeing him yet. "So...tell me. Why should I buy from Mr. Brian's apparel shop?" she said. She felt hot and restless under her raincoat. "Give me the pitch."

"Oh. Well...we specialize in men's tailoring, for sapiens and others, but I would certainly outfit a lady if she were looking for a coat, or slacks, or if it were a matter of alterations." Brian smoothed his hair and facial fur, starting to adopt his professional manner. "Wools and silks, and premium synthetics, are what we deal in primarily. Among other fabrics. I think seersucker is coming back; there were some interesting examples in a couple of the New York shows this year. But wool really is remarkable stuff and clonewool has changed things entirely."

"Yeah?" She was scanning the people coming down the gangway.

"It's about consistency. With cloned sheep you get exactly the same fiber properties from every animal in terms of diameter, strength, and chemistry, assuming you're feeding them all the same. It gives you an absolutely uniform fiber staple, which means lower production costs, and with the right nucleic acid treatments you can get every sheep to give you the fiber you want. For comfort, heat resistance, breathability, and receptiveness to those hand-dyeing processes that everybody wants these days," here Brian was gesturing enthusiastically with both of his long arms, "wool can't be topped! And of course insulating properties, which is why clonewool insulation has made such advances in construction and other industries. The Avventuroso menswear line, for instance, uses a tough but breathable clonewool fiber originally developed for aircraft insulation."

The flow of people off the ferry had ended and now only crew members were moving leisurely up and down the ramp. "Very interesting," said Autumn, feeling her pulse accelerate.

"And since it's nondestructive to the source animal, the wool industry isn't threatened by the Elevation."

"Brian." Autumn put her hand on his arm. "I'm not seeing Mack."

"No?" He stopped and looked all around. The paved disembarkation zone was looking distinctly emptier as people drained away. "Oh. Oh, dear."

Anxiety gripped her, but also a kind of indignation at the thought that Mack might have somehow deserted them. And disappointment, for some reason. Well, that was natural; they could use his skills. He knew a lot of people, and he was good at improvising. She, on the other hand, relied a lot on protocols. She missed having Carter to balance her out.

"You don't think something happened to him?" said Brian, stroking the furred back of his hand anxiously.

She didn't want that to be a possibility. And Mack always seemed so sure of himself, even if he was hard to pin down about details. "No, of course not. He's probably … scouting the area."

"Do we stay here?"

She wasn't sure. The Lady in the car had not specifically said that someone would be there to meet them. Autumn had merely assumed it. She wished Mack would show up. He had helped them big-time last night; he paid a small fortune to Urizen, and as a result they were here now to meet Jiggs.

Mack wasn't such a bad guy. She didn't want to think about how she had talked to him that first day. It had been forty-eight hours, but it felt like an awfully long time ago.

"Oh! Look over there," said Brian.

Across the street on the sidewalk there was a neatly hand-lettered sign leaning against the building saying simply "BRIAN". It had not been there two minutes ago. No one was near it.

"Hmm. I guess we go," she said.

They walked up and waited at the crosswalk for the light to change. They crossed the street in front of the stopped cars with a crowd of other pedestrians.

As Autumn and Brian made their way across the asphalt, she became conscious that nearby in the crowd a bearded man in a polo shirt was walking exactly in step with her.

She glanced back on her other side and saw that a chimpanzee in work fatigues seemed to have appeared only a few steps behind them. She glanced at Brian. He had a stiff expression on his face, his eyes far away, as if he was paying attention to other senses, as if he were well aware of what she saw—and more.

The grilles of expensive automobiles were only a few feet from their kneecaps. The crosswalk display was flashing 11, 10, 9… *Better keep going forward.* In a few seconds they would be out of the crosswalk. *It's OK. Mack's probably close by and he knows how to handle himself.*

The chimp and the man in the polo shirt were closer, almost at their sides.

She looked straight ahead. The sign saying "BRIAN" was already gone.

Inside the shaking crate, Mack was desperately bracing himself with his arms and feet, trying to keep from becoming the human equivalent of a marble rattling inside a can of spray paint. It had been more than nine minutes. A lot more.

Were they holding Brianna on the UCSD campus? The cat had made it sound that way. Hopefully Jiggs could confirm. The Tall Guy's name was Reinhardt: he would be in tactical ops at Secure-Tek's campus office. With the COR band, or even his ViewGlazzes, Mack could have put together a whole file on Reinhardt, but did it matter? Reinhardt was a hurdle, not the goal. What they needed was to get Brianna back. And the COR band of course. And Autumn's good name.

Autumn's partner they couldn't get back. That had to be tough for her. She'd be a different person after this. As it turned out, she wasn't even going to stay with the Knights. *Maybe it's better that way*, he told himself. People needed to move on.

Brian would, knock on wood, recover his wife and get back to the menswear business. Mack himself would be pretty much who he always was, floating like a bubble—or, okay, like scum—on the edge of things. The people he knew who weren't clients tended to be mostly the edge-of-things kind.

Maríqui was a bubble too, in her own way, and he had thought they were a good fit for each other. But now it wasn't clear what she was up to. The hit at the Sleepy Daze motel—was that Ivan, trying to get the jade figurine? A pillow muffling a small-caliber firearm was mob style, but too stealthy for Ivan. He'd have just beaten the guy senseless and torn the room apart. In fact, if Quan Yin was the center of some special international deal, Ivan wouldn't have had the brains to arrange it.

Mack suspected the story might go more like this: Somebody needs a courier to deliver a small valuable item from Southeast Asia—somebody operating at a much higher level than a bouncer in a small-time dance club. But this somebody knows somebody who knows Ivan. Maybe they also know Maríqui, or at least they know about her. They find out that she has an on-again-off-again boyfriend who spends a lot of time doing business on the far side of the Pacific Rim. They set her up to set him up. Oh, honey, could you please buy me this little jade thing. Good so far. Slight problem: disposable boyfriend suddenly vanishes while going through Lindbergh Transport Control. It made sense that Ivan would come looking for the disposable boyfriend and, well, dispose of him.

Did Maríqui know about whatever it was that made the necklace valuable? Was she in for a cut of the profits? Or was she as much a patsy as Mack himself? Was she mad as hell at Mack? Or was she in big trouble and desperately needing his help?

The shipping crate rocked and lurched. Mack's shoulder didn't appreciate that. Floating like a bubble would be nice right about now.

Who is Maríqui, anyway? Did he already know? Had she been playing him all along? Which end is up?

BAM. The crate hit what seemed to be a flat surface. It stayed there for a while.

Damn that ape, Mack thought. *I know he did it on purpose. He deliberately put a "This side up" sticker on the case upside down.*

Mack felt himself being turned over.

Ahhh, he sighed. *Relief at last.*

The case was opened, and Mack was dumped onto an oil-stained concrete floor at the feet of two powerfully-built chimps in fatigues.

They grabbed him, shoved him against the wall, and began searching him. They had apparently graduated from the Meat Tenderizing School of Search Technique. Verhoven had only put a gun barrel up against Mack's kidney. One of the chimps shoved a gun barrel into Mack's ear.

"Uh," Mack wheezed, "watch that…"

"Shut up or die," said the chimp.

Ho-kay, works for me.

After being searched and relieved of both his weapons, Mack was drag-walked from the airplane hangar floor up a flight of metal stairs. *At least they can't take away my COR band.*

They went down a hallway with bare pipes and ducting on the ceiling, and then into a darkened room. The chimps pushed him down onto a folding chair and he blinked at a bright light shining into his eyes. There was a desk about six feet in front of him and a dark figure seated behind it.

"Welcome to the New Island Transportation Center," said a deep male vocoder voice. "We hope you enjoyed your trip."

The lamp was then adjusted to take the light out of Mack's eyes. He could make out the head of a chimp with pronounced eyebrow ridges.

"Brilliant location choice," said Mack, "on New Island where nobody would— "

The voice cut him off. "You are the notorious Mack Davis, although I'm sure that is not really your name," the voice said. "And I am your new keeper."

The chimp with the powerful voice swung around to the front of the desk. He was taller than average, wearing khaki cargo pants and a black T-shirt fitting tightly over impressive muscular development. He held himself like a warlord. "I am Jiggs VI. You are going to tell me everything that has happened to you, Mr. Davis, starting from 6:00 a.m. Tuesday morning. Begin."

Mack didn't know how much information Urizen might have passed along, so he told Jiggs everything, pretty much, except about Quan Yin. Shadow Guy became an old friend he went to see about borrowing some money. *All of that isn't this chimp's business, and I don't want Maríqui dragged into it.*

When Mack had finished, Jiggs walked back behind the desk and sat down again.

"Lights," he said.

The main lights in the room were switched on. It was a bare space with some metal cabinets and corrugated steel walls. Mack suspected it to be a New Island airplane hangar.

Mack saw at the side of the room, Brian and Autumn, sitting as motionless as statues. One of the chimps who had searched Mack, the taller and thinner one, was holding an 8mm Tivra to Autumn's head. "Elton, stand down," said Jiggs. The chimp stepped back and stuffed the pistol in his pocket.

Mack and Autumn made eye contact. He mouthed *Are you OK?* at her. She nodded, wearily.

"I told you he was all right," said Brian to Jiggs. "Can we stop wasting time now?"

"I don't waste time," said Jiggs. "Elton, Churchill." He showed the chimps something on his desk screen. They nodded and made an exit, walking bipedally until they passed through the doorway and then swinging up into the overhead conduit and metal crossbeams of the hallway.

Jiggs pressed a button on the desk and a vidscreen across the room lit up. "This is why they kidnapped my sister. And why they will kill her tomorrow morning unless I comply."

The screen showed a photograph of a beach leading up to a concrete wall. On the concrete wall there was a sign:

SOUTHERN CALIFORNIA WATER AUTHORITY
SAN LUIS REY DESALINATION FACILITY
SAN CLEMENTE

"By tomorrow this seawater processing plant is going to be blown up," said Jiggs. "They want my cooperation."

"But that plant supplies all of North County," said Autumn. "And the public system all the way to downtown."

Water, water, everywhere, and not a drop to drink, thought Mack. *Urizen was right, as usual.*

Chapter 50

"Whoever sent you the message didn't even tell you to destroy the desalination plant?" said Mack. The four of them were now seated around Jiggs's desk, reading a message on the screen.

"They only want me to take credit for it when it *is* blown up," said Jiggs in his deep voice. "Even if we wanted, we do not have the explosives required for a job of that kind. We are not a violent movement."

"What about that business when all the deer rampaged through the Senate chambers in Sacramento?" asked Autumn. That example got trotted out, so to speak, in every conversation at White Knights about why Free Life was dangerous and had to be controlled. She saw this as a rare chance to get the other side of the story.

Brian motioned anxiously at her to be quiet. But Jiggs nodded slowly. "Some of our activists have gotten carried away on occasion. But when animals with hooves stage a protest, should Free Life take the blame for a pack of incompetent legislators who lack the common sense to move aside?" His face was twisting a little. "Or the sensitivity to listen to the animals' complaints?"

"Losing the water supplied by that plant," said Brian quickly, "would hurt us all, animals *and* humans. Who would gain by that?"

"River water is rationed and expensive," said Autumn. "When SoCal became its own state it began to get most of its water from two sources: the state-owned San Luis Rey plant, and the commercial desalinization plant in Huntington Beach."

"Would that commercial plant stand to profit?" asked Mack. "Could they have hired Secure-Tek to destroy the competition?"

"That is possible," said Jiggs, leaning regally back in his metal office chair. "But it's not the way they do business generally. I suspect that explanation is too straightforward. Something bigger is going on: a plan deeper and more sinister."

"I like the way you think," said Mack.

"Maybe it's another organization, like One-God or Open Source, trying to destroy things and get you to take the blame," said Autumn.

"Why?" said Jiggs. "Terrorist groups have goals and public images. They must present a credible threat. When they strike, they take the credit, in order to enforce their demands. They don't give it to others."

"Could someone be trying to destroy Free Life's public image?" asked Mack.

"I have been considering this," said Jiggs. "It is more plausible than the corporate competition theory. There are many players who would like Free Life discredited and out of the way. And eliminating a water source could be a setup for a later control scenario."

"Right," said Mack. "Makes it easier to control the supply and put the squeeze on SoCal. Whoever might want to do that."

"Indeed. There are some indicators that international players could be involved," said Jiggs. "Our affiliate groups around the Pacific Rim have reported seeing some activity that might be connected, but we do not yet know how, or why."

"The question," said Autumn, "is what do we do about it."

"You could go along with it to get Brianna back," said Brian. "Tell the media that Free Lifers committed the crime. Then after we get her free, you just tell the media the truth."

"Brian. Do you really think they intend to give her back?" said Jiggs. "How much easier to kill her and leave her body near the plant before they blow it up? When polisec found the body, it would confirm that animals were responsible for the explosion."

"Oh no!" said Brian. "That can't be their plan!"

Jiggs merely stared at him.

Brian paused, then looked down. "Perhaps that is their plan."

"Even if you did tell the media," said Mack, "the public would never believe you."

"Nor would the members of Free Life continue to grant me their trust," said Jiggs.

"So if you're not going along…?" asked Autumn.

"We act. We have been trying to locate where they are holding her. Your information from Urizen has narrowed the focus of our search."

A light blinked on Jiggs's desk. "Yes," he said, and the desk replied something in a chimp language. "Good. Bring him in." To the three of them he said, "My messenger has returned."

Churchill pushed the door open with his foot and swung down from the hallway into the room.

"Welcome back, Niccolo," said Jiggs to the rumpled black thing perched on Churchill's shoulder. It was a crow.

"This is bizarre," said Autumn. watching the crow walk across the large ink pad again, then dance around on the sheet of lined paper.

"For birds in the corvid family, no one has bothered to make a vocoder," said Jiggs. "Officially, no bird this size is supposed to be elevated at all. When I discovered that crows were in fact elevated, I developed a way for them to communicate with us. It's similar to musical notation used by the early Christian monks. No one understands my system except me. Unfortunately crows' spelling is pathetic."

The crow stopped dancing and flew over to perch on top of the open door. Jiggs studied the marks on the page. After a minute or two, he looked up. "What can you tell me about the Geisel Museum in La Jolla?"

"It looks like a big concrete tree," said Mack. "Gets wider with each floor as it goes up."

"I went there once in grade school to see some Vietnamese items," said Autumn. "It used to be the university library before UCSD went completely online."

"Is the university abandoned?" asked Brian.

"No, the university still has research facilities," she said. "No students, but a lot of scientists. That building is sort of isolated now. The exhibits are only on the main floor. As I recall, they use most of the square footage for storage of books and furniture and stuff."

"It also apparently contains the offices of the security company contracted to patrol the campus," said Jiggs.

Autumn looked at Mack. "Secure-Tek," she said. "Reinhardt."

"Is that where they're holding her?" asked Brian, in excitement.

"At about 10 a.m. on Tuesday, crows noticed human and baboon security agents carrying a bag of the right size through the loading dock. They had come in a burstcar up Interstate 5 from downtown. One of the humans fits your description, tall and thin. One of the baboons had a wounded arm."

"Bingo," said Autumn.

"Two had been killed," said Mack.

"Perhaps," said Jiggs, "but no bodies were brought back to the museum."

"Let's go!" said Brian.

"I am already assembling my forces. The building is a hardened target, and we can expect heavy resistance. Officer Winn, I have a plan in which your skills will be of use."

"I'm coming too," said Brian. "I'm not much of a fighter. But she's my wife."

"Stick with me, Brian," said Mack. "I'll cover you. Assuming I get my guns back."

"You are not coming," said Jiggs.

"What?" Mack tried to get up, but Elton and Churchill shoved him back into the chair. Churchill held Mack down while Elton tied him up with a rope.

"I told you I was waiting for messages. One of those messages was a check on your story. There was a murder at the Sleepy Daze Motel yesterday. Not long before you supposedly arrived."

"What?" Autumn and Brian looked at Mack.

"Something did happen," said Mack. "But it wasn't anybody I knew."

"Really? Crows are excellent spies. You were seen meeting with someone outside the building while the ambulance was present. There was evidence of drug use."

"It was a smoke break," said Mack, pleading. "And I don't even smoke."

"Who was killed?"

"I don't know who the dead guy was," said Mack as his hands were being tied behind him. "You don't think *I* killed him, do you?"

"Mr. Davis, what I know is that when you had a chance to give me the full story, you did not."

"But −" said Autumn, "that's just how Mack is. It's nothing serious. He's on our side, really. He just has, um, trust issues."

"I have trust issues with people who lie to me," said Jiggs. "So he is staying here."

"But I have to come with you!" said Mack.

"Why is that, exactly?"

Mack swallowed. "I need to get back my property."

Jiggs took a submachine gun handed to him by Elton. "We'll return anything of yours that is still intact after our operation is complete," he said. "I recommend that you not have your hopes too high." He motioned to the others, and they all filed out into the passageway.

At the door Brian suddenly turned and rushed back into the room, throwing himself against Mack and beating him furiously with his open hands. "Traitor! Traitor!" screamed Brian as he reached around Mack and pounded on his back. With his hands tied behind him, Mack could do nothing to defend himself.

"Brian!" Jiggs yelled as he came back into the room. "Stop it!" But Brian seemed not to hear. Jiggs strode over and grabbed Brian by the shoulders.

"Leave him!" Jiggs said, pulling Brian off Mack. "Don't think I don't know how you feel, brother. But Brianna is waiting. We are gone." The chimps and Autumn left, and the door slammed behind them.

Which ought to be more surprising, thought Mack. *That Brian did the slapping-me-around bit? Or that Autumn defended me?*

Mack held tightly to the object Brian had pushed into his hand while beating on his back. With his other hand, he traced the thing's outline until he recognized what it was.

It was the ultrasonic shear.

Chapter 51

Autumn was wearing a gigantic sun hat and a very yellow dress, and standing halfway up the back of a gigantic serpent.

How did I get myself here?

She was starting to get a bad feeling that this was going to get her killed. But she had told Jiggs she would do it, for Brian and Brianna as well as for her own sake.

At the top of the slope was the concrete plaza, where the coiling path of variegated slate hexagons under her feet became a snake's giant head spilling out onto the concrete plaza. It was a public artwork installed a long time ago when there were still students here. Now some of the slate tiles were cracked or missing. Above the plaza loomed the gray inverted-ziggurat-on-a-stem of the Geisel Museum.

Here under her feet was the Serpent, and there was the Tree. Just as Urizen had said.

The rough concrete pillars around the base of the building swooped up to become gigantic concrete ribs angled to support the head of the tree, which consisted of progressively wider levels of floor-to-ceiling glass stacked on top of each other with thin shims of gray concrete jutting out in between each level. There were security cameras hanging from the underside of the lowest tier, floor 4, which was one of the floors where Brianna might be hidden.

"This will be a dangerous operation in a tightly contained space," Jiggs had said, briefing his troops. They had used a canyon between the freeway and the university campus as their staging area. Squatting in the brush were chimps, monkeys, and several humans, in addition to antelope, weasels, raccoons, and an assortment of other species.

"All of you here have volunteered," said Jiggs, "and you understand the risks. You will not use unjustified violence to people or property, but if you need to shoot you will shoot to kill. Expect Secure-Tek to do the same. Their humans are wily, and their baboons are fast and unrelentingly vicious. While you are on the stairs always look above and below.

"Here is the map and the side view we will see as we approach from the east by the Snake Path. The main entrance to the Geisel building is on the south side and the loading dock is on the north. The elevator and stairwell shafts run up past the plaza level through the central stalk, the narrow waist of the building, to the tree-top made up of floors 4 through 8."

Niccolo the crow's report on the comings and goings in the building had led them to believe that Brianna's presence was being kept a secret even from most of the Secure-Tek staff, whose administrative offices were on the top three floors. *The staff must have a magnificent view of the campus,* thought Autumn, *and all of La Jolla. And the ocean.*

Her lemon-yellow dress came from the air terminal on New Island; Jiggs's people had had to open seven or eight suitcases to find it for her. It wasn't really her color but she needed something long to conceal her BioBoosters, which she insisted on wearing if they wanted her to be part of an action involving live fire. *Some 6' 1" rich lady is going be hopping mad when she gets to her hotel in Fiji or wherever.* The leather purse they provided with it was a brand she had never heard of, but when Brian saw it, he gave a low whistle. Autumn was more impressed by the .50 caliber Kālikā Automag they gave her to put in it. She had no idea where the enormous hat came from, but it would hide her face from the security cameras.

"The main entrance," Jiggs had said to his followers while they crouched in the low scrub under the blue sky, "is reached through a funnel walkway flanked by glass walls, then across a bridge over an artificial ravine which cuts down to the first floor on the basement level. This bridge is watched and guarded."

"It's like a castle with a moat," said a thin, weathered-looking blonde woman with an assault rifle. "Who designed this? Back in the 1900s, wasn't it a library?"

"As Susi points out," said Jiggs, "it is not so far from a castle. The university developed in the period of the 1960s when protesters were common. Many features of the campus were designed to protect the administration from unruly mobs."

"Unruly is *back*, Jack," grinned a lanky young man with a red goatee and a shiny aluminum jacket. A few animals grunted.

Autumn looked down to her left at the shining glass walls of the entrance walkway. She could remember coming down that funnel and across the bridge as part of a pack of Siliconian grade-schoolers on a field trip to SoCal. At that time she had never personally met an elevated animal; not many humans up in Siliconia had. The world had changed so quickly. People had grown used to rapid change, but they had thought of it in terms of gadgets, of social customs, even of climate and geography. The real changes catch you off guard. No one had had the tiniest idea of what the world would be like in fifteen years.

A week ago she had not had the tiniest idea of what her life would be like right now.

"We will not storm that main entrance," continued Jiggs. "Instead we will come up the hill on the east side to the plaza, which is actually floor 3 of the building, and enter through the emergency exit door to the stairwell in the tree-trunk. We have acquired an ally" -- he was looking at Autumn, who was holding her enormous sun hat down in front of her knees because wearing it right now made her feel ridiculous—"with the ability to unlock that door. Officer, our people will block the security cameras trained on that area in order to give you time to open it."

"Team Matterhorn," He turned to a group of long-haired red howler monkeys decked out with coils of rope and bags of equipment, "once the cameras are blocked you will climb the understructure to floor 4, use the autocutters on the glass walls, and fire the freeze gas grenades. We'll show Secure-Tek that two can play that game. Use your grappling hooks and do the same on floor 5. Once fighting has begun Secure-Tek will occupy the roof, so expect fire from above. By then, the plaza will have become a no-man's land. Our entire assault force *must* enter the building in the initial push."

Talk about different experiences of elevation, Autumn thought. These animals were working together with sapiens in a way she had never seen. She remembered how Urizen's riflewoman had behaved with the mountain lion; like a superior officer rather than an owner. Here the roles were reversed, and it seemed entirely natural for humans to get orders from a chimp—not in worship, as in the case of Urizen, but as part of a group with a shared mission. And for a group with no polisec or military experience, they were pretty organized.

"Once in the stairwell," Jiggs said, "we will divide to perform our tasks. Teams Kingpalm, Pine, and Oak will go up the stairs to rescue the hostage as previously agreed. Team Boxwood will use the graphene panels and plasma riveter to seal the door connecting the stairwell to floor 2, the main museum floor, where the bulk of Secure-Tek's on-duty guards are posted. Team Rootball will go down through the floor 1 door into the elevator lobby space at the basement level; chimps are to seal the metal double doors into the basement corridors while weasels disable the elevator at the access panel. We will then control all access to the floors above. You *must* hold that lobby against attack." He nodded at the chimp Churchill, who was crouched with Team Rootball gathered around him, and Churchill nodded back.

Jiggs went on: "We believe she is being held on floor 4 or 5, below the main Secure-Tek administrative offices for the campus. However, if we do not find her upstairs, we will proceed to the basement floor. Meanwhile Team Hurricane will be emplaced to the north and use the YongSoom tripod machine gun to guard the loading dock so Secure-Tek cannot take her out the back to the burstcar fleet."

A YongSoom! Autumn had wanted to say, standing there in the brush listening to him. *Where the hell are you getting these weapons? You said this wasn't a violent movement!* This group right here, she realized, was the organization that the scarecrow-tall Reinhardt—or someone he was working for—wanted to destroy. And she was just beginning to understand why.

"Teams Quince and Barberry will make sure Secure-Tek does not send fighters up the external stairs from the main entrance porch to the plaza level." Two pairs of marmot and antelope nodded, looking as if they knew what they were in for.

"Team Drizzle"—Jiggs addressed a ragtag assortment of lightly armed animals, including Brian—"will approach the main entrance from the south as a feint to draw Secure-Tek's attention." The expression on Brian's face—Autumn was surprised by how good she had become at reading chimpanzee expressions—showed mixed feelings: he clearly wished he could be in the main assault force to get to Brianna, but he was relieved not to be in that stairwell.

"Those of you who fought at Santa Clarita know enemy fire does not frighten me." Jiggs pulled up his sleeve to show scars puckered white on his hairy shoulder and stood there calm and still, as if showing a holy relic. "Bullets cannot pierce our soul." His poise and power were spellbinding; a magnificent leader, Autumn had to admit, even if she did not wholly sympathize with his cause.

"Free species," he pronounced as if invoking a familiar formula, "have souls."

In unison the assembled species grunted quietly, almost in a whisper, but with the same spike of group energy as if they were screaming in a packed arena: "Free Life!"

"Free species have minds."

"Free Life!"

"Free species have rights."

"Free Life!"

"That is why we fight."

"We fight!"

The briefing was over. The animals and humans picked up their gear and assembled into line.

Waiting on the Snake Path, Autumn gazed out at the glittering skyscrapers of La Jolla to the south.

Over those hills to the west was the sea from which San Diego drank. If the water supply were cut off, there would be severe rationing. And if for any reason they lost the reservoirs as well, it would be only a matter of weeks before civil authorities lost control. A good time to come in and take what you wanted, if you were Someone who would do that. If she had nefarious plans, she wouldn't want the Free Lifers around. They were just unpredictable enough that they might swing to the side of law and order.

They had to get Brianna back. And she needed to find out who was responsible for that drone missile in the tailor shop, so she could get her name cleared. But more than that: they had to stop Secure-Tek.

Autumn touched briefly once more with her fingertips the reserve .50-caliber magazines in her purse. She had to admit it: she wished Mack could have been here.

Chapter 52

Mack was walking briskly up Genesee Avenue, a few blocks from where he had jumped out of the auto-taxi at a stop light and run off. He owed seventy-eight dollars for the ride from New Island, but no problem: He had memorized the driverless vehicle's reg number. *I'll send the company the fare when I get back my COR band.*

The route for the "Village Mall to UCSD" flatwagon ran down this street, or so he recalled. He had no guns, no ViewGlazzes, and no plan, and his finger was hurting badly, but he had to get to the university campus somehow where his COR band must be.

Hey, I own an artifact on loan to a prominent museum! It's an ill wind that blows no good, as my grandmother used to say.*

And after UCSD, back to the Sleepy Daze. Maybe Shadow-Guy-who-was-no-longer-Verhoven had left Quan Yin for him in a hollowed-out motel lamp or something.

He noticed a drone in the air half a block behind him. It looked like one he had seen from the taxi back on the freeway. He crossed to the other side of the street and noticed that after five seconds the drone shifted its position, staying in view of him. He didn't like that. Time to dry clean.

He slipped behind a building, cut through a gas station lot, doubled back and went under some bushes, ran up the next street over and then hopped a fence into a residential complex and out again into the trash area behind a strip mall. As he came through the back entrance and into the front of what turned out to be a bead shop he smiled at the surprised ladies who were speaking Spanish and stringing necklaces on the counter. He walked straight outside onto the pavement.

The drone was directly across the street, hanging above a tree like a big black bumblebee, as if waiting. Probably too small to be carrying missiles. Although missiles these days were getting pretty small.

Do not run. It wasn't as if his legs were at a hundred percent anyhow, after the fights yesterday. He wondered if the earbud phone from Huero had been set up with a tracer after all. Huero had never made a false move. Yet.

Would they fire a missile at an open retail store? He didn't want to back into the bead shop to find out. He felt a strange sort of calm happiness and he wondered why. Then it came to him that he was relieved to be alone right now: *good thing Autumn's not here to get blown up too.* He was surprised to find himself thinking about her. He walked on, looking at the storefronts.

A tax preparer's office two doors down in the strip mall had a sign saying CLOSED FOR LUNCH, but when Mack tried the door, it opened. He could hear in a room off to the side a man talking on the phone while eating something. It was talk, chew, talk, talk chew, talk some more. Mack slipped inside and moved down the hall as quickly as he could without making noise. The door to the restroom was open and, conveniently, the room had a window. Mack closed the door behind him and with only a little struggle got the stuck window to open completely.

Mack pulled himself through the window, dropped to the ground, and turned around. Hovering two feet outside the window was the drone, rotors spinning.

He took a deep breath and looked around for a board or pipe or anything to use as a defensive weapon. There was none. *The word* Destiny *comes to mind.*

"Can I help you?" he asked the drone as he braced himself for fight or flight, or maybe both.

A motor somewhere inside the drone popped and clicked. A little compartment on the underside clicked open and a light blinked green. There was something thin and white in the compartment. The light kept blinking.

Mack reached out cautiously and took the white thing in his thumb and finger. He drew it out.

It was an envelope with the logo of the Sleepy Daze Motel.

The drone stopped blinking and its hatch clicked shut. It spun up its rotors and angled up, soaring over a suburban hedge and away to the east.

Mack stared at the envelope in his hand for about five seconds. Then he sprinted across the parking lot.

If I can run all the way for another block and a half I might still make my ride.

322

The flatwagon and Mack both reached the curb at the same time. The raccoon operating it, and his passengers—one emu, one Falabella pony, and a large family of long-tailed weasels— all glared at Mack. It was perfectly legal for a human to ride the flatwagons, of course. In practice, however, because Provie riders were subsidized by the city as part of the Species Opportunity Act, flatwagons were used almost entirely by animals, especially lower classifications on their way to or from menial jobs. They felt proprietary about their right to at least use some form of public transportation without having to share it with sapiens riders.

The battered DNA scanner screen by the boarding step flashed:

San Diego All-Species Transit
Please Swipe Nose or Limb across Scanner

Time for the secret weapon. During his taxi ride Mack had realized that the Meat Tenderizing search treatment Elton and Churchill had given him in the Free Life hideout, plus Brian's brief attack, had left chimp hair all over his suit. He had rubbed a bunch of it together into a tuft and put it in his pocket. You never knew when someone else's DNA might come in handy.

Now he pulled it out, holding it between his thumb and forefinger, and brushed it across the scratched sensor plate. The machine hummed briefly, and then the screen changed:

3 Chimpanzees. Subsidy Confirmed.

323

The boarding gate clicked open. Keeping his eye on the animals, Mack climbed onto the long unroofed flatbed and held tightly to the support rail that ran around its sides. It was not unknown for a human who presumed to get on a flatwagon to mysteriously fall off as it made a sharp turn.

After a few blocks, the resentful animals turned their attention to other things, and Mack felt it would be safe to open the envelope. Inside was a single sheet of paper. A mini-chip with a number printed on it was taped to the bottom of the page. The handwritten note said:

"No, I didn't kill the old guy. He was buying street drugs for his cancer pain and let his bill rack up too high and too long for the dealer's liking. So now we get polisec on the premises and that means I'm gone.

I'm heading West to East. I think I've identified the Main Man. This thing is bigger than I ever dreamed. It's the End Times for sure. Wish me.

P.S. The chip is for a locker at the TransPac Bus station."

Mack stowed the chip in the compartment in his belt buckle, then tore the envelope and paper into a hundred pieces, allowing them to fall off the flatwagon one by one as it clattered toward the university.

Chapter 53

This was it. From her spot on the Snake Path, Autumn saw Jiggs's signal in the trees down the hill. Time to go.

She strolled up the hill on the tiled path, her summer dress swishing around her ankles, looking leisurely around at the scrubby foliage in her best impression of a harmless tourist visiting the University of California. She stepped between the diamond eyes of the serpent and onto its giant forked tongue.

Earlier, right after Jiggs's briefing, she had tried to keep Brian calm as the Free Life forces made their way through the canyons around the campus. It turned out that he was calmer than she was. He was smiling slightly, in fact.

"You going to be OK?" she asked. She held the big brim of the hat with both hands as they picked their way crookedly through the brush. Her back was sweating in the afternoon sun. Or maybe it was more than the sun.

"I am well," he said. "We are going to get Brianna back."

"Good, I'm glad you're OK."

"Autumn, Jiggs is highly experienced. I trust him to succeed."

"I know," she said. "It's still all very improvised, and we aren't even sure which floor is the target, but this seems like the best that can be done. It's just a little…bewildering. Three days ago I was a polisec officer with an unblemished service record, and now I'm working in disguise with an underground movement to break into a baboon-infested polisec stronghold."

"Two days ago," said Brian, "when we were running for our lives and hiding in a garage, I was a frightened bourgeois who didn't know where to turn. I never imagined that I would see a determined multi-species army dedicate itself to rescuing my wife. Or that I would be ready to fight alongside them."

"Life is strange."

The group paused in its walking. Niccolo the crow was in the air, guiding them along the most concealed route.

She realized that the group of them plodding in single file reminded her of an image she had seen in the programs on Vanishing Vietnam: a line of villagers making their way out to the rice paddies in the morning. As motley and utopian as the Free Lifers were, they seemed to have an actual way of life, a solidity of purpose, reminiscent of traditional societies. Or maybe she was just imagining that.

"We just have to get through this," said Brian. "You have a dangerous task. You seem tense. Let me groom you."

"I don't need to be groomed. It's a clean dress."

"It's not actually about lint management. It's more like conversation. It's all about attention." He flicked a cockleburr off her knee with a practiced, businesslike gesture. "You groom me too. Find some lint on my coat or something."

"This is weird," she said as he brushed off the edge of her hat brim. "It's a little personal, you know? Even though I know that in your culture, I mean your species, it's supposed to express support."

"Humans generally don't understand," said Brian, "how crucial good grooming is for group morale and clarity of thinking in response to stress. Both receiving and giving," he said, twitching a grass stub out of her dress hem.

"It is?" She hesitantly located a grass stub in his shirt cuff.

Brian looked at her with twinkling chimpanzee eyes and his mouth pulled up into a tiny smile. "Of all the small business opportunities in Southern California," he said, "why do you think chimpanzees would open a tailor shop?"

Now, as Autumn left the Snake Path and went down the brief steps to the plaza she saw that a seemingly wild raccoon was already scratching its back on the lens of the security camera on the south parapet. In the afternoon sun the plaza was shady from the great shadow of the concrete Geisel tree. The external stairs were blocked with metal gratings. *That will help make Teams Quince and Barberry's jobs easier,* she thought.

She kept her head down and walked across the wide flat empty expanse of concrete as if heading past the huge concrete pylons surrounding the core of the building. Ahead of her was the metal door. It said EMERGENCY EXIT ONLY. The emergency alarm would be switched off automatically, however, if it received a polisec code from her lock activator.

327

As she came near enough to see the lock, something black fluttered in her peripheral vision. That would be Niccolo. She looked up and saw him swooping in against the massive angling concrete supports and the ridged underside of the lower floors. He landed on the camera that covered the door, hiding her from its view.

She swerved to the right, toward the door, and as she came in past the massive pillars supporting the building's ribs she swiveled her luxury purse in front of her and reached in with both hands. One hand gripped the Kālikā pistol and the other hand found the polisec lock activator from her utility belt. She felt the activator switch with her thumb and pressed it.

The door lock didn't open.

Chapter 54

Mack was walking quickly across the university campus and had reached a wide brick walkway, heading like a beeline for the Geisel Museum in the distance.

He said had off the cuff in Jiggs's office that the building looked like a concrete tree because it got wider with each floor as it went up. It did look like a squat tree but he'd been wrong about one point: the widest level was the sixth floor and then the top two floors narrowed again, so that the tree-head of the building was actually diamond-shaped in profile. Between the thin concrete sandwich layers, each floor of the tree was glass, gleaming blue from floor to ceiling. Somewhere in there was Brianna. And his COR band.

On a lamppost along the walkway there was a screen-printed banner. ANCIENT DREAMS: ARTIFACTS OF AUSTRALIA. NOW AT GEISEL MUSEUM. The artifact he wanted was mostly built in Iceland, it wasn't ancient, and it was no longer, he hoped, just a dream.

The walkway under his feet alternated in bands of light and dark gray brick, in sync with a long line of low concrete blocks on one side. Maybe students used to stand on them and give speeches or something way back when. It had probably been twenty years since any face-to-face classes were held on the campus. Professors still taught classes and students still took them, but in their pajamas, not here. A signpost said *Biosciences* left, *Visual Arts* right. To the left the campus looked well-kept and modern, while to the right were mostly boarded-up buildings and litter. A ghost town.

Two bunny rabbits hopped from under a bush and across the grass, white puffs of tail flickering as they bounced. When Mack was younger he had seen an old vid called *Watership Down*. He wondered if maybe rabbits were better off not being elevated. Like the giraffes in the zoo, they seemed to be plenty busy having mealtime all day long.

As he drew closer to Geisel he could see the glass walls on the ground that funneled visitors toward the entrance. A couple of figures in blue Secure-Tek uniforms were strolling into it.

On the roof of the top level there was a gleaming blue object. *A burstcar. They can bounce it right up and down the terraced roofs of the building. Mighty convenient for executive travel. Or, when they aren't busy guarding all this federally funded research, convenient for dashing off to blow up desalination plants.*

He passed a facility on his right with a dry fountain and some steps leading past a brown remnant of terraced lawn to a sunken empty courtyard area. There were still a few trees on the lawn. Birds were chirping. A pleasant breeze was rustling the branches. There was a loud metallic click behind his right ear.

"Hands on top of your head," a voice said. "Turn around very slowly."

Mack slowly turned, muscles tensed for a fast kick and disarm.

330

It was the Neo-Hipster with the red goatee and the shiny aluminum jacket.

"My man!" A broad smile broke across the hipster's face. "So cool to see you again! No one told me you were part of today's action." He lowered his gun and patted Mack on the shoulder. "This is just frosty cool!"

"I'm, uh, a little unclear on the details," Mack said as he lowered his hands. "And I don't have a weapon."

"Come on, I'll give you the spiel while we get you a rod," said the hipster. "The rescue is starting, and we have to get ourselves into po-*sit*ion. Great you could show. This is going to be the most righteous direct action we have ever done! Woo-hoo! Free Life Forever!"

The hipster led Mack down through the sunken terraced courtyard, where the big glass front of the old student bookstore was dark and swirled with dust. On the other side of the circular concrete dais there were dead neon signs advertising pizza and frozen yogurt. They came out onto a sloped bicycle pathway and crossed over into a grove of trees in a hollow just at the foot of the slopes of the Geisel complex. A group of animals and humans was already moving out of the hollow toward the main museum entrance to the left. Mack looked at them from the back as they moved stealthily up the path and he realized that one of them was a chimp in a familiar tailored suit.

Mack was about to go and talk to Brian, but the hipster tugged his sleeve.

"The Snake Path is right up there," said the hipster, gesturing to the hill beyond the courtyard. "Polly Wolly's fixing to pop the door in minutes, and then we are taking it to the *man*."

A weathered-looking blonde carrying an old M4 saw them and came up. "Apparently there's a burstcar on the museum roof," she said. "But Jiggs says we go ahead. Who's this?"

"Friend of ours, Susi," said the hipster, keeping his voice down. "Joining the operation."

"Really," said Susi. She looked at him like something the cat dragged in. *Which, after a visit to Urizen, is sort of true.* "Which assault team are you on?"

"The fun one," said Mack. "Just refresh my memory, would you, about which names went with which assignments."

"Team Kingpalm just might be the *most* fun," said Susi, stroking her rifle barrel. "Elton and his group will be putting up a defense against attack from the upper floors. You might get as far as the seventh floor before being pinned down by close-range fire on the stairs."

"OK, a total gas, absolutely," said Mack. "But which is the one that goes straight to where the hostage is being held? I'm on that one."

"Righteous!" said the hipster. "We think she's on the fourth or fifth floor. Jiggs is leading Team Pine up to floor 5. Susi and myself are your tour guides for Team Oak, all-expense-paid express travel

332

to Floor 4." He handed Mack a small .38 caliber revolver that looked like it hadn't seen oil in years. Mack felt right at home. It showed a little pitting from rust, but it looked like it would fire.

"You're probably on Team Pine with Jiggs," said Susi.

"Jiggs. Wait. Let me think. No, no, I'm definitely on Oak. That name sounds very familiar. I remember I memorized it because it rhymes with um, ah, hoak."

"Hoak?" asked Susi, staring at him. A weasel in a little flak jacket scurried past their feet.

Cloak broke smoke folk yoke. I could have picked one of those..."Yes, you know, hoak," he said, "it's that medicinal plant that grows up there in the Pacific Northwest. Little purple hoakflowers."

"I have a certificate in Herbal Medicine," said Susi, "and I've never –"

"So now we know we're all on Team Oak, why don't we just review the plan here. For all of us. On Team Oak."

"You are some hep cat, man," said the hipster. "I gotta know more about everything you *know*!"

At that moment a signal was passed from the hillside. "Positions," said Susi. Humans and animals in the hollow clustered and moved up the slope. Jiggs up the hill was ahead of them, just behind some antelopes with marmots clinging to their backs, with his arm lifted in readiness to signal. Keeping his head turned away from Jiggs, Mack crouched behind some chimps with submachine pistols. His right index finger was still sore, so he was holding the .38 in his left hand.

"Where's your filter mask?" whispered Susi in his ear.

Filter mask? Mack gave a quizzical shrug.

"For the freeze gas on 4 and 5."

Mack nodded wisely. "Right." *Holy floating carp. Where's a roll of paisley when you need one?*

"Are you —"

GO! Up on the hill Jiggs dropped his arm to his side and began running. The assault force rushed forward, chimps loping, weasels bounding, sapiens pumping their angly human knees and elbows. In the corner of his eye Mack caught the flash of the hipster's aluminum jacket.

As they crested the hill and ran up the Snake Path, Mack saw the gray mass of Geisel glowering above them. The glass walls on the fourth floor were already dripping with long-tailed red monkeys on ropes. The antelopes with armed marmots on their backs were sprinting across the plaza to the external stairwells. There was a large chimp in overalls blocking Mack's view and he couldn't see where the door was, or whether it was open. *Oak. Also rhymes with croak.*

Chapter 55

Desperate, Autumn pulled the lock activator out of the purse and looked at the tiny status screen. *SEARCHING,* it said. *TRYING ADDITIONAL CODE SEQUENCES....*

The Geisel Museum was a public building, and therefore required to have polisec-approved lock codes. However, the upper floors of this particular public building also served as the headquarters of a private security contractor. So naturally they would reprogram the code. *You idiot,* she said to herself.

LOCK CODE SEQUENCE TYPE IDENTIFIED.

Good thing Secure-Tek didn't have such secure tech. White Knights lock activators were equipped with a comprehensive code library based on inter-corporate polisec agreements for joint operations. In a moment they would be inside.

LOCK CODE SEQUENCE TYPE IDENTIFIED.
DOWNLOADING UPDATE TO CODE LIBRARY.
PLEASE WAIT...

Update?! Autumn could feel her yellow dress sticking with sweat to her arms. She looked back toward the Snake Path, but Jiggs and the others were waiting below the level of the hill, and she couldn't see them. How was he going to know when the door was open? Oh, yes: Niccolo.

PLEASE WAIT...

She looked at Niccolo. He was clinging upside down to the camera housing and preening his black feathers live on closed circuit TV. She didn't know what to tell him, or if he would even understand her.

PLEASE WAIT...

Don't time out. Please don't time out. She had not been raised religiously but she was beginning to wonder whether, if she made a bargain with God, the Episcopal church or the Reformed synagogue would be preferable as a place to spend her Sunday mornings for the rest of her life. *Wait a minute,* she thought. *The synagogue doesn't meet on Sundays.* That complicated the decision.

CODE DOWNLOAD COMPLETE.

The door lock clicked open.

Niccolo's black shape flashed out through the huge concrete pylons and back toward the Snake Path. He had left something white and sticky on the lens of the security camera.

She threw the hat away, took the Kālikā from the purse and opened the door. She stepped inside.

She was on a landing in an empty stairwell, bare except for metal railings and old florescent tube lights and metal stairs spiraling up on all four sides from two levels below. Above her they continued around the empty center space and shrank to a square whorl of stairs and railings centered around a small skylight high overhead. At the scrape of her foot the bare concrete walls echoed and then there was silence.

Pillars round the Void, Urizen had said. For a split second she wondered if he had also been right about Kyle giving Bethany an engagement ring.

She heard movement and stepped back toward the sun-washed plaza outside.

The Free Life army was charging across the concrete plaza toward her. Jiggs was in the lead, running on his feet and one hand, his face grim behind his filter mask, his submachine gun in his other hand.

Autumn stepped back politely and held the door for them.

In the midst of the assault force charging toward the building door Mack caught a glimpse of a stunning black-haired woman in a yellow dress with a machine pistol in her hand. *Another one of Urizen's female acolytes?* You never knew where his people might turn up.

As the group flattened into a single line of fighters that curved and raced through the doorway like a machine-gun belt he came nearer and realized it was Autumn.

He was going to say something friendly, but each member of the assault team was hurtling through with less than a second in between, and if he even slowed down he would be run over. He just smiled at her as he rushed past and was carried with the group up the stairs to the left. He thought, from the startled look on her face, that she had seen him.

With no mask, I can't go right away into floors 4 and 5. The building HVAC would probably take at least ten minutes to clear the freeze gas. *I'll have to go with Team Kingpalm after all. And I don't know for certain the COR band is even still with Brianna. They might have moved it to another floor for inspection. Hell, they might have thrown it away.*

At the door marked 4 he peeled off from Susi's group and went up another level. Jiggs was opening the door and Team Pine was rushing inside. As Jiggs turned to enter he saw Mack and for half a second he stared. Mack waved and grinned and passed him on the stairs and ran even faster. Jiggs turned and vanished into the floor 5 doorway.

The one thing I'm pretty sure of is that the COR band won't be lying on a stair step.

After that burst of speed Mack found himself a good deal higher up on the stairs behind a cluster of tough-looking chimps with machine guns, one of whom looked like Elton. Mack panted for breath on the metal railing.

Below, on the second floor, there was the signature lavender spark of a plaz riveter as chimps fastened flat sheets of some material over the doorjamb. Down at the basement level a chimp held the door and a weasel bounded through.

Hasn't Secure-Tek heard our whole Little League team thumping up the stairs by now? Surely we won't get to just pick up Brianna and walk out. He realized that if things went that smoothly he would have almost no time to look for the COR band.

Things didn't go that smoothly.

A door opened on the next floor up, floor 7, and someone poked their head out. It was a lady with large round glasses and a phone bud in her ear. She screamed and slammed the door. In the vast vertical cavern of the stairwell the echoes of the scream and the slam blended into one howling, haunted shriek rolling around the walls as for a lingering moment the assault teams above and below stood unmoving with their guns pointed down.

Suddenly there was muffled gunfire from below. Where was it? He couldn't see any action.

Doors flew open above them. Elton's chimps fired upward.

Below them armed baboons poured out of the basement door, most of them in blue Secure-Tek uniforms. They were already firing. From somewhere above came the two-syllable baboon bark: *Raaa-hu.* It echoed through the stairwell: *Raaa-hu.*

Concrete splintered on the edge of the stair Mack was standing on. Above them on the opposite side, baboons were firing as they poured out of floor 7.

I'm not getting anywhere on these stairs except shot.

Mack ran around to the other side of the stairwell, beneath where the baboons were coming out. He crouched, threw open the door to floor 6 and went in low, his rust-pitted .38 held out ahead of him.

Autumn heard a gunshot from the basement level, and then several more shots. Then shots overhead. She crouched low, holding the Kālikā, and looked into the stairwell. The basement door opened and two baboons in black armor jumped out, firing their machine guns. The small-caliber rounds ricocheted off the planes of concrete and whined off, one of them ricocheting a second time.

Autumn shot both baboons. The .50 caliber rounds easily penetrated their armor. *Bad news. Looks like we lost Churchill's team. Hope the weasels got to the elevator wiring first.*

She was almost sure she had seen Mack among the fighters. *How did he get here?* What was he doing? She was confused, but seeing him gave her a little more confidence.

She heard gunfire overhead as more baboons came out of the basement. *We didn't think they'd come up so soon. Those are the museum offices. What else is down there?*

She also heard shots outside the door, coming from higher up in the building. The red howler monkeys scaling the outside of the glass walls had apparently been noticed.

This concrete bottle is the worst possible place for a gunfight, she told herself, *and you are dressed like a big billowing lemon-yellow target. Get out and sprint across the plaza. With your BioBoosters you can make it back to that canyon. Get out.*

She got in.

Chapter 56

Below in the stairwell, the Free Life chimps who had just sealed the door to Floor 2 were in prone shooting position on the concrete landing. The noise of gunfire in the concrete space was deafening. Autumn saw baboons on the railing were swinging up and over, leaping across the central open shaft to the next railing and then the next floor, heading for Floor 3 in order to outflank the chimps vertically.

In other words, they were coming toward her.

Autumn's boots whirred as she bent her knees and jumped. The baboons got there a moment too late and they bared their fangs as her BioBoosters pushed her out of reach and across the shaft. She cleared the opposite railing, her long yellow dress poofing up as she came down and hit the stairs in a crouch.

A baboon appeared out of nowhere on the railing 90 degrees from hers. She shot him between the eyes.

They're working their way up.

Another boon swung up, firing at her while he was upside down, and she felt a pain in her side like being smacked with a hockey stick. *That was a direct hit on my SafeLite.* She shot the boon but saw three more leaping up, guns in hand as they flew crisscrossing the shaft from railing to railing.

Raaa-hu, echoed the baboon call all around her. A constellation of splinters burst from the concrete wall around the exit door.

I can't hold the exit alone, she thought. *Where's Mack?*

She jumped across the shaft down to floor 2 and blew away three baboons creeping up the stairs to ambush the chimps.

She saw that above her the baboons were leaping across the shaft and the Kingpalm chimp team was doing the same thing, staying in motion. With nothing to hide behind, no one could afford to stand still. She sprang upward, bouncing between stairs.

The floor 4 door opened. Susi and the guy with the goatee and the shiny jacket ran out. They were followed by two chimps carrying Brianna. She was limp and motionless from the freeze gas, but breathing.

Autumn stopped them. "Secure-Tek's on the lower floors," she shouted. "We can't get out yet." A bullet whined past.

"That's our only escape," Susi shouted through her filter mask. "We have to cut our way through." She shouldered her rifle and fired down over the railing. "Lower floors should have been easy to secure." She fired again. "Baboons aren't big strategists. Who did they have downstairs to give the orders when—" Susi stopped and crumpled slowly to the floor. Her body lay still.

Autumn yelled at the hipster with the shiny jacket. "This is a death trap! Get Brianna back inside Floor 4!" She aimed and picked off a baboon climbing down from overhead.

"Got it," the hipster shouted back through his mask. He went back up to open the door. The concrete nicked and spattered apart only a foot from his head; he ignored it and held the door open for the others. The chimps from Team Oak picked up Brianna. But then there was a BANG and one of them spouted blood and let go and rolled down the stairs. Then another BANG and the second one collapsed also.

Autumn turned. Just above them on the stairs was Reinhardt, the Tall Guy, long-barreled revolver in his hand.

She jumped aside, and his shot blasted a meter-sized crater in the wall behind her.

Reinhardt snatched up Brianna's limp body by one arm and slung her over his shoulder as he fired again. Autumn dared not return fire directly, but she began blasting holes in the wall by the exit doorway to keep him away from it.

Reinhardt stopped and looked down. He unslung Brianna from his shoulder, and threw her into the empty space of the shaft.

As Brianna fell, one of the baboons swing out from the level 2 railing and caught her. Then he swung her down to two more baboons on the basement floor.

Raaa-hu, Raaa-hu, they barked.

Reinhardt leaped over the railing and with his long arms he swung down to Floor 2. She fired at him and a red crease opened in his black tactical suit on the front of his thigh. He winced as he landed, but fired back at her as she jumped up to Floor 5. He turned and tried to open the Floor 2 door to get to the public entrance.

By now the chimps of Team Boxwood were all dead on the landing next to their plasma riveter, but before dying they had sealed the door to Floor 2 and it wasn't budging.

Her magazine was empty and she snapped in a new one. *I thought it was the good guys who get to say it's only a flesh wound.*

Reinhardt hugged the wall under the stair levels as he circled round the last flight of stairs and ran out the bottom door.

The aluminum hipster flashed down around the stairs in pursuit, leaping down two and three steps at a time.

Autumn wondered where Jiggs was. And Mack. With most of the shooters gone from the lower floors there was a momentary echoing lull.

"Autumn!" She looked around; she heard her name again. It was Mack two levels above her, across the shaft. A chimp leaped across her line of sight.

"They'll get away!" she shouted back. At the bottom of the stairwell the shiny jacket flashed as the hipster passed out of the stairwell into the basement.

"Let's go!' Mack shouted. "Catch me." Without waiting for an answer he slung a machine gun over his shoulder and swung his legs over the rail.

"Mack!"

"Your boots! Catch me!" He looked her in the eyes, and jumped.

She had to jump. With a painful lurch she caught him in mid-air in the empty center space, getting both her arms under his armpits. Their opposite horizontal forces canceled out and the two of them fell together down the shaft, turning, the stairs whirling around them. Something whined past Autumn's ear.

Her boots screamed as they hit the floor at the bottom of the stairwell, motors maxing out their burst power to break the fall. Autumn and Mack spilled apart and collapsed on the floor.

"You OK?" asked Mack, gasping and rolling onto his side.

"Yes," said Autumn, being optimistic. "Where have you *been*?"

"Looking for my COR band," said Mack. "Sixth floor doesn't know a thing about it. They're just office workers hiding under desks. Outside the glass we got howler monkeys and baboons chasing each other on the ropes."

"Where's Jiggs?"

Mack staggered to his feet, machine gun ready. "No idea." He extended a hand. "Come on!"

"Coming!" Autumn stumbled up after him. *That jump was definitely not within BioBooster product guidelines.* She ran after Mack out the stairwell door and into the lobby. The bodies of weasels and chimps lay on the floor. An open access panel showed wires that had been ripped out and, she saw, now twisted back together.

Past the lobby was a T-junction to a very long corridor in both directions, filled with shelves and boxes. Mack was creeping quickly to the right. Autumn followed him. In the corridor they passed the body of Churchill sprawled over a box.

They reached the end of the corridor and came out into another stair area surrounded by boxes and filing cabinets and shelves and rolling book carts, loaded with books and binders and old pieces of paper. The walls down here were glass but they had been boarded up almost to the ceiling.

In front of the shelves Mack and Autumn saw several dead baboons on the floor and the hipster in the aluminum jacket standing with his hands up, looking into the business end of Reinhardt's gun.

"Drop it," said Mack to Reinhardt. "Drop or I'll shoot."

"Really," said Reinhardt. He was pressing with one hand on the gash on his thigh, but his long face showed a crooked smile and his gun did not waver.

"I think you should drop yours instead," said a bland voice behind them. Autumn thought it sounded familiar. They turned around to see a pudgy man in ViewGlazzes wearing his black uniform with the White Knight chess logo on the shoulder. He was pointing a gun at them.

"Captain Heap!" said Autumn.

"I should probably say something like, we've been expecting you," said Heap. His long-barreled revolver was identical to Reinhardt's. "But the truth is, your attack has caught us off balance. I was busy in the server room."

With his free hand Captain Heap pushed up his glasses on his nose. On his left wrist there was a coppery thing like a bracelet.

Out of the corner of her eye, Autumn saw Mack stiffen.

346

Chapter 57

"And I thought it was Bickson. You've been working with Secure-Tek all along!" said Autumn, while Reinhardt took her Kālikā and Mack's machine gun.

"No, Secure-Tek is working with me," said Captain Heap. "I am working with a covert operator overseas who is paying top dollar to get rid of both a water treatment plant and the Free Life Movement. Hands on your heads and over to that wall, please."

I think I've had worse situations, thought Mack. *Later I'll make a list and rank them. This can't be more than number three or four. Lesotho is still number one. This one is pretty bad. But it's not hopeless yet because I know something they don't know.*

Namely, when he picked up the machine gun back in the stairwell, he took the old .38 the hipster had given him and shoved it into his backup holster. It was hidden under his expertly tailored suit. It still held two rounds.

I can do this. As long as my trigger finger works, because I can't draw from that holster left-handed.

As Mack and Autumn put their hands on their heads they could hear the sounds of gunfire echoing from the stairwell.

"I thought Bickson was bad, but you!" said Autumn to Heap. "You'll be caught, and wrapped, and arrested, and thrown in a Supermax for the rest of your life."

Gun in hand, Reinhardt frisked the hipster, both sides and legs and the small of the back. *Uh-oh,* thought Mack. *They actually get training at Secure-Tek.*

"Your only hope," she went on, "is to relinquish the hostage and make a run for it."

Reinhardt frisked Autumn. *This isn't good,* thought Mack, *we are heading for the wrong outcome here.*

"You're wasting your breath, duchess," said the hipster. "This cut-rate isn't coming on that tab."

"And who are you?" asked Heap, waving his gun at the hipster. Reinhardt stopped frisking and stepped back out of the line of fire.

"I'm a graduate student, Jack. Working to free animals from human oppression."

"And what do you expect to get out of that?" asked Heap.

"A Ph.D. in Animal Justice."

"Animal Justice? No kidding!" Heap smiled behind his glasses. "Congratulations. Here's your terminal degree."

Heap fired his gun, placing one round in the young man's heart. He was dead when he hit the floor.

After the thunder of the shot Autumn was silent for a few seconds. Then she got her voice working again. "You *scum,*" she said. "Heap, you are eternal, scum-sucking, diabolical, worthless, scum-sucking, gutless *scum*. You are supposed to be protecting the rights of Provisional and Human Citizens."

"And you, Officer Winn, are supposed to be dead," said Heap pleasantly. "We'll fix that soon, but I do need to know something. Why *didn't* you go into the building across from the tailor shop? Did you suspect me even then?"

"No, we had absolutely no –" Autumn began.

"We had no idea that you were working with Secure-Tek," interrupted Mack. *Keep the show going, kid.* "But you had dropped certain clues and we knew you were running your own show. White Knights will be here in minutes."

"So who *are* you, exactly?"

Think fast. "Mack Davis," said Mack Davis, "private investigator for Spade and Archer, Inc. Some of our corporate clients were concerned about the integrity of White Knights on the tech side and this sweep was a chance to test our hypothesis. There are specific indicators of your activity that you'll need to erase if you hope to stay under the radar. Let's make a deal."

"I think an ordinary PI wouldn't own something like this," said Heap. He raised his left arm a little to show the COR band on his wrist. "Because this *is* yours, isn't it?"

"Never seen it before," said Mack. "Pricey bracelet, I'm sure, but –"

"I'm sure that's why you can't take your eyes off it," said Heap. "They brought it to me for analysis and by gum, of all the prizes! This is a corker. I'll keep it."

"Looks like they got the elevator working again, Captain," said Reinhardt. "We have a burstcar on the roof. Coming?"

"Go up and send a baboon down in the elevator for me," said Heap. "When all this happened I was working on the exit diagrams for San Clemente, and I have to get those. And I'll finish up these nice folks as well."

"You've got this?" said Reinhardt.

"Sure," said Heap, "I'll take care of it. You've got a lot on your plate."

"Do we have to bring the girl chimp, or can we ex her too?"

"Don't kill her yet. Sorry," said Heap. "I can't authorize that without orders from Samajargan."

Hearing the name of Heap's client didn't make Mack feel better. *That's generally a sign they don't plan for you to leave.* Heap was standing just a little too far away to take out with a kick. Mack flexed his right hand a little as it sat on top of his head. That index finger that Vlad the fox had chewed up had lost the bandage and it was scabbed and stiff.

Reinhardt holstered his gun and picked up Brianna. "Fifteen minutes," he said. "I can't hold the car longer than that. Call me and I'll send Brack down for you." He strode down the corridor, limping only slightly.

"Jiggs won't play ball with you no matter what," said Autumn.

This girl doesn't need anyone to give her more rope to hang herself, thought Mack. *She just spins it out of thin air.*

"Jiggs won't play ball with you, no matter what," said Mack, "unless he can meet you and see Brianna alive and well. Then he'll definitely play ball."

"Well, it would have been better if he had, but it isn't the end of the world," said Heap. "We do have a vid piece to send out on the news, claiming the job for Free Life. I always have a backup."

So do I, thought Mack, rolling his shoulders to loosen his jacket. It reminded him that the shoulder still hurt from yesterday and from landing just now out of a six-story jump. "Are you really sure you can trust Samajargan?" he asked Heap. "What kind of crowd are you running with these days?"

"You think I'm devoid of ethics," said Heap. "Let me tell you something. I've already been paid the fee in full. My client is not small-time. He trusts me, I trust him. I could take the money and split. But I'm a professional. I'll complete the job as agreed."

There was noise on the main museum level above them, like the pounding of hooves. Heap blinked, but held the gun steady.

"We'll help you," said Mack. *Wait for his eyes to move away.* "We don't have a choice. You won't have an easy time getting to San Clemente now. The White Knights will be in pursuit." He heard the elevator ding and swoosh open, far down the corridor. "If you had someone who knew how to operate the COR band you could confuse their burstcars."

Wait. He's thinking it over.

"You'd have to do exactly what I tell you to do, the second I tell you," Heap said. "You'll help us blow up the plant, and then –"

"Forget it!" said Autumn. "We are *not* aiding and abetting! Mack, we... "

Autumn, no, I've got this, don't –

"You know, Winn," said Heap. "Bickson said you weren't cut out for law enforcement, and I'm forced to agree. Time for you to retire." He turned toward Autumn and shot her in the chest.

She jerked back against the wall, then dropped face forward onto the carpet.

By the time she hit the floor, Mack had already drawn the .38 and fired. Heap spun backwards.

It seemed to Mack that Heap took a long time to fall, that he *wanted* Heap to take a long time to fall, that as long as Heap was still falling the exchange wasn't over, and the deadly effects of that bullet would not have touched Autumn, that there was time to say things if only Autumn could hear him, and if he could think of the words to say. But he knew she was beyond all hope of that now. She was nearly two seconds past hope and it might as well have been two thousand years, the exploding bullet had vaporized her heart; her body was no longer her, but was now just so much mass to which gravity clung as it was clinging to Heap. As long as Mack could see Heap falling, the whole package of events would not actually have happened.

Heap hit the carpet on his back.

Mack grabbed the weapons quickly. Heap lay in a heap, bleeding in the upper right quadrant, but still breathing. Mack heard a moan behind him. He rushed to Autumn and checked for a pulse. She had one.

"I'm OK," said Autumn, face down, her voice muffled by the carpet.

She's alive. Thank you, thank you. Thank you.

"Kid, you are not OK. Let me see the —"

"Don't move me!" she said. "I think a rib's fractured. Lower down left side."

"Autumn, you've been shot with a cop-killer bullet. You should be dead, and there ought to be an unholy mess." He took her arm. "I can't see any exit wound. Designed to detonate internally. We've got—"

"Dammit, don't move me!"

"Wait a sec," said Mack. "You're not even bleeding!" He let go.

"It's my underwear," she said into the carpet.

"Underwear?"

"The blue thing. The Miss Autumn modeling outfit. It's bulletproof. Microdispersor flex tech. Wow, is it *ever* bulletproof. Ouch!" She pushed herself up a little to one side. "Go find Brianna!"

"The elevator's gone. Anyway, I can't leave now."

"I won't die!"

"But Heap will." Mack tore off his suit jacket and wadded it up, a durable Astrozzoli fiber imported from Tuscany, and put pressure on Heap's chest wound. "Maybe that's what he deserves, but we need him alive to testify, so you can clear your name."

Autumn very, very slowly walked her hands up the wall, pulled herself to her knees, and groaned. "Ohhhh. Wow, that—achh!—hurts. Gotta save Brianna."

"Jiggs will get to her." He pulled Brian's ultrasonic shear from his pocket and began cutting the front of Heap's uniform shirt open.

"Oh, wow," she groaned again. She used the wall to pull herself up to her feet. The front of her yellow dress was shredded over most of her torso, and the blue underneath was spangled with spiraling dabs of shrapnel. "Jiggs won't know, *hhp*"—she was breathing in shallow, painful gulps—"the elevator is working again. *Hhhp*. They're taking her directly to the roof, *hhp*, not through the stairwell. What do we do?"

"I don't know," said Mack, still applying pressure with one hand. The polisec officer was breathing with a sucking noise from the wound. "He's got a punctured lung. Can you find a first aid kit down here, or at least some tape?"

"I don't know," she said. "I can barely walk. I don't, *hhp*, I don't think I can climb stairs. Mack, we're going to lose, every way."

Behind them was the heavy noise of someone coming down the carpeted stairwell.

Chapter 58

"Mack! Autumn!" said Brian on the stairs. "You're alive!"

"Brian, if, *hhp*, if you hug me right now, I'll kill you," said Autumn, standing stiffly with her hand on the wall.

Brian wondered for a moment if she and Mack had had another argument, but this was no time to ask. "It's insane up there," he told them. "Our team is trying to secure the lower floors, but nobody knows what they're doing."

"He needs medical help," said Autumn. She nodded at Mack, crouched over the unconscious Officer Heap.

"Wait. Wait a minute," said Mack. He jammed his hand in his trouser pocket. He hunted around for a second and came out with a small earbud phone. "There's the old hospital across the freeway." He tapped something on the phone and jammed it in his ear.

"There are antelope and baboons chasing each other through the museum exhibits right now," said Brian, "knocking over glass cases with rare boomerangs and things. We were never supposed to get this far. The resistance at the main door just collapsed."

"Medical emergency!" said Mack loudly. "Geisel Museum, polisec officer down! Send an ambulance to these coordinates. I repeat, officer down!" He gestured to Brian. "Come here right now.

Yes, Geisel Museum! Hey, Brian—come help me," he said less loudly. "Hold his head steady and press his hand against his chest."

Brian sprang to his aid. "White Knights," he read from Heap's uniformed shoulder as he applied pressure. "A fallen comrade of yours? Autumn, I am sorry."

"Don't, *hhp*, waste your breath," said Autumn.

"YES, we have an active shooter!" shouted Mack into the phone. "Hyperactive. Many many shooters. Sister, right now everybody in the building is shooting at everybody else. We have an officer critically wounded and we need an ambulance!"

"Where is Brianna?" he asked. "Did you find her?"

"Up," and Autumn gestured with her arm, grimaced, then pointed with just one finger. "Elevator. Roof."

"They reconnected the elevator controls," said Mack. He was hunting, tearing through shelves and desks and rolling carts, his hands shaking a little. "Reinhardt is taking her to the roof."

"Has a burstcar," said Autumn.

Mack ripped a clear plastic sheet off the front of a binder and ran back with the sheet and a roll of Super Adhesive polymer labels. "Main entrance!" he shouted into the phone. "Okay, thanks, Brian." He snipped a section of plastic off with the shear, laid it flat on Heap's chest and began sticking it to the bare skin using labels on three sides. "Where's Jiggs?"

"I have no idea," said Brian. "Autumn, I thought you were with him."

Autumn shook her head tightly. "Floor 5, last seen. Maybe higher now. But stairwell doesn't connect to roof."

"Let's go!" said Brian.

Autumn shook her head. "Brian, I'm hurt. Can't help up there."

Brian looked at Mack. But Mack shook his head. "I need to keep this guy alive until we get an ambulance. For Autumn's sake. Brian—you have to go."

"Me?"

"Yeah. You can do this. And you've got to. If I leave now and Heap dies, they'll throw Autumn in prison. So it's you. Go after Brianna. Go ape."

"Right," said Brian, pulling his shoes off.

"We can offer a wide selection of pre-owned firearms," said Mack, gesturing to weapons scattered over the floor. "Machine guns with suppressors, a nice .50 caliber pistol, a long-barreled revolver with exploding rounds."

Brian looked at them. A machine gun? But he'd probably need to shoot one-handed. He picked up the Kālikā. "I think I can operate this."

"Reinhardt said they'd wait, *hhp*, fifteen minutes," said Autumn. "By now, about eight."

"Down the corridor, first left," said Mack. "Point the gun like a finger and shoot. Go."

Brian had to jump over the bodies of the chimps and weasels lying in front of the elevator. He had smelled their blood in the corridor before he saw them, and a bad feeling churned in his gut, but he didn't have time to think about it. Then he entered the stairwell.

Screams and shots were echoing and it reeked of gunpowder. In the murky concrete well above him, now suffused with drifting trails of smoke, there were two spots of daylight: up to his left, the hot sunshine from the open third-floor doorway, and high at the top, the pale square of the skylight. At every level baboons and chimps were circling, leaping between rails, always in motion.

They seemed now to be mostly holding their fire, screaming and shouting and baring teeth, trying to intimidate without risking a ricochet. *Raaa-hu!* shouted the baboons, and *Eheeaa!* screamed the chimpanzees, and the shouts all shredded and mixed together as if sound itself had been dropped in a blender. The chimps were bigger and stronger, but the baboons had better weapons and were keeping the chimps from getting out. A chimp swung for the third-floor exit and then, as shots blasted the wall, swung back out of the line of fire. A baboon somersaulted between railings and a chimp hand grabbed its tail mid-air and hurled it against the opposite wall. Baboons sprayed bullets back. The walls of the third floor, and many other places, were eaten to rubble.

Eight minutes to get through.

He ran halfway round the first circle of the stairs, climbed onto the railing, and jumped. He caught the bottom of the railing above and pulled himself up to Floor 2. His silk necktie was flapping everywhere and he stuffed the end of it in his suit breast pocket.

He jumped again. As he pulled himself up to Floor 3, a spray of machine gun fire ripped the wall to his left. He flipped up over the railing and pulled the trigger in haste before he had landed. The shot went straight up: on the ceiling, near the skylight, a section of concrete burst and rained dust down gradually from floor to floor. The sound of the Kālikā temporarily deafened him and the kick almost made him drop the pistol.

Maybe this was the wrong choice of weapon, he thought, running up toward floor 4, his ears ringing. *Too late now.*

A baboon dropped through the sifting airborne dust and landed on the railing right in front of him; then a shot boomed from somewhere else and the baboon spasmed and fell limp onto the stairs. A chimp landed on a railing higher up. It was Elton. He shouted something at Brian but in the roar of the stairwell Brian understood nothing and just kept running up. He was halfway to Floor 5.

Another baboon landed on the railing 90 degrees ahead. Brian pointed the gun like a finger and pulled the trigger. The Kālikā fired, shoving Brian's elbow into his stomach, and he stumbled a little. The baboon dropped his machine gun down into the shaft and then fell in after it.

Brian jumped onto the railing and made a jump straight up to the next level, grabbing the railing base with his left hand and firing two shots at the stairs above, swinging crazily each time he fired. Then he reached up with his feet and grabbed to get up to the upper railing. The baboons were running to safety farther up. He saw one of them turn back and aim. *Can't stop now.* He fired and then flung himself up to the railing on the next flight up, his tie flapping free. He fired again at the baboons above. One of them was sagging on the rail. Maybe he had hit him. He ran, passing the door marked 6.

Raaa-hu, echoed hoarse voices in the concrete void.

Three baboons appeared on the landing in front of him with more coming down behind them. He jumped over the rail and grabbed the base of the railing, dangling in the shaft as their machine fire tore the landing he had just been on. Then there were more shots from somewhere else and the baboons dropped, one by one. He got back up onto the outside of the railing and looked one floor down to see Elton and another chimp with their guns smoking. Elton waved him on.

He swung up and ran past door number 7. He kept running. There were no baboons on the stairs above.

As he climbed the last set of steps toward door 8 and the terminal balcony, the door opened. Coming out of door 8 was a male human in a helmet and a Secure-Tek tactical suit. The man raised a semi-automatic pistol and took aim.

Brian pointed and fired. The shot hit the man in the lower leg and he stumbled against the railing. Brian shot again, missing this time, but kept running forward. The man knelt and clutched the railing and brought his weapon up. Brian stopped and fired. The man seemed to do nothing. Brian reached the eighth floor landing. The man was hanging on to the railing; the pistol dropped from his hand and clattered down one step. Brian could not tell if the man was alive, dying, or dead. *Go on.*

Now for the hard part. He was under the yellowed square of the skylight, but it was too high. And because the skylight was out in the center of the building shaft it would be a jump forward as well as up. What now? *I need the distance to be half of that. Maybe I could shorten the distance. If I could get something through it.*

He fired two shots at the skylight and they punched holes straight through. It did not shatter but there was a crack in it now, between the holes. At the third shot the gun clicked. Empty. *Now I have something to throw.* He whipped off his silk tie and knotted it around the Kālikā, then pulled off his belt and knotted the other end of the tie around the buckle to lengthen the line. He held the weapon like a javelin and tested his arm a couple of times. *Please make it,* he thought. He threw it up at the broken skylight. *I can find guns all over this place, but I only have one necktie.*

The weapon missed the holes he had made but it crunched through the yellowed Plexiglas anyway and landed above on the roof, with the tie-and-belt belt line swinging down into the empty space a few feet up from the railing. A bit of Plexiglas tumbled down into the open shaft and disappeared from his view as it fell.

This is insane. He went back and grabbed the human's pistol from the steps, then leaped onto the top of the railing, balanced precariously. A single shot sounded somewhere a long way below him. *If I fell...* He didn't continue that thought. *Brianna, I'm coming.*

He jumped up into the shaft and seized midair the end of a top-grain cowhide Milanese men's belt. The Kālikā jerked down and smacked against the crumbling Plexiglas pieces but Brian was already up past the belt to the necktie and as cracks spread through the remnant of the window he caught hold of a shard of Plexiglas sticking out from the frame. It sprung up and down and cut his hand. He didn't let go.

Chapter 59

"The medics won't come into the building," Mack told Autumn, pressing the phone bud firmly into his ear. "It's still a combat area." To the phone he said "Matthews Lane, I don't know where that is. I'm not from campus. Can you drive at least to the museum entrance?"

"Can't wait very long," said Autumn, holding herself stiffly and trying to think about cool breezes and ice cubes. "Heap's got lung injury. *Hhp.* Protocol is ten minutes to ER."

"I know," Mack told her. "They'll meet us in front. But we have to get him out."

"How?" gasped Autumn.

Mack rolled Heap onto his side. Then he stood up, grabbed a small wooden book cart, and ran with it upstairs to the main floor. He came back, wrenched a pair of metal shelves out of a bookcase, and took them up along with a second cart.

"What are you doing?" she called up.

"Making a gurney," he panted, running back down. "Now we need a blanket. To carry him up the stairs."

"We have to?"

"His pulse is weak. If we wait till the shooting stops, he'll be dead."

"This is a museum, *hhp,* it used to be a library, don't know where they'd have blankets." She started to take off her shredded yellow dress, but the light fabric began to rip. "Nope, won't hold his weight." If she were in good shape herself she could have jumped with Heap using her boots but even then it wouldn't exactly be good for him and as things were this was out of the question.

"What else have we got? " He looked at the body of the hipster on the floor with the shiny aluminum jacket. "Yes siree." He sprang towards it.

As he rolled the body gently onto one side he talked quietly. "Hey, Jack. I imagine now you're hep to more than everything *I* know." The jacket was intact. He worked the arms rapidly out of the sleeves one at a time. "Hope it's OK if I take this. And thanks for everything. You're a righteous dude, you hear?"

He came back and worked the jacket in under Heap's shoulders. "This stuff is unrippable. Let's go."

"I don't think, *hhp,* I can carry anything," she said.

"Maybe try. Just one hand. I'll get his feet up to you." He tied the bloodstained remains of his own suit coat around Heap's ankles and lifted it up so she could reach without bending. Autumn took hold of the knot in one hand and waited.

Mack loosely knotted the ends of the aluminum jacket around Heap's arms and hauled his heavy body off the ground.

With the sudden weight, pain rang her whole body like a church bell.

"You got it?" he asked.

364

"Uh-huh," she grunted. Immediately she began to be soaked with sweat.

Once Brian got through the skylight and onto the roof he found himself in a walled service enclosure full of machinery. Holding the Secure-Tek pistol at the ready, he crept forward. There was the noise of a motor close by.

"Heap coming?" said someone. "Or not!"

"Said he was," said another. Both were hard voices, male.

It sounded like they were just on the other side of the wall. Brian hopped onto a metal HVAC housing and climbed to peek over the top of the enclosure.

On the flat roof surface, which was square with the corners indented, was a burstcar painted blue with big yellow letters saying SECURE-TEK. Its back lift door was open. Reinhardt was standing a few meters from the vehicle, talking to a baboon with a machine gun. Another man in blue fatigues was in the burstcar's pilot seat. The motionless body of a red howler monkey was lying on the landing pad.

The baboon scurried away and Reinhardt walked over behind the burstcar. He bent down and picked up something heavy and as he heaved it in, Brian caught a glimpse of Brianna's face. She was bound but her eyes were open and she looked conscious. He felt a pang of joy. *She's here. What to do now?*

He answered himself: *Keep the vehicle from leaving.* Looking for a clear shot he inched along the wall and pulled himself silently onto the top of the service enclosure. Reinhardt had closed the lift door and was now over at the south edge of the roof, looking down.

Maybe I can drop down, get up close to the vehicle and shoot the pilot, then shoot Reinhardt from behind it. He hoped the pistol's owner had not used many of the bullets. He got up into a crouch on top of the enclosure. If necessary he would—

A cry came up from behind him. He whirled around. The baboon had come inside the enclosure to reach the elevator, and was now staring up in surprise at Brian atop the wall. The baboon fumbled to get his machine gun up. Brian shot him and he fell.

Reinhardt saw him. He reached to pull something off his sleeve. Brian turned back and jumped down back into the enclosure. He was about to go around to the gate where the baboon had come in. But a thin gray double-headed snake slithered over the top of the wall.

Aaaa! Brian leaped over to the opposite side of the enclosure and scrambled to the top.

The wrapsnake Reinhardt had thrown sensed motion. In a running sine wave it crossed the space, past the fallen body of the baboon, to the opposite wall, and reared one end up like a cobra. As Brian reached the top, the very tip of the wrapsnake shot up and curled around the thumb of his bare foot, and the snake came along with him.

By the time Brian dropped onto the outer roof on the far side of the enclosure, the arcing ends of the snake were already spinning themselves around his legs.

I'm not actually sure I have enough left in me to do this. Mack was stumping backwards carrying Heap's shoulders up the carpeted steps. His finger was on fire and each step was exhausting. Autumn was gripping Heap's tied feet in one hand and the wooden banister in the other. Heap's body swayed and bounced with every step they took. Mack reached the landing halfway up and turned so Autumn could get onto the landing as well. "Rest a sec," he panted.

Autumn didn't say anything. Her teeth were clenched. She tried to rest Heap's heels on her hip just below the shredded part of her yellow dress that showed the blue underneath.

Took a cop-killer at two meters, thought Mack. *If* I'm *tired, what about* her? *Gotta keep going.* "OK, go," he said, putting his heel on the first step. They worked up one step at a time.

Hey up there, thought Mack. *Can you hear me? We need help. I'm not much, you know that.* Another step. *But for her sake.* Another step. *She needs him to stay alive so she can not go to jail, keep her job, maybe do some bigger things someday. Please.* He couldn't remember how many steps there were still to go behind him.

Brian dropped the pistol and tried to fight off the snake, but its stainless steel mouths dodged his hands as they slithered up and wound around him. Before they were even locked in, he thought, *I had her, and I've lost her.* An awful nauseating feeling of failure swept over him.

Then something came to his memory: *It will avoid your neck and head.*

As the wrapsnake passed the top button of his suit coat Brian threw both arms up and clutched them tight over the top of his head. The snake's mouths curled around his shoulders and pulled to cinch its wrap together, but Brian's chimpanzee strength was enough that the snake could not yank his arms down. Instead the snake's mouths swooped around to his back, found each other, and clicked shut between his shoulder blades.

At the same moment he heard, from the inside of the enclosure, the swish of the elevator door opening.

With his long arms mostly free he could reach over his back and feel the connecting point. He just had to untwist it. Trying it one-handed didn't work. He stretched to get both hands back there and twisted again. *How did Mack do it?* Just a twist. It had looked easy. Maybe for primates with a more precise grip than a chimpanzee's it *was* easy. Maybe it was a push-and-twist. His fingers slipped on the smooth metal of the connection.

From the other side of the enclosure there was machine gun fire, and the bang of Reinhardt's long revolver answering back. From somewhere farther away, an ambulance siren.

OK, try the other way. Brian twisted in the opposite direction. Almost effortlessly, the wrapsnake came apart.

He reeled its slithering length off his torso and legs and hurled it away; it bounced and slid, still twitching, but found nothing on the flat roof to hook onto and slithered helplessly off the edge.

Brian snatched up the pistol and ran around the east side.

Ahead of him he saw Elton and Jiggs firing machine guns, covering each other and taking turns advancing in short hops across the roof toward the burstcar. The pilot leaned out of the vehicle and fired a pistol. Reinhardt dived to the ground on the far side of the car, stumbling with his wounded leg, but he came up again with his gun in hand,.

Brian steadied his arm against the enclosure wall, lined up the gun sights on Reinhardt's head, and fired.

A gray flower bloomed on Reinhardt's body armor around the collarbone, and he dropped the pistol and went to one knee.

The pilot fired. Elton dropped, his leg bleeding. Ignoring bullets, Jiggs sprang to close the distance with the pilot and as he landed he seized the pilot's head and arm and gave them a lethal snap. Then he vaulted over the top of the burstcar, touched down behind it, and began trying to rip the doors off the back to get to Brianna.

Still kneeling, Reinhardt unclipped something long and gray from his other sleeve.

Brian pulled the trigger again but the pistol clicked empty. *Only two shots?*

Reinhardt threw the wrapsnake. It skidded underneath the vehicle, looping and twisting, looking for a mammalian heat signature. It found Jiggs's foot.

Brian ran towards the burstcar.

Reinhardt scrambled to the car, yanked the pilot's body out onto the roof, and jumped in.

Jiggs was on the ground, struggling with the snake in vain.

As Brian reached the burstcar, its jets switched on with a *bwrrrshhh*. Jiggs had peeled up the edges of the rear doors, leaving little wrenched gaps all around, but the center part with the latch wouldn't budge even when Brian jerked and hammered on it. Through the back window he caught a glimpse of Brianna's terrified face.

The car lurched a few inches, going into hover mode. In moments the burst function would be powered up and ready to bounce down the terraced levels on the west side of the roof.

At the top of the stairs Mack and Autumn heaved Heap onto the metal shelves Mack had thrown on top of the library book carts.

Must keep going, thought Autumn, but she really wanted to rest for a second.

"Frankenstein's cart. It's all we have," said Mack. "I push, you steer. Go!"

The frankencart wobbled and shook precariously on its small wheels as Mack rolled it double-time down the broad carpeted hallway; at the front end Autumn was jogging backwards and looking over her shoulder as much as the pain would let her, trying to steer around shattered museum exhibit cases and boomerangs lying scattered on the floor. A few animals were picking their way through the debris, taking no notice of them. A vidscreen was still playing a looped explanation of the Dream Time as part of Australian Aboriginal life.

They reached the sliding glass doors of the entrance. With a grimace Mack lifted and eased each end of the contraption over the threshold, then again through the outer set of doors, and they were outside in the sun, rolling faster now on the concrete bridge but going uphill and rattling badly. Mack had to bend down and hug the frankencart to keep it together. Autumn kept a hand on it to steer.

Ahead of them, past the passage with the glass walls, there was a big white ambulance parked by a spindly metal tree.

Brian grabbed a machine gun and fired off its remaining rounds into the air as he dashed back to the burstcar's rear door. He wedged the gunstock into the gap Jiggs had peeled up and used the weapon as a lever, trying to pop the latch open. He hammered with both hands on the gun barrel and the door groaned and bent but it didn't pop. He tried again in the gap above the latch. *I need more force, more leverage, more tools.* Reinhardt was revving the burstcar engine. Brian looked around. *There are no tools here. Nothing.* There was only Jiggs on the ground, the snake twisted tightly around him.

Twisted, thought Brian, and in his mind he saw the coin purse in the souvenir shop. *Be honest on your own time. Damage to merchandise.* He had an idea.

Brian leaped over to Jiggs and flipped him over on his stomach. There behind his back was the steel wrapsnake connector. Brian disconnected the mouths and with a jerk he yanked the snake off, reeling Jiggs out of it as if unrolling him from a carpet. He went

371

back to the burstcar rear doors, shoved one end of the writhing snake through the gap above the latch, and then stuck his hand through the gap underneath. With his other hand he slammed the machine gun flat against the latch.

Jiggs was on his feet, running to the front of the vehicle, pounding on the TefPlas windows, but they were too strong for him to smash. Inside Reinhardt was gripping the steering unit and moving his hand in the orange light of the holodisplay, configuring settings for the vehicle's burst system.

The wrapsnake surged into the burstcar latch and looped around Brian's wrist and looped around it. He drew the snake out, used his foot to pluck it off his wrist, and fed it over the machine gun and tempted it into the gap again, letting it pour in after itself.

He was sewing the gun onto the car doors.

Jiggs was back at his side. "What's this?" he shouted.

"Help me turn it!" shouted Brian back. The carbon-fiber body of the snake was coiled closely now around the gun and the latch. The steel mouths were searching around the latch for each other. "Come on, snake!" He grabbed one end of the gun. Jiggs took hold of the other.

The snake's steel mouths found their last embrace and clicked together tight around the gun.

"Now turn!" shouted Brian to Jiggs. With full ape strength both of them cranked on the gun as if wrestling the wheel of a ship in a storm. The torque on the snake-wrapping squeezed the latch area where the warped doors still met. "More!" The metal around the latch twisted and wrinkled and bulged and tore.

The burst jets fired.

NO, screamed Brian.

Reinhardt lifted the vehicle with a jerk two feet into the air, pulling Brian and Jiggs off the ground, still holding the ends of the machine gun. They kicked in the air like swimmers and got their feet braced against the bumper and gave one more heave against the gun.

The burstcar roared forward. The latch broke loose. The doors flew open and Brian lurched backward, clinging to the door as the gun spun away. Jiggs was thrown off; Brian scrambled and reached into the back of the burstcar, and he clutched at Brianna. He got his fingers around the snake she was wrapped with and pushed off with his feet and Brianna slid and he was out and she was out and they were free, falling back onto the roof.

Suddenly relieved of the weight in the back, the vehicle bucked as it accelerated, and the front end dipped and struck the lip of the roof. It plowed a section out of the roof's concrete edge, crushing one of the ringjets on the car's underside, and slid downward and out of sight.

The EMTs were opening the ambulance as Mack and Autumn struggled to roll Heap up the path from the building entrance. *They have to stay a safe distance from the building*, thought Mack.

But the EMTs saw the officer in uniform lying on the cart and didn't stop. Instead they grabbed their gurney and ran down the bridge walkway, running all-out, hunched down as if they were launching a bobsled. As they rolled up to Autumn they jumped in to take Heap by the knees and shoulders, slid him lightly and quickly off the frankencart onto the gurney, then reversed course to get back up to the ambulance.

Mack and Autumn continued to stagger forward slowly. They let the frankencart spin away and clatter to pieces. The hem of her shredded yellow dress fluttered in the breeze.

"OK, you should stop," he said. "Sit down. There's benches. There." He gestured feebly with the aluminum jacket he was still dragging in one hand.

"Can't," she said, holding her side and taking small steps. "Worse than standing up."

"Let's get you to the wall at least."

"Don't need that now, you know," she said, glancing at the jacket.

"I'm keeping this damn thing," he said. *A memento of the fallen.* "Here. Let me help you." He placed her arm around his neck and lifted.

"OW!"

"Sorry, kid. This any better?"

"A little."

There was a noise of destruction behind them. With an effort the two of them linked together turned to look.

Way up on the top of the Geisel building, a Secure-Tek burstcar was sliding off the western edge of the eighth floor. The eave under it crumbled and the burstcar nosed straight into the terrace roof of the seventh floor.

It flipped over and scraped upside down off the edge of the sixth-floor roof, then slid off and somersaulted freely through the air, swirling out from one end an expanding pinwheel of black smoke, and completed one end-over-end rotation before it crashed in a pile of smoking metal on the ground near the plaza.

As Brian's hand touched his wife's, her fingers took hold and held his hand tight. He looked at Brianna. Tears were streaming down her furred cheeks and his as they spoke each other's names.

Mack helped Autumn lean up against the glass wall at the top of the walk. "That okay?" he asked. "You OK there?"

"Mm-hm," she replied, leaning back with her eyes closed and letting the pain do its thing. It was a little better when she wasn't lifting, carrying, pushing, or walking. Or breathing, really. There was a part of her mind that seemed to be working now. *We did it.*

"Sure glad you made it, kid," said Mack. "I was pretty worr...well, anyway, I'll call for another ambulance and get you to the hospital." He pressed her arm gently for a moment.

"OK," she said. "And you too. You look awful."

"I'll be all right. Nothing a little trip to Huero's won't take care of."

"Who's Huero?"

"Friend of mine. You'll have to meet him sometime. Helped me out. I was in a real fix because—wait a sec. Hold on just a —well, I'll be damned." He started to laugh.

"Mm?" She cracked open one eye.

Mack was rocking back and forth with laughter. "That's too funny!" He leaned his back against the glass wall next to her. He wiped away a tear, shaking his head slowly. "I forgot. Wasn't even thinking."

"What?"

"I still have to go get that thing off of Heap's wrist."

Chapter 60

It was a beautiful morning in San Diego, as usual.

Mack left the locker area of the TransPac Bus station, took the little package into the comm lobby, and found an empty vidstream chair. He draped the aluminum jacket over the arm of the chair and eased himself in, trying to avoid making any contact with the bruised and bandaged parts of his finger and his legs and his shoulder and his hip and a few other places.

He closed the vidchair wings around him for privacy, and the chair screen flashed at him:

WELCOME
BLINK TO START
$17.79/MINUTE

He flicked his wrist to activate the control system on the COR band. He overrode the vidchair and shut off the flashing welcome screen.

Ahhhh. It felt good. He settled in and adjusted the aluminum jacket next to him. *Copasetic, man.*

He turned the package over and over in his hands, feeling every part delicately with his fingertips like a safecracker. There was a small bump under the brown wrapping on one side. It might be a tiny poisoned thorn that would kill instantly if the wrong person tried to open the package. Or a spray capsule of nerve gas. The guy was certifiably nuts.

After about five minutes Mack was fairly confident that the bump was probably a defect in the polyboard box. He held his breath and peeled off the wrapping. The bump was only a drop of glue.

Inside the box was the figurine of Quan Yin. The jade pendant and its silver fitting looked like new. Well, almost like new; the silver had exactly the same smudge of tarnish on the back as when he bought it.

Under the necklace was a note with a chip taped onto the bottom of the paper. The chip was just the right size and color to have been invisible inside the figurine.

The note had no salutation. It was just a list of names and numbers. What they meant, however, in that particular order, Mack knew.

The company the data had been stolen from. A number with a squiggled symbol indicating how fresh the data was, meaning how long since the theft. The name and address of a discrete intermediary, whom Mack had heard of, if he wanted to either return it for a reward or sell the chip to a third party. The amount of the reward. The approximate price if sold on the black market.

Those last two amounts were the reason Mack spent another ten minutes sitting there in the vidstream chair, staring at the paper and the chip taped at the bottom. Eventually he found his jaw and managed to close it.

It was not until the next day that he was able to get Maríqui to answer. On the vidscreen she looked old and tired, with bags under her eyes.

"Hi, beautiful," he said from the vidstream chair. "I got back in town this week. You probably know that."

"Yeah," she said. She didn't sound like she wanted to talk about how she knew. "Hadn't heard from you. Everything OK?"

"I picked up your necklace, if that's what you mean. Nice little figurine. It's coming to you by express mail."

She smiled. It wasn't a big smile; it showed resignation and disappointment. But not anger.

That smile is the tip-off, he thought. She wasn't relieved, the way she would have been if she'd actually only wanted a jade necklace. That meant she was in on the plan somehow. But hearing that Mack had entrusted it to the dubious care of the postal emus should have made her furious—if she had known how valuable the figurine was. *So it was somebody else's plan, all right. And that plan didn't involve cutting her in on the proceeds.*

"I'm happy I was able to retrieve it for you," he said. "Don't lose it, OK? I almost got arrested getting it into the country. All a misunderstanding, of course."

"Sure," she said, gathering her long black hair on one side with both hands.

379

"And how is Ivan?"

Her mouth moved a little. "OK," she said wearily.

"Also, I sent you the number of a fellow who has a shipping company. He's looking for big, strong loaders. In case Ivan wants to take a break from bouncer life and try out a quieter career."

"Okay," she said in a subdued voice.

If a random Transport Control worker hadn't happened to recognize him at Lindbergh, he wouldn't have had to go to the tailor shop, and instead of running all over town fighting baboons, he would have been having a candlelight dinner gazing into Maríqui's eyes, just the way he had wanted. Very briefly. Because even though she hadn't been planning to kill him, her friends probably had been.

Nice how it all worked out. Thanks, you up there.

At this point he didn't care who had set up the plan. But he did care about Maríqui, a little, for old time's sake. He was glad he had decided to have some better news ready for her.

"Maríqui, listen. I did something else for you. I arranged for you to get one of those bank accounts where you are the only person who can touch the money, no matter what. Not even a husband can get to it, if you marry. An account sole, it's called."

"Oh." She looked puzzled. "Why?"

"Well, you'll need to sign a few things, of course. It's all in the package I sent you. Once you do that, there will be ninety thousand in the account in the name of Maríqui Valle."

380

Her eyes widened, then she glanced quickly at something offscreen. When she looked back, she spoke more quietly. "Mack! Why?"

"Let's just say the Goddess of Compassion and Mercy has smiled on my finances. And I had a sense that maybe you could use some extra money. In case you wanted to move to Ciudad La Raza, or even farther away. Get a fresh start. Make new friends."

Once you get wise to your current friends, you'll want to move out, and fast. But he didn't say that out loud.

"Mack! I don't know what to say. Thank you. I mean—maybe we could—"

"I have to be going now. I'm pretty certain we won't be seeing each other again," he said, "but I wish you the best. I really mean that." He closed the connection.

He actually did have to be going; he was headed to Huero's to pay his tab. But before he stood up from the vidstream chair, a message alert flashed on the screen. It was addressed to Mack Davis.

He had used a secure connection, and the vidchair could not possibly know the name of the public user. He paused, then double-blinked to accept the message. It said:

Now in Bhutan.
The truth would blow your mind. It's all about history, Mack.
Come soon. Clean and oil them this time.

Mack sighed.

Chapter 61

When Autumn reached the door of her apartment she was wearing her White Knights uniform with the shirt hanging out, and she was shuffling in flip-flops too small for her. She was carrying a big bag marked *UCSD Medical Center* in one hand and her jump boots in the other. To enter her key code she let the boots drop to the carpet because bending to set them down was medically not advised this week. Then she noticed that at the foot of the door there was a small, brand-new box of earplugs. There were also some freshly chewed indentations low down on the door jamb.

She leaned for a minute with her shoulder against the door looking at the chew marks before going in. She shuffled the boots and the earplugs over the threshold.

Inside the apartment it was dark. She had left the blinds closed when she caught the SpeedRail on Tuesday before sunrise. She turned the control knob to open the blinds, and light flooded in long stripes into her small studio showing her unmade bed, her plastic plants, her com-phone, the travel bag she hadn't taken to Fresno. She touched a leaf of the plastic pellonia by the door and rubbed it slowly between her fingers.

On the nightstand were the pieces of the mug saying *San* and *Diego Padres*. She tossed them in the trash.

She emptied her utility belt and other belongings out of the UCSD bag onto the bed. She checked her messages; there was one from Kyle last Tuesday night. *"Hey there Autumn. Hope you're not too bored down there giving out traffic tickets. Listen, call me back as soon as you get this. I have new-ews...about what Bethany's wearing on her fiiiin-gerrr....Tell you more tonight. Okay, bye."*

Autumn walked stiffly over to the kitchen sink and poured herself a tall glass of desalinated water and drank it.

I bet I could get a recommendation for a nice building for the porcupines to move to. I bet I could find another apartment. I bet I could just hang on for my last five months in San Diego. If I'm leaving.

She felt a pain in her toe. It was the tip of a little porcupine quill stuck in her flip-flop. She started to bend down and immediately remembered why she couldn't.

How will I get out of this one, she thought.

As she stood on one foot and worked her toes out of the flip-flop, she smiled.

EPILOGUE
One Month Later

Mack and Autumn were having lunch at Zhou's Imperial Spendour. It was on the 30th floor.

"Wow, Mack," Autumn said, looking into the white gift box. It contained a brand-new SafeLite protection ensemble in Delicate Cider. "Thank you. You did not have to do this."

"I wanted to show you the real me," said Mack, dressed in a brand new suit, gesturing around at the white-draped tables of the restaurant. He had spent twenty minutes in the restroom trying to get his hair to lie straight before she arrived. He was now lounging in his chair with something like the utmost nonchalance.

"You mean the real you? Not another one of your fake identities?" she smiled. She was in uniform, although it was cleaner and more crisply pressed than when they'd first met.

"A *Mutabilis* by any other name. I also picked this place because it has a great view of the biggest vidwall in downtown." He nodded toward the windows. Beyond the buildings and vidscreens and traffic-snarled streets far below lay the glittering blue of San Diego Harbor.

"Why is that a plus?"

"You'll see. Keep your eyes on it."

"Any news on our John Q. Covert?" asked Autumn, sipping carefully from her elegant water glass.

"Nothing big," said Mack. "The name Samajargan comes up a few times—some financial transactions clearing through Mumbai, a manufacturing deal in Bekasi—but it's spotty. His trails always turn out to be dead ends, same as the contact info Heap coughed up. It could be that Samajargan is someone who only makes a move occasionally, but I wouldn't be surprised if the name is one of many handles used by a covert operator."

"Did you see Urizen yet?"

"I did go have a little talk." Mack smoothed out his napkin on his lap. "Urizen is supreme in his local sphere, and it still surprises me what he can tap into overseas, but overall his visibility into Asian operations is shallow. Before I ask him to run large-scale searches I need more to go on. Or at least a paying client. As you know, that cat doesn't give discounts."

"Samajargan probably still wants San Diego, or Free Life, or both."

"Probably. The deal with Heap seems to have been one piece of a larger strategy that we've only glimpsed. Right now, though, the trail is cold." Mack knew who he would have to ask about it sooner or later. He just didn't feel like going to Bhutan yet. He liked the idea of staying around San Diego for a while and maybe having lunch with Officer Winn on a more frequent basis.

The waiter brought their lunch plates.

"How's business on the legit side?" he asked.

"Actually I wanted to tell you—I have a problem," said Autumn, picking up the sterling silver chopsticks.

"You getting tired of those early mornings?"

She smiled a little. "It's more of an existential thing. Mixed emotions."

"Hey, hey, hey! Wait a second. Look at the vidwall!" said Mack. "Look right now. There it is!"

The advertisement on the forty-foot screen showed, in dramatic perspective, a chimpanzee in an impeccable suit leaping heroically between skyscrapers. The text above and below the image read

AVVENTUROSO

Tailoring For Today's Successful Action Species

at the famous

MR. BRIAN'S

The vidwall flipped to a map of the tailor shop location and a photo of Brian and Brianna side by side, beautifully dressed, with their arms tightly around each other.

"Oh, *Mack*," said Autumn. "I'm really happy for them."

They began eating, not saying anything for a minute or two.

"So I told you Bickson's leaving, right?" said Autumn.

"Right. Availing himself of an early retirement opportunity," said Mack. "Rather than be fired for not watching Heap more closely. Seems like a happy outcome for you."

"But listen. They've tapped Chavez to replace him as TAC Captain."

"Also not a problem, right? You get along with Chavez." He wasn't sure where she was going with this. "And you said Lucille's taking on more responsibility as part of the transition, and you're happy for her."

"Listen to me." She sounded pained. "Mack, Chavez is getting me early promotion to Sergeant!"

"Wow." Mack sat back in his chair. "Congratulations. That is great news. Really great. Why didn't you say so? You deserve it, of course."

"And they're giving me a one-year credit toward Lieutenant rank. Oh, and I get a raise. My parents are on cloud nine."

"Huge problems. Ginormous. So what's bothering you?"

On her plate she sketched out with her chopsticks an outline faintly like a chess knight. "I was planning not to be *in* anymore."

"Ahhh. Yeah, I get it." Mack adjusted his napkin. "Whether to accept. You're afraid you're selling out."

"My parents have had the same little CPA firm for twenty-one years. I don't think they have dreams any more. It's all about just keeping it going. I can't live that life. I want to get better connected to where I came from. On the other hand, if I stay and take the promotion I'll …you know…bring honor to the family name. Very culturally important."

"That's a dilemma."

"Well, it *is*, you know? Although to be honest, I was starting to wonder whether now was exactly the right time to leave anyway."

"Sometimes just keeping something going for a while is OK. Besides, you're young. You still have options." Mack had the undeniable feeling that he was not keen on the idea of Autumn leaving San Diego.

"Here's the thing, Mack; I feel like I'm at a transition stage. I have to do something differently."

"Sure, you can do things differently. Anybody can change."

"Don't you think I should beware of getting stuck?"

"Well, nobody wants to do the same thing forever." As he set his wrist on the table the COR band lit up faintly with the READY display, showing a tiny picture of a mountaintop in Idaho. "You might want to run the numbers. I mean, before you quit your job to become Heritage Girl. Do you know how much you need in savings?"

"Unfortunately I have a rough idea."

"Yeah. Well, it's not selling out to stick around and play it cool for a while, bask as local hero, stay out of trouble. Read more books."

"Mm-hm," she said, finishing a bite. "Kind of what I've been thinking. Lucille says basically the same thing. I want to make a change in some way, though. I have an idea."

"You're planning to start carrying a backup weapon, right, Autumn?"

"How about if you don't call me Autumn any more."

Mack blinked. "OK," he said. "I understand." He pushed the rest of his rice slowly to the center of his plate. He didn't understand, not a bit. He thought they had mended all the fences and come out okay. But maybe it made a lot of sense to her. She was going places and she didn't need to mess with some smart-aleck with a shadowy line of work. She had bigger dreams. Better ones.

"I get it," he said, keeping his voice steady. "You're moving on, building your identity, your career. And by jingo, you've earned it. I wish you the best, Sergeant Winn." He motioned to the waiter. "Check, please."

"No, Mack, that's not what I meant." She smiled. "I mean I'd like it if you tried calling me Thu. My Vietnamese name."

"Oh," said Mack. He blinked again. "Thu." He smiled back at her.

Both of them were smiling.

"No problemo," he said. For once, all he was concealing was how much brighter he wanted to smile. "That is, if I remember."

"Just between us. I'm not ready to tell my coworkers yet. They already ordered my name plaque anyway. And I get my own deskpod on the third floor."

"Congratulations," he said. "Going to decorate your office *alla Vietnamese?*"

"I was thinking," said Autumn, her eyes bright, "maybe I'll get a plant. A real one. The kind you have to water."

"It's a start," said Mack.

THE AUTHORS

Robert McGraw has had several professions, but his most difficult job is convincing his wife he's actually working even when he's just staring out the window. He is the author of many magazine and newspaper articles, as well as four books. Two of his television scripts won awards from the International Television Association.

A former professional symphony musician, Robert worked on his Ph.D (all but dissertation) in music. He has also studied art at The Ruth Prowse School of Art in Cape Town, RSA, and his art has been shown in numerous galleries and shows.

Darrin McGraw has been a writer, software developer, university instructor, library manager, and assistant art school director. He served for eight years as the writing director of the Culture, Art and Technology Program at UC San Diego. He is a graduate of Stanford and UCLA.